Ms. Kearney's strengths is her deft use of characterization, which instantly vests readers in the perilous quest."

—*Romantic Times BOOKreviews*

PRAISE FOR *THE ULTIMATUM*

"From the first reluctant coupling to the final lovers' tiff, romance readers will feel right at home."

—*Publishers Weekly*

"In this third chapter of Kearney's outstanding futuristic series, Xander from *The Challenge* is all grown up and major hero material. Sizzling sex is a major component in Kearney's books, and, once again, she manages to find unique ways to increase the tension and sexuality. With all this fast-paced action, sensuality, and adventure, you can't go wrong."

—*Romantic Times BOOKreviews*

Dancing
with Fire

SUSAN
KEARNEY

TOR®

A TOM DOHERTY ASSOCIATES BOOK
NEW YORK

This is a work of fiction. All of the characters, organizations, and events portrayed in this novel are either products of the author's imagination or are used fictitiously.

DANCING WITH FIRE

Copyright © 2008 by Hair Express, Inc.

A Tor Book
Published by Tom Doherty Associates, LLC
175 Fifth Avenue
New York, NY 10010

www.tor-forge.com

Tor® is a registered trademark of Tom Doherty Associates, LLC.

ISBN-13: 978-0-7653-5845-5
ISBN-10: 0-7653-5845-X

First Edition: July 2008

Printed in the United States of America

0 9 8 7 6 5 4 3 2 1

Logan—this book is for you. Logan not only keeps my computer running, in crunch time, he always comes through. In the son department, this mom certainly lucked out. I don't just love you, I'm very proud of you.

Acknowledgments

I'd like to thank Anna Genoese for buying this book and Heather Osborn for editing it. In addition, I'd like to thank Seth Lerner and Tara Kearney for the cover.

And to Tara Nemitz, who pitches in, helping to mail ARCs, starting the Susan Kearney MySpace page for me, and even being an extra in the book videos, I want you to know—you are very much appreciated. You're already like one of the family.

I also want to acknowledge the Tor sales team, who went to extra efforts for me on many occasions. I don't even know all your names. But for those who I've met, I'd like to send special thanks to Steve Kleckner, Stuart Miller, Rebecca Wik, Paul Kilber, Tom Espenschied, Bob Williams, Dianne Boldt, and Jeff Willmann.

Thanks Leslie and Elena for all your hard work. And to the production staff and the people up and down the line who helped this book make it to the store shelves, thank you.

And to my readers, thanks for reading my books. Please feel free to contact me through my Web site at www.susankearney.com.

breath whistling out of his lungs. Instead of precise spins and regulated moves that he would have expected of the Kaylin he thought he knew, this Kaylin's body ebbed and flowed like a wave, the rhythm provocative, the beat primal. The effect she had on him was druglike, tantalizing, like a whitecap swelling, breaking, sweeping him under.

From outside the studio, the full impact of her skill hadn't been as apparent. Her stomach muscles, emphasized by a slick gleam of sweat, shimmered and flexed as she spun a complete rotation. As she twirled, she caught sight of him and went still. If he hadn't been watching closely, he wouldn't have seen her bristle, her nostrils flare, her lips tighten, her eyes narrow—just a bit. Then she flicked off the music, picked up a towel and draped it around her graceful neck, and raised an imperious eyebrow.

Dabbing her face with the towel, she shot him a you-better-have-a-damn-good-reason-for-invading-my-space look. "Yes?"

"That dance . . . wow." He could tell by her expression she wasn't sure whether to take his words as a compliment. She bit her lower lip, the confidence and sensuality of the dance hidden, replaced by invisible armor she'd wrapped around her taut frame. She appeared as unhappy as he'd be if a stranger intruded on one of his experiments.

Uncertain if he'd offended her, he combed his fingers through his hair. "Sorry. I didn't mean to come in uninvited. I knocked. You didn't hear. Those moves you do . . . that's not classical ballet, is it?"

Kaylin chuckled, her green eyes brightening, her lips breaking into a wide and playful grin. In that one moment, her barriers shredded and her inner self shone through. "That was tribal belly dance. An experiment."

"If you want my opinion," and he wasn't sure she did, "your experiment's an unqualified success."

"Thanks, but as you aren't a dance critic . . . what are you doing here?"

She hadn't taken long to redirect his personal comments. She did it smoothly, giving him a gentle brush-off. He had to give her credit. Kaylin Danner was outwardly consistent. Her tribal dancing—a wild aberration in her normally staid character—had shocked and intrigued him. To his frustration, the Kaylin he'd occasionally seen around her father's business had returned, the one who was a master at keeping Sawyer at an emotional distance. "I'm looking for your father."

She frowned. "Isn't he at the lab?"

Twenty-five years ago Henry Danner had built his lab, a nine-thousand-square-foot steel building, on the one-acre lot next door to the house he'd inherited from his grandparents. Back then, the zoning laws had permitted industrial building in the area, allowing Henry to construct his lab in the middle of the neighborhood, and it had since been grandfathered in. Henry could work on his inventions literally in his own backyard. Although Kaylin's studio shared land with her family's home and stood about a hundred yards behind her father's laboratory, Sawyer hadn't been here before.

Since Henry had made Sawyer a partner in an exciting new business, they'd stayed busy at the lab. Lately, their results had been encouraging and Sawyer had just returned to Tampa after an interesting consultation with researchers at the University of Michigan. With technology growing exponentially, Sawyer and Henry couldn't afford not to stay apprised of the latest developments.

"Your father didn't answer the phone or my knock." Sawyer pulled a key from his pocket and held it up. "My key didn't work and he didn't answer his cell phone. I heard your music, and thought you might know where he is. So I came over. Why'd he change the locks?"

"He upgraded security." Kaylin went from uptight to thoughtful. "You were gone last week, right?"

"Yeah. Why the upgrade?" Sawyer was surprised she'd noticed his absence. Kaylin didn't come over to the lab much, if ever. She preferred her dancing. According to Henry, she'd been all set to head for New York and ply her talents on Broadway four years ago. Then her mother, Danielle, had died and Kaylin had given up a serious boyfriend and her dreams. She'd stayed home to help raise her younger sisters and undoubtedly pick up the slack. Henry, who would be the first to admit he was a better inventor than businessman, needed Kaylin's help to pay the bills. Though with Sawyer on board, that was about to change.

Still, he understood why Kaylin was so prickly. As much as he admired her loyalty to her family, he thought it a shame that she'd given up her ambitions to stay home and teach ballet to five-year-olds. Anyone who could move like she did should be sharing her talent with the world.

"Would you like a glass of water?" Kaylin asked, then headed toward an alcove she used as her studio's office.

The apricot-painted walls showed off framed pictures of her students as well as posters of famous ballet stars from the New York City and Moscow Ballet companies. A pair of threadbare toe shoes hung from ribbons on a hook, signed by some ballerina whose name he couldn't read. She opened the mini-fridge beside her desk, removed a pitcher of water, poured two glasses, and handed him one.

She sighed. "Dad told me this morning he has the biodiesel formula all worked out. He was waiting for you to return to fire up the plant's reactor. But when I walked my students to their parents' cars, I heard the generator go on. I assumed you were with him. You think he started without you?"

"I doubt it. It takes both of us to make fuel. He was probably just warming up the power." However, the generator hadn't been on when Sawyer had discovered his key didn't work. He hoped the power wasn't on the fritz.

Kaylin's shoulders slumped as she let down her guard again, allowing him to see her concern. "Dad's been working too hard. Sometimes to relax, he sits by my mother's rose bushes. Did you check out the backyard?"

Kaylin stood and pulled open the sheer curtains so they could both look out the window. Sawyer's gaze swept over the lot that Kaylin's students' parents used for parking. Spiked grass with Mexican heather, blooming yellow, pink, and orange zinnias, roses, and variegated ginger decorated the yard. Her students and their parents were long gone. And Henry wasn't there.

His gaze shifted to the Danners' back porch, a cozy deck with a potted pink grapefruit tree and hanging baskets of white and pink orchids. Their mutt, Randy, lay curled and lazy on a lounger, sunbathing in a beam of Florida sunlight that filtered between palm fronds. The grass needed mowing, and the orange trees required pruning, but the ferns beneath the moss-laden granddaddy oaks shone green and healthy. A swift perusal of the fading olive colored paint along with the curling shingles and sagging shutters of the family's two-story home reminded Sawyer that the house needed repairs to squeak through another hurricane season. He didn't see Henry anywhere.

Kaylin went to her big yellow purse on a hook by her desk. "Let's see if he's in the lab." She pulled a key from her purse but it snagged on a piece of paper. An airline ticket fell to the floor.

"Going somewhere?" he asked.

"Maybe." A muscle in her jaw tightened, and she picked up the ticket and replaced it in her purse.

"Maybe?" His eyebrows rose in surprise. "But you've already bought the ticket."

Kaylin helped support the family with her dance studio. She was practical, full of common sense, and managed the family checkbook like a seasoned accountant and financial planner. And she never, ever went anywhere.

Not to the beach with friends. Not over to Disney or Universal Studios for a day trip. Certainly not anywhere that required air travel. It was so atypical for her to buy an airline ticket, never mind one that she wasn't certain she'd use, that she'd piqued Sawyer's curiosity. And from the flush of color in her cheeks, she didn't want to talk about it.

"I haven't—"

One moment she was placing her purse strap onto her shoulder, the next a thunderous roar rocked them. The glass panes of her studio's windows shattered. Sawyer yanked her to the floor with him and caught a glimpse outside. A fiery inferno.

"Oh God," he breathed.

The lab had exploded.

2

§

Kaylin and Sawyer shoved up from the floor and dashed out of the studio. Her view of the hellish flames was up-close and perfect. Just like her fear.

God.

Oh, God.

Dad had started up his lab and something had gone terribly wrong. Rectangular, made of gray and rusted metal, the entire building had burst into flames. The red-hot metal walls flickered with orange fire and the roaring flames devoured the two-story flat roof. Even from here, the heat beat on her face.

The fuel—Dad's biodiesel—must be burning, the black smoke curling into an ugly death plume. As Kaylin stared in growing horror, a second explosion rocked the building, spitting flames thirty feet into the sky.

"Call for help," Sawyer told her, his face drawn and hardened, his jaw set as if clenching his teeth. "I'll check the back of the building."

As Sawyer sprinted around the lab, she prayed the other side wasn't on fire, too. Hands shaking, she reached into her purse, plucked out her phone, and dialed 9–1–1. On autopilot, she gave her name and address. "Hurry. Please hurry."

No one could survive that inferno. Yet, Dad might not have been inside. After all, Sawyer had been at the lab before he'd come to her studio and no one had answered his knock. Her father could have gone to buy more caustic soda, used in the biodiesel production process, or to see his attorney. Or maybe he'd had a dental appointment he'd forgotten to mention.

Kaylin looked right and left, and didn't see her father in the backyard. Not on the back deck. Not beside her mother's rose bushes.

Don't panic.

She had to hold herself together. For her sisters. Perhaps Dad had stepped out to get the mail. Or returned to the house for a file or a wrench. Or gone to his car to run an errand.

Randy scampered by on his short little legs and started barking at the fire from the relative safety of the back porch. A neighbor shrieked for her children to come inside. Even from her studio the air reeked with the stench of burning fuel, causing Kaylin's eyes to water.

Her sixteen-year-old sister, Lia, sprinted across the yard with Billy, her best friend, in tow. Lia had lost her usual flirty and sassy expression. She now wore a wide-eyed look of horror. Billy hung back, and his normal teenage cockiness had vanished. And when, for a moment, Billy and Kaylin locked gazes, she could have sworn he looked guilty as hell. When he took off running toward the house, her suspicions spiked.

But then Lia was tugging Kaylin toward the lab with surprising strength. "We have to get Dad out. He was in there."

Please, no. "Are you sure?"

"Billy and I were just there, talking to Dad. He got a phone call and then his line went dead. We left. We have to get him out."

No way would she let her sister walk into that blaze. "Sawyer's checking the lab." Kaylin tugged Lia back toward the house, a relatively easy task since her sister's initial strength seemed to have vanished. "If Dad's phone went dead, maybe he went to the house for his spare battery or to recharge it on the cigarette lighter in his car."

Kaylin and Lia raced across the yard to their home.

Together they searched the downstairs, kitchen, office, and dining and living areas, shouting for their father. And all the while she wondered if the explosion had been sabotage. After two hard-looking men had paid them a visit last week, they'd had a break-in. Afterward, her father had changed the locks.

Now, she wondered if those men had threatened him. Had they returned and blown up the lab? Or was the fire an accident?

"He's not answering," Lia half yelled, half sobbed.

He'd have to have been deaf not to have heard them. "Maybe he's on the phone with 9-1-1." Kaylin sprinted upstairs, Lia on her heels. But again, they didn't find him. Kaylin spun around, grabbed Lia's hand, and clenched it tight. "Let's check the garage and his car."

Panic urging her onward, Kaylin opened the door that led from the house to the garage. She flipped on the light. Dad's ancient Oldsmobile sat parked on the right. She held her breath, hoping he'd pop up from under the dash with his lopsided grin.

Lia's voice trembled. "He's not here, either."

"Let's go back outside. Maybe he's with a neighbor. Or he's searching for us while we're looking for him."

"I'm scared. I'm so scared, Kaylin."

"We'll find him." Kaylin wrapped her arm around her sister's thin shoulders. She was scared, too. But she had to clamp down and lock out the terror. It was her job to take care of Lia and Becca. After Mama's liver had shut down and she'd died, she'd left Kaylin her love of dance, her roses, and her job. So Kaylin couldn't give in to her own fear. She had to be the adult, even when inside she was crying.

They hurried outside. The flames had grown higher, the heat more intense. Neighbors congregated down the block, holding their children tight, fear reflected on their faces. Kaylin didn't see her father or Sawyer anywhere.

Sixty feet away, the flames consumed the lab, the heat forcing them to retreat. Neighbors on the far side of the block gawked from their yards as if the Danners were a Florida side show attraction. Kaylin heard the squeal of car tires, the driver clearly eager to avoid the flames near the street. Even Randy had the sense to stay back from the fire and sat cowering by the studio door, whining uneasily.

Kaylin led her sister away from the house—even as she prayed that, too, wouldn't also go up in flames. She began to advance around the backyard when her sister planted her feet and stopped.

"Look!" Lia pointed to a man running like an Olympic sprinter straight toward the flames. "It's Sawyer."

Her father's partner bolted across the side yard. With a crowbar in hand that he must have fetched from his vehicle, he ran, no hesitancy in his stride. But a black cotton T-shirt and hip-hugging jeans were no protection from the heat or the flames. Eyes narrowed in determination, lips tight with resolve, Sawyer's tan face was red—too red from his proximity to the fire. Sparks landed on him but he didn't so much as bat them away. Arms pumping, biceps bulging, he raced straight for the burning lab's side door.

"Sawyer, stop!" No one could enter that building. No way. Kaylin's throat tightened with fear. Either Sawyer hadn't heard her or had paid no mind. He was about twenty feet from the burning lab when a third explosion blasted open the door, ripping it from its hinges and knocking him off his feet. The crowbar flew from his hand.

The force of the blast slammed him to the ground and the industrial-sized door missed crushing him by only a few inches. Flat on his back, he didn't move. Blood trickled down his forehead and into his dark hair.

Lia gasped, hid her eyes against Kaylin's chest and wailed. "He's dead. Oh, God, he's dead."

Praying Lia was wrong, Kaylin stepped away from her sister. "Stay here."

Ducking to keep stray embers from her eyes, Kaylin sprinted to Sawyer. She drew hot air into her lungs and tried not to wince at the increasing heat. He sprawled on his back, one arm flung over his eyes. Blood trickled from his sliced scalp, seeping over his temple and ear, and she hoped that meant his heart still beat.

When sparks threatened to ignite his clothing, she grabbed the towel that was still around her neck and used it to flick embers and ashes from his legs and chest. Flames danced up his shoulder and she smothered them with the towel.

"Sawyer. Get up." She grabbed his calloused hand, surprised at the warmth and size of it. Kaylin tugged, but the guy didn't budge. Not an inch. This man was fit. And muscles were heavy. Too heavy for her to pull him to safety.

Something burning drifted onto his jeans and began to smoke. She snapped the towel at it, but wasn't quick enough. The flames caught. What did they teach kids in school? Stop, drop, and roll.

He was already down. "Sawyer," she screamed and shoved him onto his side. "Roll."

He moaned, opened eyes that were clear and blue and stared straight at the burning building. By his sad gaze, she could have sworn he'd awakened clear-headed and immediately recalled what had happened at the lab. The explosion. Her father still missing.

"You're on fire. Burning up. Roll," she ordered, shoving him with a strength that came from years of dance training.

He tightened his fingers on hers, pulled her down. "You're burning, too."

He kept his wits, rolling in the grass with her in his arms. They both swatted the flames with their hands. Randy kept barking. Lia shouted for help, her voice surprisingly shrill and loud. But working together, Sawyer and Kaylin finally beat the fire on their clothing into submission.

For one long second, he lay on top of her, his chest against hers. Their gazes locked, and she couldn't look away. She couldn't read his expression. Couldn't guess his thoughts.

Then he rolled aside and helped her to her feet. He now possessed several charred holes in his jeans and his ripped shirt looked like he'd gone through a shredder, but the flesh beneath didn't appear to have blistered.

"You okay?" Breathing evenly, he stood, towering over her, his broad shoulders slumped, head bowed.

She blurted the first thought in her mind. "That was crazy. For you to try . . ."

"I had to." His massive hands closed into fists.

He'd had to try. Something about the rawness in his voice at that moment cut through her fear and touched her heart. Kaylin had always kept Sawyer at a distance. For one, he was too damn good-looking. For another, she wanted nothing to do with a dreamer like her father. And lastly, she didn't intend to put down one more root that might keep her from leaving town.

Still, she didn't hate him, either. Her father had told her his history. After losing his own parents in a car accident, he'd grown up with his grandmother, without a father figure. Sawyer and her father had bonded, the two of them working in the lab, fishing, bowling, fixing cars, and drinking beer. Even when he'd been away at college, he'd returned and worked with her dad during the summer. No doubt her father had wanted a son—and Sawyer had needed a father. Case closed.

They'd fit. Not by blood, but by common interests. And mutual respect. Enough for Sawyer to risk his life on the chance her father was still inside the lab.

Fire engines with alarms wailing roared down the street, arriving with sheriff's cruisers, their red and blue lights flashing. Deputies made the neighbors move back.

Lia, her round green eyes dilated with shock, ran over and hugged Kaylin. "Hold me. Please. Dad's gone. He's not in the house. Or your studio or across the street. Hold me and don't let go."

Her little sister had always been on the delicate side, like their mother, and with her blond curls blackened and streaked from the ashes, her frail bones trembling, Kaylin feared Lia was about to collapse. All three of them backed away from the heat toward the curb, with Kaylin supporting Lia. "We're okay. I'm all right. Sawyer has a cut on his head, but he's fine, too."

As she embraced her sister, she couldn't help thinking that if her father had been out of the lab, like Sawyer, they would have found him by now, too. Between the smoke, the oncoming sirens, and the stench, her hopes of finding her father alive dwindled, especially as she stared at the ruined lab.

Sawyer raised his head, and he was anything but defeated. His blue irises burned with sorrow and fury and in that moment, if his rage had been a hurricane, the storm would have taken out the state of Florida. The force of his rage was almost palpable, and she took a step back. Then another. She knew the moment his anger and helpless frustration turned to something else. She could almost smell his determination to find out what had happened, a consuming intensity that canceled out the reek of the fire.

Kaylin didn't know Sawyer well, but he wouldn't have headed into that inferno unless he believed her father had been inside the deadly fire. Despite her terrible fear for her father, she'd never forget that Sawyer had risked his life to try to save him. Still, that didn't mean her father *had* been inside. A tiny part of her refused to give up hope. Maybe there was a safe pocket inside the building that had protected him from the fire. They might yet find her father safe.

3
♪

As Fire Rescue rolled out water hoses, a deputy approached Kaylin, Sawyer, and Lia. Kaylin pressed the towel into Sawyer's hand. "Put this on your head to stop the bleeding."

He ignored the towel and faced the deputy, who introduced himself. "I'm Deputy Bryant. Are you all right? Do you require medical attention?"

Sawyer made quick introductions and refused any treatment. Blood dripped into his left eye. Finally, he pressed the towel to his scalp and it quickly soaked up blood. Too much blood.

"Ma'am, can you tell us who might have been in the building?" Deputy Bryant asked.

"My father, Henry Danner. And he's missing. Lia and Billy had just left him before the explosion."

"Lia's your sister?"

When Lia didn't speak up but trembled at her side,

Kaylin nodded, her throat raw from the smoke. "And Billy is Mitzy's son."

"Mitzy?"

Lia began to tremble so badly, Kaylin feared she might faint. "Sweetie, why don't you sit right here by the curb." She lowered Lia until she was sitting. When a paramedic began to fuss over Lia, mostly comforting her, Kaylin stood and answered the question. About a year after Kaylin's mother's death, the family had needed a house-keeper and they'd hired Mitzy. When money had gotten tight, Mitzy had taken an outside job, but by then, Mitzy and her Dad had grown close, and she and her son had stayed. "Mitzy's my father's friend. She lives with us. So does her son, Billy."

The deputy made notes on a pad. "And where is Mitzy today?"

"She works as a cashier at Wal-Mart. Her shift is almost over and she'll be home soon."

And Kaylin would have to explain all over again, to Mitzy and to Becca, Kaylin's sister, what had happened. By then, hopefully they'd have found her father. She must have paled because suddenly Sawyer gently put an arm around her shoulder to lend her strength.

"Give her a minute."

Grateful for a few moments to collect herself, she ap-preciated his kindness. Sawyer's voice, so gentle for such a big man, reminded her that her father had decent friends, starting with Sawyer and Mitzy. Mitzy had effortlessly joined their household three years ago, but only recently, when she was sure they would welcome it, had she attempted to assume a motherly role.

Still, Mom had left Kaylin in charge. If Dad hadn't survived . . . she couldn't go there. Couldn't give up on him. Not yet.

Lia seemed to be okay, talking quietly to the paramedic and that calmed Kaylin, too. Slowly Kaylin regained her composure and nodded at Sawyer. "Thanks." She seemed to be thanking him a lot.

Deputy Bryant returned to his questions. "Did you see anyone else enter or leave the lab today?"

"Sorry. I never pay much attention."

"What exactly does your father do here?"

Kaylin let Sawyer answer. In truth, she didn't have the energy. Until she knew if her father had been in that burning building, she could barely focus on the conversation.

"Dr. Danner was making biodiesel fuel," Sawyer said.

"Biodiesel. From corn oil?"

"Soybean."

Deputy Bryant paused. "Biodiesel's the stuff the president says is going to help solve our fuel crisis, right?"

Sawyer nodded. "Trucks can take it right into their fuel tanks without any modifications."

"Were there other employees inside?"

"We haven't hired anyone yet. Actually we haven't even started operations. We're still working out the kinks."

Sawyer went on to tell the deputy that her father's

invention might be valuable enough for someone to make him a target. The deputy wrote everything down but looked skeptical. He turned to Kaylin. "Does your dad have any enemies?"

Kaylin shook her head.

"Have you had any trespassers or threats or—"

Sawyer cleared his throat, but his voice remained roughened from smoke inhalation. "Kaylin, why did your father upgrade security while I was gone?"

The urgency in Sawyer's tone made her refocus on the conversation. "Last week two strange men rang our bell. Dad brought them inside, but he didn't look happy about it. They looked pretty hard-edged."

"They came to the house?" Sawyer urged and after Kaylin nodded he spoke to the deputy. "Dr. Danner always conducted business at the lab. Since I was out of town last week, I don't know what was discussed. But our project might be very threatening to people in the oil business."

"Do you have their names?" Deputy Bryant asked Kaylin.

She shrugged. "Sorry. I don't remember."

"What did these men look like?" the deputy asked.

She tried to pull herself together. "They looked Middle Eastern, with dark hair and swarthy skin. Dark eyes. Cold eyes. They spoke English with thick accents. One even sported a shiner that had to be painful."

"What were they wearing?"

"Business suits."

"What did they talk about?" the deputy asked.

"I don't know. After the introductions, Dad ushered them out."

"Did the men threaten you or your father?" Deputy Bryant asked.

She shook her head. "It was just their appearance that spooked me. Oh, I almost forgot. Both men were clean shaven. They spoke broken English. But what really freaked me out is that when Dad introduced us, they didn't acknowledge me. The silence was awkward and not just because of the language barrier." She shivered. "They creeped me out. And even Dad must have noticed. He quickly escorted them to his lab. To tell you the truth I was relieved to see them go."

"Did you ask Henry about the men later?" Sawyer asked.

"He promised they wouldn't come to the house again. But then he clammed up. I'm certain he changed the locks because of them."

"Did Dr. Danner tell you that was why he changed the locks?" Deputy Bryant asked.

She shook her head. "He's been really tight-lipped about the meeting." Kaylin looked at Sawyer. "You know how he is when he goes into full-avoidance mode."

"Do I ever." Sawyer spoke to the deputy. "Dr. Danner is brilliant, stubborn, eccentric, and secretive."

"So you enjoy working with him? You and Dr. Danner have a good relationship?"

Kaylin sucked in a hard breath. If the deputy's words were meant to make Sawyer uncomfortable, he didn't appear to notice.

"Dr. Danner thinks outside the box," Sawyer continued, his tone full of admiration. "And he has a passion for his work, an enthusiasm that makes working with him a pleasure."

Sawyer had pegged her dad, all right. Meticulous about his work, protective of his family, yet naive when it came to judging people, her father was a mass of contradictions. While her father exasperated her at times, Kaylin didn't just love him. She admired and respected him as well.

Deputy Bryant looked up from his notes at Kaylin. "These men who came to your house. Have you seen them again?"

"No. A few days later someone broke into the lab, but they didn't take anything. I thought the break-in was tied somehow to our visitors, but we had no proof. Dad may have been suspicious, too, because he changed the locks and beefed up security. He filed a report with the Sheriff's Office."

"I'll check on the report. When you said your father beefed up security, do you mean he hired a guard?"

Kaylin wondered if they'd ever know what had caused the explosion. "Dad installed extra security cameras inside the lab. They must have burned up." She glanced at the smoking building. The roof had caved in. Two of the metal walls remained upright at one corner, but the rest was a heap of charred metal. And smoke obscured the remains like a shroud.

"The security system may not be a total loss," Sawyer contradicted her. "Henry was meticulous about removing the footage from the camera and backing it up onto his computer."

"Can we talk about this later? My father's missing." Kaylin stared into a second deputy's face as he joined them and she prayed for good news.

"Fire Rescue found a body inside," the deputy, a black man with kind eyes, told them. Then he quietly conferred with Deputy Bryant.

A body? Blood roared in her ears. She forced words through a throat raw from smoke and from holding back tears. "Was it my dad?"

"Was your father wearing any identifiable jewelry?" Deputy Bryant asked.

"A watch and a wedding ring."

"And a class ring from the University of Florida?" the second officer asked.

She nodded and sorrow welled up in her throat. They'd found her father. Still, she didn't want to believe it.

When Deputy Bryant didn't say anything else, she forced another question through a mouth as dry as sand. "Was it him?"

"I'm sorry." The truth was in his sympathetic eyes, there for all to read.

God. They'd found his remains. Kaylin swallowed hard. Her father was dead.

Dead.

Like a jab to her gut, the pain radiated outward and she swayed on her feet.

Sawyer slipped an arm around her waist to steady her and she was grateful for his heat, because her flesh had gone ice cold. A cold that made her shiver and her teeth chatter.

"You're wrong!" Lia leapt to her feet and screamed at the cop, her pretty features contorted with tears. "Dad was right at the door when Billy and I left. He could have walked out . . . couldn't he? You found someone else. Not him."

Kaylin stepped away from Sawyer's side and held her sister tight, easily wrapping her arms around her.

Her heart agreed with Lia. Their father couldn't be dead. It had to be a mistake. Kaylin had spoken to him on the phone only a few hours ago and he'd been so happy, telling her that his formula worked. He just couldn't be gone.

But her head pointed out the facts. Her father had been inside that building. He never took off his ring. Never. They'd found his body.

Oh . . . my . . . God. He was dead.

The loss seemed to squeeze her lungs so that breathing was an effort. Anger and grief spun her thoughts so fast that nausea hit. Dad was dead. The Danner girls were on their own.

Her sister shook Kaylin in desperation. "Do something."

Kaylin couldn't flip out right now. She had to get a grip.

Lia needed her.

Hugging Lia, Kaylin shielded her from the ashes and the tiny fragments of metal still falling from the sky.

"Do something," Lia repeated her demand. "Maybe the medics can save him. Make them try," Lia sobbed, her tone high-pitched, tears streaming down her face.

If the medics could have saved him, they would have. They'd gotten here too late. Or maybe he'd died instantly. She prayed his death had been quick, painless. Not like her mother, whose liver had slowly shut down. Kaylin kept the thought to herself as she tied the grief down tight. Wrapped it in bands of steel.

Don't think about losing Dad. Don't think about never seeing him again. Don't think about him never calling. Don't think about anything but helping Lia.

Focus on her. And Becca.

Surely this couldn't be happening to them. Not again. Their mother had died four years ago. Now, Dad was gone, too. He might not have been practical but he'd been an extraordinary man. Without him she didn't know how she'd keep it together.

But she had to. She couldn't let herself think about the fear. She didn't have time to come apart. She had to stay strong for poor Lia, who wasn't going to make it out of her teenage years with even one living parent.

Kaylin didn't know what to do or say to make this right.

Nothing could make this right. Parents weren't supposed to die and leave their families until their kids were grown.

Daddy was dead. Kaylin's throat tightened in grief and tears choked her. But she couldn't release her emotions. Lia needed her. So would Becca when she came home.

Her sister couldn't hear about their father's death from a stranger. His death. God. She still couldn't believe it— even though she'd seen the building blow up, even though Fire Rescue had found his body and his rings. She still expected the laws of physics to bend for her.

Damn. Damn. Damn.

When her sisters didn't need her so much, Kaylin would grieve. Later, when she was alone. Not out here on the lawn with all the neighbors looking on. For now she repressed her tears. Her horror. Her fear.

Flames that danced across the backyard broke through Kaylin's shock. The fire had leaped from the lab to the bushes.

Her mother's rose bushes were on fire.

"I'll be right back," she told Lia, then sprinted across the yard.

If Kaylin could hook up the hose and turn on the water spigot, she could save her mother's roses. The firemen were concentrating their efforts on the lab as well as the roof and walls of the house. The east wall was blackened, but nothing burned there. But the garden behind the back deck was another matter. She had to save the roses. Her Dad loved those roses. *Had* loved the roses. Her mother had given them into her care on her deathbed.

Hands shaking, Kaylin screwed the hose to the spigot. But the threads refused to align and her hands shook with frustration.

Sawyer approached and took the hose from her useless fingers. "Let me help."

"My mother's rose bushes . . ." She pointed to the flames burning the first three bushes.

For a moment, she was afraid Sawyer would mock her. Her father had just died and she was worried about rose bushes?

His face remained gentle, his tone soft and serious, as if he understood exactly how much those bushes meant to her. "We'll save as many as we can."

Within seconds his clever fingers had attached the hose and with an efficient twist he fixed the spray nozzle into place. When she spied the raw patches on the backs of his hands, guilt stabbed her. He should be getting medical treatment. "Your hands. Let me do it." She reached for the hose.

And was slightly startled when he gave it to her. He actually understood she needed to act, to do something.

As the hose sprayed water, all her careful control burst. Tears cascaded over her cheeks. Tears of frustration and fear and sorrow. As she put out one fire and watered down her mother's rose bushes, her eyes overflowed. Then she was crying, out of control, shoving the hose into the ground and digging through the mud with her hands so the water could reach the roots, unable to hold back deep, racking sobs.

At twenty-four, she was head of the Danner family. Everyone had left her. Her grandparents were long gone. Then Mom. Now, Dad. There were no aunts and uncles. Her parents had had no sisters or brothers. There were no cousins. Just Kaylin, Becca, and Lia.

But they would manage. Kaylin would keep it together. She'd promised her mother to watch over the girls. And Kaylin didn't break her promises.

With a muddy hand she wiped away her tears. When she finally regained a measure of control she looked up to find Sawyer beside her. He'd removed his tattered shirt and handed it to her. "Here. It's ruined anyway. Go ahead and wipe off the mud and blow your nose."

She couldn't believe she'd actually forgotten he was there. He'd remained so still. Hadn't said a word. Just allowed her grief to pour out without intruding. And she liked that he didn't mutter platitudes—like it was going to be okay. Because it wasn't ever going to be okay. Not with Dad gone.

She sniffled and accepted his shirt. She wiped her face and eyes, blew her nose, and breathed in the smoky scent of Sawyer's shirt along with a faint earthy scent that she found as comforting as his presence.

She mashed his shirt in her hands. "Thanks. I need to go to Lia. I shouldn't have left her."

"Take a minute. She's safe with Deputy Bryant."

"She shouldn't see me like this." God. Oh . . . God. What was she going to do now?

4

❧

Saturday morning, the day after Henry's death, Sawyer set up a ladder and rolled primer over the scorched side of the two-story Danner home. The physical labor gave him an excuse to stay close by . . . in case anyone tried to bother the women, but it also left Sawyer with too much time to think, to mourn.

Through the open window, he heard Kaylin phoning her students and canceling dance classes for a week. Then she took a break and came outside to offer him a cold glass of water.

Dressed in jeans and a tank top, she looked young, fit, and strong, but one glance into her eyes told him she was hurting. She looked exhausted, and he suspected she was coping with her grief by keeping busy. The artistic and playful Kaylin whom he'd seen dancing two days ago had entirely disappeared. Although his heart had ached for her, and he thought about giving her a hug, he didn't. She'd reeled her emotions in tight and any intrusion into her private grief clearly would not be welcome. So he accepted the water with a nod. "Thanks."

After handing him the glass, Kaylin gestured to the fresh primer. "I should be thanking you." Then as if uncomfortable with accepting his help, she changed the subject. "What will you do now?"

"Wait for the primer to dry and apply paint." He could have easily drained the entire glass in one swallow but sipped, suspecting the moment he finished she'd take back the glass and retreat into the house. With her shifting uneasily from foot to foot, no doubt she'd come outside out of obligation, out of politeness, not because she wanted to talk.

She shook her head. "I meant with Dad gone. . . ." She bit her lip and changed the subject. "The medical examiner called with a preliminary finding and said Dad died due to the fire. They couldn't be more specific until final tests come in, and that might take weeks."

"What about the cause of the explosion?"

"That's yet to be determined, but I can proceed with the funeral arrangements. I picked out a casket and headstone to match my mother's." She swallowed hard and brushed away a stray tear, then got herself back together.

"Henry would have liked that."

"But what will you do without him?" she asked, recognizing she wasn't the only one in this conversation who would dearly miss her father.

Losing Henry might not just be the end of his friend, but the end of Sawyer's dream. The idea of working with Henry had motivated Sawyer through many lonely nights of hitting the books, of studying. "I hope to continue Henry's research."

"But the lab's gone." Her gaze floated over the burned

building and caved-in roof, what was left of the walls a poignant reminder of their loss.

"I'm not giving up."

"Maybe you could get a job with—"

"I've never wanted a corporate job."

Kaylin made a face. "Neither did Dad."

He could tell by her tone she didn't approve of that choice. Was that why she'd never come around the lab much? He'd assumed she'd been busy. Not interested. But maybe she'd disapproved.

He tried to keep censure from his tone. "Surely you of all people understand that owning your own business gives you a certain freedom?"

She avoided a direct answer but rolled her eyes, revealing skepticism. "The dance studio gives me the freedom to starve if I'm not successful. It doesn't automatically supply health insurance or a steady paycheck."

"You seem to do okay."

"But if a hurricane blows through or I twist an ankle and have to shut down for a month or two, I won't have the financial resources to recover."

"Sure, it's a risk." But life was a risk. And Sawyer yearned to control his own destiny. "If I do research for a big company, then they own my work and any patents that come from it. I don't want my ideas to belong to stockholders who might or might not appreciate my creations."

He could see doubt in her eyes, and with the burned-out lab a fresh reminder of risk gone wrong, he didn't blame her. She glanced at his water glass as if willing him to finish. "What will you do for funding?"

"I haven't figured that out yet." He downed the rest of the water and shrugged out the aches in his shoulders, determined not to give up. Perhaps he could apply for a grant or attract financial backing. Somehow, someway, he would continue. "Maybe we'll find Henry's laptop with his latest formula. Do you have time today to search the house?"

"While Billy mows the yard, Mitzy, Becca, Lia, and I are going to clean the house top to bottom. We intend to search as we clean."

"I could help," he said.

Kaylin accepted his offer, and after he rolled out the last coat of primer, he headed inside, where under Kaylin's supervision the Danner sisters and Mitzy cleaned and all of them searched for the laptop. Sawyer's hunt began in the attic, and he worked his way down through the house. He rummaged inside every closet and cabinet in each room, even the pantry. They opened old suitcases and boxes. They'd been through the garage twice and checked his car as well as the trunk. And then they all switched rooms and searched again. But no one found Henry's laptop.

Frustrated, Sawyer went back outside and touched up the primer.

Still, even without Kaylin in sight, his thoughts revolved around her. He admired her strength, the passion he'd glimpsed when she danced that she'd again buried so deep that only family or a good friend would know was there. Sawyer used a brush around the eaves, and thought about the contradictions in Kaylin. She seemed so strong, but her fear of spraining an ankle or a hurricane showed her vulnerability. She seemed to put her family first, and yet, he kept thinking about Kaylin's airline ticket. The one she hadn't wanted to talk about. Where was she going? Had she canceled her plans?

ON SUNDAY, the day of Henry's funeral, Sawyer awakened early and walked through the charred ruins of the lab before the church service. The fiberglass tanks that had held the soybean oil had melted. Ditto the wash tanks. The pumps, the generator, the methanol and caustic soda . . . all of it was gone. Sawyer hadn't needed to check on the insurance. This year money had been tight and they'd let the policy lapse, gambling that disaster wouldn't strike. Talk about starting from scratch. First he'd have to clear the charred ruins of the metal walls from the lot. He'd scheduled demolition for Monday. The sooner the better. He didn't want any of the neighborhood children exploring and hurting themselves.

During his tour of the lab, he said his own good-bye to Henry. The man had been father figure, mentor, and friend, and Sawyer would miss not only his wisdom but his gift for seeing possibilities when everyone else believed a project couldn't happen. Henry's personal mantra reverberated through him.

What would you attempt if you knew you wouldn't fail?

Borrowing Henry's optimism would help him go on.

A hundred failures didn't matter. Not if experiment one hundred and one brought success.

As Sawyer's feet crunched over the ruins, Henry's spirit reached out to infuse him with hope. And Sawyer vowed to rebuild. He didn't know where he'd acquire the funds, but he would find a way . . . as a tribute to Henry. To the legacy a brilliant and caring man had left behind.

Saying good-bye to Henry reminded Sawyer of the loss of his own parents. Not that he recalled the actual car accident that had taken their lives when he'd been little, because he hadn't been with them, but he knew about loss, a constant companion through his childhood and into his teens. Luckily his grandmother had raised him, and then he'd found Henry. Henry had given Sawyer's life a purpose.

Sunday morning the Danner sisters buried Henry beside their mother, Danielle. They'd sat together, Kaylin in the middle between Becca and Lia. She'd been courageous and outwardly stoic. But Sawyer had only to look at her red-rimmed eyes with dark circles beneath to see her grief. Yet despite her own grieving, she'd always seemed to know when Becca needed a tissue, when Lia needed a comforting hand on her shoulder, or when Mitzy needed bolstering. Coping with her father's death had obviously drained Kaylin, but she kept up a brave front, even whispering kind words to friends of Henry's during the burial.

After the funeral, the clean house was ready to welcome mourners. The chandelier in the foyer glistened, as did the hardwood floors. Wearing black slacks and a pale gray blouse and charcoal pumps, Kaylin stood in the foyer graciously greeting neighbors and friends, introducing her sisters to her father's friends when needed, and directing traffic. Time and again as the line moved forward, she pointed people to the kitchen. Many had arrived with plates of food, fried catfish, hush puppies, coleslaw, cornbread, pork cassoulet, fried chicken, greens, black beans and rice, cherry pie, and peach cobbler. At least no one would have to cook for a week.

The scent of food actually made Sawyer's stomach churn. He had yet to regain his prodigious appetite. He couldn't help thinking that if he'd been there when Henry had switched on the systems, he might have stopped the spark that had likely caused the fire. Then again, the generator hadn't been running just before the explosion, an indication that Henry *had* waited for him to do the first test run of the fuel.

With a beer in hand, Sawyer strolled through the house, now filled with friends and neighbors, and out onto the back deck, where Randy slept on the lounger. He sat beside the rose bushes and gazed across the lot at the burned lab. When Kaylin sat beside him, he was a bit surprised.

"I needed a break," she admitted.

"Me, too."

But she obviously had something on her mind. "Just after the explosion, I heard a car drive away. Did you happen to notice if it was a neighbor?"

He shrugged. He'd heard a vehicle's tires squeal, but his focus had been on getting inside the lab to Henry. "I didn't see any . . ." Her question had his mind shooting in new directions, directions that made his stomach clench into a roiling knot. Had someone caused the explosion?

Kaylin gently swatted away a pair of love bugs, careful not to hurt them. "My father was intelligent, methodical, and careful."

"I agree. Henry knew that methanol is flammable and every machine inside that lab was explosion proof. That means—"

"No sparks." He liked that she'd picked up some scientific knowledge, but wished she knew more about the business. Kaylin continued, her voice softening. "I was talking to Dad that morning. . . . He was so excited. He sounded certain he'd discovered a workable biodiesel formula."

"He called me, too."

Kaylin turned to look at him, her green eyes wide and curious. "So you know the formula?"

He wished. "My cell phone dumped him into voice mail. But even if we'd touched base, your father was way too careful to reveal secrets over a cell phone connection."

"But if you were already planning fuel runs, wouldn't you have known the formula for a while?"

Sawyer shook his head. "We'd run a batch, test it, then modify. We didn't expect to get it right on the very first run."

"But you must have some idea of his research direction?" Kaylin asked.

"We'd been getting closer all month. Tweaking this, adjusting that." Sawyer frowned. "I can't help wondering if the attempted break-in last week is connected to the explosion."

"But no one got in," Kaylin argued. "At least Dad was fairly certain they didn't."

"But suppose he was wrong?" Sawyer's voice was grim. "Did he search the lab top to bottom? They could have planted an explosive device behind a ceiling panel or in an air vent and he'd never have seen it."

Kaylin stared at him. "But the break-in was days ago."

"Maybe they had a timer. The driver of that car you heard could have set it off with an electronic device."

"But why? If Dad had a formula, it disappeared with him."

"Unless they stole it before they blew up the lab," Sawyer suggested.

"You think someone else wanted that formula badly enough to . . ."

"Steal it and kill him? That would have to be a yes."

Randy inched over and put his head in Kaylin's lap. Absently, she scratched behind his ears. He took her attention as an invitation to curl into her lap, put his head between his paws, and close his eyes.

"I don't know, Sawyer. The idea sounds farfetched. Like a movie plot. Nothing that would happen in sleepy Riverview."

"Yeah. I know."

"And yet, I keep thinking the same thing. Those Middle Eastern guys . . . were scary. I wouldn't be surprised if they came back and—"

Lia ambled outside and interrupted the conversation. She'd swept her blond hair back in a ponytail, revealing a pixyish face with swollen green eyes that had known too much sorrow. She sat tentatively, right next to Kaylin, as if she was afraid to let her get too far away. "I miss him, Kaylin. I miss him so much."

"We all do." Kaylin hugged her sister.

"Daddy's not going to see me in the school play," Lia sobbed. As if sensing that Lia needed him, Randy scooted from Kaylin's lap to Lia's. Her sister clutched the dog, who didn't seem to mind as he tried to lick tears from her cheeks. "He's not going to see me graduate from high school."

"I know you're hurting," Kaylin sighed, her voice choking up. "But I'll be there, sweetie. Becca and I will be there."

"You aren't my mother."

"We're your family. We'll be there for you," she murmured, her tone strong and gentle.

Lia buried her face in Randy's fur, anger in her voice. "It's not fair."

"No, it's not fair," she agreed.

Sawyer bit back the words he wanted to say. Henry's death *wasn't* fair. But it wasn't fair that Kaylin had stayed home to take care of Lia and Becca when she could have been auditioning in New York. Of course, Kaylin didn't say the words. She didn't seem to have a selfish cell in her body. Besides, Sawyer supposed someone had to be the adult.

He also couldn't help being proud of her. Henry had told him how Kaylin had promised her mother to take care of her sisters. And she'd kept her word. Sacrificing her goals to do so. And from the way Lia leaned on Kaylin both physically and emotionally, the kid obviously needed her big sister's strength and love.

The door banged open again and Randy growled, but when he saw Becca hurrying toward them, he went back to cuddling with Lia. Unlike Lia, Becca was built curvy and strong. Wearing too much eye makeup for Sawyer's taste, a crisp white shirt over a navy tank top, brown capris, and wedge sandals with black ribbons that criss-crossed up her calves, Becca didn't just look upset, she was tensed with anger, her makeup was smeared as if she'd been crying. "What's going on?"

"We were taking a time-out." Kaylin twisted sideways and took Becca's hands in hers. "Before Lia came out, Sawyer and I were discussing whether or not the fire was an accident. Until we know, I want you both to be very careful."

Becca wrenched away from Kaylin's grasp and gestured to the blackened lab. Of his three daughters, Henry had claimed Becca thought most like her father. He'd said she had the brains, but she often let her emotions lead her. Right now grief and anger battled across her strong, feminine face.

Anger obviously won out as Becca pointed at Kaylin. "This is all your fault. It's your fault he's dead."

"What are you talking about?" Kaylin demanded, even as the blood drained from her face. Sawyer felt as confused as Kaylin looked. How could this be her fault? She hadn't been inside the lab in months.

"Becca's still in shock," Sawyer muttered. "She doesn't know what she's saying."

Becca frowned at him. "You aren't part of this family. Butt out. And I know exactly what I'm saying." Becca shook a finger in Kaylin's face. "Dad needed money for a methanol recovery system. And you wouldn't mortgage the house."

"Huh?" Clearly stunned, Kaylin probably didn't understand the technology and had no idea what Becca was talking about. But she knew she'd been attacked. Hurt and anger blazed from her eyes. *"What?"*

"Focus." Becca snapped her fingers in her sister's face, her eyes narrowed in anger. "Methanol is dangerous. It's one of the chemicals that blow up crystal meth labs."

"Crystal meth?"

Sawyer knew that Becca was real smart, except when it came to common sense. She'd even earned a college scholarship—only she hadn't put in the work and had let her grades slide until she'd dropped out. At age twenty, she now worked as a waitress at a local restaurant, helping the family as much as she could with her meager earnings.

Kaylin's voice revealed her skepticism. "Surely Dad didn't have crystal meth in the lab." Her gaze shot to

Sawyer for answers. "Are you saying our father was making drugs?"

"Of course not." He chose his words with care, refusing to say that the process could be dangerous if done incorrectly. "The methanol is combined with caustic soda to make methoxide. In the final stage of the biodiesel process, impurities are cleaned out and that cleaning can be done in many different ways."

"Dad wanted to buy a centrifuge so the process would be safer, but you wouldn't sign on the loan," Becca accused her again.

"I wouldn't sign the loan because no way could we make the payments."

Becca tossed her dark hair over her shoulder. "If Dad made the fuel, *he* would have made the payments."

Kaylin threw up her hands in disgust. "When was the last time Dad made a house payment? I'm the one who earns the money to pay the bills—"

"I help," Becca interrupted.

Kaylin started again. "*We* couldn't afford—"

"Says you. And you like playing the martyr—"

"I do not. And please keep your voice down." Kaylin glanced toward the guests still inside. But no one seemed to notice as they ate, drank, and talked among themselves.

Becca's voice sharpened. "You're a control freak. My God, you hide in your studio—"

"I earn a living in that studio," Kaylin's voice was threaded with steel. "A studio that helped Dad—"

"Dad's dead. It's your fault he blew up because you wouldn't let him buy the centrifuge." Becca pivoted on her heel and returned into the houseful of guests, slamming the door behind her, leaving Lia sobbing and Kaylin shaky.

The two sips of beer Sawyer had swallowed roiled in his gut. Didn't Becca know how lucky she was to have her sisters? He'd give anything to have a brother or a sister. He had no aunts or uncles, no siblings. Only his grandmother. And Henry, who was gone. This family should be pulling together, not fighting.

Apparently, Becca was hurting so badly she couldn't stop from lashing out. Still, the damage was done. He doubted Kaylin would ever forget her sister's nasty accusations.

Lia raised her head to peer at Kaylin through her tears. "It's not true, is it?"

Kaylin seemed to draw on an inner strength that was bottomless. "Becca's just angry because Dad's dead. She's taking it out on me . . . because she can." Kaylin sighed, her eyes sad, but she seemed already to have forgiven her sister. Amazing.

Then Sawyer saw doubts begin to cloud Kaylin's eyes. By God, he didn't care if Becca was hurting. She had no right to say such terrible things to Kaylin, who'd sacrificed her own dreams to be there for her sisters. He wished he could say something to comfort her. Anything.

5

§

Monday morning, Kaylin emptied the dishwasher, her mind on her sister. She and Becca hadn't talked since their argument on Sunday. Could Becca have been right? Becca might fly off the handle, she might be impulsive, but she was smart. Had Kaylin refused to sign for an additional bank loan because she really was the control freak Becca accused her of being?

Sure, Mitzy and Becca helped when they could, but Kaylin was the primary family provider and took pride in her role. Despite that, she would have welcomed more help. She sure as hell would have applauded her father's success and she still wished Becca had completed college so she could find a better job. Becca might be smart but she was an underachiever. Yet her criticism remained, like a raw and open wound that would fester if left untended. Kaylin didn't know how to heal the damage.

The three sisters were so different. Lia, delicate, sensitive, and young, was almost Becca's opposite. Becca was strong-willed, physically fit, super-intelligent, yet it was almost as if her ability to see every side of an argument left her unable to make good decisions.

The doorbell rang and Kaylin answered it to find Sawyer and Deputy Bryant on the stoop. Sawyer was obviously taking a break from directing the lab demolition. Bulldozers were currently loading debris into dump trucks, a job that shot ashes into the humid air.

"Please come in."

"Deputy Bryant came by with more questions," Sawyer explained, dusting off his shoulders where black flakes had settled on his brown T-shirt, before he stepped inside.

The deputy removed his sunglasses and placed them in his front pocket. "Ma'am, I was wondering if I could take a look at your father's home computer."

"Why? He didn't keep his lab data there."

Sawyer nodded. "True. But every few days, Henry backed up the digital security footage from his laptop to the desktop at the house—at least that's what he told me. He said the footage took up a lot of room and he didn't want to slow down the laptop."

Kaylin had always thought three computers was overkill. But her father had insisted he needed one at the lab, another at home, and a laptop for presentations. Her frustration over her growing suspicion that the laptop with his formula had blown up with the lab warred with the hope the data might be on the home computer.

"Can we check?" Deputy Bryant asked.

"Sure." She gestured down the hall, past the wedding picture of her parents that hung next to baby pictures of the three girls. "I'll take you to his office. Has anyone figured out how the fire started?"

"Not yet." The deputy followed her down the hall and through the formal Florida room. Her mother had decorated in soft greens with bold tangerine pillows that had faded a long time ago, but Kaylin hadn't had the heart or the funds to replace them. On the other side of the room was a side porch and her dad's office. The deputy paused and surveyed the office, then headed to the desk. "It could take up to six weeks for the forensic evidence to come back."

"And in the meantime?" she asked.

"Anything we can get off the security footage might help our investigation. If we can identify his visitors, we'll talk to them as well as your neighbors, and perhaps the family attorney . . ."

"Mr. Lansky." She offered the name.

"We'll find out if anyone saw or heard anything unusual." The deputy caught Sawyer's eye. "If you could make a list of all of Dr. Danner's business associates, that would be helpful."

Her father's desk was immaculate, his pencils sharpened, a picture of Mitzy in a silver frame next to one of Kaylin dancing, another of Becca at a high school track meet, and one of Lia with Randy in her lap. It looked as if he'd just stepped out for a moment and would return momentarily.

But Dad wasn't coming back. Ever.

Seeing her father's empty coffee cup hit her full force as she stepped into the room. Or maybe it was the family pictures that dominated the dark paneled walls. A photo of her parents at a fancy restaurant. One of the entire family at Fort De Soto Park, on the beach, where they all looked tanned and happy. They'd dug for clams, roasted them over a campfire, and spent the night in a tent.

Her gaze moved to another photograph of her dad and Sawyer fishing. A more recent one of her father in the lab with Mitzy and Billy, who at only sixteen was already several inches taller than his mother. Billy had Mitzy's coloring, but his dark hair was ragged and showed off several earrings which had recently been a bone of contention. Next to that picture sat her father's prized possession, a framed engineering blueprint of his first invention, a machine used in paper mills to process paper. The family had lived off the royalties for years. It had been his most successful invention to date. His legacy.

They certainly hadn't been rich. But Becca and Kaylin's babysitting, plus her mother's jobs and the royalties from her father's invention, had supported them all through Kaylin's teens. Unfortunately, the paper process was computerized now, his machine dated, and the royalties had dwindled to almost nothing.

"Did your father have any arguments with anyone lately?" Deputy Bryant asked. "Did he have business competitors? Another lover? Any enemies?"

"Sorry. Nothing like that." She shook her head and opened the top drawer of his desk, where he kept his laptop. Although they'd already searched here, she tried to keep her impatience toned down. To her it was obvious that foul play was a factor, and though she understood the authorities needed proof, it was difficult to keep her tone even. "Why aren't you investigating those men I told you about? The foreigners who showed up right before we had the break-in?"

"We're working on it, but without names or better descriptions, you haven't given us much to go on."

Sawyer raised an eyebrow. "Actually, Kaylin, Henry did have business competitors."

The deputy raised his pen over a pad to begin writing. "You have names?"

"I'll make you a list," Sawyer said.

"What kind of competitors?" Bryant asked.

Sawyer shrugged. "There are other biodiesel plants in the area. And also an ethanol plant."

"Why would the ethanol plant be a competitor? They sell gasohol—not biodiesel, right?" Kaylin asked.

"We compete for tanks as well as for government funding. There's a scarcity of both right now."

"Can you tell me more about Dr. Danner's work?" Bryant asked.

Sawyer shrugged again. "We were working on a patented process to convert soybean oil into biodiesel."

"Would that be profitable?"

"Yes," Sawyer said.

No. But she didn't say it out loud. Kaylin sighed. "The process is unproven, and quite frankly, over the past thirty years my father only had one profitable invention."

"But if he'd discovered a new process?" Deputy Bryant asked.

Sawyer rubbed his temple. "Profitability depends on how efficiently the process works. Many people are turning soybean oil into biodiesel fuel. What matters is how many gallons a minute can be made, the cost of the components, and the quality of the end product."

I think Dad took his laptop with him that morning," Kaylin said. "That's why we can't find it."

"But you aren't sure, right?" Sawyer asked.

She frowned in thought. "Dad didn't take it with him every day, only the days he backed up the security footage or when he had a presentation. The day he died . . . I packed his lunch and I thought I saw him put it in his briefcase. But he did stop here in his office before heading to the lab. I was hoping he'd left it behind, but if he had, we would have found it during our search."

Deputy Bryant rubbed his forehead. "We checked the lab site thoroughly. There was no evidence of a laptop, and those things are surprisingly sturdy. Even after the explosion, we should have found pieces. However, the team hasn't finished sifting through all the evidence we gathered Friday night." The deputy paused, then asked, "You think your father might have gone somewhere else that day?"

She shook her head. "Dad rarely left the lab. Once he was at work . . . he was focused. Totally absorbed."

"Maybe he put the laptop in his desk?" the deputy suggested.

"My father kept everything in its place." Nevertheless she opened every drawer, searched the closet and a magazine rack next to his coat stand. Nothing.

Deputy Bryant made a note. "I'll ask the forensics team again if they found anything. Maybe we'll luck out and recover a readable hard drive in the unprocessed evidence."

"May I?" Sawyer gestured to the desktop computer. When she nodded, he sat behind the desk and booted it up. The machine asked for a password.

Despite the minor blisters on the tops of his hands, Sawyer typed with confidence.

"You know Dad's password?" she asked.

"D-A-N-N-E-R-K-K-B-L-B-I-O-D-I-E-S-E-L. Unless he changed it. Nope. We're in." Sawyer seemed as at home at the computer as he had on their roof repairing the shingles last summer. She found his knowledge of her father's password odd since he'd never been at the house much. But he'd been nothing but helpful since the fire began. Too helpful?

Could he want access to her father's computer for reasons of his own? Kaylin didn't know if her father's claim of finding a secret formula to make biodiesel was for real, nor did she know if her father had shared all his research with Sawyer. However, she suspected that if her father *had* discovered something, he would have backed it up on this machine—if the explosion hadn't happened before he'd had the chance.

Had his formula died with him? Was it on the missing

laptop or this desktop? And if it had been on the laptop—where was it? Frustrated and confused by her father's actions on the day he'd died, she held her breath, wondering if Sawyer was about to open a file that would reveal not only who had been in the lab this past week, but the formula itself.

She watched carefully as Sawyer pulled up the security files, burned them to a new disc, and handed it to Deputy Bryant. Meanwhile, on the monitor, she saw people come and go, in and out of the lab; some she recognized, others she didn't, but it bothered her that Sawyer had known the password. But then, her father probably had used the same password on all his computers.

Later, she intended to ask Sawyer questions about the biodiesel formula and the people caught on camera, but this wasn't the time. She tried to put everything out of her mind, concentrating on watching what Sawyer brought up on the monitor.

As far as Kaylin could see, Sawyer had found nothing useful on her father's desktop. The security footage was three days old and hadn't been backed up since then. The Middle Eastern men her father had ushered from the house to the lab weren't there. He'd bought the additional interior cameras after their visit. She did see one bald-headed man with silver-rimmed glasses and tattoos who didn't seem to be a businessman, but she had no clue to his identity.

"Any chance you can trace that man from his tattoos?" Sawyer asked.

"We can try," Deputy Bryant said.

On the security tape, another man strode into the ware-house and shook Henry's hand. "That's Dean Witman. We buy containers from him." Sawyer pointed to the man beside Dean. "And that's Mr. Lansky, Henry's attorney."

"We'll check them both out, too." Deputy Bryant wrote the names on his pad.

Sawyer searched the system. "From what I can see so far, the formula for Henry's biodiesel isn't here."

Disappointment flooded Kaylin. Apparently, her father had figured out the working formula on the day he died and hadn't had time to make backups.

Unless they found the laptop, his biodiesel formula had burned with him. A formula that may not have worked, she reminded herself.

As she escorted the deputy and Sawyer from her home and closed the door behind them, Lia, with school books in her arms, came running into the foyer. She bit her lower lip and spoke softly. "Mitzy's not right. She's acting . . . weird."

"I'll go talk to her. You'd better head to school."

"Maybe I should quit school. Get a job," Lia suggested, setting down her books.

Kaylin picked up the books and thrust them back into Lia's hands. "Absolutely not. You keep up your grades. You're going to college."

"But if we need money . . ."

"We'll manage. Lia, you know a college education is important. Dad wanted that for you."

"Okay. Okay. It was just a suggestion." She shifted the books in her arms.

Kaylin thought it would be best for Lia to resume her normal activities as soon as possible. Still, she'd allowed her sister to sleep in late this morning before heading back to class.

But now her offer to quit school and get a job scared Kaylin. It was bad enough that Becca had dropped out; she didn't want Lia to follow in her footsteps. Lia's offer to find a job showed she had a good heart—if not the judgment that went with it.

At least she hadn't argued too much about heading back to school. Lia didn't need to be around to deal with Mitzy's grief. The teen had enough to manage on her own.

With a sigh, Kaylin headed into the house to find Mitzy, who hadn't been herself since she'd watched the emergency rescue people load the body bag containing Henry into the medical examiner's van. She'd wailed, a long piercing cry like a wounded animal about to die, and had fainted. Her son Billy, totally wasted, probably from pot, had nevertheless helped his hysterical mother to her bedroom, where except for the funeral, she'd kept to herself, mourning in private.

Kaylin hurried into the kitchen to find Mitzy collapsed at the table. Tiny, rounded, and wearing smudged, dark-red lipstick, she sobbed noisily. Her mascara ran and made her appear as if she had two black eyes. Since Henry's death she'd aged a decade. Her red-rimmed and bloodshot eyes looked unfocused. Her faded blue blouse was stained with tears. "I need whiskey," she demanded.

Kaylin didn't mention that it wasn't even lunch time. Mitzy's coworkers had all pitched in to cover her shifts, but the time off didn't seem to be helping her over the grief. Clearly Mitzy hadn't slept last night. Kaylin poured two fingers of amber liquid from a decanter in a cupboard and placed the glass in front of Mitzy, who picked up the liquor and downed it in one swallow. A bit of color returned to her cheeks.

Kaylin half expected her to demand another, but she didn't. She sat perfectly still, except for her shaking shoulders, and allowed the elephant tears to fall. The tears turned into a waterfall, her large chest rising and falling with giant sobs. Kaylin didn't know a lot about Mitzy's past. But she'd lost Billy's father to cancer and now she'd lost Henry. Clearly, she'd cared a great deal. However, like a thunderstorm that blew in, darkened the skies, and was quickly over, she suddenly grabbed up several tissues and blew her nose.

Kaylin should try to console her—but what could she say? Nothing would bring Daddy back. Not tears. Not pleading. Nothing. And Kaylin's emotions were tapped out.

Still, she asked. "Is there anything I can do?"

Mitzy didn't answer.

Kaylin placed a hand on her shoulder. She hadn't slept well last night and exhaustion washed over her. "I'm going upstairs and back to bed. You could use some rest, too. Come upstairs with me."

Mitzy nodded. "Go ahead. I'll be up after a while."

"You sure?"

"Go on. I have to get over him. I forgot how hard it is." Mitzy looked up and shooed Kaylin. "Go on. I'll be fine. And don't worry, I'm going back to work soon. I know we need the money."

"Thanks." Kaylin left Mitzy and headed upstairs to her room to take a nap. Kaylin ached to lie down, close her eyes, and rest. She might be too wired to sleep, but she needed to gather her strength. She didn't bother removing the coverlet as she sat on the bed. Between the loss of her father and her uncertainty over her sisters, her mind whirled. Was Lia ready to return to school? What was the best way to get past the nasty argument with Becca?

And she also worried about Billy. She suspected he felt left out, not a real part of the family. She wished she could talk to her dad. Only he was gone. And they didn't even know why the lab had exploded. . . .

Before she could lie down, the phone rang. Kaylin unplugged it. Voice mail could get it. Later she'd return calls from neighbors and friends. Right now, she so badly needed to close her eyes, to pull herself together.

She must have fallen asleep. At a knock on her door, Kaylin jolted awake. Becca opened the door and walked in. "It's an emergency."

6

"An emergency?" Kaylin shouldn't have turned off the phone. Kaylin sat up so fast that dizziness made her close her eyes. "Is Lia—"

"Lia's fine." Becca stalked into the room, her body language innocent, as if they'd never fought. But that was Becca. She lived in the moment. "Mitzy had a panic attack and Billy gave her what he thought was a Xanax. It put her to sleep."

"That's the emergency?"

"Well . . . no."

Kaylin rubbed her eyes. "I'm too tired to play twenty questions, Becca."

Her sister strode to the window and peered out. Kaylin knew she was stalling. Uncomfortable. Since Becca had practically accused Kaylin of murdering their father, Kaylin wasn't inclined to be patient or congenial. With a sigh, she reminded herself that Becca had just lost her father, too.

"What's wrong? What's the emergency?"

"Maybe now isn't a good time."

"In my experience, emergencies never come at a good time."

"Why do you do that?" Becca asked.

"Do what?"

"Talk like you're the mom. Talk like you're twenty years older than me."

Kaylin scooted upward on the bed until her back rested against the headboard and she could pull her knees to her chest. "Maybe I feel older. And you're stalling. Spill it."

"I have a problem."

Kaylin just waited. She didn't have the energy to prod. Becca had come to her. Eventually she'd talk. Unless Kaylin blew it and asked too many questions and they started yelling at one another. She didn't want that. With Dad gone, they had to pull together. But why couldn't Becca have waited until she'd slept a little longer, or at least had time to really wake up?

Of course, even if Becca left right now, sleep was out of the question. Kaylin's raging curiosity had spiked enough to short-circuit any chance of returning to sleep.

Becca moved from the window and perched tentatively at the foot of the bed. "First, I want to apologize. I should never have accused you of . . . it was a terrible thing to say. I'm sorry, Kaylin."

"Come here." Kaylin moved over and patted the bed beside her. "If I had known buying that centrifuge would have saved Dad, I wouldn't have cared if we lost the house. I'd have mortgaged this place to the leaking attic."

"I know. I wasn't thinking. I was scared and angry and the funeral was more than I could handle. I've been in over my head lately." Becca bit her lip. "I think I'm in love."

In love? The conversation seemed weird. Inappropriate. It was as if Becca was already done with her grieving and ready to move on to normalcy. Kaylin wasn't there yet, but with Becca reaching out to her, she wasn't about to criticize, either. Everyone grieved and mourned differently and at their own rate. Perhaps Becca was stronger than Kaylin, ready to accept their father's death and move on. But it also crossed her mind that Becca might not be able to deal with such a painful loss, so she'd manufactured another problem. She'd said she *thought* she was in love.

Please God, don't let her sister be in love with a married man. Kaylin took her sister's hand. "Being in love can be scary."

"I'm terrified. I was going to talk to Dad but . . ."

"Now you have to settle for me." Kaylin said what she knew her sister was thinking. There was a long awkward silence. Finally Kaylin found the words she wanted. "You know, since Mom died, it hasn't been easy for me, either. I try to look out for you and Lia but I don't always know what to do. I'm not Mom. Neither is Mitzy, but we're both here."

"I want Mitzy to stay," Becca told her. "And she has nowhere else to go."

"I agree," Kaylin said quickly, anxious to have common ground. Her sister was impulsive, but she could also be generous and loving. "You know that no matter what you tell me, I'll be on your side."

"You'll disapprove of him."

"It won't be the first time. We're still sisters. We'll always be sisters. Besides, being in love should be a good thing."

"Yeah, it would be if I knew . . . oh, Lord . . . I made love with Shadee Sumad and now I'm afraid it was a mistake."

Uh-oh. Kaylin knew now was not the time to play the mom card. Right now, she was Becca's sister and had to be nonjudgmental. However, she didn't know if she was qualified to give any advice.

Four years ago when Kaylin had broken up with Kevin, she'd messed up her own love life. At the time she'd believed she loved him, had intended to go to New York with him. Then her mother had died. He'd left for New York without her.

But if she'd loved him enough, wouldn't she have found a way to go with him? Kaylin still didn't know the answer to that question and hardly felt qualified to talk to her sister, never mind give advice.

Becca shifted restlessly. "I've been seeing Shadee for a year. He's kind and when Dad died he was gentle and compassionate. He cares about me."

"But?"

"Shadee's parents are from Lebanon. His father's a professor at USF."

"Hold on. I'm not following you. What does his family—"

"Shadee's going to think I'm not good enough for him."

"Oh, for heaven's sake. Why would he think that?"

"Don't you see, it's because I made love to him and no, I'm not pregnant." Becca paused but Kaylin said nothing. Her sister was already upset, and there was no point in heaping more blame on her head—she'd already done that to herself. Besides, Becca was a grown woman, entitled to do what she wished with her life. Obviously, she cared about Shadee. Although it was news to Kaylin that her sister had been seeing him for a year, and it was clear this was no one-night stand. Besides, there could be no undoing what she'd done. Kaylin wasn't even sure what she'd have advised if Becca had discussed it beforehand. "Shadee's culture and morals are different," Becca continued. "I should have waited. His family is probably conservative."

"Probably?"

"That's what's so strange. I've met his family, of course." That was more than Kaylin could say about Shadee, but she bit her tongue. "But after we started hanging out, he kept me away from them. Kept me apart. I think he's concerned that they won't like me. And now that we've made love, he'll probably think I'm not good enough for them."

"You don't know that." Kaylin didn't know the family, but had heard neighbors mention them, always favorably. "And haven't they lived in this country for years?"

"I guess."

"Some of our culture may have rubbed off. Besides, it wasn't all your fault. He could have said no."

Becca sighed. "I'm so into him, I *couldn't* have said no.

But no guy is going to blame himself. And I really, really like him. I may have just blown my long-term chances with him."

"Back up. Start over. Why do you think you blew it? I think you need to begin at the beginning."

"There's not that much to tell. We had chemistry right from the moment we met. I was hanging out with Shadee about a week when we exchanged sweatshirts." She smiled at the memory, the passion in her eyes reminding Kaylin of their father. "I'd bought mine at a concert and they only had size large—so we traded. I got his Tool and he got my Chili Peppers."

"And?" If Becca had given away her Chili Peppers sweatshirt she must adore the guy.

"We've spent a lot of time together. And I love everything about him. His smile. His hands. His sense of humor. And the way he really cares about me. Last night I pulled up to his family's driveway and he was bent under the hood of his car, checking the oil. I asked if he was ready to go. He said sure and hopped in my car. We ate burgers at DQ and then parked. One thing led to another and . . . God, he was wonderful. Sweet and tender and . . . well, anyway, everything was perfect until I took him home, and his brother, Tariq, walked up to the car and glared at me as if he knew. . . ."

"He couldn't possibly have known what you'd done," Kaylin tried to reassure her.

"But Tariq hated me on sight."

"That's his problem."

"I wish." Becca paused. "He looked upset. Asked why we'd left without him."

"That doesn't mean anything."

"He disapproves of me. I know it. And Shadee told me they're tight."

"So we'll think of a plan to win Tariq over."

"You'll help?" Becca paced, her long dark hair flying over her shoulder as she spun. "You think I need a makeover?"

"You look fine." With her dark curly hair and curves, what man wouldn't want her? "Why don't you find out his favorite food? Then maybe you and Mitzy can make whatever it is and take it over there as a peace offering."

"But if Shadee's ashamed of me, he might not want me to show up on his doorstep."

With their relationship so tenuous, Kaylin thought carefully before she replied. "You know how you're always telling me that I don't have the experience to tell you what to do?"

"Yeah?"

"Well, I don't have that kind of experience. Only you can tell if Shadee has real feelings for you, enough to introduce you to his family, enough to stick by you no matter what others think."

"But what if I can't tell? What am I going to do?"

"Why do you have to do anything? Why not just wait and see what happens?"

"Because I can't stand not knowing what he thinks about me."

"You could ask him." Kaylin raised an eyebrow. She sympathized with her sister, she truly did. But Becca only had a few choices. And she didn't seem to like any of them.

"I'm not like you, Kaylin. I'm afraid to ask. I'm afraid of what he might say."

So much for the strong front Becca put on to face the world. Her sister might appear secure on the outside, but deep down, she was full of uncertainty.

"Maybe you need some time apart. To get your head together. Give him time to miss you."

Becca frowned, obviously not liking that idea, either. "I don't know."

"You could bring him over and let us check him out."

Becca grinned. "Maybe. But I don't know when. I'm waitressing Saturday and Sunday nights. With Dad gone, I'll work extra as long as you need me to."

"Everything helps. Thanks."

Interrupting the conversation, Lia, blond hair bouncing in a ponytail, skipped into the room, Randy on her heels. Her collar bones seemed too sharp, her face pale, but Lia's energy seemed up. "I could work, too. Maybe get some babysitting jobs."

"What are you doing home from school?" Kaylin asked.

"I didn't go. I wasn't ready."

"Okay." Kaylin and Becca exchanged long looks and then made room for their sister, which wasn't difficult considering she was a size zero. Kaylin plumped a pillow for her. "But no schoolnight babysitting jobs. You won't be able to stay awake in class."

"Whatever." Lia wormed into the bed between Becca and Kaylin. Randy followed suit, curling up in a spot by Kaylin's feet. Lia, like a snuggly puppy that had run around excitedly and then collapsed, closed her eyes and almost immediately fell asleep.

Kaylin must have fallen asleep again, too. She awakened later that afternoon, her neck stiff and cramped. Leaving her sisters asleep in her bed, she rolled out, shooed Randy downstairs and out the dog door to do his business, and then returned upstairs to hit the shower.

She was finally ready to face the blinking message lights on her phone.

7

Before Kaylin could fix a cup of coffee or listen to messages, the kitchen phone rang. She recalled unplugging her bedroom phone this morning before her nap and guiltily answered. "Hello."

"Ms. Danner. Kaylin Danner?"

"Yes."

"This is Francis Lansky, your father's attorney," he introduced himself, his voice kind. She'd met Mr. Lansky after her mother's death and again when the house title had been transferred from her parents' names to Kaylin's and her father's so they could qualify for a refinance. She liked the elderly Southern gentleman, appreciated how he spoke simply and understandably about the law, without putting on airs or making her feel dumb. He'd also come to the funeral, although she hadn't spoken to him. "First of all, I'd like to offer my condolences."

"Thank-you." And so it began. The awkward calls and strained silences that had punctuated the weeks and months after the loss of her mother started anew. Just because she'd been through it before didn't make it any easier.

"Would you like me to take care of the corporate details?" he offered.

"Yes, thanks." The fewer calls she had to make, the better.

"Your father was a friend, and it's the least I can do." Her father had found friends in all walks of life and it saddened her that she hadn't known he and Mr. Lansky had been close. He cleared his throat. "Do you have time to meet me this afternoon? I can come to you."

"Now?"

"It's about your father's estate. I believe you should know what he wanted."

"I understand." She checked her watch. "I should have time to ask my sisters to join us."

Mr. Lansky cleared his throat again. "I'm sorry. You and Sawyer Scott are the sole heirs."

"What!" What had her father been thinking? For a moment her suspicion of Sawyer rose. If he'd inherited any-thing . . . would that be a motive to blow up the lab? She doubted it. Likely whatever Sawyer had inherited had blown up.

Mitzy stumbled into the kitchen. Looking hung over, her eyes bloodshot, she headed for the coffee pot.

"So I'll see you at four?" Mr. Lansky asked.

"Four o'clock will be fine." Kaylin had one last ques-tion. "Will you notify Sawyer?"

"I'll make all the arrangements. And again, I'm very sorry. Henry was a good man."

Kaylin swallowed the lump in her throat. Mitzy slumped at the kitchen table, her gaze on her coffee cup. If she'd slept, she didn't look it. By her expression one would never know that cheerful Florida sunshine poured into the kitchen along with the scent of orange blossoms. While the faint reek of smoke still clung to the cleared lot, the balmy breeze was either blowing in the other direction or the smell was already fading.

Mitzy, sitting up straighter, spoke carefully. "I suppose you'll be wanting Billy and me to move on."

Glad that she and Becca had already spoken about the matter, Kaylin felt free to have this discussion. In truth, if Becca had wanted Mitzy to leave, Kaylin didn't know what she'd have done. But all she had to do was think what her father would have wanted. He'd adored Mitzy. She'd made him happy after their mother passed on. Becca liked her, too. And she paid her and Billy's own way, helping out with the electric and grocery bills.

Kaylin placed her hand over Mitzy's shaking one. "This is your home. You're welcome to stay."

She hoped the words would relieve Mitzy. But like a tropical rainstorm that opened up out of a cloudless sky, she started to cry. "I didn't expect . . . I'm very grateful. Thank-you."

Kaylin supposed she should have spoken to Lia, too, but she already knew Lia's mind. She and Billy were friends and she didn't need to lose her friend along with her dad. Still, Lia was growing up. Kaylin should start including her younger sister in the decisions.

Kaylin topped off Mitzy's coffee and poured herself a cup, then pulled up a chair at the table. "Mitzy, now may not be the best time, but we have to talk about Billy. I'm concerned."

"He's a good boy."

"Billy needs help. He's using drugs."

Mitzy shrugged and mopped her eyes with a napkin. "He's a kid. All kids experiment."

"He's doing more than experimenting." Half a dozen times in the last few months Kaylin had seen him high.

"I'll have a word with him," Mitzy promised, and sighed. "Henry and I wanted him to finish high school. Maybe go to trade school after that. Car mechanics make good money."

The phone rang. Kaylin awkwardly patted Mitzy on the shoulder. "We'll talk later."

She picked up the phone. "Hello?" This time she was surprised to hear a voice she didn't recognize. "Ms. Danner, my name is Dean Witman. I'm sorry for your loss, and I know this may be too soon to intrude on your grief . . . but I wanted you to know that I'm interested in purchasing your father's business." He quickly reeled off his phone number and automatically she wrote it down.

"I'm not sure there's anything left to sell."

"Just promise me you won't do anything with his assets, that you won't sell them to anyone else until I have a chance to make an offer."

Like people would be coming out of the woodwork to purchase a black patch of earth? "Sure. I'll do that."

Kaylin hung up the phone and stared down at it, trying to process the exchange. The man had sounded kind enough, eager. Maybe too eager? Before she had a chance to come to a conclusion, the phone rang again. As if on cue, the bell on the front door chimed. She ignored the phone. Mr. Lansky had arrived and she wanted to get this meeting over with.

Only when she opened the front door, the family attorney wasn't there—it was Sawyer. But he wasn't dressed for any lawyer meeting. He was bare-chested again. Either his skin was naturally bronzed or the guy had an incredible tan. All that skin plus his powerful shoulders and that triangular dusting of hair drew her gaze downward. Where it didn't belong. She tried to keep her eyes on his face, his brilliant blue eyes, the wide jaw, the stubble already shadowing his chin, although she was fairly certain that he'd shaved this morning.

As she stared into his face, she recalled his hard chest

against hers as they'd rolled on the lawn, his arms protecting her, his hands gentle as they'd snuffed out embers. Her thoughts were inappropriate and she stuffed down the memory. Packed it away where it couldn't see daylight.

Sawyer was a gentleman. Her father's partner. He'd simply been kind. And she was relieved to see him.

In jeans too low cut to be decent, he stood on their front stoop with a sharp expression in his eyes. "Would you happen to have any spare rollers?"

"Rollers?"

He held up a paint roller, the rounded end caked with old paint. Someone had forgotten to wash it after use. From the dark green color, it appeared to match the house's shutters. She'd forgotten he'd planned to paint this week after the primer dried.

"There's extra paint in your garage," he explained with patience, as if he didn't expect her to remember. "I thought I'd touch up the scorched side of the house. But this roller's seen better days." He looked her straight in the eye—as if he had nothing else on his mind but the task at hand.

"Did Mr. Lansky call you?" she asked.

He frowned, the crinkles at his blue eyes deepening. "Why would your father's attorney want to talk to me?"

That's what she'd like to know. "He'll be here shortly and he requested your presence at the reading of Dad's will."

"Okay. I'll be here for the meeting." When she didn't

say anything more, Sawyer raised an eyebrow. "What about the rollers?"

Her hand fluttered toward his chest then back down to her side. "Don't you want to put on a shirt?"

"It's hot. Upwards of eighty-five in the sun." He grinned. "And I'm working on my tan."

His tan already looked great to her. Which was damn annoying. She had no business noticing that—however, she couldn't exactly help it when he showed off those pecs right in front of her. *So don't look.* Yeah, right. Like that was possible.

She turned around and headed for the laundry room. Sawyer followed her through the foyer and kitchen and down a short hall. It had only been a few days since her father's death, and she had no business appreciating so much as one glance at all that bronzed and toned skin.

She turned on the laundry room's light and peered above the washer and dryer, where shelves held an assortment of tools, cleaning sprays, paper towels, and various hardware that had overflowed from the garage. "We might have an extra roller in here."

Sawyer reached up to the top shelf and pulled down several plastic baskets crammed with broken knobs, string, scissors, an old lunch box, and all kinds of junk. In the close space, his male scent drifted to her—earthy, with a hint of spice.

She scooted forward to avoid touching him. But she was aware of his every movement as his strong hands efficiently moved aside a crock pot, two kites, mosquito repellent, and a spare dog bowl left over from Randy's puppyhood. Sawyer seemed to have absolutely no idea that they were only inches apart, that she could feel heat radiating off his body, that when he stretched to reach the back of the shelf, his jeans dropped lower on his hips.

She swallowed hard.

Barking, Randy ran through the kitchen, his paws scrabbling on the hardwood floor. In his eagerness to reach them, he knocked into the laundry door, shutting Sawyer and her inside the small room, which suddenly seemed tinier than a mouse trap. Randy kept barking and scratching the door, demanding they let him in.

Kaylin would have reopened the door, but with space so tight, she couldn't do so without turning around and reaching past about an acre of flesh. Very male, very sculpted flesh.

God.

What was with her? So what if he didn't have a shirt on? So what if he was chiseled? So what if he looked more mouthwatering than fresh berries with whipped cream at the Florida Strawberry Festival?

She didn't know the man. Before a few days ago—when they'd rolled around in the grass—they probably hadn't spoken ten words in the last five months. Suddenly they were in a space so tight, that with each whiff of his primal scent, she couldn't stop her nostrils flaring. Her pulse was up. Her stomach a tight ball of nerves.

"Here they are." His voice sounded casual, yet triumphant. He reached to the very back of the laundry shelf and his chest cradled her back, his hips nestled intimately against her butt. "Excuse me."

Was that amusement she heard in his tone?

Outside Randy kept barking. Someone yanked open the laundry room door. "Randy, I swear," Mitzy scolded the dog, "there's no one . . . Sawyer? Kaylin?"

Kaylin turned and peered around Sawyer. Mitzy's eyebrows shot up until her forehead wrinkled. Her eyes widened in shock. "What's going on?"

Great. Just what Kaylin needed. Mitzy jumping to conclusions. Mitzy loved gossip. Lived for gossip. From her expression, no doubt she believed she'd just discovered a juicy story to share at Bonnie's Hair Express. No doubt the incident would hit every home in Riverview by next week.

Mitzy looked from Sawyer to Kaylin, grinned, then winked at Kaylin with approval. "Don't worry," Mitzy said as if reading Kaylin's mind, "I won't say a thing."

"There's nothing to say. Sawyer needed a paint roller. Randy slammed the door shut." Kaylin would have brushed by Sawyer—except there was no room. Now that she'd spun around she and Sawyer were face to face, her chest almost brushing his, she was certain there wasn't enough air in here, despite the open door. The guy was big. Too big. Too attractive.

For one moment, she prayed Randy would slam the

door shut again and Mitzy would disappear, then she'd be free to lean into him and absorb some of that heat. Some of his strength.

Oh, for heaven's sake. She really wasn't herself. She put down her inappropriate thoughts to Sawyer's scent playing with her libido.

"Is that the doorbell?" Kaylin asked, her voice worried, but worried was okay. She had a lot on her mind. "Mr. Lansky must be here. We need to go." She placed both palms on Sawyer's chest and gave him a little push. He didn't budge. He simply peered down at her, his eyes bright with amusement.

She prayed she hadn't acquired a new habit of turning red when she was embarrassed or that he could read her momentary discomfort. However, he appeared distracted, so maybe he hadn't noticed anything unusual. Like her yearning to run her hands across his . . . his everything. What the hell?

Impatient with herself, she let an edge creep into her tone. "Come on, Sawyer. Move."

Mitzy took two steps back, but not enough to let Sawyer pass by. Her gaze speared Kaylin. Her eyes might still be bloodshot but she appeared clearheaded. "Did you say your father's attorney is here?"

"Yes. He wants to talk to me."

"And Sawyer?" Mitzy guessed. But how? Unless she'd overheard the conversation at the front door.

It didn't matter. Kaylin shrugged. "Mr. Lansky's following Dad's request."

Mitzy nodded, her eyes calm, the circles not as dark as earlier. She'd repaired her makeup and hair and maybe she'd slept. "Your father counted on Sawyer with the business. I'm sure he'll be helpful to you, dear." She stepped back with a pleased look on her face. As if she knew something Kaylin didn't.

With the doorbell ringing and Randy barking, there was no time for conversation. Kaylin hurried to the front door. But Lia, Billy, and Becca had already beaten her to it.

Her sisters were speaking quietly to Mr. Lansky, a tall, thin man with graying hair and bushy eyebrows in need of a trim. Billy hovered, half in and half out of the foyer. Kaylin took a good look at him. For once, he didn't look wasted, not the least bit high.

He wore clean pants and a new shirt. A fourth earring marked a new piercing. His shirt hid his latest tattoo. Billy almost looked . . . *respectable* and Kaylin wondered if cleaning up had been his idea or his mother's.

Her sisters turned to her with frowns. Becca folded her arms over her chest and tried to hide her hurt. "Mr. Lansky wants to talk to you and Sawyer alone. What's going on, Kaylin?"

"I have no idea. But whatever's mine is yours. Don't worry, Becca. You either, Lia. We're in this together—no matter what. Okay?" Kaylin leaned forward, hugged both sisters and Billy slunk further into the shadows.

When Kaylin saw Sawyer outside on the porch, heading toward her and the front door, she blinked in surprise. She hadn't realized he hadn't followed her through the house. Instead, he must have gone out and around the back. He now wore a shirt. She caught his eye and nodded her thanks.

And reminded herself to have another talk with Mitzy about Billy. They had to see what they could do to make him feel more a part of the family. She didn't approve of the drugs and believed he used them to bolster his self-esteem. And she worried about where Billy got the money for drugs since he didn't have a job. She prayed he wasn't dealing, because they couldn't come up with money for bail, or even rehab for that matter.

However, she shouldn't borrow trouble. She had enough on her plate. And now with Mr. Lansky here to discuss the estate, she suspected more problems could be coming her way.

8

Kaylin settled Mr. Lansky and Sawyer in her father's office and served iced tea along with Mitzy's home-baked chocolate rum-raisin cookies. Kaylin and Sawyer sat side by side on the sofa, carefully not touching, and the attorney took the wing chair across the coffee table.

After setting down his sweet tea, Mr. Lansky opened

his briefcase and removed a thick sheaf of documents. Kaylin wasn't surprised her father had his estate in order. He'd always kept meticulous records. If he used cash, he had a receipt and filed it in the correct expense account folder. He kept books the way he kept his journal: neat, precise, and up-to-date.

Tense, Kaylin tried and failed to relax. She didn't want to discuss her father's estate. She just wanted the pain to be over. But she had no choice. This was her responsibility.

The attorney cleared his throat, eyeing the paperwork through thick black-rimmed glasses. "You'll be pleased to know your father had a life insurance policy left over from his teaching days at the university. While not a large sum, it should cover the funeral expenses."

"I didn't know Henry had taught," Sawyer said.

Mr. Lansky handed over the life insurance documents to Kaylin. She closed her fingers tightly on the papers without reading them. "After graduation, Dad worked exactly one semester at the University of Florida in Gainesville before running into political differences with the department head. He must have bought the policy back then."

Sawyer leaned over and peered at the policy limit. "If that won't cover it, I'll help."

"Thanks." His offer was kind, generous. Sawyer had always been thoughtful. As if cognizant of how much of her father's time he'd taken up, Sawyer hadn't intruded into family time. He'd avoided their house—women's territory, her father had said he'd called it. Sawyer didn't come around for supper or to celebrate Christmas with them, not even to exchange gifts.

Although last summer when the roof had leaked, they'd returned from church to find him patching a hole with tar paper and shingles. She'd recalled he'd gone shirtless then, too, and the sun had bronzed a chest that was glistening from honest labor, calling attention to a fine dusting of hair that added to his sex appeal. His short dark hair had spiked with sweat, his five o'clock shadow emphasizing his cut cheekbones. The man was damn attractive but he seemed to accept it much as he did everything else— with a shrug. He didn't seem to have one pretentious atom in his body. When he'd caught her looking at him, his lip had curled in a satisfied half smile—part challenge, part interest that had caused her stomach to flutter. At the time, she'd chalked up her attraction to him as due to having gone too long without a man.

They hadn't had many face-to-faces since then. She kept to the house and her studio, he to the lab. But when they'd rolled across the grass to put out the fire on their clothing, she'd felt the power of him, the way he'd instinctively cradled her body to protect her, how his hands kept her head from slamming into the ground. Although part of her cherished the memory of his kindness, she also resented it. Because one thing she knew for certain— if she let another man back into her life, it sure as hell wouldn't be a man like her father and Sawyer.

Kaylin was too practical to fall in love with a dreamer

like her father. She wanted solid and down-to-earth. A man who had health insurance and knew he could pay the mortgage. And Sawyer had told her straight up that he didn't want a corporate job. Even with no resources he hadn't given up on the biodiesel. She'd seen the fire in his eyes when they'd discussed it, heard the determination in his tone. Despite losing Henry, despite the lab explosion, Sawyer wasn't giving up and she feared that, like her father, Sawyer would spend his life chasing a dream that would never happen. She really didn't want to be around him, didn't want to give the attraction she felt any room to grow.

She had to remind herself that Sawyer hadn't asked to be here. And he'd just offered money to help with funeral expenses. She stared at the condensation on her glass of tea. Swirled her fingers through the wetness. And wished she could be anyplace but here. Under any circumstances but these.

The attorney rustled the papers. "The house, Henry's car and personal belongings go to you. It was your father's wish that you take care of your sisters and allow Mitzy and Billy to remain at the residence, but it was a request, not a requirement of inheritance."

"I understand. My sisters and I will share the house, and I've already invited Mitzy and Billy to stay."

"The business part of the estate is more complicated. Basically, Sawyer gets half, the rest is yours."

"Half?" Sawyer was clearly shocked. And touched. "That was good of him." He paused, then asked softly, clearly baffled, "Were you privy to Henry's reasoning?"

"He was counting on you to make his venture profitable. He felt Kaylin would do better with fifty percent of something, than one hundred percent of nothing."

"I'll do my best to get the business going again," he told Kaylin. "But it won't be easy."

"Was there property insurance?" Kaylin asked, unable to suppress all hope. She understood her father had trusted her to do right by her sisters, and she would. Whatever he'd left Kaylin would be equally shared with Lia and Becca.

"Yes, but the policy lapsed last year," Sawyer told her. "Your dad—"

"—didn't have the funds," she completed his sentence for him and stood. "Obviously, continuing the business is impossible."

"Not necessarily," Sawyer disagreed. "I know the direction of your father's research. I might be able to find backers or get a government grant."

Kaylin looked in Sawyer's eyes and saw fierce determination, but she also recalled how many times her father had had that same mind-set, yet had never attained his dreams. "Well, if that covers everything—"

"I'm afraid there's one more item on the agenda." Mr. Lansky raised his eyes to Sawyer. "Your presence here is no longer necessary."

Sawyer nodded and shoved to his feet. "If you need me, I'll be outside." She must have had a blank look. He added, "Painting."

"Right. Thanks." Kaylin sat down abruptly.

What could Dad have left her? The extra life insurance money would come in handy. As far as she knew, he had no other assets. She didn't understand and didn't like surprises.

After Sawyer left, the air in the room grew tense. Mr. Lansky placed the large stack of papers on the coffee table, but held one envelope in reserve. "Kaylin, what I'm about to tell you may come as a shock."

She sensed he hesitated to speak out of kindness. But waiting for bad news had her stomach clenching into one giant knot. "Nothing you can tell me could be worse than what's already happened. I'll be fine." She braced her back, squared her shoulders, and raised her chin, hoping he couldn't discern her trembling. "Just tell me."

"Your mother's mother, your grandmother, is still alive."

He had to be wrong. "She died of an illness before I was born."

"That's what you were told." Mr. Lansky nodded in agreement. "But your parents lied to you."

Stunned and shocked, she didn't know what to think. "I have a living grandmother? You're certain?"

"Yes."

"I don't understand. Why would my parents . . ."

"They had their reasons. Apparently your mother's folks, the Carstairs, did not approve of their daughter's marriage to your father. They considered him a bad choice and threatened to disown your mother should she marry him."

"The Carstairs are wealthy?" she guessed.

He nodded. "Apparently, despite the threats, your parents eloped."

"My mother loved my father very much." Enough to leave her own parents. Kaylin couldn't imagine such a thing. No wonder her mother had sometimes looked sad during family get-togethers. How different all their lives might have been if the Carstairs had helped out financially—just a little.

If the family could have afforded medical care, her mother might have been vaccinated for hepatitis B. And if she hadn't so badly needed to work three jobs, she might not have ignored her own health. But after Mom had gotten sick, she'd continued to work and come home exhausted, insisting she just had the flu. By the time her mother had finally seen a doctor, her liver was too damaged for medicine alone to work. Her immune system had been compromised and she'd been too weak for a transplant.

Even her father might have had better lab equipment and not have blown himself up if they'd had financial help. At the thought of a wealthy grandmother, resentment buffeted her. No wonder her parents had shielded them from such a narrow-minded woman.

"After your parents wed, the Carstairs cut Danielle out of their lives."

Kaylin, Becca, and Lia had a grandmother. And while she might not be someone Kaylin wanted to meet, she might have other relatives. "Do I have aunts and uncles and cousins?"

"I don't know. However, I do know that after Danielle's liver shut down, when she was on her deathbed, your father went to her parents. They refused to come to the door."

How horrible. Her poor mother. It made her stomach knot just imagining her father frantic with grief and going to those horrible people for her mother's sake—only for them to rebuff him.

"Why are you telling me this now?"

"Your father thought if anything happened to him that you should know the truth." He peered at her through his thick glasses. "There's more."

Kaylin braced herself. "I'm listening."

"Your grandfather has passed away. But your grandmother sent me a note after Henry's death."

"I don't understand."

"I've always been your father's attorney. A little research would be all it would take to find me. In the note, your grandmother asked me to tell you that if you ever needed her, she'd be there for you."

"My grandmother offered help? The same woman who wouldn't go to her daughter on her deathbed?"

"Yes."

"I'd have to be insane to contact her."

"Kaylin, I can't tell you what to do, but years have passed. She could have changed. It's also possible that although she disliked Henry, she doesn't hold that against you."

"If she were a forgiving woman, she would have contacted my mother after she married my father."

"What will you do?"

"I don't know." Talk about being shocked. She hadn't realized her parents were capable of keeping such secrets from their children. She wondered what else she didn't know. "I'm not even sure if I should tell Becca and Lia. We might be better off alone."

"My dear, the decision is strictly yours. If you wish to contact her, and if I can be of service, please don't hesitate to call on me."

"Thank-you."

Kaylin wondered if she was better off thinking she had no relatives. Ugh. She couldn't imagine disowning a daughter because she disapproved of her husband. What kind of people would refuse to make amends with their own child on her deathbed?

Kaylin, in a daze, saw Mr. Lansky out the door. Although she wanted to share more of the responsibilities and decision-making with Becca and Lia, she didn't want to hurt them. They'd just lost their only living parent. Yet, her father had made certain she knew about her grandmother. He'd opened a door. And her grandmother had sent a note. Still, contacting her and being rebuffed would only increase their pain. She wanted to think about what to do. None of them needed more disappointment right now.

9

§

Sawyer removed his shirt and started on the other side of the gable eave with the brush. He reminded himself to paint slowly, because he enjoyed working with his hands and found the repetitious labor soothing. Especially after that meeting. He could tell from his conversation with Kaylin that she hadn't believed one word he'd said about getting the business back on track. But proving himself to her wasn't his biggest concern. Between the missing laptop, the Middle Eastern visitors, and the attempted break-in, he didn't need to read the forensic report to suspect something was wrong. He'd known Henry too long to believe the lab explosion had been a careless accident. So after Sawyer finished the paint job, he'd have to find other reasons to stick around and watch over the Danner sisters.

He hadn't expected Mitzy, Lia, and Becca to come outside and pump him for information about Henry's will. So instead of enjoying the fresh air and the exercise in the April sunshine and relatively low humidity, he was trying to keep his answers short and vague.

"So what happened in there?" Becca asked. Dressed in

a blouse, jeans, and spiked sandals, she was about to lean against the fresh paint.

"Look out," Sawyer warned from atop the ladder. "That paint's still wet."

Becca jerked away, her dark hair barely missing the paint, but when she twisted, her heel snapped off her shoe with a loud crack. Becca swore. Lia held back a grin. Mitzy put a motherly arm over her shoulder. "Are you okay?"

"I'm fine, thanks." Becca gazed up at Sawyer and shaded her eyes from the sun. "Tell us. Did they kick you out?"

"You could say that. Mr. Lansky wanted to talk with Kaylin alone."

"How come?" Lia asked, her tone curious, uncertain. Kaylin's sister always had looked younger than her sixteen years. With her lack of self-confidence she looked as if a strong wind could blow her away.

"I don't know a thing," Sawyer answered truthfully and began to sweat, although it had nothing to do with work or the heat. He enjoyed being around the Danner women. Their house smelled good. Something in the kitchen was always cooking on the stove or in the oven. And the women were just so feminine, each in her own way. However, right now he wished Kaylin would show up. Then he'd be off the hot spot and she could answer all these questions.

"So what *do* you know?" Becca asked, her annoyance coming through in her question.

"If I keep talking, I won't finish today," Sawyer kept his tone light. He required more paint for the roller but didn't relish the job of climbing down the ladder. It wasn't his place to tell them the terms of Henry's will.

"Is there anything left of Daddy's business?" Becca asked.

"Anything besides bills?" Mitzy added.

"I'm not sure." In truth Sawyer now owned half of a corporation that received dwindling royalties on an old paper mill patent and a bunch of unproven biodiesel formulas . . . if only they could find Henry's laptop. With the lab gone, the records burned in the fire, the business's primary asset remained the land the building had stood on, a lot that had been mortgaged several years ago with the house. There likely was little equity.

But Sawyer would find a way to build it back up. Henry was counting on him to do right by his daughters and he'd known Sawyer's dreams had coincided with his own. By giving him half ownership, Henry had given him a way to continue. If he could find Henry's laptop or duplicate his work, Sawyer could start over.

Keeping his thoughts to himself, Sawyer stalled, praying Kaylin would come soon. Instead of climbing down for more paint, he pretended he'd missed a spot, and kept smoothing the roller over the same area.

Finally Kaylin and Mr. Lansky came outside. She walked him to his car and shook hands before he drove away. Kaylin had her purse strap over her shoulder and her keys in hand as if she intended to head somewhere.

Her face composed, her steps quick, she walked with the grace of a dancer. For a moment Sawyer feared she was going to take off without stopping to speak to her sisters, but when she spied them with Mitzy and Sawyer, she headed over.

Kaylin wore an expression Sawyer couldn't read. Part angry, part thoughtful, part sad, she seemed such a mix of emotions—no way could he predict her state of mind. If he had to put a name to her primary sentiment, he would have said uptight. And since she'd been fairly relaxed when he'd left, he guessed Mr. Lansky must have revealed something alarming.

"So tell your sisters what happened and put their minds at ease," Mitzy urged, her tone kind, as if she understood the undertones of Becca's jealousy and Lia's uncertainty.

Kaylin's voice was surprisingly upbeat. "Dad left his affairs in good order. All three of us will share everything, except half the business goes to Sawyer."

But she was hiding something.

On her one good heel, Becca hobbled over to Kaylin. "The business is gone, isn't it?"

Kaylin gave a careless shrug, almost as if the business wasn't on her mind, and she had other troubles on her shoulders. "We'll be fine. Dad had a small life insurance policy that will cover his funeral expenses."

"What did Mr. Lansky say after Sawyer left?" Lia asked.

Before Kaylin could answer, Becca stumbled on her broken heel. To steady herself, she reached for Kaylin and knocked her purse from her shoulder to her elbow. A paper flew out. "Sorry."

"I've got you." Kaylin balanced her and noted the broken heel. "You should take those off."

Lia reached for the paper, picked it up, read it. "Oh . . . God. What's this?" Lia shook the paper in Kaylin's face. Sawyer recalled the trifold paper with its distinctive orange sun, the same image he'd seen on the airline ticket jacket in Kaylin's studio. Lia's voice rose an octave. "You're leaving us? You're going to New York?"

Sawyer climbed down the ladder. Lia was close to hysteria. She looked white enough to faint.

Kaylin plucked the airline ticket from Lia's hand. "I'm not going anywhere."

Becca peered at the ticket and pointed. "But your name is right there. You were leaving and not coming back? When were you going to tell us?"

"Never." Kaylin's mouth tightened. She ripped the ticket in half and tossed it into the bushes. "I'm not going. End of story."

"Kaylin, Becca, Lia, all of you calm down," Mitzy pleaded. "We can talk about this without letting the neighbors know our business. Please . . . the last few days have been—"

Lia paid no attention to Mitzy's plea. "Mama left us. Daddy left us. Now Kaylin wants to leave us, too."

Kaylin looked like she was going to be sick. She swayed on her feet. One person could only take so much. Sawyer wanted to sweep her into his arms and carry her away from her sisters. From all this responsibility. From their accusations. This had been one hell of a week. Her father had died and then she'd had a nasty fight with Becca. The attorney had dumped more stress on her and now Lia was tearing into her.

Sawyer knew Kaylin probably wouldn't appreciate him coming to her defense but he couldn't stop himself. "Excuse me, ladies, but Lincoln freed the slaves over a hundred years ago. If your sister wants to take a trip—"

"Becca's right. That ticket was one-way . . . she wasn't coming back." Lia's face turned bright red with fury and tears brimmed in her eyes.

Kaylin exchanged a glance with Sawyer and shook her head. Obviously, she wanted him to leave the arguing to her. He nodded. Fine. But he was on standby, ready to jump back in if she needed him.

She faced her sisters and kept her voice calm and firm. "The ticket was one-way because I couldn't afford to pay for round trip. I was coming back, Lia. I had lined up a short gig in New York. A friend of mine pulled a tendon and she recommended me to take her place. I would have earned enough dancing to pay for a ticket home."

"When were you going to tell us?" Becca asked, her voice sad.

"I was waiting for the right time. And then with Dad . . . I canceled."

"How long was the gig?" Becca asked. "Maybe you can still go. I could look after Lia."

"I don't think I should leave now. It might have been

for a month. It depended on how long it took her injury to heal."

"Mom would never have left me alone for a month," Lia sniffed.

"You wouldn't have been alone. Mitzy and I would have been with you," Becca told Lia.

Mitzy nodded. "I already feel like we're related. I wouldn't mind looking after you, along with Billy."

Sawyer took in the pride in Kaylin's face as Becca and Mitzy offered to help. These women might fight, but they were also strong.

"Lia, when Mom died, I was the same age as Becca is now," Kaylin reminded her sister, defending her position with a maturity that he admired. "And New York is only a two and a half hour plane ride away. If you'd needed me, I could have come back."

"That's not the same as being here," Lia muttered, but she was clearly getting over her shock.

Kaylin rolled her eyes and Sawyer almost grinned. "I won't leave right now. Not since we all just lost Dad. But I'm entitled to a life, too. Get used to it. It doesn't mean I don't love you, but I've put my dreams on hold—"

"So it's my fault that you aren't dancing on Broadway?" Lia asked, her tone pitiful.

"I didn't say that. But I'm giving you fair warning. I'm not staying here forever."

Wow. Talk about being firm. Kaylin had never abandoned her dream of dancing. She'd just put it on hold. Good for her. Sawyer couldn't have been more proud of her if she'd been his woman. And there was the rub. The more he knew about Kaylin, the more he liked her. But she'd just told them all she fully intended to leave.

How ironic that when he'd found a woman who interested him, who intrigued him, she was determined to head out of state. Up north. Where it snowed. Despite the heat, he shivered. Sawyer didn't like snow. His parents had died on an icy street, on a snowy gray day, during a vacation up north. He still remembered the cop coming to the hotel room door where he'd been holed up with a sitter. He couldn't remember the cop's words, just the frosty blast of air from the open door, the snowflakes swirling into the room and chilling him. Sawyer had eventually gone to college up north, but he much preferred southern weather. And Southern women.

But now he understood Kaylin better. No wonder she'd isolated herself from having many friends or dating. She didn't intend to stay.

And now he was undecided. Because as much as he wanted to get to know her better, Sawyer didn't want her to change her mind about dancing. Not when there was so much joy in her when she danced. How could he or her sisters deny her that pleasure? She had floated across that dance floor as if she defied gravity itself. He recalled the sensual sway of her hips, the erotic undulations of her body. He might not be an expert judge of dance, but he knew star quality when he saw it, and Kaylin had it in spades.

Becca went inside to change her shoes and then left for work. Mitzy headed for her shift, too. Kaylin and Lia went inside, the ticket forgotten. Sawyer climbed over the bushes, picked up the two pieces, and stuffed them into his pocket. He wasn't sure what he intended to do, but unused tickets could be exchanged. Now might not be the right moment, but someday Kaylin would get a chance at her dream.

He only hoped he could make the biodiesel plant viable again while she was still young enough to have a shot at Broadway. Her father had always intended for Kaylin to leave to follow her dreams, and had regretted he'd needed her too much at home to make it happen. Sawyer couldn't help but want that opportunity for her, too.

Damn, she was a fine woman. Gutsy. Independent. Sexy.

At the same time, he didn't see why they couldn't spend more time together while she was here. It wasn't like he wanted to hold her back. She might not see it that way, but Sawyer could be convincing once he set his mind to something. And he was set like concrete when it came to Kaylin.

10

"I hope it's not too late to call. I was wondering what you know about Dean Witman?" Kaylin asked Sawyer over her bedroom telephone, pleased when he'd picked up on the first ring.

Earlier, with Lia upset over the airplane ticket no one was supposed to have seen, Kaylin hadn't had the chance to ask Sawyer about the man who'd phoned about buying her father's business. And when she'd looked for him outside later, intending to invite him for dinner, he'd already left. Disappointed that he wasn't there, Kaylin realized how accustomed she'd become to Sawyer's presence. Over the last week he'd become part of her life, an increasingly important part, one she was beginning to count on.

Although it was after ten, she had too much on her mind to watch TV or sleep, and she wanted to settle her father's affairs so she could get back to teaching dance next week. At least that's what she'd told herself when she'd picked up the phone and called Sawyer.

"It's not too late to call," he said. "We bought plastic tanks for storing the finished biodiesel fuel from Dean. He owns Witman Container. He supplied the soybean oil tanks as well as the methanol and wash tanks. Why do you ask?"

"He called a few days ago. He asked me not to sell the business until I spoke to him."

Sawyer's Southern accent strengthened, a trait she'd learned was a strong indication that he cared a lot about a subject. "You want to sell?"

"Do you?" she countered.

"I hoped we could make a go of the business." Sawyer's optimism sounded so much like her Dad that she had to swallow the lump in her throat. She couldn't believe how much she already missed her father. She needed him so much. But he was . . . gone.

She ached for one last conversation. One more argument.

So what if they argued sometimes? Who didn't? Just because she and her father often disagreed didn't mean she hadn't loved him. Just because she was furious that he'd blown himself up didn't mean she didn't miss him. She missed their early morning talks when he'd read interesting bits from the newspaper to her. She missed filling his thermos with coffee, packing his sandwich, either egg salad or turkey with cranberry sauce (spread between the meat slices so his bread wouldn't turn soggy), and adding a few of Mitzy's cookies. She missed the twinkle in his eyes when he announced his next invention, one that would never come to fruition now. And she missed his excitement and passion for his work, which had been contagious. Living with Daddy was like always living on the verge of winning the lottery. Any day he might hit the jackpot.

But as much as she loved and missed her father, he'd been a dreamer . . . and so was Sawyer. Her father could have easily taken a company job. So could Sawyer. They had the degrees to work in corporate America and earn a steady paycheck. But both of them wanted to go it alone. They were alike in so many ways. Too many ways for her ever to allow herself to be interested, despite the strong connection she felt with him.

"Biodiesel has tremendous potential. Do you realize we can sell every drop we make?" Sawyer asked.

"But can you really make it? Without blowing yourself up?" she replied. Kaylin didn't mind working toward a dream, but she wanted one that was attainable. She believed in hard work. In what was possible. She wouldn't hang her future on moonbeams and end up like her mother, working three jobs and dying an early death. When Kaylin fell in love, she was going to choose a man who lived in New York, someone who had health insurance and maybe a retirement plan.

No way was she getting caught up with a dreamer who always believed his next invention would make them rich. She'd been disappointed too many times to believe anymore.

Sure, Kaylin wanted her shot at the big time and Broadway. She and her mother had always planned that career for her. But she was also practical enough to know dance would always provide a living. If she couldn't be the star, she might be in the chorus. If she couldn't perform, she could teach. Her backup plans had backup plans.

"Making the fuel is not the problem. Making it cost effective has been our goal. And between the break-in at the lab and your father's suspicious visitors, I'm not ready to concede that the explosion was an accident. We should keep an open mind until we have all the facts," Sawyer spoke carefully, his voice tight, his accent thick. "But . . . why don't we speak to Dean and see what he has in mind?"

She could tell by Sawyer's tone that he didn't think the offer would be a good one. Yet he was being reasonable. She couldn't fault him for that.

Sawyer's voice changed, hardened slightly. "Dean also visited your father while I was gone."

"That's right. You said he was on the security footage, wasn't he?" She recalled the images of several men who'd visited her father. But she hadn't remembered Dean Witman because they'd never met.

"He was there and had a brief conversation with your father. Too bad we only had visual. No sound. I have no idea what they spoke about. However, your dad intended to buy more tanks."

"You're sure?"

"We were going to streamline the process. Use a better filter and replace the five hundred gallon wash tanks with larger ones."

"So Witman's not in the biodiesel business?"

"He's a supplier. Not a producer. But it sounds like he may soon be our competition."

"Not if he buys us out," she countered.

"How about I pick you up for breakfast? Afterward, we'll go talk to Dean, together."

"That would be great."

"See you at nine?" His voice was all business and yet she sensed Sawyer was holding back, trying not to say more.

"Nine's good." Kaylin hung up the phone, glad that Sawyer would prep her on the business before they went into a meeting, and consult with her afterward if they got an offer.

But although Sawyer hadn't said much, she suspected that he would try to talk her out of selling. Trouble was . . . they owned it fifty-fifty. What happened if she and her sisters wanted to sell and he didn't?

She wished she'd asked Mr. Lansky that question. She could call him in the morning. Or maybe wait until after she'd heard Sawyer out. Perhaps she could talk him into selling or maybe into buying them out.

Kaylin had finally drifted off to sleep when the phone rang. Groggy, she reached for it in the dark. "Hello? Hello?"

At the hang-up, she swore and pressed the Caller ID button. No number came up. Just "private caller."

Probably just a wrong number.

To be certain they didn't disturb her by calling back, Kaylin unplugged the phone and pulled the pillow over her head. She went back to sleep and slept without dreaming.

The next morning, she woke up refreshed and glad to find that Lia seemed ready to return to school. Apparently Billy had talked her into going back. Billy seemed to have cleaned up his act, but Kaylin couldn't be sure since he wore dark sunglasses and she couldn't see his eyes. They walked out the front door, gossiping about a mutual acquaintance, almost like normal.

Mitzy left for work and Becca had some errands to run,

so Kaylin had the kitchen to herself. She poured a cup of coffee and drank half before she noticed the blinking light on the phone message machine.

She hit playback. Five long silences. Five hang-ups. All of them the "private caller" ID. Kaylin wondered if someone thought their phone was a fax. That happened sometimes and the programmed machines just kept dialing. Six seemed to be the magic number.

Still, she got up, called Randy inside, and locked the doors. Until they knew exactly what had happened at the lab, she planned to be careful. Perhaps she should have driven Lia to school . . . but she hadn't been alone. Billy and Lia walked together. And Becca . . . was twenty. Old enough to take care of herself. However, with the care Becca had taken with her appearance this morning, Kaylin suspected her errands including dropping by to see Shadee.

Maybe that was a good thing. Kaylin would feel better knowing Becca wasn't alone either.

LIA DREADED HER return to class. She hated being the center of attention. She detested other people's pity and there'd been enough stares over the years. She was the poor Danner kid whose mother had died. Now with Dad gone, the pity party would be even worse.

If not for Billy walking beside her on the sidewalk through their neighborhood, she might have bailed and headed back home again. However, Billy wasn't being a friend this morning. He'd smoked some pot in the garage right before they'd left the house.

"You're going to get caught. I can smell the weed on your jacket," she'd complained after they were out of hearing range of the neighbors.

"It'll be gone by the time we get to class." He grinned, his tone mellow. "And I'm not wasted or anything. Just had to take off the edge." He reached into his pocket for a joint. "Want some?"

Take off the edge? That would be awesome, but she didn't dare mess with her mind. Lia already had enough to deal with. Kaylin had common sense and was good at dance and making money. Becca had the brains. Lia was the dumb, pretty blonde. She couldn't afford to lose any brain cells.

She flicked her fingers at the joint and it sailed into a hedge. "Lose it. If you get caught, Kaylin might make you move out. She's tougher than she looks." Lia had yet to get over that airline ticket. Kaylin had been ready to leave. Sure, she'd said she'd come back but she might have gotten all caught up in glamorous New York and forgotten about her family.

And didn't Lia sound lame? Most kids her age wanted nothing to do with their parents. They didn't latch onto an older sister for courage. But those kids had parents. Lia didn't.

But she did realize how much Kaylin did for her. She was both mother and sister. Lia got it that she had her own dreams. That someday she would leave. She just didn't want it to be now.

"Stop for a sec."

At first she thought Billy meant she should stop thinking along those lines. But he'd halted, kneeled, and parted the greenery in search of his dope. Apparently he wanted her to wait for him. She grabbed his arm and yanked him up. "Imagine a sheriff's cruiser rolling by."

Billy looked both ways down the empty street. "There's no one here."

"I'm here."

Billy laughed at the idea of tiny Lia stopping him from doing anything. "You going to arrest me?"

She sighed. "I like you better when you're thinking straight."

"And I like you better when you aren't telling me what to do." He unclipped his skateboard where it hung from a short chain attached to his jeans, placed it on the sidewalk and shoved off. On foot, no way could she keep up with him, and her eyes brimmed with tears.

Lia didn't want to show up at school. Arriving alone was the worst. Kaylin would understand if she stayed home one more day. After all, she'd canceled dance classes for the entire week. Why should Lia have to go back this soon?

11

§

Just as Kaylin hopped into Sawyer's truck, her cell rang. "Sorry," she tossed out an apology to Sawyer, then fumbled for her seat belt and answered the phone. "Hello."

Kaylin clicked in with one hand as Sawyer reached over and helped hold the seat belt. Then he backed out of the driveway and drove down the street. The neighborhood children had already left for school but bikes, balls, and a catcher's mitt were strewn across front porches, yards, and sidewalks. A neighbor out mowing the yard waved, another stared as she retrieved her *Tampa Tribune*.

"Ms. Danner, this is Deputy Bryant."

"Yes?" Kaylin clutched the phone tighter.

"Your father's death has been ruled to be of undetermined origin."

"Undetermined? Does that mean you're still investigating?"

"Not unless we discover a solid reason for us to do so. We need more evidence to continue. I thought you'd like to know that the ATF found no evidence of his laptop. According to the official report, the explosion wasn't severe enough to disintegrate his laptop. In other words, if it had been with him, we'd have found at least a few of the parts."

"So that's it?"

"The explosion has been ruled an accident. But if anything else comes up, please don't hesitate to call."

"Thanks."

Kaylin snapped shut her phone and stared blindly out the windshield. Just like that the investigation was over, and her thoughts whirled as frustration roiled in her gut. "Deputy Bryant says that without any evidence, they have to rule the explosion as an accident. And he said if the laptop had been with Dad in the lab, they would have found pieces, but there weren't any."

"The good news is that we might still find his laptop," Sawyer's tone was gentle, as if uncertain of her mood.

"We've already looked everywhere." Kaylin wasn't sure she had a mood. Should she be relieved no one had deliberately set out to harm her father? Or should she be upset that he hadn't been careful enough to stay alive? Should she be frustrated that they hadn't found evidence of murder? Or relieved? Either way her father was gone, but sorting out her own feelings had her head spinning worse than after an hour practicing pirouettes.

"You okay?" Sawyer asked.

"I'm trying to figure out what I should feel."

"You can do that?"

"What?"

Sawyer's eyes narrowed. "My feelings just *are*. I can't decide what they should be."

She sighed. "Mine are conflicted." She leaned back into the seat, glad she didn't have to focus on driving. Sawyer was a good driver, his competent hands steady on the wheel, and when he braked for a red light, he came to a smooth stop. "On the one hand, if I believe Deputy Bryant and the team of forensic experts, then I'd be angry that Dad was careless enough to accidentally set off the explosion."

"But—"

"On the other hand, I'd be relieved to know those Middle Eastern guys had nothing to do with his death." She sighed again and tried to shrug the tension out of her shoulders.

"You don't believe the official report?"

"Their theory doesn't account for the missing laptop or that Dad's formula might have been valuable. They're treating him like an amateur. He did have a doctorate in chemical engineering. He was brilliant."

"Can you think of any place else where Henry could have left his laptop?" Sawyer turned right onto Highway 301 and merged into traffic behind a vegetable truck that had a hand-drawn *Ruskin Tomatoes* sign on the back window.

"I've been racking my brain." Kaylin didn't believe her father had mislaid his laptop. He wasn't the absent-minded professor. He'd been extremely careful with his data, meticulous about his work. But he was human and she supposed he could have slipped up.

Sawyer drove to the local waffle house. They chose a

table in the back where they could talk quietly without being overheard. The morning rush of nine-to-fivers was over and the snowbirds, retirees from up north who came south for the winter, were mostly gone. He ordered his breakfast, waffles with blueberries and a large glass of orange juice, and she chose waffles with fresh strawberry topping and coffee.

Sawyer grinned at her order. "My grandmother loves strawberries."

"You could have invited her to join us." Kaylin floated her napkin over her lap. She'd never met his grandmother but knew she'd taken him in as a kid, something she doubted her own grandparents would have done.

"Gran's off on a seniors singles cruise." His grin widened. "She told me she has her eye on a nice young man of sixty. She's eighty."

"She sounds full of life."

"You have no idea. Last summer Gran decided she wanted to learn karate."

Kaylin laughed. "Every woman should know how to defend herself."

"That's what she said." Sawyer's easy grin faded. "Do you and your sisters know how to defend yourselves?"

"Dad insisted we all take a self-defense class. But it was a long time ago and I don't remember as much as I should." She turned and stared at him. "Why? You think we're going to have more trouble? Should I be worrying about Becca and Lia?"

Sawyer looked her straight in the eye. "I don't know."

A man who didn't mind saying he didn't know something? How unusual. In spite of herself, his admission kicked her impression of him up another notch. Over the last few days, he'd earned a lot of notches. Sawyer couldn't have been more helpful, less intrusive. At times he fit into their family so easily he became a part of it—even when the sisters were arguing.

She recalled how he'd stepped off the ladder to defend her against Becca. How he'd seemed willing to fight her battles for her. Not that she needed a man to defend her, especially when the weapons of choice were words. Kaylin could do that herself, thank-you very much. Still, it was nice, sweet really, that he'd made the effort.

Kaylin rested her forearms on the table and leaned forward. "So tell me about Dean Witman. What part of Dad's biodiesel business is left to buy?"

"Dean's probably after the formula."

"Which we don't have."

"But he doesn't know that," Sawyer reminded her.

"Unless he stole it, blew up the lab, and is covering up his actions by pretending to want to buy what he already took."

"Damn." Sawyer eyed her with new respect. "That's quite a theory. Do you read mystery novels in your spare time?"

"Actually I'm a *CSI* fan." She held her breath, waiting for him to poke fun at her. When he didn't, she began to breathe normally again. "What else do you know about Witman?"

"He runs his father's multimillion dollar business. On the surface, he doesn't appear to need to resort to underhanded tactics. He drives a Porsche and lives in River Hills, an expensive community—"

"South of Brandon. Okay," she agreed. "But he could be mortgaged to the hilt. Or he might want out from under daddy's thumb. Or he could have two ex-wives who have left him strapped for cash."

"You ought to write TV shows." He peered at her, his lips curled with amusement. "For such a practical woman, I never figured you had such a vivid imagination."

"There's a lot about me you don't know. But there's even more I don't know about you." She speared him with a curious look.

The waitress returned with their orders, interrupting the conversation. He skipped the butter but drowned his waffles in syrup. Impishly, he plucked a blueberry off the top and held it up to her lips. "Want a taste?"

"No thanks." The idea of eating from his fingers seemed way too intimate. She busied herself by adding cream and sugar to her coffee, then dribbling syrup over her waffles. She speared a strawberry with her fork and offered him the first bite.

Eyes full of amusement, he didn't hesitate, taking the strawberry into his mouth without his lips touching her fork. He chewed and swallowed. "Good choice." Then he surprised her, returning the conversation to her earlier comment. "So what do you want to know about me?"

Everything. The silly thought popped into her head.

She banished it fast, before it could settle in. "I never ran into you in high school."

"That's because I'm three years older than you."

"We still overlapped one year."

"After my freshman year, I dropped out."

"Oh?" He didn't seem the kind to quit. In fact, he seemed kind of laid back, with a steel core. Steel honed for whatever life threw his way. He was one of those rare men who was so self-confident, he didn't need the fake macho BS to bolster his image.

His blue eyes twinkled. "Gran wasn't too happy, but she forgave me when I did home schooling and ended up earning my diploma within a year."

She should have figured his education process hadn't been normal. Her father had been like that, too. "Then what did you do?"

"I got accepted into MIT."

"At sixteen?"

"Yeah. I was a nerd." He didn't sound proud of his accomplishments. "Socially I was so not ready for college, but I thrived academically."

"Let me guess. You have a doctorate in engineering?"

"Chemical engineering and physics." He nodded, a mischievous please-don't-hold-my-brains-against-me eyebrow rising.

"So you're a genius?"

"At MIT geniuses are as common as nerds."

She laughed. He had a way about him that was just as charming as her father. A similarity that reminded her that friendly was good, too friendly was a real bad idea. Long ago, she'd decided to swear off dreamers. Now she was certain. Dead certain.

"What's wrong?" he asked. "You look as if you just bit into a rotten strawberry."

The guy was perceptive. True, she'd never been great at hiding her emotions. Showing what she felt was a part of the dancer in her. Because dancing wasn't just technique. The best dancers portrayed emotion. Too bad hers leaked out at the most inconvenient times.

She shook her head. "Sorry. Dad had a similar attitude towards his intelligence and when I thought of him . . ."

"No problem. While I wouldn't mind telling you my life story, especially about my childhood cat, Fuzzy, we need to prep for our meeting."

"Agreed." Although his owning a cat named Fuzzy seemed incongruous with his masculine image. Sawyer really was the total package. Sure he had a great face, but it was his intelligent eyes and gentle charm that lured her. Not that she had any intention of allowing him to reel her in.

Keeping the conversation on business would be good. Not as interesting, but safer. She needed to think of Sawyer as her father's business partner, not as an attractive, kind, and amusing companion. "So where do we start?"

"Let's consider this meeting preliminary."

Again she sensed his reluctance to accept an offer. "What does that mean?"

"It means we don't agree to anything without first talking it over in private."

"Agreed. What else?" She picked up her coffee cup and sipped, looking at him over the rim. His eyes caught hers and the intensity she saw there tugged at her.

"I'm not sure where to start."

Although his tone sounded casual, she suspected he'd already worked out this part ahead of time. He obviously didn't want to sound as if he was telling her what to do. Nevertheless, it's what he was doing.

She didn't mind. He knew a heck of a lot more about biodiesel than she did. "Just assume I know nothing about Dad's business and go from there."

"The government is pushing alternative fuels big time. They've created tax incentives to buy, sell, and produce biodiesel. The soybean farmers are powerful lobbyists, fully behind growing soybeans and turning the crop into diesel. Our government likes the idea of homegrown as opposed to importing oil from the Middle East."

"Got it."

"If the tax incentives alone weren't enough to make it attractive, the environmentalists jumped on board. Burning this fuel doesn't pollute the air."

"Sounds wonderful . . . in theory."

"The industry has gone beyond theory. Any diesel vehicle can run on biodiesel without mechanical alterations, although they might have to use more fuel filters in the beginning."

"Biodiesel clogs the engines?"

"Just the opposite. The fuel actually cleans out the old gunk. Old residues clog the filters, but after using biodiesel two or three times, the old gunk is gone and the engines run even better. There's extra lubricity, so less wear and tear on the engine's moving parts."

"Okay. I get it. It's a great product. So why isn't everyone making it?"

"Because the process is complex and slow. I won't bore you with the chemistry."

"Thanks."

"Basically, your dad was working on a catalyst. A way to make the chemical reaction faster."

"But if we don't have his work, we don't have anything to sell."

"In general, I know what he was working on. If the lab were still there, I could probably duplicate his experiments and figure out what he discovered."

"So even without the final formula it would be a big help to anyone else to have his research?"

"Exactly. But I'm not sure we want to reveal any information to Dean in our meeting."

Again his hesitancy told her he didn't want to sell. But to her it was a no-brainer. She didn't want to own a business that had killed her father. And she wasn't convinced they could really produce biodiesel and make it profitable. Besides, even if they had the knowledge, they didn't have the means. Not unless Sawyer was wealthy. "Why do we want to keep silent about the only thing we have to sell? I understand we don't want to go into specifics unless we have a contract, but why not tell Witman we know the direction of Dad's research?"

"My gut instinct is saying to keep this between us."

"Excuse me?" She'd expected more business analysis. Or a scientific reason. Not his gut instinct.

"We aren't sure what really happened in the lab or if Dean could be connected. I just don't think we should reveal too much."

"That won't be hard for me. I don't know a lot. However, if the man makes us an offer—"

"We'll discuss it after the meeting. Over dinner?" He made the suggestion with a casual air, but the glint in her eyes told her he was thinking about more than business.

"Dinner could be arranged. Especially if you don't mind leftovers."

Kaylin suddenly realized she was foolishly grinning. This wasn't a date, just business. Yet never before had she looked forward to a business discussion. Her smile faded.

She needed to keep her priorities straight.

12

§

No one was home. Lia used her key on the front door, pleased when Randy greeted her with a friendly wag of his tail. With Mitzy and Becca at work, and Kaylin gone, the house seemed empty, better than school, but lonely.

Lia entered the kitchen, poured herself a cola and

snagged some homemade pistachio muffins left over from the weekend. With Randy on her heels, she headed up to her room. Posters of her favorite stars greeted her. She kicked her PJs from the floor, pleased when they landed on top of the pile in her clothes hamper. She'd have to do laundry soon. Maybe later.

The house seemed quiet. Too quiet. Lia plopped on her bed, turned on her iPod, placed the headset over her ears, and closed her eyes. Right now she wasn't up to appreciating the awesome black walls with white trim that Kaylin and she had painted together a few months ago. Right now, black reminded her of death, of her father's black suit when they'd laid him to rest. The black coffin. The black burned patch of grass where the lab used to be.

Randy jumped onto the bed and snuggled against her side, no doubt hoping she'd drop a few muffin crumbs while she listened to one of her all-time favorite albums. Usually pop ballads soothed Lia, but today she seriously couldn't get into the music.

Perhaps she should have gone to school. Sooner or later she'd have to face the stares, the silent questions, the pity. But not today. Opening *Seventeen*, she thumbed through the pages, disgusted with the Photoshop-perfect models who never had a pimple or a bad hair day. If she ever grew tall enough, Lia had thought about modeling as a career, but those girls looked so confident, so intimidating, that she knew she'd never fit in.

Randy wagged his tail and Lia removed her headphones. She broke off a piece of muffin and shared. When she heard a thump on the stairs, her adrenaline kicked in. Oh . . . God. Was someone in the house?

She must be imagining things.

But she heard another thump. Then a footstep.

Someone was here. And making a lot of noise. Her heart sped up and her stomach churned.

Kaylin had told her not to go anywhere alone. Although Kaylin was a worrywart, this time she should have listened.

Should she call out? Maybe one of her sisters had returned early. But if it wasn't Mitzy, Becca, or Kaylin, if there was an intruder, letting them know she was in the house wouldn't be a good idea.

Lia picked up Randy, tucked him under her arm, and headed for her window. Already half open, she easily slid the window all the way up.

More footsteps on the steps urged her to hurry.

Placing her foot on the sill, she started to slide outside onto the roof, not the easiest maneuver with Randy in her arms. Half in, half out, the blinding sun made it difficult for her to see past her door into the dark hallway.

God. Someone was there.

Keep going.

Maybe they wouldn't see her. For once her tiny size might work in her favor. Maybe they'd continue looking down the hall to Kaylin or Becca's room. Damn it. She should have taken her cell phone with her. But it was sitting inside her backpack, right where she'd left it on her nightstand.

Fire-breathing dragons couldn't have tugged her back inside.

"Anyone home?" a voice called out. Then someone stepped into her bedroom.

Heart pounding with fear, Lia almost dropped Randy, who barked and wagged his tail. Talk about a welcoming committee, Randy liked everyone. Even an intruder.

Lia scrambled out the window, scraping her leg in her haste.

"Lia. Where are you going?"

"Billy?" Mouth dry, Lia squinted back into her room, suddenly feeling foolish that she hadn't recognized his voice right away.

He poked his head out the window. "What are you doing?"

Randy barked again. Lia had never been so happy to see Billy's punked-out hair and his cheerful grin. But she didn't want him to know she'd been freaked out. "I thought I'd come up here and work on my tan."

He climbed out the window and joined her. "Cool."

Actually it was hot. But she couldn't exactly complain since she'd just claimed she was out here to lie in the sun.

She settled her back against a gable that was part of the attic. "What are you doing here?"

He shrugged. "I came back for more weed."

"Liar." He'd come back because of her. She and Billy were tight, and it was good to have company. Being alone sucked. "More likely you wanted me to do your homework."

Lia wasn't the best student, but Billy was downright terrible. He didn't have much ambition either. If not for her, he might not have passed last year.

"You know I might not always be able to help you." Lia placed Randy on her lap.

"Why not?"

"Kaylin wants to go to New York. I wouldn't be surprised if she upped and moved me there."

"She told you she was staying," Billy reminded her.

"I know that's what she said . . . but with Sawyer and her planning to maybe sell Dad's business, she could afford New York. Of course, they'd get more money if we could find Dad's laptop."

"Really? Why?"

Billy had to be the greatest friend. He loved to talk about her family. And he loved to talk about Lia's problems. Her clothes. Her hair. Her sisters. In some ways, she realized, he desperately wanted her family to be his family. And that was cool with her.

She liked to pretend Billy was her brother. He did look out for her. Last year, one of boys at school had pressured Lia to go out and then he'd wanted more than Lia had wanted to give. Billy had put a scare into the guy.

He kept her secrets. And she kept his. Only she wished he'd quit the drugs. He'd picked up some new friends who scared her. But she could never convince Billy he was flirting with danger.

A black van pulled into the driveway and two men walked right to their front door. Billy peered at Lia. "Is your TV broken?"

"Not that I know of. Why?"

"Before the van turned into the drive, I thought I read TV repair on the sign."

"I suppose I should go inside . . ."

Billy grabbed her hand. "Stay here and be quiet."

"What's wrong?"

"They didn't ring the bell and they're inside the house."

Damn. Billy had exceptional hearing. If he'd heard them go in, then she believed him, and the tension in her neck tightened her muscles into knots. She heard glass breaking, thumps, thuds. "They're wrecking the house," she whispered. "We have to do something."

"No."

"But—"

"No. You go in there, they might wreck you, too."

"We could jump off the roof. Go for help."

"We're twenty feet up. We jump, we'll break bones and they'll find us."

"So we should stay here and do nothing?"

"I'm good with that." Billy placed an arm over her shoulder.

They heard pounding, like hammers on walls. Even an electric drill. More thuds, metal slamming and plates pounding on the floor.

Between the hot sun and her fear, Lia began to sweat under her arms, between her shoulder blades. Strangers were tearing apart her home. Ruining their things. "I'm going to be sick."

"Shh. We can't let them find us."

Randy started to bark.

The banging and drilling stopped. *Oh . . . my . . . God.* Male voices rose in a heated discussion, but Lia couldn't make out the words. Had they heard the dog?

Were they searching for Randy? Searching for them?

Billy and Lia exchanged a look of horror. She patted Randy's head. "Shh, baby, shh. Don't bark. Please don't bark."

13

§

Becca didn't have errands. How could she think about banking and picking up her skirt from the dry cleaners when she was so upset?

Besides, she desperately needed to see Shadee. He hadn't called all week. While she told herself he was giving her time to grieve, the thought still niggled at Becca that he'd somehow thought she'd gone too far. She shouldn't have made love to him.

It would explain the lack of phone calls. In fact, going

over to the marina where Shadee worked might not be a very good idea. She'd just stop by. Say hello. Gauge his mood.

From Riverview, she drove south on the interstate to Apollo Beach. In the last five years the area had boomed with new housing, especially along the waterfront. Condos and single family homes nestled along man-made canals that provided boating opportunities for residents along Tampa Bay. Those who lived inland could also enjoy the multitude of islands and beaches by keeping a boat at the marina.

She parked and got out, appreciative of the salt tang of the water, the seagulls diving into the harbor for fish. A stiff breeze cooled her skin and dried her lips. Nervously, she searched for Shadee among the boats at the marina. If he was on the dock, he'd be easy to spot. Just under six feet, with cropped dark hair and dark sunglasses, he should stick out easily among the families that frequented the place. She saw powerboats, sailboats, and houseboats cradled on land and docked in the harbor. But the marina seemed deserted, and she realized she'd never been here during the week, but only on busy weekends. She didn't see Shadee, either.

She hoped he wasn't working in the warehouse today. Inside, he'd be with coworkers. Outside, they'd have more privacy for a quiet chat. Becca headed for the docks. Sailboats and motorboats were tied to slips. Almost every slip was full.

Sailboat halyards clanged against their masts and the

protected harbor had a slight chop due to the southwest wind that blew in from the bay. Her hair tracked over her eyes and she swept it up with one hand.

There. She saw a dark-haired man duck into a large sailboat all the way at the end of the third dock. Stomach churning, she prayed Shadee was alone, not working with another mechanic. Prayed even harder that he wouldn't be furious with her for having . . .

God. Surely he wouldn't hold it against her that they'd made love?

A dolphin arced through the water, accompanying her down the dock. Sometimes manatees swam through here but most preferred the warmer waters by the local Tampa Electric power plant. Fish raced ahead of the dolphin, eager to get out of the way. Her hair whipped her face. Great. Not only was her hair going to be a pathetic mess, her makeup would be smudged and smeared by the time she arrived.

You're only stopping by to chat.

Yeah, sure.

She'd spent half an hour deciding what to wear, another half hour on her hair and makeup, and driven ten minutes out of her way just to say hi. Her gut churned. Maybe she should have waited until lunch. That might have seemed more natural.

Becca was certain her social skills would have been much better if their mother had lived. Not that Kaylin was a nerd or anything, but she wasn't a social animal. Their house was usually quiet, not party city. Becca had to go out and make her own fun.

Fun with Shadee was the best kind.

She closed in on the sailboat. The fiberglass glistened and the spotless chrome shone in the sunlight. An open hatch was a portal to a cabin below, but because of the contrast between the bright light outside and the dark cabin interior, she couldn't see down there.

Should she wait for Shadee to come up? Call out? Why not?

She heard a clang down below, like the sound of a metal tool striking another piece of metal, and the sound of him speaking Arabic. At least she thought it was Arabic. Uh-oh. Suppose he wasn't alone?

"Shadee?"

"Down here."

Okay. Now she had an invite. This wasn't hard. So why was her mouth so dry, her pulse unsteady? She didn't even know if Shadee had recognized her voice.

She ducked into the cockpit, and the wind stopped tearing at her. Taking a moment to smooth her hair and let her eyes adjust to the shadowy cabin, she looked below but didn't see anyone. She climbed through the hatch and found herself in a kitchen—no, a galley, it was called on a boat—to starboard. Opposite was a luxurious white leather wraparound bench and a kitchen table made of a light-colored wood. There were lots of matching light oak cabinets and another cabin up ahead. But as she peered forward, she still didn't see Shadee.

"Where are you?"

"Here." His voice, dark and gruff, was behind her. He

was slipping his phone into his pocket. Since no one else was there, she assumed he must have been on his cell.

She spun to see two bunks, one on either side of the hull and behind the hatch where she'd entered. An open panel revealed he'd been working on the engine.

From the bunk Shadee peered at her but said nothing. She swallowed hard. Why couldn't he say that her visit was a nice surprise? Even a what-the-hell-are-you-doing-here question would reveal his mood. But he said nothing.

"Hi." How lame was that? *Get it together, girl.*

He frowned and stared at her with those big brown eyes. "Is everything okay?"

"I guess. Why?"

"You aren't smiling."

"Huh?"

"You're always smiling."

"I am?"

He stood, ducking his head slightly in the cabin. "So what's wrong?"

"Nothing." Sheesh. He wasn't giving her any clue at all about the other night. If he was angry, he was keeping it inside. If he wasn't, he wasn't being his normal friendly self.

His lips quirked. "Nothing?"

And what was this? Now he was acting as if she were hiding something.

"You're working on the engine?" she asked, wishing that with all the gauges she'd seen on the boat, she had one to determine his thoughts.

"A tune-up." He leaned into her. "You smell good. Like jasmine and oranges."

"A new shampoo. I'm glad you like it."

He brushed her bangs from her eyes, tilted up her chin. She locked gazes with him. Heat flamed from his soft brown irises. Then his mouth angled down over hers, and he was kissing her, deep, hard, needy. She wound her arms around his neck, loving the feel of his warm flesh and corded muscles. The boat floated over a wave, and she used the excuse to lean into him, until all her curves slid against all his hardness.

She so needed to be held. Kissed. Loved.

Last week had been terrible. She didn't want to think about losing her dad. She didn't want to think about losing Shadee. She didn't want to talk. She only wanted to feel.

And Shadee knew exactly what she needed. He kissed her back, his mouth teasing, taunting, tasting. Oh . . . my . . . he felt delicious. But the open hatch . . . anyone who came to the dock could board the boat. Find them kissing. However, it wasn't much of a risk. The place was deserted.

Besides, the idea of his willingness to risk his job to kiss her excited her. She must mean a lot to him. But it was hard to think with her blood simmering through her veins.

He ran his hands up and down her back. "Does this feel good?"

"Yes." She didn't want him to stop. Whenever she was

with Shadee he always made her feel good. Wanted. Precious. Pretty.

"Tell me you want more."

"Tell me you want me," she demanded right back at him.

"I want you." Shadee leaned into her and held her close, his grip both tender and fervent. "You have no idea how much."

For a moment she hesitated. Yes, he wanted her body. But was that it? But then his lips claimed hers. Damn, the man could kiss. They could talk later.

Much later.

14

$

Witman Container consisted of ten impressive industrial acres along a railroad spur. Steel, delivered by train car, was unloaded by forklift and overhead cranes then moved the material into a massive open-air warehouse. Machine shop workers cut and bent flat plated steel. Welders, steel fabricators, and painters in hardhats and steel-toed boots worked on tanks in every stage of manufacture.

In addition to steel tanks, the company also manufactured fiberglass ones. Kaylin wrinkled her nose. The odor of the process wasn't something she'd like to breathe on a daily basis.

Sawyer led Kaylin along a sidewalk toward the office. The brick building was set to one side of the plant and from the substantial number of cars parked outside, she realized Witman Container consisted of several departments—a multimillion dollar operation. If the owner was interested in buying out her father, and she believed Dean Witman had been serious or he wouldn't have called the day after her father's death, then they could certainly afford to make a decent offer.

Her excitement rose. "Have you been here before?"

"Once. Witman delivered a tank with a hole cut through the side. We didn't discover the mistake until after they'd unloaded the truck."

"Did they take care of it?" She was curious. Whenever she had a customer relations problem at the studio, she'd found her best move was to ask questions and do her best to fix the situation immediately. Ignoring problems usually made them worse.

"They picked up the damaged tank the same day and gave us a ten percent discount on the new one for our trouble. Back then, Witman Senior was in charge."

Sawyer sounded as if he'd been pleased with the company's service. However, his tone implied that the son didn't run the business in the same competent fashion as the father. She wondered if both Witmans would be at the meeting.

Sawyer opened a glass door for her and she entered

and approached the front desk. After they'd given the receptionist their names, she immediately ushered them through a set of double doors down a hallway into a spacious office with oversized windows that overlooked the outside operation. On other walls blueprints of tanks dominated the room, their spec sheets pinned to the wall and rolled up on shelves, spilling over to the desk and onto the floor.

A tall, well-groomed, brown-haired man in his mid-thirties rose to his feet as they entered. Dean Witman Senior was nowhere in sight.

"Come in." Dean Jr. shook hands with her and Sawyer, and then swept more blueprints from two chairs. "Please have a seat. Can I get you anything? Water? Coffee?"

"We're fine, thanks," Kaylin said.

With his sleeves rolled up, his nails clipped short, and his hands smudged with ink, Witman looked like he worked for a living. Streaks of dust on his neck and dusty boots indicated he'd been inside the plant this morning. Pictures that Kaylin assumed were of his wife and kids were proudly displayed on his desk. From first appearances, the guy seemed legit. Solid.

Right now, to her, any offer would be a good one. It wasn't as if she wanted to go into the biodiesel business. She glanced at Sawyer. His face had a friendly expression, but his eyes were guarded, reminding her that selling out would be the end of his dream.

Dean settled a hip on his desk, ignoring his chair. "Before we talk business, I just want to say that I'm sorry about your father. He was a good man."

"Thank-you."

As if realizing she had to crane her neck to look up at him, Dean moved around his desk to his chair and took a seat. He didn't ignore Sawyer but directed his remarks to her. "I understand your father was close to working out a formula? Did he finish?"

Wow. Talk about direct and to the point. Kaylin leaned back. "I'm not that familiar with my father's business, so I'll have to leave that question to Sawyer."

"Fair enough." Dean folded his hands and waited.

Sawyer spoke easily, as if he weren't weighing his words carefully, but she knew better. "If Henry had completed the formula, you'd be interested in purchasing it?"

"Yes." Dean didn't hesitate. "We have the room and the resources," he gestured to two empty acres out back, "to put Henry's formula into practice. I'd like to see his work come to fruition. Of course I'd have to verify with other scientists that his formula actually worked."

Sawyer kept his tone pleasant and nonconfrontational. "And why should we sell to you? Why not take his formula to Mobil, Chevron, or BP and let them bid?"

Dean shrugged as if he'd already thought of that and had dismissed it. "First, they might not be interested. Second, those big companies take a week to send a memo, and it might be months just for you to do lunch. To get them to make an actual offer might take years. In the meantime, they might steal the formula from you just to squash it. Or if you wait too long, someone else may come up with the same formula or a different process that makes Henry's obsolete. I'm ready, willing, and able to act right now."

Dean Witman had made very good points. But Sawyer's expression didn't change one iota and he kept his voice level. "After what happened at the lab—"

"Big companies might believe Henry blew himself up."

"He didn't," Kaylin insisted.

"Can you prove that?"

Kaylin shrugged.

"Then you have nothing to sell."

"Not necessarily," Sawyer said. "After what happened at the lab, you can understand that we're reluctant to admit what Henry did or did not discover."

"Look, if Henry blew himself up—you have a problem. And if it *wasn't* an accident, you're talking corporate espionage, and you still have a problem. Whoever owns this secret could be in danger. While I can protect myself and my family, can you?"

Was that a warning or a threat? Kaylin didn't know. She was having trouble reading Witman.

But at the implication of danger to her family, Kaylin would have shuddered if she didn't have a dancer's control over her body. She'd promised Sawyer she wouldn't undermine his negotiations. She'd keep her word. However, that didn't mean he was going to talk her into anything. She'd make up her own mind.

"We are willing to consider a sale." Sawyer held the other man's gaze. "So here's what I suggest: make us an offer, with all your contingencies, and we'll consider it."

"You want me to make you an offer based on a formula that might or might not exist?"

"Obviously, if it does exist, we'll provide you with proof before money changes hands."

Dean didn't look happy. But he didn't argue, either. Instead he stood, signaling the end of the meeting. "All right. Let me see what I can do."

They exited the office and strolled to the car. All in all, Sawyer's skill in handling the conversation had impressed her. He'd told Dean nothing. And that helped to protect her family. At the same time, he'd urged the man to make them an offer, giving them time to hunt down the missing laptop. Too bad she didn't know where else to search.

Not only did selling the business hinge on convincing Sawyer to sell, they had to find the formula. Kaylin's cell phone rang and caller ID told her someone was calling from home.

Maybe Mitzy or Becca had come home early.

"Hello."

"We've been robbed." Lia spoke in a hysterical rush. "They tore the place apart. With hammers and shit. Our house is ruined. They broke everything and—"

"Are you all right?" Oh . . . God. Lia should have been in school. Kaylin prayed she hadn't come home in the middle of the robbery.

"Yes, but—"

"Where are you?"

"At home. You need to be here."

"I'm on the way. Hang on, Lia. I'll be right there. Give me twenty minutes."

15

§

After Kaylin explained to Sawyer in a shaken voice that their house had been robbed, he drove back to the Danner home in ten minutes, running yellow lights and speeding. Sawyer knew Kaylin wouldn't really believe Lia was all right until she saw her sister and checked her out herself.

Glad that Lia was unhurt, his thoughts turned to the latest break-in as he drove. According to Kaylin, Lia had said that the robbers had torn the house apart—as if looking for something.

The most valuable thing in the Danner home was Henry's formula. It wasn't like the women had expensive jewelry or art. Their electronics, cameras, and DVD player were old. And he didn't believe it a coincidence that the house just happened to be robbed less than a week after the lab had exploded. Apparently the thieves hadn't gotten what they wanted from Henry and had resorted to breaking in and trashing the place during their search.

These were organized pros. He kept the chilling thought to himself. Kaylin was already upset. Until she knew her sisters were safe, he refused to alarm her any further.

But Sawyer was kicking himself for not insisting on a more thorough search of the house for the laptop. They hadn't checked the walls for secret compartments. Had the thieves found one?

Sawyer pulled into the driveway. Deputies had yet to arrive. Kaylin opened the car door and the scent of jasmine, fresh paint, and plaster dust hit his lungs. Lia and Billy sat beside one another on the stoop's front steps. Lia clutched Randy to her chest. Her tears had dried but the smeared mascara remained behind, evidence of her former panic. Still, she rose quickly to her feet and hugged Kaylin, her shoulders trembling.

Red and blue lights flashing, a sheriff's cruiser drove up. Deputy Bryant exited his vehicle and walked up, his eyes grave. "Is anyone inside the house?"

"No, sir," Billy answered. "The thieves left in a black van. They had a TV repair sign on the side of their vehicle."

"Any idea of make and model?" Bryant asked.

Lia sighed. "Sorry. We couldn't see it very well."

"Do you remember the name of the TV company on the sign?" Bryant asked.

Lia and Billy both shook their heads.

"Can you describe the intruders?" Deputy Bryant flipped open a pad and began taking notes.

Billy shook his head again. "We never saw them. They broke in while Lia and I were on the roof."

"The roof?" Kaylin asked.

Billy and Lia exchanged a glance. Lia finally spoke. "I came home from school. I . . . I'm not ready to go back. Billy came with me. I wanted to work on my tan."

"On the roof?" Kaylin asked again.

"Yes." Lia pointed. "My window opens up and it's easy to climb out."

"All right. Please continue," Deputy Bryant said.

Sawyer sensed Lia had edited the truth and knew that the cop and Kaylin suspected it, too.

Billy bit his bottom lip but didn't contradict her. Sawyer wondered what the boy would say if he took him aside and asked questions. He seemed to be hiding something.

Once Billy started talking, he kept it up in a rush. "Randy started barking and we thought the thieves might find us. But then Lia fed him a muffin and he settled down. We didn't go back into the house until after we were sure they were gone."

"That was smart thinking, son."

At the cop's praise, Billy's eyes lit up with pride. Sawyer clapped his hand on the kid's shoulder. "You did good keeping Lia safe."

"I think there were two men," Billy added.

"I thought you said you didn't see anyone?" Deputy Bryant shot Billy a curious look.

Lia was quick to come to Billy's defense. "He's right. We didn't see them, but we heard them talking."

"What can you tell me about their voices? Any accents?"

Lia shook her head.

Billy hesitated. "They were hammering and sawing and making a lot of noise, but they might have spoken French."

"French?" Kaylin sighed. "That would rule out a Middle Eastern conspiracy."

"Not necessarily," Sawyer argued. "French is spoken in Morocco and Lebanon, and Lebanon can't be the only Middle Eastern country where it's spoken."

Billy's eyes narrowed. "They went from room to room, as if hunting for something."

"Did they take anything to their van?" Deputy Bryant asked.

"I don't know." Lia shrugged.

"We hid so they couldn't see us," Billy explained.

Lia added, "When we came out, it was hard to tell if anything was missing. The house is a wreck."

"All right." Deputy Bryant snapped shut his pad. "I've got a forensics team on the way. We'll dust for prints. See what we can find. In the meantime, I'll take a look around. You folks stay here, please. We don't want to contaminate the crime scene."

The deputy pushed open the front door and Kaylin gasped. Sawyer didn't blame her. The house looked as if a tornado had hit the interior. Lights had been ripped from the ceiling, and wires now dangled dangerously. Drywall, plaster, and debris peppered the foyer floor. The carpeting on the stairs had been ripped, the padding shredded. They had destroyed the banister and the wooden stairs beneath it.

Kaylin's knees seemed to give out and she sank to the grass. She placed her head in her hands and took several deep breaths. Sawyer hurried to her side. "I know that house has been in your father's family for three generations but everyone's okay and the house can be repaired."

"You're right. But property insurance won't cover everything, and if the rest of the house looks that bad, we'll need another place to live in the meantime."

"You can all move in with me," Sawyer offered. "Gran would love to come home to a houseful of people."

Before she responded, her cell phone rang and she answered. He didn't think her face could go any whiter, but she paled even more and her hand trembled. Then she snapped the phone shut and didn't say a word.

"What's wrong?" he asked, his voice quiet.

"Not now. We're being watched," she whispered.

Watched?

Sawyer placed an arm over her shoulder. Becca was the only Danner sister not present. Could she be in danger? What had happened to shake Kaylin so? And that reference to being watched? Was Kaylin talking about Lia and

Billy, who were within earshot? Or Deputy Bryant, who was coming back outside?

Hell. Sawyer could feel Kaylin trembling beneath his fingertips. If only he could sweep her away for a day to relax. Maybe if he could get them all to safety . . . and have Kaylin to himself.

THE FORENSICS TEAM took several hours to finish. Not that they spent much time at the Danner residence. They'd been busy on a murder investigation and had to process that first.

So it was late afternoon before the Danners, Sawyer, Mitzy, and Billy trudged inside to see what they could salvage. Sawyer still hadn't had a moment alone with Kaylin. After her initial reaction to the mess, she'd dismissed the destruction. Obviously something worse was bothering her, something that was taking her mind away from the utter chaos inside the house.

They'd all gone upstairs and Billy and Lia went to their rooms to check for damage and spare clothing. In the hallway Sawyer had his first opportunity to speak to Kaylin alone.

He kept his voice low. "What's happened?"

Eyes anguished, Kaylin didn't pretend to misunderstand. "Someone called and told me that if I talked to the cops, they'd kill my sisters like they killed Dad."

So her father's death *had* been no accident. Murder. Rage whipped Sawyer's temper into knots. And now they were threatening Kaylin's sisters? Every protective instinct caused his body to produce adrenaline. But there was no one to fight, not that he'd ever used his fists. Sawyer much preferred to use brains over brawn.

Finally he settled down enough to ask, "What aren't you supposed to talk about?"

"They didn't say."

"What did they want?" he asked.

"They said they'd call again."

"That's it?"

Kaylin's face tipped up to his, her eyes fierce. "Isn't that enough? Whoever called probably murdered Dad and now they're threatening . . ."

"Dad was *murdered*?" Lia asked, Billy beside her.

Damn. Sawyer had been so concerned with Kaylin he hadn't heard the kids come up behind them. He turned to face them. "You're both going to have to keep this a secret." He waited for them to nod. After they did, he continued. "Kaylin got a phone call that said if she went to the cops, whoever did this might strike again."

Lia gasped. "They threatened to come back? But they've already destroyed everything."

But not everyone. Sawyer didn't want to tell Lia they'd threatened to hurt her. He let Kaylin do the talking.

"Even if they return, we won't be here. Sawyer said we can all move in with him while the repairs are made."

"How will we know when it's safe to come back?" Lia's hushed voice rose to a wail. "Will we ever be safe again?"

Kaylin hugged her sister. "Of course we will. Maybe they just called to scare us."

"Well, it worked. Consider me scared," Lia said.

"We'll be fine."

"Right." Clearly Lia didn't believe her.

Kaylin looked to Sawyer for help. But he had no answers for them. "The only good thing to come of this is that they didn't find Henry's laptop."

"How do you know?" Lia asked.

"We already looked for it. Unless Henry hid it in a secret compartment, we would have found it. But neither did the intruders." He rubbed his neck and ear. "Because if they had found what they wanted, why make a threat?"

"I don't know." Kaylin's brow furrowed. "I think they came after Dad for the formula and when he didn't give it to them, they killed him. Then they came here to look for the laptop. Or maybe the lab explosion was an accident and they figured without Dad here to protect us and the house, we'd be easy pickings."

"You don't believe that," Billy said with a perceptiveness far beyond his years.

Kaylin's eyes found Sawyer's. "They said they'd call back. Maybe they'll ask me for the laptop then." Kaylin slumped against the wall and stared at Sawyer. "And then what do I do?"

"You lie. Tell them you have it."

"And then what?" Kaylin asked, her voice confused and unhappy.

Sawyer wished he had an answer. "I'll think of something."

16

§

Kaylin looked at the massive heap of plastic garbage bags filled with broken possessions and hoped the insurance agent who'd inspected the destruction would come up with a fair replacement value on the damaged items. The intruders hadn't missed smashing one dish, glass, or coffee mug. Not that the kitchen cabinets would have held glassware even if they'd found something unbroken: the vandals had ripped the cabinets half off the walls, leaving them dangling dangerously.

Obviously no one expected to find her father's missing laptop in a coffee mug or inside a dish. The destruction here was more than a search, it was malicious. Unnecessary. Was it possible the home invasion had had nothing to do with Dad? But what else could it be? She tried to think of possibilities—no matter how farfetched. Could Billy have gotten into trouble with drugs? Could Shadee's brother have ruined the Danner home because he didn't approve of Becca and Shadee? Could her grandmother have anything to do with this mess? Nothing made sense. Everything seemed implausible. Kaylin might as well have blamed Martians for the senseless destruction.

While Kaylin swept broken glass from the floor, Sawyer

nailed up the cabinets. Talk about helpful. Kaylin didn't know how she would have managed without Sawyer. With her sisters and Mitzy upstairs going through their personal possessions, Kaylin stopped the cleanup for a moment and brushed aside the damp hair plastered to her forehead.

Sawyer wore low-slung jeans and a carpenter's belt filled with assorted tools. Whether hammering or sawing, he didn't seem to have one uncoordinated muscle in his body. For a man who'd spent his life hitting the books, he had an extraordinary physique and coordination in spades. And unlike her father, he was proving himself amazingly practical.

When he spotted her staring, she grinned. "For a nerd, you're downright handy."

He winked. "Thank-you, ma'am. You'll still need to replace the cabinets, but at least they won't fall and damage the countertops."

"I really appreciate your help." She had to stop staring at him. The way the sunbeams played over his skin had her heart thundering, her blood sizzling as if she'd never seen him before. What was up with that?

Nothing.

Absolutely nothing. He was an inventor, a dreamer, a man who wasn't for her. Even if he knew what to do with a hammer and screwdriver.

Forcing herself back to work, Kaylin tackled the refrigerator. The entire contents had been emptied. Frozen meat, fresh vegetables, shelves and drawers had been strewn across the broken glass. None of the food was salvageable.

"Who would hide a laptop in the freezer?"

Even his voice was deep and sexy. "Maybe they were after jewelry and the vandalism had nothing to do with—"

"You don't believe that."

"No, I don't."

Kaylin carefully picked up each drawer and shelf, wiped it down and replaced it in the fridge, but her mind wasn't on her work. No doubt she was just feeling vulnerable, out of sorts—that's why she was so preoccupied with Sawyer. Carefully, she steered her thoughts away from the too-attractive Sawyer to much more important matters.

Like what was she going to do when whoever had done this called back? Should she refuse to talk and hang up? Claim she had no knowledge of what they would ask?

Jumpy as oil skittering in a hot frying pan, she used the excess energy to wipe the fridge clean. She hated waiting for another phone call. Hated the threats made against her family. If the caller asked for the laptop, she couldn't tell the truth. They'd never believe she didn't have it.

It worried her that whoever had done this might still be watching them. Should she risk going to the authorities? She had to consider her decision with more care than any she'd ever made in her entire life. The Sheriff's Office was still investigating the break-in, so would telling them about the phone call help them figure out who was threatening them?

If she spoke up, the cops might protect them—but for how long?

She did have proof of the phone call since her cell phone had recorded the number. But these men were pros. The call had likely been made from a public phone. So even if Kaylin risked telling the Sheriff's Office, she doubted they could do anything more than they were already doing.

But she didn't know for certain. Did she have the right to make a decision that might place her sisters in more jeopardy?

Was there anything else she could do to protect them? Would keeping silent do any good? Or would they be safer if she defied the orders in that phone call and went to the Sheriff's Office?

She wished her family was wealthy. She wished they could pick up, go somewhere, and hide. But she needed to keep the dance school open to pay the bills. They didn't have any other resources or relatives or . . . wait. They did have one relative.

For a moment Kaylin had forgotten that Mr. Lansky had told her that she had another family member. Although her grandmother had written a note, it seemed unlikely she would take them in, and Kaylin wondered if she should ask. She hated to go begging for help from a stranger, especially one who'd treated her parents so badly. But if they could find a place to hide, her sisters would be safer there. And for her sisters' sake, Kaylin would do what must be done.

"What are you thinking?" Sawyer raised an eyebrow, the sunlight streaming off his bare chest and incredible shoulders. It didn't seem to matter how many times Kaylin saw him half dressed, the man's hot body kept taking her by surprise. Because if she had to sum up Sawyer in one word, it would be *gentle*.

Yet with all those muscles he looked raw, savage, primal. All pure male animal with smooth sinews and honed pecs.

"I'm thinking I need to talk with my sisters, but I wanted to thank you again for everything you've done." She wished she didn't sound so prim. For just that moment, she yearned to lean into his arms, kiss him on the lips. She shouldn't even be looking at him. He was a dreamer like her father. Kaylin still wanted substantial and solid. And New York.

Still . . . just because he was all wrong for her didn't mean she couldn't appreciate him.

He finished screwing a hinge back into place, the muscles on his back cording. "Thanks aren't necessary. If the situation had been reversed, your father would have helped me out. And to tell you the truth—" He paused. "I feel a bit guilty about inheriting . . ."

"You've been helping my father for years. He wouldn't have left you part of the company if you didn't deserve it. Besides, none of us know how to run a biodiesel plant." Kaylin wanted Sawyer to understand that she didn't resent her father's bequest. In fact, she approved of his very practical decision.

Sawyer peered at her, his blue eyes twinkling. Standing with his hip cocked, one hand on his waist, he shot her a sensual grin. "You really don't mind that he gave me half the business?"

Did he have any idea of the effect he had on her? Was he deliberately acting provocatively or was she seeing signals where there weren't any? It had been a long time since she'd so much as taken a second look at a man. But now with Sawyer her eyes were darting back, not just for seconds, but for thirds and fourths.

Her mouth went dry. With his sharp cheekbones and expressive eyes, he could have been an actor. To calm her raging hormones, she reminded herself he was unemployed, with few or no prospects of ever earning a steady living. Sure, he had degrees from MIT, but her father had had a degree, too. At any time, her father could have taken a corporate job, but he'd never considered it. In his eyes that would have been selling out. And she suspected Sawyer wouldn't give up his dreams for financial security, either. Besides, he had roots here in Tampa. He wasn't what she wanted for her future.

But she couldn't seem to stop herself from taking a step closer to him. He was drawing her with a magnetic power she couldn't resist. As if she were a princess, he held out his hand to help her cross the last few steps. She took it, and with a gentle flick of his wrist, he tugged her into his arms. With no hesitation, his mouth came down on hers.

He felt warm and strong—heat mixed with a multitude of rich flavors that seeped deep into her core and oh, yum, he smelled good too, his scent freshly cut wood with a hint of male sweat.

The warmth and texture of his skin pulled her out of her normal caution mode. Sawyer was everything she didn't want, but he felt so right. Smooth and supple, framed with muscles, his skin felt rich and luxurious beneath her fingertips. She couldn't seem to stop herself from wrapping her arms around his back, couldn't stop her fingertips from trailing up and down his neck, couldn't seem to stop her palms from creating a slick friction.

This guy might think like a nerd but he didn't kiss like one. He knew exactly how to taunt, entice and seduce, using his sensuality to keep her wanting more.

It was Sawyer who pulled back first. Sawyer, whose eyes narrowed as if he were as surprised by the way she'd felt in his arms as she'd been. His lips tipped into a charming grin. "I'm not the least bit sorry about that."

"You aren't?"

"The only thing I'm sorry about is waiting so long to kiss you."

"Then why did you stop?" she demanded.

"Because you don't feel real."

"Excuse me?"

"No kiss can possibly be this good."

"So you stopped in order to analyze . . ."

He shook his head, a lock of hair spilling over his

brow, eyes bright. "I stopped to savor the moment." His tone was soft, husky, and threaded with a deep Southern accent. "I wanted to see the woozy expression in your eyes. I wanted to watch the way the light sparkled in the red highlights of your hair. I wanted to remember exactly how you look at this moment so I can store it away in my memories forever."

With her pulse thudding in her ears, her lips plumped and ready for more, she didn't understand anything beyond wishing she was back in his arms. She didn't know if he was the most romantic man she'd met . . . or the strangest. "So you're telling me you were willing to cut short our first kiss to file me away as a memory?"

He licked his lip where hers had touched his, as if to get a last taste of her. "Something like that."

She leaned back into him, thoroughly intrigued as well as turned on. "Well, now that you have me properly filed, do you think we could create another memory? A longer one this time?"

"I think that could be arranged."

Before he could kiss her again, her cell phone rang. The Caller ID said private caller. As much as she wanted to ignore it, she couldn't. If the intruders were calling back, she'd have to give them whatever they wanted . . . because she wasn't about to place her sisters in danger.

"Hello."

"It's Dean Witman. I'm sending you my offer. However, it's contingent upon you turning over your father's formula."

"I understand." The fax machine was broken. So was every computer in the entire house. "Would you mind sending it to Sawyer's e-mail address?"

"Of course not." Sawyer gave her his address, she repeated it to Dean, and hung up.

"He said the offer's only good if we have the formula."

Sawyer nodded. "So we'll tell him your CPA and attorney have to review the contract. That will buy us some time to search."

"Search where? We've looked everywhere but Dad's safety deposit box and that's not big enough to hold his laptop." She gestured to the messy kitchen, wondering why her pulse was still elevated. It had just been a kiss. But the word *just* shouldn't ever share the same sentence with kiss—not when it was one of Sawyer's kisses.

"We'll start there."

"All right." She paused. "Sawyer, I appreciate all your help, but that kiss . . . we can't do that again."

"Of course not," he agreed and took her back into his arms.

She scowled at him. "I mean it."

"So do I." He leaned down and kissed her forehead. "Absolutely, no more kisses."

"Sawyer—"

He kissed her nose. "No more kisses ever again."

"You're impossible."

"Agreed."

He kissed her mouth. And Kaylin stopped fighting herself. Being in his arms felt too good to think much farther than this moment. Damn, the guy could kiss. He didn't rush. He didn't crowd her. And yet she wanted to crawl into his skin, draw him closer. Much closer.

Finally, she found the will to break away. "This doesn't mean anything."

"Right."

"We can't go any farther."

"Uh-huh."

He wasn't taking her seriously. "Sawyer, I want to sell Dad's business."

"I understand."

"So there's no point in you and me . . ."

"Yes?"

"I don't want to get involved."

"Okay." He agreed with her . . . and then he kissed her again.

17

Sawyer's grandmother's home was nothing like the Danner residence. The neighborhood and exterior structures might have been similar, but his house fronted on the Alafia River with a huge lawn that swept down to a dock with a motorboat. The front doors were inlaid with an unusual stained glass landscape and inside, the house was anything but old-fashioned. Right off Kaylin had noticed ceiling fans that turned in a breeze from the river that cooled down the house. A huge flat screen television and a luxurious white leather sectional placed on hardwood floors with a shiny finish made Kaylin realize how shabby and dated the Danner house must have seemed to Sawyer. White sheers framed the windows as a counterpoint to dove-gray walls. Colorful runners and glass art lampshades made the home warm and inviting. The mix of contemporary pieces and antiques worked, especially with the inviting green plants in various ceramic pots scattered around the home that imparted a delightful scent to the air.

Mitzy twirled around the kitchen, making Kaylin smile as she obviously fell in love with the modern upgrades, a double oven, Corian countertops, and a double sink. The fresh coat of deep red paint set off white woodwork and a black tile floor, and white oak cabinets with black knobs gave the room a decorator feel. Yet mail sat out on the counter, along with several magazines and a pot of herbs. His grandmother's house wasn't a showplace but a home.

The move actually went more smoothly than Kaylin had anticipated, since the big old house had plenty of extra bedrooms. Mitzy had her own room, as did Kaylin. Lia and Becca doubled up, sharing a bedroom over the garage looking out on the river. Billy ended up on a couch on a side porch with Randy, who liked curling up in a sunny spot on a braided rug.

They'd salvaged what they could after the home invasion and their house was now boarded up, waiting on the insurance company to compute damage estimates and process a check. With a new roof over their heads, Kaylin turned her thoughts to keeping the family safe. The threatening phone call weighed on her. Was she doing the right thing by remaining silent and not going to the Sheriff's Office?

Kaylin placed toiletries on the dresser in her bedroom, which was directly across the hall from Sawyer's, and thought again about her grandmother's offer. If the intruders had found Lia at home, she could have been injured . . . or worse. As much as Kaylin wanted to keep her sisters with her here, they'd probably be safer elsewhere—if their grandmother would take them in.

But before she said anything to her sisters about moving them again, she needed to ascertain whether or not her grandmother would welcome them. Kaylin called Mr. Lansky and learned her grandmother lived in Orlando. That was perfect. About an hour and a half's drive from Tampa, Orlando was far enough away for her sisters to hide, but close enough so they could visit. Hopefully they could all move back home soon, but Kaylin couldn't count on the deputies finding the intruders quickly.

Perhaps if the business were sold to Dean Witman, moving her sisters would be unnecessary. She made a mental note to ask Sawyer if the e-mail offer had come in.

Meanwhile, she hung jeans in her closet, placed dance clothes in her bureau, and considered her options.

A move to Orlando would mean Lia changing schools, but . . . she'd be safer if no one could find her. And that had to be Kaylin's priority. Finished unpacking, she made Becca and Lia promise to stay together and explained that she needed to take care of the estate, implying that she was meeting with Mr. Lansky.

All set to head to Orlando, Kaylin snatched up her keys and headed through the garage to her car parked in Sawyer's driveway. She could drive to Orlando and be back before—

"Going somewhere?" Sawyer exited his truck.

At his sudden appearance, she jumped. "You scared me."

Wearing jeans and a blue shirt that brought out the color of his eyes, he held a newspaper folded under one arm and a bag of dog food in the other. Obviously, he'd just returned from the corner store with food for Randy. The guy was thoughtful, she had to give him that.

"What's up?" His tone was casual, but his perceptive gaze took in her slacks and blouse, the extra care she'd taken with her hair and makeup, and his eyebrows rose.

"Just running some errands."

"I'll go with you." He set the dog food and newspaper inside the garage, strode across the driveway to her car, opened the passenger door, and slipped inside.

"It's not necessary for you to come with me." Damn.

She hadn't issued an invitation. One kiss—okay, maybe two or three—didn't mean he could assume she wanted his company. She opened her car door.

He didn't budge, but buckled his seat belt. "You shouldn't be alone."

Probably not. But just because he was right didn't mean she didn't resent it. And it wasn't like her grandmother expected her. She'd decided not to call first. She didn't want her to have time to prepare for a meeting—she wanted to gauge her true reactions. But it was one thing to arrive unannounced all by herself, another to show up with Sawyer in tow.

He wasn't family. But they were living together. Sort of. She really didn't want to go there—not with a woman who'd refused to see her own daughter on her deathbed because she hadn't approved of her husband. Kaylin didn't need extra complications, and Sawyer was definitely that. There could be no mistaking his latent sexuality, his masculinity, the way his eyes gleamed when he looked at her.

Kaylin kept telling herself he was simply helping them out because he was her father's partner. Because he was a good guy. But she didn't want to have to explain that to her grandmother the first time they met.

She placed her hands on the steering wheel but didn't start the car. "I'm going to Orlando."

"Okay."

Sawyer could be the most frustrating guy. He didn't

ask questions. He didn't try to talk her out of the trip. He didn't tell her Interstate 4 would be a parking lot at this time of day. He didn't give her one reason to ask him to get out of her car.

She twisted in her seat. "Look . . . I appreciate everything you've done for us—"

"But you don't want me with you." He said the words without resentment.

Her hopes rose that she wouldn't have to lie . . . or explain. "Thanks for understanding."

"Sorry, darling."

"I'm not your darling."

"Sorry, sweetheart."

"I'm not—"

"You're stuck with me." He didn't raise his voice. But he didn't get out of her car, either. She could see determination in the stubborn tilt of his jaw, the oh-too-casual tone on his voice, the simple challenging gesture of slipping on a pair of sunglasses and easing back into the seat.

"Fine." She didn't have time to argue. Twisting the key in the ignition, she fired up the engine and backed out the driveway, trying hard to keep her temper under wraps. She understood his high-handed tactics were due to his concern about her safety, but she didn't like it. "If you want to waste an entire afternoon with me—"

"Time with you is never wasted."

She glared at him. "You don't even know where I'm going."

"I'm fine with Orlando." He grinned. "The specifics don't matter."

"Maybe I'm going to . . . to see my lover." She said the most outrageous thing she could think of.

He chuckled.

And that made her all the more furious. He didn't believe her and wasn't the slightest bit jealous. "Why is that funny? I could have a lover."

"But you don't."

"Really?"

"If you had a lover, you wouldn't have kissed me." How did he know that? "You just want to make me angry so you can justify pushing me away. It won't work."

"So now you're into psychobabble?"

"I'm into you. I like you, Kaylin."

He'd seen right through her. She wanted to hit him, and not just for his perception but for telling her straight up that he liked her. He wasn't giving her maneuvering room. He wasn't allowing her to tell herself that their kiss had just been one of those momentary things. He wasn't allowing her to tell herself that she didn't mean anything to him. He wasn't letting her misinterpret his feelings.

He wasn't playing games. And he wasn't giving her any place to go.

So she did what any intelligent woman would do when cornered. She decided to think about it later.

18

§

Lia finished putting away her clothes, left Becca and headed downstairs in search of Billy. Moving to Sawyer's house was awesome. She liked getting away from her home and the constant reminder of her father. That someone had murdered him made her start at tiny sounds, fear all the shadows. But in Sawyer's home she felt safe for the first time in a while. She still missed her father terribly, but the memories weren't as sharp here.

She didn't dread seeing her father's toothbrush in the bathroom, or his magazines in the rack, or his coat hanging on the back of a door. She felt lighter, as if she had room to breathe.

As she walked onto the sun porch, Randy lifted his sleepy head and woofed a greeting, but Billy was nowhere around. He hadn't bothered with his stuff, just dumped his skateboard and clothes on two rattan chairs and bailed.

You'd think he'd make an effort to be neat, but the guy *had* been acting weird lately. Even before Daddy's death, he'd been secretive. She'd walk in and catch him on the phone and he'd suddenly hang up. She supposed he could have a girlfriend, and she wasn't quite sure how she felt about that. Lia liked Billy as a *friend*. A friend was easy and comfortable. But another girl might get in the way.

She strolled down the hall lined with framed photographs of cats and Randy followed at her heels. Poor little dog. He'd been uprooted and likely felt lost in the new house. She passed the bathroom but the door was open and no one was inside. Perhaps Billy was in the den.

"Billy?"

He didn't answer and she wandered through the kitchen, the coolest room in the house, snagged a few cookies and headed down to the dock. Lia was drawn to an umbrella with several lawn chairs beneath it that overlooked the river.

She sat in a lounger and Randy jumped onto her belly, circled and lay down, his ears perked up, his eyes on her cookie. Absently, she broke off a piece and fed him. She'd picked a perfect spot to relax. The river flowing by in front of her, an occasional boat motoring past. A breeze kept flies and mosquitoes away. She caught sight of a heron, several catfish and bass in the clear river, and some box turtles sunning on a log.

When she heard Billy's voice, she looked around for him, confused because the sound drifted to her from the water. But she had a clear view of the river and didn't see him. Her gaze veered to a shed at the property's edge.

Suspecting he was on the phone, she brushed Randy off her lap, stood and strolled over. But before she saw Billy, she heard several other voices—dark, secretive voices— and refrained from calling out. What was going on?

She couldn't make out the conversation, but Billy's tone revealed he was playing it cool to cover uneasiness. Before Lia could decide whether to approach or turn around and pretend she'd never been there, Billy and two other guys walked around the shed.

Both guys were older than Billy and she'd never seen them before. One looked like he could have played defense for the Tampa Bay Buccaneers. He had a massive chest, powerful biceps, and he was at least six foot five. The shorter guy was darker skinned, Hispanic, with tattoos that rippled over the skinny arms that hung out of his khaki army vest. Around his neck, he wore a multitude of gold chains, and when he saw her and frowned, his front tooth showed off a gold cap.

"Hi," Lia said, trying to stay cool. Randy barked and she scooped him into her arms. The dog stopped barking but continued to quiver.

"What are you doing here?" The gold-toothed guy sneered at Lia.

"Looking for Billy. What are you doing here?"

"Business."

She stared at Billy, her stomach knotting. He was sixteen. He had a part-time job at the local convenience store, but if this was business, it was bad business.

Billy jammed his hands into his front pockets, a sure sign he was uneasy. "It's okay, Lia."

"Two days. If you want your collateral back, you've got two days," the big guy said in a threatening tone, then both strangers headed up the side yard to where they'd parked their car, started it and left.

Lia put Randy back down and handed Billy a cookie. "What was that about?"

"Nothing."

"What collateral? Did those guys loan you money?"

"It's nothing. Really."

She sighed. "It didn't sound like nothing. And what's with the two-day deadline?"

Billy didn't meet her gaze. "You don't want to know."

"You don't want to tell me," she countered, hurt and confused. It seemed everyone had secrets these days. Kaylin tried so hard to protect Lia, trying to pretend their financial situation was stable. And Becca, Becca was so into Shadee that she rarely talked to Lia, either. Mitzy still wasn't herself and they had to tiptoe around her. If Billy shut her out, she wouldn't have anyone. "Don't you trust me?"

"You won't like it."

"So. That doesn't mean I won't hang with you anymore."

Billy finished the cookie, ambled to the dock, and picked up several stones. He tossed them toward the river, skipping them across the surface. "I needed money for weed, so I got some extra to cover my expenses."

"You're dealing?"

"No."

"Come on."

Billy rubbed his forehead. "The weed was in the house, in the back of my closet. The intruders stole my stash and now I have to pay—not just for mine but for the three ounces I was going to sell."

"I've got a hundred and fifty dollars saved. You can have it," she offered.

"I owe twelve hundred."

"You're kidding."

He wasn't. "It goes for three hundred an ounce."

"Twelve hundred dollars?" It might as well as been a million. Sweat broke out on her forehead and she bit her bottom lip. "What happens if you can't pay?"

"Nothing good." Billy's voice trembled.

Lia pictured that big dude. And the other guy had had mean eyes. In a fight, Billy wouldn't stand a chance. "Maybe you should go to the cops?"

"Then I'd be dead. Those guys are the delivery boys."

"Huh?"

"They deliver the message from the boss."

"Then you have to tell your mom."

Billy shook his head. "She doesn't have any money. And before you suggest telling Kaylin, we can't. If she finds out, she'll kick me and Mom out."

Lia sat on the dock's edge and stared into the river. "This sucks. What are we going to do?"

"You are staying out of it."

Lia glanced at Billy. He had a hard look in his eyes. "You're scaring me."

"Sorry. I told you you didn't want to know." Billy was

silent a long while. "As far as I can see, I only have one option."

"What's that?" Her hopes didn't rise, not even a little. She knew that whatever he came up with would be bad news.

"I'll work off the debt."

"How? It'll take weeks at the convenience store and they said you had—"

"Two days. But I know another supplier. If he'll front me some good stuff and I work fast, I can earn the difference. At least make a serious down payment."

"I don't like it."

"I'll be gone a lot. Will you cover for me?"

Lia sighed. "Don't I always?"

19

§

"**H**ey, Shadee." Becca had phoned him right after Lia left the room. Knowing guys didn't like girls who clung, she made her voice easy-breezy. "I can't make it tonight."

"Okay."

Shadee didn't sound the least bit upset or disappointed, almost as if he didn't care if he and Becca got together or not. He didn't even ask why and that worried her.

"Is this a bad time?" she asked, and could have sworn she heard giggling in the background. Female giggling.

"Hold on a sec." Shadee's voice was muffled, as if he held the receiver with his shoulder and his hands were busy. But busy with what? Was he with someone else? Doing to her what he did with Becca? "Stop it," he hissed.

"Excuse me?"

"Sorry. Wasn't talking to you."

So he was with someone and Becca fumed. They hadn't discussed exclusivity. Still . . . if he was cheating on her already, she should hang up and lose his number for good.

Memories of how good they were together made her eyes tear up. She'd miss him. She'd thought he might be the one, the one who would change her life. Had she gone too fast for him? He seemed so Americanized, but his culture could be different. God. Making love had seemed so right when they were together, but now that she thought about it, Shadee never talked much. Had she made the wrong assumption that he'd liked her as much as she did him? Was he ashamed of what they'd done? No. He'd been just as ready to make love as she'd been.

"Still there?" he asked.

"Yes." But she wasn't sure why she was hanging on. She wasn't a loser. She deserved better. Certain that whatever he said next would be a lie, she slumped onto the bed and squeezed her eyes tight to hold back tears.

She would not cry.

She wasn't a wimp.

She was too smart to let him treat her badly.

"I'm going to be busy for a few days," Shadee came back on the line.

"Really?"

"My cousin's visiting and my brother Tariq and I have to show her around."

His cousin? Yeah, right.

"She wants us to take her to the beach."

"The beach?" She felt like a parrot, repeating what he said, but she couldn't help but feel down. He was ditching her to spend time with another girl. She wouldn't be human if she wasn't hurt.

"I was thinking about Clearwater Beach. Want to come?"

Had Shadee just invited her to go, too? She'd been trying so hard not to cry into the phone that she wasn't certain. But as usual, she'd assumed the worst. No wonder her last boyfriend had told her to lighten up. In truth, she couldn't. Becca wasn't made that way. When she loved, she loved with her whole heart, or what was left of it, since it had been broken a bunch of times.

"Sorry, Randy barked and I couldn't hear you," she fibbed. "Did you say Clearwater Beach? When?"

"This weekend."

Relief poured through her. Shadee wasn't dumping her or lying. The other girl had to be his cousin. If he'd wanted to be with someone else, he wouldn't have invited her along. She was an idiot. But after her last fiasco with Anthony, who'd cheated on her twice, then told her she was insecure, Becca was no longer certain she was a good judge of men. Especially men as good-looking as Shadee. Something about the guy had gotten to her in a real short time.

She wanted to go with him. "Kaylin's got me looking after Lia but maybe I can break away."

"If you can swing it, that would be wonderful. I don't know a damn thing about five-year-olds."

Sheesh. She'd been jealous of a five-year-old? Mortified, Becca said goodbye and put down the phone. She really had to find some backbone and some self-esteem. Kaylin would see the beach outing as an opportunity to win Tariq over. Why couldn't she be more like her? Her sister always seemed to know exactly what to do and where she was going. And Kaylin had determination. Once she picked a goal, she stuck to it. Becca never seemed to have a goal. Just desires. Unfulfilled desires.

But Shadee wanted her . . . and that was what mattered.

"I THOUGHT YOU said we're going to Orlando?" Sawyer eyed Kaylin as she pulled into the bank. Touchy after their argument, she'd driven in silence for a while. No longer sure of her mood, he nevertheless was pleased. He liked being around Kaylin. She smelled good, like fresh citrus, and she looked good, with her crisp white shirt and dark brown slacks.

"We're still heading to Orlando. But Mr. Lansky gave me a key to Dad's safe deposit box and I wanted to see what's inside first."

"If you're hoping your father left the formula in his safe deposit box, it's very unlikely."

"How do you know?" Smoothly, she pulled into a parking space and placed a sun screen in the window to protect her dash in the Florida sunshine. She checked her hair in the rearview mirror and smoothed the gloss on her lips with her pinky, almost as if she didn't want to look at him. She'd composed herself and withdrawn, putting up that barrier she kept between herself and the world.

But after that kiss he could never let her go back to treating him as a business acquaintance, not and respect himself in the morning. He'd always suspected Kaylin hid a passionate nature, and then he'd seen her dance and known for certain she had unexplored depths. He'd never forget the way she moved, silkily, sensuously.

And Sawyer could be both friend and lover. He saw no conflict there. Nor did he intend to back off just because she preferred it. If she hadn't been attracted to him, she wouldn't have kissed him. He could work with attraction. She'd left him operating room. While he'd give her time to think about his interest in her, he had no intention of holding back for long. Sawyer had punctured her defenses and now that he knew it could be done, he enjoyed the idea of doing so again. And again.

Still, her determination and energy intrigued him most. This woman wouldn't give up or give in.

As she parked, Sawyer unclipped his seat belt. "Henry adjusted that formula daily. And I made his monthly deposit for him before I left town."

"You're probably right." Kaylin exited the vehicle and

locked the car, her heels clicking as she strode across the parking lot. "But we still need to check."

Sawyer opened the bank's door for her and noted several men inside turning their heads to appreciate her walk. The angle of her head, her graceful neck, her dancer's body didn't just say *I'm fit*, but *I'm self-assured*. Sexy. But now that he'd insisted on coming along, he didn't want to crowd her. "You want me to wait in the lobby?"

She hesitated, then looked him in the eye. "Actually, I wouldn't mind the moral support."

She acted as if she were reluctant to open the box, more averse than excited. Yet, she quickly signed her name at the front desk.

"You don't have to do this now." He took her hand in his, not surprised to find it icy.

She squeezed his hand and pulled back, giving mixed signals. "I need to get it over with."

"Maybe Henry left you a stack of cash, bonds, or stock certificates," he teased.

"We'll see."

He'd expected a smart comeback. Instead she lifted her chin as if fighting an inner battle.

"Kaylin Danner." A bank employee checked Kaylin's driver's license against the bank's records, pulled up a signature card on file, and asked for the box number. Apparently, Kaylin had always had access to her father's box. The clerk led them past an open vault door into a medium-sized, windowless, gray room with metal boxes of various sizes lined against the walls.

Sawyer followed Kaylin to the far right corner. The clerk inserted Kaylin's key along with a master bank key and withdrew the box. He gestured to a door. "There's a private cubicle there. Just let me know when you're done."

"Thanks." Kaylin compressed her lips and her hands shook, but she marched toward the cubicle without hesitation.

"What are you so worried about?" Sawyer asked. In her place he would have been really curious. But she obviously dreaded this as if she expected bad news. Perhaps the loss of her father was too recent, too painful for her to feel anything else.

"I . . . don't . . . know. But do you ever have that pit-of-your-stomach feeling that something is about to upset your life?"

"Chemical engineers aren't known for their intuition or sensitivity," Sawyer joked, but she didn't grin. If anything, she'd paled a little more. He shooed her into the cubicle. "Maybe you should just open it."

She placed the box on the counter and shoved it toward him, the metal squeaking. "You do it."

"You sure?"

She grabbed it back. "No. I'll do it." She tugged the box closer, snapped open the lock and tipped back the top. She acted as if she half expected to see a bomb in there. Instead there was an innocent-looking cardboard box with a rubber band around it sitting on top of several ordinary-looking envelopes.

She reached for the box first. Fingers trembling slightly, she fumbled and opened it. A gold wedding band and a string of pearls gleamed in the light. As if familiar with the items, Kaylin snapped the box shut and set it aside. Next, she opened the envelope. This one held an assortment of documents, Henry's passport, birth certificates for him and the girls, a marriage certificate, her mother's obituary, and the deed to the family property. Henry had also saved a crayoned Father's Day card from the girls.

Kaylin's drawn expression curled into a tiny smile. "I remember us making this and giving it to Dad. He raced around the kitchen table kissing each of us, acting as if we'd bought him a new car."

"He thought the world of you girls. I used to be jealous of that," he admitted.

"You? You saw him more than we did."

"But you were family." He shrugged and said no more. Gran had done her best, taking him in, keeping a roof over his head, but she wasn't the motherly type. She had her gardening club, her stained glass projects, and her widowed friends. He'd spent a lot of his childhood alone. Henry had been . . . a substitute father. A partner. But Sawyer had always been an outsider to the Danners' family life.

Next, Kaylin opened a manila envelope and drew out yet another official document, this one with the pages yellowed, the edges frayed and curling. "This looks like an old will. It's dated before my sisters were born."

"His new will supersedes that one, but I wonder why he kept it all these years?" Sawyer saw white paper sticking out of the envelope. "What's that?"

Kaylin turned the envelope upside-down and a picture of a woman fluttered out. She looked enough like Kaylin to be her sister. The red highlights in the woman's chestnut hair and her wide eyes weren't the only clues to her identity. She was dressed in a tie-dyed T-shirt, short-shorts, and sandals. "Your mother?"

"I've never seen this picture." She flipped over the old Polaroid and read the back. "Thanks for setting me straight. Love, Quinn."

"Who's Quinn?" Sawyer asked.

"Uncle Quinn was my Dad's best friend."

Henry's best friend? "I've never met him."

"Funny, I haven't thought about him in years. But when I was a kid, he was around a lot. He gave me a silver locket for my seventh birthday and I still have it—or I do if the thieves didn't steal it."

Why hadn't Henry ever mentioned him? "Did he move away?"

Kaylin frowned. "I don't know. He was like part of the family and then . . . he was gone."

"Did he die?"

She shrugged. "I don't think so. My parents never spoke about him. I asked Mom about him once and she just shook her head and refused to answer. Her eyes were sad."

Kaylin thumbed through the old will and found another document stuck between the pages. "This is odd."

"What?" Sawyer wasn't concerned. Henry had been of sound mind and body when he'd redone his will, which provided a clause that nullified the previous ones, but Kaylin sounded upset and her eyes were filled with turmoil.

Kaylin held up the document between two fingers as if reluctant to touch it. "This is an agreement between Quinn and my father stating they'd share the proceeds of any patents or formulas my father developed during his lifetime."

His lifetime? Why would he sign such a document? Had Quinn been blackmailing his friend? Something wasn't right. In his will Henry had said nothing about Quinn. He'd left half to his girls, the other half to Sawyer.

Kaylin squinted at the messy handwriting. "This is dated about a year after Dad's paper mill patent but there's no termination date. It's open-ended." Kaylin handed Sawyer the old agreement, her brows knotted. "Why would Dad have signed this?"

Sawyer tried to think of something positive and couldn't. "Maybe Quinn was an investor in your father's business."

"This was years ago. Is this claim still legal?"

Sawyer didn't know. He supposed they could check old bank records for canceled checks from Quinn to see if he'd bought a stake in Henry's business. "If this agreement is legitimate, it could mean that if the biodiesel formula works, Quinn would be entitled to a share."

She peered hard at the document. "One half. We'll have to ask Mr. Lansky where we stand." Kaylin sighed. "I wish I knew what this is about."

"You think it's possible that Quinn got tired of waiting for a return on his investment?"

Kaylin eyed Sawyer with a troubled expression. "He wouldn't be human if he hadn't gotten impatient after waiting all those years. I don't know how my mother stood it, day after day, month after month, year after year, living on a shoestring and promises that never came true."

"You sound angry with her."

Kaylin sighed. "I suppose I am. If she hadn't been working three jobs, she might not have gotten sick. She might still be alive."

"I used to do the same thing."

"What?"

"Play *what if* about my parents' car accident. What if they'd stayed home with me that day? What if the drunk driver who hit them had been ten minutes later or earlier? What if I'd been in the car? Would I have seen the drunk coming and warned them?"

"You probably would have died with them."

"Yeah. At some point I just accepted they weren't ever coming back and moved on. It's not easy." Sensing her discomfort, he changed the subject. "Maybe Quinn killed Henry and stole his formula to cash in."

"After twenty-plus years?" Kaylin shook her head. "We don't even know if Quinn's still alive."

"With a little effort we could find out. I think we should look him up. See what he's doing now."

"It'll have to wait. I still need to go to Orlando." She closed the box and locked it away, taking only the letter of agreement between Quinn and her father.

Looking through the box seemed to have tired her emotionally. He held out his hand for the keys. "Want me to drive?"

She cocked her head to one side. "You know how you said you felt like an outsider with our family?"

"I didn't say that."

"Yeah, you did. It was in the subtext."

"Huh?"

"Every dancer knows body language. You were still, too still."

"So?"

"So, this could get nasty."

"Nasty?" He had no idea what she was talking about, but he was more certain than ever he didn't want her to face any nastiness alone. "I never figured you for a pessimist."

"I'm a realist. If my grandmother didn't want to see my mother on her deathbed simply because she hated my father, what are the chances she'll be open to meeting his children?"

He'd assumed her grandparents weren't alive. Her statement rocked him. He'd never figured Henry had so many secrets. "Henry never said a word—"

"Yeah, well, Dad lied to us, but I'm guessing he had good reasons. Mr. Lansky filled me in and my grandmother sent a note to him, offering us her help. I haven't told Becca or Lia yet. Until I meet our grandmother and decide what to do, they don't need to know, at least not right now. They've been through enough."

So had she. But she was protecting her sisters again and he admired her for it. Between their father's death and the robbery, they'd suffered enough grief. Yet Kaylin had been through that, too, and he wished he could spare her some of the pain. "So why are we going there now?"

"Because if she'll take in my sisters for a while, they'll be safe." Her tone was grim, determined. And he hoped for her sake her relative had changed.

20

Kaylin's first view of her grandmother's home was of a driveway of gracefully arching brick pavers lined with royal palms. All this money, and yet Kaylin figured the woman couldn't be happy. What kind of person could disown her own daughter? Despite the heat, she shivered.

The huge house had a many-gabled roof covered in an

acre of barrel tiles. Sweeping balconies, lush landscaping, and a sculptured lawn made the house picture-perfect for the cover of *Architectural Digest*. Kaylin, already jumpy after Sawyer had tailed another car through the entrance to get past the electronic gate, half expected security to pull up at any moment and escort them off the premises. Or arrest them.

They were trespassing. Uninvited.

"Did Witman ever e-mail you that offer?" she asked, realizing she should have questioned him during the drive over and maybe saved herself a trip. With a deal, with the promise of a contract and funds, she might not have to go inside. With enough money, she could afford to send her sisters someplace safe.

"Nothing came in, but I could call him." Sawyer sounded reluctant. "But we don't want to seem eager or he'll lower his price."

"So I have to go in." She shoved open the car door.

"I'm not letting you go inside alone."

"That's not a good idea." She shook her wrists as if to shake away the tension.

"You don't want me?" He raised an eyebrow.

"It's not that." She bit her bottom lip. "I don't know how to explain our relationship."

"I'm your father's business partner. That's all anyone needs to know."

She nodded, giving in. She really wanted him there. She trusted his judgment and knew he'd back her. Kaylin straightened her spine, squared her shoulders, and headed for the front door, wondering if she'd be allowed to step one foot inside.

"Ready?" Sawyer asked.

"Yes."

Sawyer rang the bell.

Rosebushes on both sides of the grand columns led to the entrance. She was no expert, but they appeared to be the same variety her mother had planted. God. Was that why her mother had loved them so? Had she brought cuttings from home? Had tending those bushes made her feel closer to the parents who'd rejected her?

Kaylin's throat tightened and she started to reach for Sawyer's hand, when the door opened. She placed her hands behind her back to hide their shaking and prepared to talk her way inside.

A tall, slender woman with immaculately coiffed white hair, pearls, and a designer suit stood there, her piercing green eyes shocked, her face paling. "Kaylin?"

Her grandmother recognized her. "Mrs. Carstairs?"

In one short movement, Mrs. Carstairs swept her into her arms. "Call me Grandmother."

Kaylin was suddenly enveloped in a fierce embrace and a cloud of expensive scent. Despite her grandmother's offer of help in the note to Mr. Lansky, of all the scenarios she'd imagined, a warm, teary-eyed welcome hadn't been one of them. Stunned and confused, she nevertheless felt the tension inside her ease. For the first time in a while, Kaylin dared to hope the family relationships could move in a positive direction.

Her grandmother released her and stood back, but kept a hand on her shoulder. A tear glimmered in the corner of her eye. "Sorry. Here you finally come to visit and I'm smothering you. You'll think I'm senile. Come in. Come in. Let's sit down and be comfortable."

She'd *finally* come to visit? That sounded almost as if she was expected. Baffled by the greeting, Kaylin looked at Sawyer. He shrugged but gave her a smile and then motioned her to follow her grandmother, who clearly expected them to come along. Kaylin took a deep breath and released it slowly, totally curious.

She knew she looked like her mother, but not only had her grandmother recognized her, she'd known her name. At least the woman had been happy to see her. It seemed unbelievable, and though Kaylin didn't understand what was going on, her curiosity raged.

She barely glanced at the old black-and-white photographs of oil wells on the walls that seemed almost out of place among the expensive decor. The house was filled with contemporary classics and fronted an artificial lake. But Kaylin's mind didn't focus on the decorator's skills or the setting, but on the woman leading her into a casual living room.

Her grandmother possessed smooth skin, devoid of wrinkles or brown spots. No doubt she could afford star-quality spa treatments to preserve her youthful appearance. Fit, she clearly was also in great physical shape, moving like a person twenty years her junior. The swimming pool and tennis court out back might account for her physique, but staying that fit also took determination. The same kind of determination it took to study dance.

"I have lemonade." Her grandmother disappeared for a moment and returned with a tray and a crystal pitcher, glasses filled with ice and a plate of strawberries, raspberries, and pineapple. Wow. She couldn't have fixed it in the short time she'd been gone but had it been ready . . . in case company arrived?

"Are you expecting guests?" Kaylin asked, fingers crossed, hoping they weren't about to be interrupted.

"I keep fresh fruit on hand at all times. It helps keep me away from my secret vice. Chocolate." She didn't smile as she spoke but set down the tray on a coffee table and poured them each a glass. "You going to introduce me to your young man?"

Kaylin's young man? "This is Sawyer Scott. He was Dad's business partner."

Kaylin braced herself for questions about her personal life. But it didn't happen. Instead, she accepted an icy glass of lemonade and sipped. The sweet-tart flavor told her the drink was made with freshly squeezed lemons and lots of sugar. Nothing but the best for her grandma.

Her grandmother looked Sawyer in the eye, shook his hand, and turned back to Kaylin. "I'm sorry about your father."

"Are you?" Kaylin couldn't keep the sharpness out of her tone and set down the glass. How had her grandmother even known about his death? The explosion had made the local news, but had it reached all the way to Orlando?

Her grandmother's tone remained crisp and vibrant, but her eyes revealed sorrow. "Years ago I realized I'd made the biggest mistake of my life by cutting my daughter out of my life. I loved Danielle. Your mother and I were very close."

Either she was genuinely sorry for her actions or she deserved an Academy Award. Kaylin wasn't inclined to forgive so easily, although she could almost feel Sawyer urging her to do so. To his credit, he remained silent.

Kaylin thought of her dying mother and kept her back straight. "But you disowned her."

Her grandmother folded her hands in her lap. "Danielle was my only child. I wanted the best for her. And I didn't believe Henry—"

"Was best?"

"Was good enough." Her grandmother's fingers tensed, the manicured nails biting into her own palms. "You must understand, I didn't *hate* Henry. I just wanted Danielle to have financial security. I wanted her to have what I had." She gestured to her fine home and furnishings. "But Danielle loved him. And she claimed *things* weren't important to her. She loved living his dreams. But dreams didn't pay the bills." She sighed. "I wanted what I thought was best for Danielle, but I went too far."

"When you kicked her out?"

"I thought if your grandfather and I didn't help her, she'd come running back home. That she'd see that a life of struggle was hard. Danielle grew up with a horse, a tennis court, a pool in the backyard, and European vacations. Henry couldn't keep her in the same lifestyle. Unless he got lucky and circumstances changed financially, we didn't believe she could be happy."

Despite herself, Kaylin sort of understood. She'd come here with every intention of taking her mother's side, yet Kaylin had been responsible for her sisters for too long not to comprehend what had driven her grandmother. After all, Kaylin didn't really approve of Becca's guy, Shadee. Although she knew how ridiculous it was to think that, just because Shadee was Middle Eastern, he might be connected to the men who had come to see her father. He might not even be from the same country. Besides, if Becca liked the guy, there had to be a good reason.

But she and Becca were sisters, not mother and daughter. If Kaylin were Becca's mother, would she have tried harder to influence her decision?

She honestly didn't know. But she would never let things deteriorate to the point where they couldn't work things out.

"Why didn't you write or call or get in touch with Mom after she married? After she had children?"

"I wanted to." Her grandmother's voice dropped, then she picked up her chin in a gesture that reminded Kaylin of herself. "But the stress of losing Danielle took a toll on us. When your mother eloped, Garrett, your grandfather, had a stroke. I spent my days and nights caring for him. Blaming her for putting us through hell."

"Garrett might have had a stroke even if Danielle had done as you wished," Sawyer pointed out.

"I didn't say my thoughts were rational. My only excuse was that Garrett was a demanding patient. He wanted only me bathing him. Only me feeding him. Only me giving him his meds. I'm not excusing myself, I'm just telling you how it was."

"And you never once had a spare minute to pick up the phone?" Kaylin didn't buy the story.

"Danielle could have called, too, made the first step to reconciliation, but she didn't."

"She was busy taking care of her children and working three jobs." Kaylin spoke the truth but each word seemed like a slap at her grandmother.

"I always thought we'd have time to set things right. And I didn't want Danielle to feel guilty about her father's health, and Garrett didn't want her to see him like that. So I let things stay as they were. For too many years. Wasted years."

"And when my father came to you, when my mother was *dying* . . ." Kaylin choked up and she couldn't even finish her question. Her stomach twisted so tight, it hurt. Sawyer held her hand and she hung on, waiting for an answer.

"I didn't know your father came here until months later when the house sitter remembered to tell me."

House sitter? How bad off could her grandfather's health have been if he was traveling? "You were away?"

"In Europe."

"On vacation?" Her eyes hardened.

Her grandmother shook her head. "We were seeking a stem cell treatment to cure Garrett's paralysis. But it didn't work, it killed him. I lost my husband and daughter within weeks of one another." She hung her head and spoke without looking at Kaylin. "I never came to you girls because Henry would have refused me. He had every right to blame us for not helping out. But I didn't know Danielle was struggling and sick. If I'd known, I would have given everything, the oil wells, the house, the private jet to save her. I should never have presumed to know what was right for Danielle. That one stupid decision cost me my entire family. My daughter, my husband, my grandchildren."

She stopped talking as if she couldn't bear to say more. Kaylin's heart ached. Wealth certainly hadn't made her grandmother happy. She seemed filled with pain.

Her grandmother blew her nose on a tissue and spoke hesitantly, "I heard that Danielle and Henry were happy."

"They were." Kaylin could barely speak past the lump in her throat. There had been too much silence. Too much stubbornness. Kaylin made the first step toward reconciliation. "You weren't all wrong. My mother thought she had the flu and kept working. By the time she sought medical attention and learned she had hepatitis B, it was too late. Her liver had begun to fail. We all loved Dad . . . but he didn't earn enough to pay the bills and that's why Mom worked even when she was sick."

"Not a day goes by when I don't blame myself. If I

hadn't thought I knew best, Garrett might not have had a stroke. If I had known Danielle's situation, she might still be alive. I've ruined everyone I've ever loved." Her grandmother said the words softly as tears of guilt and remorse trickled over her face. "I never expected anything to come of the note I sent to your attorney, but still . . . I prayed you might call, and when I actually saw you on my doorstep . . ." She cried harder.

Kaylin cried with her and it seemed natural to move into the other woman's arms. "It's time you got to know your granddaughters."

"I'd like that. More than you could possibly know. But . . ."

Her grandmother tensed and Kaylin lifted her head, and perused her grandmother's face. "What?"

"There's more."

Kaylin looked at Sawyer for help. She wasn't up for more. She felt drained. Exhausted. Emotionally wrung out. Dealing with another terrible secret might just push her past the point of remaining on an even keel.

"Why don't we take a break?" Sawyer suggested, as if reading her mind. At that moment she could have kissed him as he graciously changed the subject. "Maybe you could show us the house?"

"Of course." Her grandmother led them through a series of rooms. Tastefully, expensively decorated rooms.

Kaylin took the time to regain her equilibrium. As she regrouped, she realized that her grandmother had plenty of extra bedrooms. She could easily take in Becca and

Lia. Her sisters could be safe here and she believed her grandmother would enjoy their company.

But perhaps just as importantly, Kaylin and Sawyer seemed to have bonded in a way she'd never expected. Without her asking, he'd been there for her. He'd been incredibly supportive. He hadn't mocked her for being emotional. Hadn't chided her or teased her. He hadn't even tried to convince her she was fine when she wasn't. He hadn't tried to solve her problems or tell her what to do. He'd been there, saying the right thing. He'd been . . . exactly what she needed.

Too wrung out to be scared that she might become dependent on him, she was simply glad he'd come with her. And she accepted that his being in her life now felt right. They had something too good not to explore further.

Being with him didn't mean she'd give up on New York. She wouldn't stop thinking ahead. Planning. However, she'd just heard what planning with the best of intentions had done to her grandmother. Kaylin didn't want to make similar mistakes. For once she'd live in the moment. Go with the flow. Enjoy these days with Sawyer for however long they lasted.

So he might not be the right guy long term. But he might be the right guy for now.

They headed outside. A waterfall from an elevated whirlpool trickled over rocks and into a pool. The soothing sound calmed Kaylin's ragged nerves. Although the temperature outside had to be in the mid-eighties, overhead fans cooled the shaded porch.

Now that she'd begun to forgive her grandmother, she didn't know if she wanted to hear what else she had to say. Yet, she couldn't get over the past if she didn't hear her out. They took seats around a patio table and she thought Sawyer would settle in beside her. But he strolled around the pool, dipping a finger into the waterfall to test the temperature, skimming his hand along the slide.

"What else did you want to tell me?" Kaylin asked her grandmother.

The older woman moved aside a *Florida Architecture* magazine and settled into a lounger and donned a pair of sunglasses. "I'm not trying to hide anything, but the sunlight hurts my eyes."

"I understand." Kaylin recalled her mother's eyes had also been sensitive to bright light. When she'd worked outside with her roses, she'd worn dark glasses and a hat. Her car always had a dark tint on the windows.

"After what happened with Danielle, if Henry had ever needed help with you girls, he would never have come to me—not that I blame him. But I decided I couldn't have on my conscience any more illnesses that weren't treated properly. So I . . ."

Kaylin leaned forward. "Yes?"

"You aren't going to like it."

Kaylin simply waited.

"Ever since Danielle's death, I've paid someone to watch you girls and report back to me."

"You were spying on us?" Kaylin raised her voice and

as if on cue, Sawyer came up behind her chair, placed his hands on her shoulders and began to knead her tense muscles.

"If I'd known your mother was sick, I would have paid her medical bills, gotten her top-notch care. Money couldn't save my Garrett, but it might have helped Danielle. Or her children. I refused to repeat my mistakes."

"So you pay a private investigator to watch us?" No wonder her grandmother had recognized her on sight. She'd been having her watched for the last four years. Kaylin bristled at her immediate feeling of violation. How far had her grandmother gone? How closely had they been watched?

"I suppose now you'll hate me. But I don't want there to be any more lies or secrets between us."

Kaylin didn't cover up her own feelings. "I certainly don't love you for it."

"I can live with that. In fact, you can hate me all you want, but unless you promise to call me if one of you gets sick, I won't call off—"

"This PI. How often did he check on them?" Sawyer asked.

"Every few days." Her grandmother's gaze narrowed on Sawyer. "Why?"

"Did he notice people who came by the house? Who visited? Where we went?"

"I have no idea. I asked for a few harmless pictures and to be informed if any of the girls took a serious dive, healthwise—nothing more."

"I'd like his name, please," Sawyer asked.

Her grandmother didn't hesitate. "Lyle Jackson."

"What are you thinking?" Kaylin asked Sawyer, curious and uncertain how she felt about her grandmother's snooping. On the one hand, she understood how after losing her mother she wouldn't want to lose a grandchild. On the other, it creeped her out.

Sawyer spoke, his tone thoughtful. "Perhaps Lyle Jackson saw Henry's Middle Eastern visitors and noticed details no one else did. Like the make or model of their vehicle. As a trained observer, he might have taken photos and gotten a tag. Or maybe he checked out their names."

Her grandmother opened her purse, took out a business card, and handed it to Sawyer. "Call him. I'll tell him to give you whatever information he has."

"Thank-you."

"I have a request." Kaylin figured now would be a good time to change the subject. She might not like that her grandmother had spied on them, but she would reserve judgment. The woman had been through a lot. And she certainly seemed to have their best interests at heart. Paying a PI to watch over them to see if they needed health care might be weird, but Kaylin understood her need to look after her grandchildren however she could. So Kaylin proceeded with her plan. "Would you mind letting my sisters stay here with you?"

"Mind?" Her grandmother's lower jaw dropped. "Of

course not. I'd love it." She lifted her sunglasses to peer at Kaylin. "They can stay as long as they like."

"That would be a big help. Thank-you. I'll feel better knowing they are out of Tampa. After Dad died, men broke into our house and vandalized it. We believe these men are connected to the lab explosion, but we have no proof. We aren't living there right now—we're staying at Sawyer's grandmother's house. However, we may still be too easy to find. I'll feel better if my sisters are in another city." She didn't mention the threatening phone call since she couldn't be certain her grandmother would follow her wishes and keep the authorities out of the situation. However, Kaylin already felt better knowing her sisters would be welcomed here.

"If there's anything I can do, please don't hesitate to ask. Garrett's oil wells aren't producing like they once did, but I'm quite comfortable."

"Did you know Henry's last project concerned biodiesel fuel?" Sawyer asked.

"Biodiesel? I've never heard of it."

"That's odd for a woman in the oil business." Sawyer made the comment with a casual air, but his eyes were piercing.

Her grandmother held his gaze. "Oil was Garrett's business. Not mine. I never got involved."

Kaylin didn't know her grandmother well enough to decide if she lied or told the truth. But how could anyone who listened to the news and read the newspapers not have heard of biodiesel? However, for all Kaylin knew, her grandmother only read astrology predictions and the advice columns of the newspaper, or maybe she didn't read much at all.

But at the realization that her father had gone into a business similar to his father-in-law's, she wondered. Had her father intended to best his father-in-law? Or was that mere coincidence? Had Henry been trying to compete with his wife's family—even after his wife had died? It seemed too extreme a motivation for her father.

Yet, if her grandmother was lying about her knowledge of biodiesel, she might also be lying about the PI. Had her conversations with her investigator been only about their health, as she'd claimed?

Perhaps bringing her sisters here might not be such a good idea after all. While her grandmother's tears had seemed real, and Kaylin might forgive a quarter century of estrangement and misunderstanding, was that good enough? Could heartfelt words make up for the past? Enough to trust this woman with her sisters?

Usually Kaylin didn't keep changing her mind. But she didn't know what to think. She wanted Sawyer's take. But even if he remained wary, she figured her sisters were better off with their grandmother than at the mercy of the man who'd threatened to hurt them.

Bringing her sisters here might not be the ideal solution, but it was the best one she had.

21

§

While Sawyer drove back to Tampa, Kaylin slept. Although he enjoyed talking to her, he didn't mind the silence. Before she'd fallen asleep, he could tell from the exhaustion in her gaze that the emotional meeting had worn her out. Even when she slept, he still enjoyed her presence. And he believed that reconciling with her grandmother had been a good choice. The Danner sisters needed family, and so did their grandmother.

When Sawyer pulled into his own grandmother's driveway and shut off the engine, Kaylin opened her eyes and stretched sleepily, her back arching, her breasts rising. She peered from the dark house to the clock in the dash. "It's late. I'm sorry for conking out on you."

"I'll let you make it up to me," he joked, trying to keep his eyes above her neck. Because the curves below were too tempting. Not that he found it a hardship to look into her big green eyes framed by long black lashes. With her graceful neck and elegant torso, she was built to dance. Practically born to be on Broadway. But that didn't stop him from aching for her. Didn't stop him from yearning to enjoy her while she sat next to him in the car.

"I'd like that."

Huh? Like what? He'd been lost in his daydreaming and had to backtrack. But Kaylin's response—that she'd like to make it up to him for falling asleep—startled him. From Kaylin those words were a most enticing comment. However, she probably meant she'd fix him a sandwich. Although his stomach growled, food was not what he had on his mind. It didn't matter that Kaylin's hair needed fixing, or that her lip gloss needed reapplication. She had a sexiness about her that made his fingers itch to tear off her clothes. Her hair's red highlights glinted as the garage motion detector turned on a light. Her hair curled softly around her face and neck, emphasizing her high cheekbones. But the heat in her gaze set his pulse rocketing and gave him hope that she might actually be flirting with him, encouraging him.

At the idea she might want him, blood downloaded straight to his groin. Wincing as his jeans tightened, he shifted in his seat. If he exited the car, she'd see exactly how he felt about her. He wanted her. Oh, yeah. A few kisses had only been the appetizer. He wanted a twelve-course, six-hour gourmet feast that included a fabulously rich dessert that he could savor for . . . forever.

He reminded himself she'd had a trying day. A terrible week.

His body paid no attention.

He told himself to be patient. But he'd run low in the patience department.

He leaned forward to kiss her and she met him more

than halfway, flinging her arms over his shoulders, grabbing the back of his head and tugging him closer.

Damn, she smelled good, like the promise of summer rain, like the electric wind before a storm, like suntan oil on Clearwater Beach. He kissed her and she tasted of lemonade, tart and sugary, a mixture that sharpened his senses and his hearing. Surely he couldn't hear her heart pounding? That roar had to be his own blood rushing as he ran his hands through her hair, the texture rippling over his fingertips.

Her lips were soft, seductive, sizzling hot. The woman didn't just kiss, she invited more, and he slid his hand to her trim waist, under her shirt. She pulled back and he figured she was done.

But he was so wrong.

With a sexy grin, she pulled her shirt over her head and tossed it aside. Kaylin wore a violet lace bra and at the sight of the material cupping her toned flesh, his mouth dried. Her curves complemented her slender body to perfection.

Making out in the car did nothing to alleviate his erection, but he no longer cared about her discovering how much he wanted her. Although he tried to go slowly, his kiss must have communicated his urgency.

She ripped off his shirt, the buttons flying under the dash, into the back seat, and against the windshield. He would have suggested moving to more comfortable quarters, but she pressed her palms to his chest and he lost his train of thought.

Good . . . God. He didn't care where they were. He couldn't think about what would happen next. He could only feel her silky skin, her fresh scent, her eager mouth. And what she did with her hands on his chest had to be classified as sinful.

Proper, careful, practical Kaylin had almost disappeared, replaced by the creative, bold, and passionate Kaylin that he craved. Whatever she did with her fingers, a light skimming flicker that left rivulets of tingling flesh behind, had him raring for more. But the two front seats were hampering his getting closer, his size preventing him from climbing over the console.

But moving to a new location meant he'd have to release her. And the idea of letting go ripped at him, shredded him. He finally had his hands on her and releasing her just wasn't an option. She solved the dilemma by scooting over the console, moving his seat back, and straddling him.

"Mmm. Much better." His head dipped toward the edge of her bra, and he traced the lacy path with his tongue.

She threw back her head, arched her chest into him, and moaned. "That tickles."

He unsnapped the front clasp of her bra and nudged it aside with his mouth. "You have beautiful breasts. You're gorgeous."

She leaned forward and nipped at his neck. "You're not so bad yourself."

As his nerves tingled straight from his shoulder down

his spine, she licked away the pain until the sting merged with pleasure. Ah, two could play that game. And with her breasts conveniently even with his face, he took his time. As he lightly scraped his five o'clock shadow over her delicate skin, her flesh, so whisper soft, quivered.

"Does that feel good?"

"Your mouth would feel better."

At her eagerness, he grinned and used his lips, testing the flavor and firm texture of her skin. "Such impatience."

She wriggled her bottom against his erection. "Look who's talking."

"I'm . . . enjoying." He licked her nipple, blew on the wetness, and adored the tiny goose bumps that arose.

She reached down to unsnap his jeans, not an easy task with her on his lap. Somehow, she succeeded, but his pants stopped her natural progression. "We need to move."

"You do that," he agreed, then took her nipple into his mouth to hold her still.

She tensed beneath his hands. Squirmed but couldn't escape. He had her right where he'd always wanted her . . . restless, edgy, impatient.

She purred into his ear. "You *so* don't play fair."

If she could still talk, he hadn't done his job properly. Keeping his mouth on her breast, he sucked in the nipple, flayed his tongue over the tip.

She moaned, melted, and although her fingers clenched his shoulders, he didn't stop. Soft coos of pleasure escaped from deep in her throat. And he was loving every second of her excitement.

Kaylin finally wanted him and he intended to make this last as long as humanly possible. He'd ached to be with her but he'd feared the reality wouldn't be as good as the fantasy. But she was better than his best dream. Soft, exciting, so female. With her scent rising up to him and her breast filling his mouth, holding back, waiting, caused sweat to bead on his forehead. His blood simmered and bubbled through his veins and his hips tensed to thrust.

At the same time he refused to give in to his need to go faster. He was with Kaylin. Beautiful, graceful Kaylin. She tasted so sweet, so hot, so spicy. And her toned dancer's body had him so ramped up he began to let instinct take over.

A dog barked. Scratched the door between the house and the garage. Then more barking. At this rate, he'd wake up the entire household and they'd come investigate.

It took all his willpower to pull away from her. "Randy hears us. If he wakes your sisters and they find us . . ."

"Damn." Kaylin swore and opened eyes clouded with passion. "I don't want to wait."

"Come on." He popped open the door and helped her slide from his lap. She scooped up her shirt but didn't put it on. He led her out the back of the garage, toward the lake.

"Where are we going?" she asked, slightly breathless.

"By the river, where we can have some privacy." He plucked a cushion off the chaise lounge.

She laughed and raced ahead of him, kicking off her

shoes and hopping up and down as she removed her slacks and panties. Then, like a pagan goddess, she twirled naked on the dock, her hair flying, moonlight caressing her skin.

He could have caught up to her in a heartbeat, but instead, he paused to enjoy the spectacular sight. Dancing and spinning to a beat only she could hear, she gyrated, her hips making figure eights as her arms beckoned with a come-hither gesture. Entranced, he walked toward her, trying to slow his steps.

He wanted to remember this moment, the wildness in his heart, the heavy need in his groin, his excitement that Kaylin was letting go. With him. She was going to make love to him under the stars and a canopy of Spanish moss that draped the granddaddy oaks.

Crickets and frogs set the beat. And Kaylin pulled his strings like a master puppeteer. At that moment he couldn't have refused her anything.

Light and airy, she advanced and retreated in a seductive rhythm that set off a spiraling need. He thought they'd kiss, work their way down to the chaise cushion, but she spun circles around him, her palm caressing his cheek, her hair blowing in his face. And as she danced, she undressed him.

He barely had the presence of mind to pull a condom from his wallet and put it on before she placed both hands on his shoulders and jumped onto him, taking him inside her. No slow easing into lovemaking for Kaylin. She was like a wild woman, all tongue and touch and flaming heat.

"You're insane," he groaned, slowly lowering them to the chaise cushion. "I could have dropped you."

"You didn't." She leaned over him and laughed, a slow, delighted laugh that echoed over the river. "Just lie there and let me do what I want. Can you do that?"

"Yes, ma'am." He raised his hands to her breasts and feathered her flesh with soft caresses. Then she rode him as he lay on the chaise, the sounds of the river floating in his ears.

"You feel so good," she whispered and tilted her hips to provide friction along his length. "Ah . . . that's better. Yes?"

"Yes." He would have said anything if it encouraged her to keep doing what she was doing. Stronger than she looked, Kaylin clenched him with her thighs, gripped his shoulders with her hands.

And she felt so good that he didn't know how much longer he could hold on. She leaned forward and he skimmed his hands over her back and buttocks. Her breasts stroked his chest, her breath against his neck.

Not yet.

His muscles tensed. Gathered.

Hang on.

She rode him hot and hard. His blood pumped furiously. His breath caught in his throat even as his lungs gasped for air. He actually went light-headed. And still he held back.

He wanted this to be good for her.

He would wait.

And wait.

Even if the waiting killed him.

And it very well might. Lord help him, she was so strong. So determined. So damned lovely that he was going to burst.

He bit his bottom lip. But she took that tiny bit of control away, too, kissing him, her tongue lashing his, demanding, giving, taking.

He yanked his head away. "Stop."

"No."

One more move and he'd be a goner.

"I need you now," she demanded. "I'm . . . ah . . . ahh."

Her muscles clenched around him and he let loose with a savage groan. His thoughts splintered. His whole body lunged upward with the explosion. They were damn lucky he didn't tumble them into the river.

She didn't stop moving throughout her pleasure. Didn't stop kissing him as they lay on the padded cushion. It was as if passion had annihilated her usual reserve. "This is good. Good. Good. *Good.*"

Her words inspired him. Although he'd orgasmed, he stayed hard. Hard enough for her to keep riding him. Hard enough for his head to spin. Hard enough to realize that they didn't have to stop.

Wow. She was lovely. Insane. Amazing. And hot. Plus, oh could she move her hips. But she'd had her fun with him for long enough.

"My turn."

"Huh?"

"My turn to play with you." He placed his hand between them and parted her slick folds.

"Wait," she whispered. "I'm so sensitive—"

"Good."

He slid his finger back and forth as he pumped in and out of her. Now that she'd taken off the edge, he controlled the pace. "Faster," she urged.

"Sure," he agreed but kept up the same exact slow pace. And he watched her eyes widen, as she realized he had no intention of speeding up. At least not yet.

"I'm . . . not sure . . . I can—"

"You can. You *will*." He didn't change his speed at all. Instead he let the tension build until she squeezed her eyes shut, until her breath came in pants, until he ramped up his own needs to the max.

And when he could no longer control his hips, he moved faster, his fingers more urgent. She might have remained on top, but he controlled the action. If the first orgasm had been solid gold, this went platinum. Pleasure slashed over him, under him, through him. His breath spilled in a rush and he tipped up his chin, his gaze taking in the stars. And as he burst free inside her, he knew that in the entire universe, he was meant to be right here, right now, with this woman.

He lost track of everything. For long moments, there were only Kaylin and Sawyer. And an infinite sky.

"That was fun."

Fun? He sighed. To him she was everything. To her . . . he was *fun*.

They weren't playing on a level field and he reminded himself to give her time. Time to catch up. Because he was in way over his head. And he didn't want to go under all by himself.

22
§

Kaylin felt Sawyer stiffen and withdraw from her, but she didn't have a clue why. "What's wrong?" she asked.

"What could be wrong?" He chuckled, his tone light and playful, and she relaxed as he tugged her against him.

The dock tipped beneath her, but she quickly readjusted her balance. "You were wonderful. Thank-you." She snuggled against him and placed her cheek against his chest, loving the stars over their heads, the sounds of the river rippling against the dock, and the gentle breeze on her bare skin.

But when his arms closed around her again, he did so a beat too slowly. Either something was bothering him or she was over-analyzing.

While they made love, everything had been fine. But now, as silence lapsed between them, the awkwardness left her confused. Something was wrong. She could feel it.

What had she done? She *had* been on the aggressive side.

"Did I shock you?"

"You can shock me like that any time," he teased.

Kaylin didn't know what to think. Perhaps it would come to her later. Right now, she simply wanted to snuggle a bit, then shower and go to bed. It had been a long day. A memorable day. Between finding her long-lost grandmother and Sawyer's lovemaking . . . she'd go to bed happier than any night since her father had died.

Her father. She hadn't even thought about him tonight. But she didn't need to swim in guilt. It wasn't as if she wouldn't always save a place in her heart to love him. But she was beginning to heal, to push back the pain, to live once again in the moment while planning for the future. Dad would have wanted that.

"What are you thinking?" Sawyer asked.

"After Mom died, Dad helped us get through it. He told us we'd always miss her, always remember her, and that she'd live on inside our memories. And when I missed her most, I'd pretend she was in the next room, that when I spoke to her she listened to me."

"I barely remember my parents. Just scents. Voices. I'm not even sure if my memories are my own or made up from looking at pictures of them."

"We're a mess, aren't we?" She picked up her shirt and yanked it over her head, stuffed her panties and bra in her purse and donned her slacks.

Sawyer stood and dressed, too, but remained silent. She'd probably pulled down his mood with her comment. "I'm sorry," she muttered. "I know I shouldn't feel guilty for enjoying myself, but—"

"It's normal." He sounded sympathetic, understanding. "After my folks died, I ate a piece of cake and thought it was delicious. Then I felt terrible because my parents were dead and couldn't eat cake." He'd been so young when he'd lost his parents, but the pain must have been awful, maybe worse since he couldn't take in what had happened. "It's not rational, but I've never eaten cake again."

"Saying sorry seems inadequate." She slipped her arms around him and hugged him, then let go.

"I'm not immune to pain, Kaylin. I get it. You don't need to hide your feelings from me. They are what they are." He took her hand in his, and gently cupped her cheek with the other. Moonlight glinted in his eyes. "You'll muddle through the grieving process the best way you know how."

"When does it end?"

"You know the answer to that."

She thought of her mother. She still mourned her death. Her chest tightened. "It doesn't end."

"But we adapt. We go on. We love and we live. What else can we do?"

"We make love like there's no tomorrow." Kaylin wasn't certain in the darkness, but she thought he stiffened. She didn't intend to hurt him. "I didn't mean to imply I made love because I wanted to escape the pain of my father's death. It wasn't like that. In fact, I sort of forgot about it, that's why the guilt hit me. I'm alive and he isn't."

He spoke gently. "It's okay."

But it wasn't okay. She had the feeling she'd missed something important, as though an idea was just beyond her grasp. She probably just needed sleep. Maybe she'd figure it out later.

After they'd gone inside the house, she showered, towel-dried her hair, pulled on PJs, and slid between the sheets. She wasn't used to sleeping anywhere but home. Every wind-creaked branch slapping the house, every drop of water in the pipes, and every hum of the AC kept her awake.

Maybe it was her fault. She shouldn't have slept on the way home from Orlando. Perhaps a glass of milk would help her relax. She tossed off the covers, slipped into a robe, and opened her bedroom door. Sawyer's room, right across the hall, had no light reflecting under the door. Unwilling to risk waking him or anyone else in the house, she didn't turn on a light.

Instead, she padded barefoot down the hall and kept her hand on the banister as she descended the stairs. She didn't want to wake Billy on the side porch, either, so she felt her way past the foyer and dining area and headed for the kitchen.

The tinkling sound of glass falling behind her had her spinning around.

Someone was breaking in.

She jerked forward to run upstairs and warn her sisters, but that would mean racing past the front door, where it sounded like the intruders were coming in.

She could shout. But would anyone hear her? And if

they did, would her sisters end up heading straight toward the intruders?

Calling 9-1-1 for help seemed the wisest choice.

She'd left her cell phone upstairs in her purse. A thud that sounded like it came from the dining room shot her into double time.

Heart slamming her ribs, Kaylin dashed for the land line in the kitchen. She'd seen a phone on the counter. Or had it been on the wall? She didn't dare turn on the light and reveal her presence. Didn't dare make a sound. She had to get help.

If the same people who'd broken into her house had already found them again, they must be watching them constantly. Moving here, staying in the same neighborhood, had been stupid. They were all in danger. She should have just packed up her sisters and left the state.

Where the hell was the phone?

Her fingers skimmed the counter. She bumped into a potted plant, a blender, a phone book. An object rolled. A pen. In the darkness she heard it skitter and ping as it hit the floor.

Damn.

She held her breath. Didn't move a muscle.

But they'd heard it. A flashlight beam hit her in the face, blinding her.

"Don't move or I'll shoot." It was a man's gruff voice.

Terrified, she held still, so scared her throat tightened and she couldn't utter any warning. And with the light in her eyes, she couldn't see anything.

"Turn around."

Shaking so hard she almost fell, Kaylin turned around, her back to the intruder. Any moment she expected to hear a gunshot, and braced for the agony of a bullet ripping through her.

At the same time, she prayed her sisters would stay safely asleep. That whatever these intruders wanted they would take from her instead.

Approaching footsteps made her tremble. A man grabbed her hands, yanked them behind her back and used heavy tape, maybe duct tape, to bind her wrists. Next he slapped more tape over her mouth, forced her to kneel, and bound her ankles.

And then he walked away.

God. He hadn't raped her. Hadn't hurt her. Hadn't asked even one question. But everyone else was asleep, and he appeared to be heading upstairs toward her sisters, Mitzy, and Sawyer.

She'd failed to warn them. She'd been too scared to shout a warning, waited too long. Now they'd left her gagged and bound, but she had to get help.

Getting to a knife and sawing through the duct tape would take too long. She had to move fast.

Kaylin inched toward the side porch. If she could get to Billy, wake him up, maybe he could slip away and call for help. Kaylin tried to stand, but learned she needed a wall to lean on. She rolled to a corner, wedged her back against two walls and pushed to her feet. Then she jumped forward, the sound of her feet loud in her ears.

Without her arms to balance her, she almost toppled. But thanks to her dancer's muscles, she stayed upright.

But she couldn't hop quietly. Surely they would hear her? But what else could she do? Her sisters were in danger. She needed to do something fast.

She jumped her way down the hall and fell once, knocking the wind from her lungs. From the dining room, she saw the shadows of several men sneaking upstairs.

Go, Kaylin. Get down. Roll.

Kaylin inched, rolled, and squirmed to Billy's room to find his door locked. She kicked with her feet, praying he'd wake up. But either he was a deep sleeper or she didn't make enough noise.

Kaylin placed her back against his door, shoved to her feet, twisted the knob with her hands, and pushed. The door opened and she fell into the sun porch. She couldn't see much in the dark, but Randy woke up, came over and licked her face.

Where was Billy?

Kaylin scrambled to the bed as the moon came out from behind a cloud. The bed was empty.

Billy wasn't here.

And she'd wasted all that time. All her energy. On nothing.

She heard a short scream. Lia. And Becca crying. Thumps. Then a deep voice issuing orders. Randy started to growl.

Lights came on all over the upstairs. She saw masked men wearing dark clothing and gloves marching her sisters and Mitzy, their hands taped behind their backs, down the stairs. Anger and frustration ripped through her.

Hope that Sawyer had escaped died when he clumped down next. He must have put up a fight because blood poured down the side of his face. She had only seconds to do something before they realized she'd left the kitchen.

Kaylin made her way to the outside door. She found the knob, opened the porch door that led outside, and toppled through it. Then she rolled like crazy, bumping down the steps, over the lawn. Shouts all over the house warned her they'd discovered her absence. Frantic, she rolled toward the river. If she could make it to the water and hide long enough to soak the stickiness off the duct tape, she might free herself.

Her plan was a long shot. But it was better than doing nothing.

Almost there, she tumbled over stickers and what was most likely an ant hill. The fire ants stung, the agony of the bites making her eyes water. Too many ant bites could kill her, the poison rendering her unconscious. But the pain, while severe, kept her going. Finally she made it to the sea wall and tipped over the edge, splashing into the river.

The water, cool and dark, soothed her at first. But between her spinning head, the ant bites, and her tied hands and feet, Kaylin lost track of up and down. She pumped her feet in a dolphin kick and shot back to the surface. She drew air in through her nose and sank.

Damn. Had she rolled herself into the river only to drown? Now was a fine time to consider that possibility.

She jerked her wrists, trying to twist the tape back and forth to allow the water to dissolve the stickiness. But if her plan was working, it was too damn slow for her to notice. She gasped more air and somersaulted, threading her hips and feet through her bound arms and coming up with her hands in front of her. She clawed the tape from her mouth and drew in desperately needed deep breaths.

Men swarmed into the backyard shining their flashlights, the beams sweeping over the grass, the dock, and the water. She ducked and surfaced beneath the dock. Swimming with her hands in front of her was easier. She no longer feared drowning and tried to use her teeth on her taped wrists. But it didn't work. She kept sinking and having to come up for air.

Kaylin ducked three times before she succeeded in using her bound hands to undo her feet. Progress. She could kick better now. While she waited for the men to leave the backyard, she worked the duct tape at her wrists with her teeth. Finally she found an edge. Peeled.

And she was free.

Now what?

She eased up the ladder and onto the dock. A man stood guard on the driveway, just outside the open garage door. Solid fences lined both sides of the yard.

She either had to call for help or go in and save her sisters herself. Getting to a phone didn't look like it was possible.

But what could Kaylin do against at least four armed men? She recalled an oar leaning up against the boat house and grabbed it. Not that an oar would do much good against a gun. Still, she felt better with the makeshift weapon in her hands.

If she could take out the guy on the driveway, she could run across the street for help. Clutching the oar, she moved along the fence line, where her shadow merged with the darkness. Several times she stepped on sharp things, a rock, a branch, but she didn't cry out.

Her heartbeat battered her ribs. Every sound seemed too loud. The guy on the driveway was facing her, but paid no attention as he lit a cigarette. In the flash of his lighter, she could see he wore a dark mask, dark clothing, and gloves. She didn't see a weapon but he could have one tucked into a pocket or in the waistband of his pants.

She edged closer. Despite her soaked pajamas and the light breeze, she broke into a sweat. Inch by inch, she stalked her prey.

When he angled his back slightly and leaned against the car, she made her move. She lifted the oar, but she must have made too much noise, because he turned. Kaylin slammed him upside the head and he dropped like a rock.

She hit him again, making certain he wouldn't get up anytime soon. Then again. Inside the house, Lia screamed.

Kaylin's plan to run across the street for help changed. That scream chilled her to the bone. It sounded as if someone was hurting the girls. She frisked the downed man for a weapon but found nothing except the guy's lighter, which she kept. It gave her an idea. From the garage shelf she swiped a can of WD-40. As she raced through the garage and kitchen, she prayed the can wasn't empty.

In the great room, Lia and Mitzy sat on the couch, bound and gagged. Becca was still free but a masked man was about to tie her, too. Another intruder was slapping Mitzy; the sickening sound of his leather glove against her face made Kaylin furious. Randy had hidden under a corner table and barked frantically.

Ragged and bloody, Sawyer somehow freed himself. The man beside Becca drew his gun but she slammed his arm into a wall and he dropped the weapon. While Becca tried to prevent the man from regaining his gun, Sawyer fought two others. He ducked under a blow, knocked over a lamp, and slammed his fist into a throat. His injured opponent staggered toward Kaylin.

Without hesitation, Kaylin sprayed the lubricant into the air and lit the lighter. The makeshift torch worked better than she'd expected, setting his sweatshirt on fire. Flames blazed up and burned his face, and as he screamed and dropped to the floor to put out the fire, she charged with the torch straight toward the man who had been slapping Mitzy.

He drew Lia against his chest and backed toward the front door, using her sister as a shield. "Let's go."

At the same time, Sawyer put his fists to good use, driving his other opponent back. But Becca's opponent had shoved her into a wall and retrieved his gun. He fired into the ceiling. "The next person to move takes a bullet to the head."

Sawyer froze. So did Kaylin. But the masked leader still had Lia. He was forcing her to go with him, and although she fought, her delicate body was no match for his brute strength.

"He's taking Lia," Kaylin screamed.

Sawyer dived behind the counter that separated the kitchen from the great room. The man fired at him twice. Fearing she'd be the next target and concerned he might bleed to death if he'd been shot, Kaylin leaped over to him. "Oh, God. Sawyer, are you all right?"

"Go. Go. *Go,*" the leader of the intruders called for a retreat.

Kaylin, realizing Sawyer hadn't been shot, peeked out from behind the counter and saw the masked leader drag her little sister with him.

Lia would only slow them down. Surely they'd release her after they got outside.

Kaylin grabbed the phone. The line was dead.

Refusing to watch in horror as the four men, one badly burned, took her sister out the door, she tried to stand up, go after them.

One of the men fired at Kaylin, and Sawyer pulled her back. "Stay down."

"Let me go!"

Sawyer rolled on top of her. "Getting killed won't help your sister."

She pummeled his shoulders.

He grabbed her wrists and held them to either side of her head. "Calm down."

"I said let me go!"

He didn't budge. "As soon as it's safe, we'll get to a phone."

As an engine roared to life in the driveway, rage and fear blasted through her and she snapped. "Don't tell me what to do. I was going to check on *Becca*."

"Fine." He released her wrists and moved aside so he no longer pinned her.

She stood up to see a van's taillights fleeing the driveway. Kaylin sprinted to the window, praying Lia would be standing on the lawn.

The van passed under a street light. For one moment she saw Lia's terrified face in the back window. Then the van rolled down the street. They'd taken her sister.

"They've kidnapped her and the license plate was smeared with mud. I couldn't get even one letter or number." Shaking, Kaylin spun around and went to Becca. She kneeled by her sister. "Are you hurt?"

"Just banged my head. Give me a minute and I'll be okay."

Sawyer helped Mitzy free herself of duct tape. The moment she could move, Mitzy ran to the sun porch. "Billy!" In a moment, she returned to the great room in tears. "They must have taken Billy, too."

"Try his cell," Becca urged.

"He's not going to answer," Kaylin said. "I saw his phone on the floor under the bed."

Earlier, Billy hadn't been in his room, but the intruders might have taken him from his bed before she'd rolled in there. During a struggle he could have dropped his phone. So it was possible they'd grabbed him first and placed him in the van.

She thought hard. Had she seen Billy in the vehicle? She'd focused on her sister, not on the others in the car. She couldn't remember seeing Billy, damn it. But she didn't have to shut her eyes to see Lia's horrified stare.

I'll find you, Lia. Hang in there.

Kaylin had thought she'd had more time to protect her family. After the initial phone call, she'd followed the vandals' instructions. She hadn't contacted the authorities.

While she'd waited for a phone call that had never come, she'd given the bastards time to plan a kidnapping.

And now . . . she didn't have a clue how to find Lia. Perhaps she should have called the cops. The FBI. But even now she doubted they would have believed her. After all, the authorities still thought her father's death had been an accident, and she had nothing except her word about a threatening phone call as evidence. Would her unsubstantiated claim have been enough for them to act? And if they had believed her, what would they have done? Put them in the Witness Protection Program? She didn't think so, not when the callers themselves had never said what they wanted.

She still believed she'd had nothing to gain by going to the authorities and everything to lose if there'd been a leak. Still, if she'd spoken up, perhaps the authorities would have protected them. Now, the bad guys had Lia. Poor Lia, she'd looked so scared. Kaylin's guilt ate at her. If only she'd hidden her sisters sooner.

Now it was too late.

23

§

"I heard you lost your last stash." Drano McVaino, nicknamed for his designer drug of choice and his collection of Air Jordans, sneered at Billy. "Why should I front you anything, dude?"

"I have buyers, ready, willing and able to pay cash." Billy tried not to sound desperate. In truth, he'd begun to wonder if scoring this weed from Drano was such a good idea. If word hit the street that Billy was an easy mark, the buy wouldn't go down at all.

The dilapidated warehouse in Tampa that sat corroding beside an old railroad spur was the perfect site for a meet-up. Cops couldn't approach by vehicle. No one would see them make the exchange. If Billy scored the dope, sold it, and returned with cash, he'd want a weapon next time. Homeless people slept along these tracks and camped out under the railroad bridges. There was no telling who else might be around. Watching.

"I don't know." Drano cracked his knuckles. "Convince me I won't lose out if I go with you."

Billy turned around and walked. "Forget it. I've got other sources," he lied. He took five long steps before Drano caved.

"All right. I'll front you a pound. You be back here tomorrow, same time with my cash, or I send my boys looking for you."

Billy turned and made his voice confident. "My customers except primo—"

Drano pulled a large bag from beneath his hoodie. "I only carry sensimilla. The best."

If Billy moved the entire pound, he'd make just enough to pay back his first dealer. Last week he would have been certain he could handle the business, but last week he hadn't yet been ripped off. Last week he hadn't realized the dangers on the street. Taking the weed made him a target. Selling it made him a target. But he already had a big fat bull's-eye on his back.

So he opened the bag, pinched off a bud, appreciating the sweet scent and the sticky green that told him Drano hadn't lied. His quality was top grade. Billy realized he should have brought a scale. He had no way to weigh out the bag and hoped it wasn't light.

He had to smarten up. For now, he'd bluff his way out of here. "I'll trust you on the weight." He slid the bag into his backpack. "But if you're light—"

"I'm not."

"—we won't be doing business no more."

"Just bring me my money." Drano snapped his fingers and he melted into the darkness.

Billy hurried off the track, feeling exposed. Vulnerable. Selling a little dope on the side to support his habit had turned complicated.

Yet as the scent of the sweet stuff lingered in his nostrils, he wished he'd brought rolling papers. After that meeting, he really wanted to take off the edge.

But he couldn't afford to smoke the profit. Since he didn't have wheels, he already owed a dude a few joints for the lift to this side of town.

Nothing was free. Not even his home.

If he wanted to live with the Danners, he had to fix the mess the best way he knew how. He just prayed nothing else went wrong.

24

§

Lia twisted in time to see Kaylin fling open Sawyer's front door. At the sight of her sister receding into the distance as the van roared away, tears poured down Lia's cheeks. When her nose began to run, she quivered with fear. With her mouth taped, if her nostrils clogged she wouldn't be able to breathe. She could suffocate in the car and these men wouldn't care.

Oh God. She wanted to go home.

These guys in their black masks didn't speak. The injured guy they'd picked up off the driveway looked unconscious. In the dark, she couldn't be certain. She sat in the back seat, wedged against a window, trying not to draw any attention to herself.

The burned man seemed out of it. He slouched, his head resting on the seat, his eyes closed. His moans of pain were all the more chilling because no one else seemed to notice or care. And if they didn't treat one of their own with kindness, that didn't bode well for Lia.

She wondered if she should try to escape. When the van stopped at a light, she could attempt to scramble over the half-conscious guy and out the door before the big man stopped her. But she didn't think she could make it. Not with her bound hands.

Yet she had to do something. Twisting at the tape, she tried to stretch it, work herself free.

When the man beside her took out headphones and placed them over her head, cutting off all sound, she shook her head but he paid no attention. When he placed a hood over her head so she couldn't see, she freaked.

She didn't know which terrified her more, the blackness or the lack of sound. It was like being dead. So scared she feared she might pee in her pajamas, she clamped her thighs tight. *No. No.* This couldn't be happening. If only it were a nightmare. But nightmares always scared her into waking up. But this time . . . she was already awake.

When a hand clasped her thigh, she jerked. She couldn't scream. She couldn't hear. She couldn't know what they planned to do to her.

She had no idea who these men were, what they wanted, or where they were taking her.

She told herself not to cry.

But she couldn't stop the tears.

And her nose began to clog again. Frantic, she twisted and thrashed in the seat. Her movements didn't help. She couldn't escape. Couldn't get the bag off her head. But a corner of the tape on her mouth came free.

She worked the tape with her tongue.

She lost track of time as they drove, but she could breathe better now, and that helped a little, lessened her panic, gave her hope that these men didn't control everything.

She'd lost track of their direction almost from the start. She should have paid attention, but how could she think when she was so scared? These men could do anything they wanted to her and she couldn't stop them.

But with the extra air, she held onto one thought like a lifeline. Kaylin would call the authorities. And her sister would never quit looking for her. Even now the cops might be about to stop the van and release her.

Lia just had to stay calm, keep breathing. Just like Kaylin, she wouldn't give up, either. She might cry. She might be afraid. But she would *not* give up.

25

§

"**K**aylin." Sawyer hurried to the window and closed the shades. He ached to comfort her, to hold her in his arms and tell her everything would be fine. Instead, he had to pile on another problem. He held up his phone. "When I answered this, *he* asked for you."

"He?"

Sawyer hated to shake her up any more. Her sister had just been abducted and Kaylin already looked ragged, pale and trembling.

He held out his cell. "I think it's the kidnapper. The call came in with a private caller ID and I put him on hold."

"The kidnapper?" Kaylin snatched the phone from his hand and turned on the speaker. "I want to talk to Lia."

A mechanical device, one of those machines that changed a voice from female to male or added an accent, responded, "You go to the authorities and she's dead. You will do what we say. Do what we say or—"

"You hurt one hair on my sister's head and you'll never get what you want." Kaylin hung up the phone. Her hands trembled and she looked sick with worry.

"Are you crazy?" Mitzy leapt off the couch and attacked Kaylin, shoving her back against the wall. "What have you done? How could you hang up on them?"

Kaylin lifted her chin and stared Mitzy down, but didn't lift a hand to defend herself. "I'm not talking to those bastards unless they prove to me that Lia is okay. And don't you think I want her back as much as you want Billy? But whatever they ask for—we don't have it. We don't have Dad's formula. We don't have any money. We need to stall—"

"Like stalling is going to get us money? Or the formula?" Becca spoke softly, brokenly.

"Give me another option," Kaylin snapped.

Sawyer shouldn't have been surprised when she hung up on the kidnappers. This was a woman who'd defended her sister like a fire-breathing dragon. He'd never forget the sight of her charging into a room full of kidnappers, lighting a can of oil, and turning it on a kidnapper like a blowtorch in order to save her sister.

Becca lifted her head and spoke quietly. "We could go to the cops."

"Even if we wanted to risk it, what would we tell them?" Kaylin argued. "Masked men wearing gloves came and took Lia? We have no description, no fingerprints. I couldn't get the license plate since they'd covered it with mud and I'm betting that even if I told them the van's make and model, we'd find out it was stolen. We have no clues for the cops to chase down."

"We can estimate their heights and weights," Mitzy argued. "We should call the cops."

"No, Kaylin's right." Becca had obviously changed her mind. "We saw four men—"

"Five. I knocked out the guard on the driveway with an oar."

"Okay. We saw five men between five-foot-eight and five-foot-eleven. I think one of them may have had a Greek accent, but I'm not certain. That's not going to narrow it down a bunch. If you think the cops will have them locked up by morning, you're dreaming."

Mitzy didn't look convinced. "But—"

"You think they aren't watching us?" Kaylin argued. "They found us here—at Sawyer's house. You want to bet Lia's life—"

"Billy's, too," Becca added.

"You want to bet Lia and Billy's lives that the kidnappers won't tap into our phones, watch our every move?" Kaylin argued.

"So we just wait?"

"I'm done with waiting." Kaylin raised her chin. "I've had it with our family being victims. Someone murdered our father, vandalized our home, threatened all of us, and now they've taken Lia. We have suffered enough. It's time to fight back."

"How do we fight, when we don't know who they are?" Becca asked.

"We have to outsmart them." Kaylin's voice hardened with determination. "And I want help, official help. But we can't just go running to the Sheriff's Office when we're being watched. So right now that means we need time to figure things out. Maybe find a go-between to do it for us."

Sawyer rocked back on his heels, impressed. It was as if Kaylin had gone from dance teacher mode to antiterrorist mode. She sounded so certain. A few minutes ago she'd been falling apart. She amazed him. To save her family, she'd knocked a guard unconscious with an oar. She'd set a man on fire. How had she pulled herself together so fast? Where did she find the strength?

"How do you know what to do?" he asked.

"I watch TV at night when I can't sleep. Cop shows, mysteries, action adventure. You name it, I watch it. Of course, a lot of TV shows aren't accurate or are exaggerated, but I've learned some things from them."

"So you're telling us we can figure this out because you watch TV shows?" Mitzy asked, incredulously. "You think we can get them back?"

"I know we need time to figure out what to do," Kaylin said softly. "I just bought us some. And we can't keep reacting to them. We have to do something. Get ahead of the curve. Find a way to notify the sheriff or the FBI without jeopardizing Lia."

"I have a few ideas." Sawyer rubbed his forehead to keep blood out of his eyes. If only his head weren't pounding, if only he didn't feel light-headed.

Kaylin went to the kitchen sink, grabbed a clean cloth and dampened it. "Let me look at that cut, Sawyer. You might need stitches."

She made him sit at the table and as she went to work on his head, Sawyer winced. "Easy."

Kaylin peered at his scalp. "The wound is long and thin but not too deep. If I can stop the bleeding, you'll be fine." She pressed harder.

He suppressed a groan, grateful his grandmother was away on a singles' cruise and hadn't been there during the attack. "How about an aspirin?"

"Bourbon's better." Mitzy poured herself a glass.

Becca stood. "Where's the aspirin?"

"The cabinet above the sink," he directed. "Second shelf."

Becca returned with a glass of water and the aspirin. He took two, but he wanted four. All his life he'd avoided fights. They looked painful, but they felt worse. His cut might not be deep, but the bruise under it was. He had one hell of a headache. It felt as if a marching band had used his scalp for a practice field.

Kaylin took another dry towel, folded it, and pressed it against his head.

"Ow."

"It's really just a scratch."

"I think you missed the egg-sized knot."

Kaylin moved her fingers and gasped. "Oh . . . my God. This bump's the size of an orange. Ice. I need ice. How did this happen?"

"Probably when the bad guy coldcocked me with his gun," he muttered.

Kaylin bent down and looked at his pupils. "Did you black out? You think you have a concussion?"

How the hell should he know? Angry he hadn't been able to protect them, furious his efforts hadn't stopped the kidnappers, he was in no mood for Kaylin's questions. But he still had enough sense not to say so. "Two aspirin should fix me."

Becca brought ice in a plastic bag. Kaylin smashed the bag on the counter, breaking up the pieces. "Here, maybe this will help the swelling."

"Thanks." He accepted the ice. "There's a pad and pen over there."

Becca brought that, too. "So what's your idea?"

Kaylin shook her head. "You should lie down."

"Aspirin's already kicking in," he lied. "I'm fine."

"So what's on your mind?" Kaylin sat, clearly upset but holding it together.

"We need a secret way to contact the authorities so we can get Lia back."

"Yeah, right," Mitzy said.

Kaylin shot Mitzy a look that could have frozen the sun's corona.

"Sounds good to me," Becca muttered.

"All right." Sawyer focused on writing notes. "We think they want your father's formula. That's why they killed Henry, robbed your home, and now kidnapped Lia. Chances are, they want to trade Lia for the formula."

"We don't know that," Becca argued.

"True, but why else would they take her?" Kaylin defended his idea. "After all, Lia doesn't know anything and it's unlikely they think she does."

"Exactly." Sawyer nodded, then wished he hadn't as pain exploded behind the bridge of his nose. He closed his eyes and waited for it to pass, then opened them. "So when they call back to trade her for the formula, we have to be ready."

"How?" Kaylin asked.

"We give them the formula."

Kaylin rolled her eyes at the ceiling. "But we don't *have* the formula."

"They don't know that." In spite of his head pain, Sawyer grinned. "We give them a fake formula."

"You can do that?" Becca asked, lifting her head and straightening in her chair.

"That's brilliant." Mitzy's eyes glinted with hope. "They won't know which formula works until they test it."

"These men are not stupid." Kaylin sighed. "Suppose they hold Lia until they test the formula?"

Sawyer shrugged. "If I give them a formula that's close to the real deal, any chemist worth his degree will recognize its value."

"You really think you can fool them?" Kaylin asked.

He didn't know. But what other choice did they have? "I can try. . . . But they'll want to verify your father's findings. I'll use old research to extrapolate, falsify the data, and manufacture fake records. At least enough to convince them to trade the data for Lia."

"And Billy. Why do you all keep forgetting Billy?" Mitzy asked.

Sawyer's mind moved on. "Kaylin, I want you to think back to the security footage. Do you recall the men's faces?"

"Yes, but . . ." She jumped ahead. "I didn't see the kidnappers' faces on the footage. I can't identify them as Lia's kidnappers."

"I'm not asking you to." He started to shake his head and remembered to stop before the pain hit again. "I want to know if any of those men was Quinn."

"Quinn?" Kaylin looked thoughtful.

"Who's Quinn?" Becca asked.

"An old friend of your father's," Sawyer explained as Kaylin closed her eyes. "We went to the bank and in Henry's safe deposit box we found a document giving half the rights to your father's patents to Quinn."

Mitzy frowned. "He never mentioned this Quinn to me."

Kaylin opened her eyes and spoke slowly. "It's been years since I saw Quinn, and I don't remember the men on the footage well enough to say if Quinn visited Dad the week before the explosion. I need to look again."

"I'm calling Shadee," Becca told them. "I'm supposed to go with him to the beach tomorrow."

"Are you thinking about telling him about Lia and Billy?" Mitzy asked. "Because that's not a good idea."

"Why?" Becca fisted her hands on her hips.

"Because Shadee's Middle Eastern," Mitzy pointed

out. "And the men who visited your father a week before his death were Middle Eastern."

"So any Middle Easterner is suspect? Come on. Shadee grew up in this neighborhood."

"Ever hear of a sleeper?" Mitzy countered.

Becca rolled her eyes at the ceiling. "I've spent more time with Shadee than Kaylin has with Sawyer. And you're paranoid."

"I have every right to be paranoid. My son and your sister have just been kidnapped."

Mitzy and Becca both turned to Kaylin. Becca's face stayed defiant, her body stiff with outrage. If Kaylin nixed the idea of Shadee coming over, Sawyer sensed it might lead to a permanent breach between the sisters.

The air crackled with tension. Sawyer didn't envy Kaylin her choices. She had to weigh Lia's life against Becca's judgment of her lover. As much as his head ached, he felt for Kaylin. Talk about being between a rock and a hard place. In her position, he didn't know what he would do, and he was glad he didn't have to make that decision.

"Seems to me it would be a good thing to have another guy around the house," Kaylin said. Becca's relief was evident as she dropped her combative stance. "But . . . I don't want him or the authorities—if we find a safe way to contact them—to know we're falsifying the data," Kaylin added. "You can tell Shadee everything else but that."

"Okay. But Shadee's trustworthy. He was in the U.S. military, for God's sake. He served in Iraq."

Kaylin's eyes narrowed. "How come you never mentioned this before? And just how old is he?"

"He's twenty-six and I never mentioned it because it never came up. It's not like his past is a secret. He's proud of serving his country. *This* country."

Sawyer and Kaylin exchanged a long glance. He could see the uncertainty in her eyes. She'd just lost one sister and didn't wanted to lose another.

For all their sakes, Sawyer hoped Becca's judgment was on target. And that Kaylin's faith in her was justified.

26

§

Becca hung up the phone and joined Kaylin and Sawyer at the kitchen table. He furiously typed data into the computer, his fingers a blur, while her sister studied faces on the security footage.

"Recognize Quinn?" Becca asked, feeling better with Shadee on the way over. The man didn't just make love like a stud, he lent her strength, and that support meant everything.

"I don't know." Kaylin pointed at a middle-aged man on the screen. "I remember Quinn from when I was a kid. Comparing these images to a twenty-year-old memory isn't easy." She shrugged her dancer's shoulders. "But it's possible this is Quinn."

The man—average height with thinning black hair and silver streaks—appeared nonthreatening. Becca frowned. "What's next? Have you figured out a way to contact the authorities?"

"What about asking Shadee to do it for us?" Kaylin suggested.

"You trust him?"

"I trust your judgment."

"Thanks. I love you, too." Becca gave Kaylin a fierce hug. "Then what's next after I talk to Shadee?"

"First Sawyer falsifies the data, and if the kidnappers still haven't called, then we check out Quinn." Kaylin jumped at the sound of a car, then peered out the window as the vehicle's headlights turned into Sawyer's drive.

"It's Shadee." Becca stepped lightly toward the front door. "After I called, he insisted on coming over." She paused and frowned over her shoulder at Mitzy. "I expect you to be nice."

Mitzy didn't answer. Just stared into her bourbon.

Before Shadee had a chance to ring the bell, Becca ran to the door and opened it. He'd never looked so good. Wearing jeans, a T-shirt, and a baseball cap pulled on backward, he was all hard male. She flung herself into his arms, gave him a hug and a kiss, and tugged him into the kitchen to introduce him. Kaylin and Sawyer offered handshakes. Mitzy never looked up from her drink.

"I'm afraid you've caught us at a bad time," Kaylin

apologized as she returned to studying the footage and
Sawyer entered more data into his laptop.

Shadee removed his cap and stuffed it into his rear
pocket. "What can I do to help?"

"Watch over Becca," Kaylin suggested.

Shadee placed a protective arm around Becca's shoulder, his voice soft, yet threaded with determination. "I
can do that, but are you certain you don't want official
help?"

"Actually we're hoping you can do something for us."
Becca spoke quietly, urgently. "The same men who took
Lia may have killed our father and broken into our home.
They told Kaylin they're watching us. But if you went to
the authorities for us . . ."

Shadee agreed. "I can do that."

"You have to do it in secret," Kaylin stressed.

"If the kidnappers find out you've gone to the authorities, they'll . . ." Mitzy shook her head, cutting off the
rest of the threat as if she couldn't bear to repeat it.

Kaylin added, "We're not just counting on the authorities. We're going to figure out how to save Lia and Billy
ourselves."

Shadee nodded and Becca steered him through the
house and onto the back deck. Sawyer had a huge patio that
spanned the entire rear of the house. Planters with flowers
and potted herbs broke up the wide expanse of decking, as
did an umbrella with chairs and two chaise lounges.

Becca drew Shadee to a hammock wide enough for
two. She rolled in and Shadee hesitated. "As much as

I like the idea of getting in there with you, I need to leave."

Becca held back tears. "Not yet. If someone's watching and you go tearing off right away, it'll look suspicious." She ached for Shadee to hold her, to tell her Lia would be okay, that they would find her soon, unhurt.

"All right. If I'm going to get help, give me as much information as you can."

"What do you want to know?"

Shadee spoke quietly, standing beside the hammock. "Did anyone get a make and model of the vehicle?"

"Kaylin saw the van, but the license plate was smeared with mud."

"What about fingerprints?"

"They all wore gloves." Shadee's questions seemed professional. And she was now certain that bringing him in to help was the right thing to do.

"Were they white? Black? Hispanic? Asian? Middle Eastern?"

"I already told you, they wore masks. I thought one of the men spoke with a Greek accent, but I'm not sure."

"What aren't you telling me?"

"It might also have been Arabic. I'm not up on foreign accents." Becca held out her arms to Shadee. When his hand touched hers, she grabbed it and tugged him into the hammock. He didn't resist, rolling against her and feeling so good, solid, warm.

"Think about eyes and the skin around the masks' eye-holes. What were the shapes of the eyes? Was the flesh white, black, or somewhere in-between?"

"I guess none of them were African-American or Asian." Becca snuggled her head against his shoulder and then felt bad that she was taking comfort from Shadee when poor Lia had to be scared out of her wits. Billy, too.

"What were they wearing?"

"Dark clothes. Long-sleeved shirts. Dark pants. Boots."

"Were they in uniform?"

Becca squeezed her eyes shut. Had the men all worn the same thing? "Everything happened so fast. I was asleep. I'm a heavy sleeper. I think I heard Lia scream the same moment I felt a hand on my neck. He held me down by the throat and slapped duct tape over my mouth. I couldn't breathe and thrashed around, not seeing much. He flipped me over and taped my hands, then marched me down the stairs. On the way, I got my hands free. Lia, Mitzy, and Sawyer and the intruders were all behind me. I thought they were going to kill all of us." She shuddered.

"So you led the way downstairs?"

"Yes."

"Then what happened?" Shadee asked.

"Sawyer got free and started kicking and punching. He was like some kind of action hero and almost saved us by himself. I twisted around to see him fighting two men. Another guy pulled a gun. He was going to shoot Sawyer and I knocked the gun from his hand. He shoved me into a wall. Then Kaylin ran inside. She was dripping wet, her eyes wild. She had a can of WD-40 and she lit the spray on fire and burned one of them. Sawyer kept fighting. They retreated, but they took Lia."

"What about Billy?" Shadee asked.

"I never saw him. No one saw him. But Kaylin said he wasn't in his room earlier. We assumed they took Billy first, Lia later, but we don't know. It's terrible of me to hope he's with her. But then Lia wouldn't be alone."

Becca didn't like being alone. She'd felt abandoned after her mother died, and now she was turning to Shadee after losing her father. She sighed. Nobody ever said there was anything wrong with comfort, did they?

She trembled and gently he rocked her against him. The hammock swung back and forth. His heat warmed her flesh, but inside Becca felt frozen. She couldn't relax, not with Lia missing. Not when she was waiting for the phone to ring.

"Did either Billy or Lia have a cell phone with them?"

Becca shook her head. "Lia was in her pajamas. And Billy's phone was on the floor."

"So what's the plan?" Shadee asked.

"Plan?" Becca stalled. She didn't know what to say. She hated lies. But she'd given Kaylin her word.

"To get Lia back?" he prodded.

God. She'd promised Kaylin she wouldn't tell. Becca didn't always listen to her sister, but she wouldn't go against Kaylin with Lia's life at stake. Shaken, too confused to know what was right, Becca relied on her sister's judgment. Besides, Kaylin had street smarts from years of looking out for the family. Still, that didn't mean she was right to keep the plan from Shadee, but of one thing Becca was certain: she would not risk hurting Lia's chances to come home.

"Sawyer and Kaylin are trying to come up with a plan," she lied and tried to make her voice soft and breezy.

"So you don't know? Or you don't trust me?" he asked, his tone still mellow but the words cutting.

"Sawyer believes the kidnappers will demand we give up my father's formula in exchange for Lia. He's getting the information ready right now."

"So you do know." He raised an eyebrow.

Becca swore. "I'd hardly invite you over here and ask you to go to the authorities for us if I didn't trust you."

"Unless you intended to pump me for information."

"*You're* the one asking all the questions," she retorted, confused where his attitude came from. She'd expected support and comfort, not an argument.

His next words sounded flat, formal. "Actually, a deputy stopped by my house and asked questions of his own."

"Deputy Bryant said they planned to talk to all the neighbors to see if anyone had heard or seen anything suspicious. So what?"

"My family's Middle Eastern. Apparently, your father had some Middle Eastern visitors before he died. Now you think one of the men spoke with a Greek or Arabic accent." He threw the statement out there and she let it die in silence.

Uncomfortable, she placed her palm under her cheek to support her head so she could look at him. Finally, he spoke softly. "I'm not what I seem, Becca."

Becca stiffened. "What the hell does that mean?" Was he saying he wasn't American? Had dual loyalties?

"Just believe that I want to help you find Lia."

He sounded sincere, but she didn't like it. Didn't totally believe him. He sounded mysterious, strange. Almost as if he wasn't himself.

She glared at Shadee. *I'm not what I seem.* What was he trying to tell her? "Now who's keeping secrets?"

The back porch door opened and Shadee didn't answer her question. Becca turned her head, surprised to see Kaylin walking over, pulling up a chair. Even in the moonlight Becca read the worry on Kaylin's face.

"Did they call again?" Becca asked, sitting up in the hammock. Shadee sat up with her and kept an arm over her shoulder.

"No. There's something I need to share with you. Mr. Lansky—Dad's attorney," Kaylin added for Shadee's sake, "told me that we have a grandmother."

"What?"

"Mom's mother is still alive." Kaylin told Becca and Shadee the entire story of what had happened earlier that day. At first shocked and suspicious, Becca thought their grandmother had duped Kaylin to gain her sympathies, but as she heard the entire story, she changed her mind.

Kaylin was sensitive and perceptive. If she believed her grandmother then Becca would, too. And as Kaylin explained, Becca slowly took in the news and her hope of finding Lia increased. They had a wealthy grandmother, who'd offered to take them in. A grandmother who regretted the past, who'd suffered enough, according to Kaylin.

"Do you think our grandmother might help us find Lia?" Becca asked.

"I don't know." Kaylin sighed. "I'm worried that out of the belief she was helping, she might go directly to the authorities and blow everything."

"So why did you tell me?" Becca asked, for the first time realizing the tremendous weight on Kaylin's shoulders.

"If anything happens to me during the exchange, I thought you should know."

Kaylin was worried that if the kidnappers called and she had to bring the formula in exchange for Lia, she might not come back. Becca reached out to her sister and took her hand. "Whatever you decide, I'm with you."

Because Becca was very glad she didn't have to make the decision.

Kaylin turned to Shadee. "You still willing to help us?"

He nodded.

"Helping us could be dangerous. My father is dead, my sister's been taken. I hate putting anyone else in danger."

Shadee stood. "I'll do my best."

27

§

After a night dealing dope, Billy hoped to return home before morning, no one the wiser for his absence. And if he sneaked back into the house early enough, Lia wouldn't even have to cover for his absence. But he'd have to hurry, it would be daylight soon.

Meanwhile, luck seemed to be going his way. After he'd left Drano without incident, he'd broken up the pot into ounces. And his other business had gone down smooth as sensimilla smoke. With the pot quality high, he'd had no trouble moving the weed or getting his price. If his luck held, he'd be out of debt and danger by daylight.

And he'd smartened up. He no longer walked around with his cash or his stash. Nope. He'd hidden it. So if the worst happened and someone ripped him off, it wouldn't be for the full amount. He had an econ teacher who'd called that "hedging one's resources" and realized that maybe some of the stuff he'd learned in school might be somewhat useful after all.

He had one more stop on his list before dawn. If he could hit Jimmy Shaddack's before his parents woke up,

Billy would have time to take a breather. The guy had appropriated a garage behind his parents' house for his bedroom. And Jimmy usually hung out with his friends and played loud music until dawn. But the guy was unpredictable.

Billy had called before coming over and Jimmy, already wasted, had assured him he'd caged his Rottweilers. So when Billy heard the loud barks, he didn't back off.

He parked his bike by the fence and headed down the side yard. The houses sat close together in this neighborhood and in the side yards, the roofs blocked out the street lights as well as the moonlight. Crickets chirped, frogs croaked, and mosquitoes buzzed. At the reek of the dog kennel, Billy held his breath and walked faster.

Jimmy's parents raised Rottweilers and the cage needed hosing. Damn. No wonder Jimmy smoked dope. Who wouldn't prefer the sweet aroma of weed to the stench of dog shit?

At the sound of a low growl, Billy jumped and ignored the hair on his neck rising. He kept going. Next time Jimmy would meet him at the front fence or he'd refuse to sell to him. So what if the garage was more private? This place stank. It was dark. Spooky.

A spider web caressed his face and he ripped it away as he reached the backyard. Although the pounding of the heavy metal music reassured him, the howling, growling, and barking dogs had him on edge. A huge male lunged at the fence and probably would have ripped out his throat if the chain link hadn't held. A motion detector turned on the side light and Billy halted. But Jimmy's parents were either gone or oblivious to the racket.

Rounding the corner, he headed toward the garage. Motorcycles, several cars, and a truck had pulled through the back lot and parked on the property. He should have come that way. But he'd never been here before, just clicked with the dude at school. He bragged a bit too much about his extracurricular activities for Billy's tastes, but, hey, no one was perfect. No one was outside in the yard, either. Inside, the blackout shades were down. Billy hurried to the door and knocked. No one answered.

Why would they? How could they hear his knock above the decibel level? He'd be lucky if his head didn't ring for a week after he left. He couldn't imagine why the neighbors hadn't complained.

Billy banged harder on the door. Just as someone opened it, and the whiff of pot hit him full force, Billy caught sight of a sheriff's cruiser, red and blue lights darkened and heading down the street.

"Cops!" Billy shouted, spun and raced back toward his bike. The dogs lunged against the fence, but he kept running. He had to get out fast. Prayed the deputies weren't raiding the place from both sides.

As he ran, he debated on whether or not to ditch the ounce. But he couldn't afford the loss. He had to risk a getaway. Besides, his fingerprints were all over the plastic bag. If he threw it away, they'd find it and charge him anyway.

Best to just run like hell.

Jimmy must have shut down the music because the noise stopped. Billy had made it past the motion detectors and yard lights and almost reached his bike when the blue and red lights of the cop cars behind him flashed.

Surely he had to be far enough away that they couldn't see him? Two cop cars converged on the garage just as Billy reached his bike. Now what?

He could try and go slow. Look innocent. But what kid on the street at 4 A.M. was innocent? He could say he had a newspaper route but if they caught him, they'd check his story. And he had an idea his fleeing alone might be good enough reason for them to search him.

Damn it. He should have listened to Lia. She'd told him he'd been heading for trouble. Getting high was cool. But it wasn't worth jail time, a record, or getting kicked out of the Danner house.

Heart pounding, Billy sprinted alongside his bike, then hopped on. If he cut through a neighbor's yard and headed to the next street, he should be fine. He pedaled hard and after his run, his lungs strained for air. Another bad thing about smoking. If he made it through this weekend, he was going to quit.

Billy hit a crack in the sidewalk and almost tumbled. Good balance saved him. That and the adrenaline that kept his muscles pumping despite his fatigue.

Huffing and puffing, he cut through an unfenced yard. Momentum carried him through the front. After he slowed, he hopped off the bike and pushed. His calves cramped, his chest hurt, and he had a massive stitch in his side, but he kept going.

Shouts behind him, as well as neighbors waking and turning on the lights to see what was happening, spurred him on. The last thing he needed was someone calling 9-1-1 to report a kid fleeing through their yard.

Finally, he made it to the next street. But he still didn't feel safe. If the cops caught Jimmy, and they must have, Jimmy might sell out Billy to lighten his own problems. Billy could still be in big trouble. Sheesh, if the cops just showed up at home to ask questions, Kaylin would freak. Even if they didn't find anything . . . she'd assume he was guilty since she seemed to know when he was high.

Don't panic.

It would be his word against Jimmy's. And he hadn't sold Jimmy anything. He hadn't even showed him the goods. He couldn't be arrested for knocking on a door.

Besides, Billy had hidden his stash and the cash where the cops would never find it. He'd been careful and it looked as if he'd gotten away. Sweat streamed off his body and he stank almost as bad as the dog pen. He didn't think he'd ever needed a shower as badly in his life as he did right then.

But he couldn't go home.

Not until he'd sold this last ounce. Not until he had the money to pay off his debts.

Not only was Billy running out of darkness and time, he'd run out of buyers. It wasn't like he bragged about his activities at school. He kept a low profile. Only sold by referral.

So his list of safe choices on where to sell his last ounce tonight had diminished. He needed to stop, rest, clear his head. He just couldn't think straight—he was too nervous, too hyped, too worried about recovering his collateral.

Maybe he'd pull over on the next street and roll a joint. Just one or two tokes and he'd be good to go.

Sheesh. He'd evaded arrest. Gotten away clean.

He owed it to himself to celebrate.

28

Lia didn't want the van to stop. Stopping meant her journey had come to an end. Stopping meant the men would do . . . whatever the hell they wanted. And she had no idea if they were driving into the woods to rape or murder her. As frightened as she was, no one could stay at the highest state of terror forever. Her body ever so slowly began to unwind. The trembling stopped. Either she'd become accustomed to the fear or had accepted that she could do nothing to change her fate. No. She hadn't accepted that. She'd fight. But with her hands tied and her eyes blinded, she couldn't have harmed a flea.

So her stomach remained twisted and tense. Her heart still pounded too hard. But she'd twisted about enough to dislodge the headset so that it no longer blocked her hearing and started to take in the sounds around her. Despite the blindfold, she could already identify the men by their voices. The injured guy spoke in grunts and groans. The leader, the one who sat next to her in the back, barked short commands in a language she didn't understand or recognize.

The driver possessed the solid assurance of a soldier while the fifth guy seemed younger and alternately elated, then scared. She'd given up trying to figure out where they were taking her. Or why.

She needed a bathroom real bad. Since she'd freed a corner of the tape from her mouth, she could speak, but hesitated to do so. She didn't want to alert them to her tiny victory. After all, she might get the chance to scream.

So far, they hadn't stopped. But maybe they'd be careless enough to push her down and drive through at a fast-food joint. No. They wouldn't. But maybe they'd stop for gas. And when they opened the door, she would scream and scream.

If only her bladder would wait.

But when they finally stopped, she didn't hear the sounds of pumping gas or people talking. Or the sound of traffic. It was so quiet, they must be out in the country. She didn't hear any airplanes or dogs barking.

She breathed in through her nose but didn't smell anything that would help her figure out where they'd driven. One of the men dragged her from the van and she stumbled, her bare feet hurting as her toes came down on a rock. They made her walk for a long while over uneven ground that cut up her feet when she stepped on rocks, sticks, and debris, but the worst part was not knowing what would happen next.

She tried not to cry out from the pain and told herself they wouldn't have gone to all this trouble to kill her. They needed her alive. She thought about struggling but didn't want to give them a reason to hurt her any more than they already had.

When they stopped, she heard nothing beyond her own harsh breathing. It was quiet. Too quiet. And despite her exhaustion, she tensed. Began to shake.

A man pushed her to her knees.

She hit the ground hard. She heard a gun cock.

Oh, God. She'd been wrong. They didn't need her alive. They were going to kill her.

Lia didn't want to die. She was only a kid. It wasn't fair.

When warm liquid trickled down her leg, she was too scared to care that the men were laughing. Too scared to move, she braced for death.

29

§

That she could do nothing for Lia tore at Kaylin. Her sister and Billy had to be terrified. For the tenth time in the last half hour, Kaylin checked her watch, wondering how long it would take Shadee to contact the authorities and return to the house. Her gaze scooted to Sawyer's phone, which sat on the table between them. Still green. Good to go. But neither her cell nor his repaired land line had rung.

After Sawyer had finished his data entry and fallen asleep at the kitchen table, Kaylin covered him with a jacket. She didn't have the heart to wake him. At least one of them would be thinking with a clear head. Even now, she wondered if she'd made a terrible mistake. Had sending Shadee to the cops been a good idea? Should she have contacted her grandmother? Should she have hung up on the kidnappers?

Any mistake could cost Lia and Billy . . . everything. Damn it. Who were these people who had murdered her father, invaded her home, and kidnapped her sister and Billy? What right did they have to rob and steal and murder? Why didn't they just work for what they wanted like decent folk?

Randy padded up and leapt into Kaylin's lap. Poor little guy. He didn't know what was happening, but he sensed the tension in people. Kaylin scratched behind his ears, and he circled and settled with his snout between his paws.

She stared at the phone, willing it to ring. Hours had passed. Becca was still outside in the hammock on the back porch. Mitzy had taken the bourbon to her room. And Kaylin sat at the table thinking that if she didn't get Lia and Billy back safe, she wouldn't be able to live with herself.

Half a dozen times, she reached for the phone to call Shadee. Each time, she stopped. Suppose they were watching? Or had tapped Sawyer's phone? And even if the authorities cooperated, what could they do for Lia when Shadee could hardly give them any new clues to go on?

Doing nothing, second guessing herself, not knowing if Lia and Billy were okay, began to drive her insane. She had to do something. Search for them. But she didn't know where to look.

Maybe she should have jumped in the car and chased after the kidnappers. But if she had, they might have killed her, too.

Stop it.

She could do her sister and Billy no good if she kept blaming herself. Second guessing herself.

The kidnappers would call. And she and Sawyer would hand over the fake documents and get the kids back. Kaylin had to believe the plan would work. She had to.

And if the kidnappers didn't call, she and Sawyer

would find her father's old friend Quinn. She wanted to know why the man owned half her father's patents, and if he'd gotten greedy and now wanted them all. Kaylin had already left a message on her grandmother's private investigator's phone. Becca and Shadee could follow up. If he'd been watching the house, maybe he'd seen something.

Shadee returned just before dawn. He slipped into the kitchen and Kaylin fixed him a cup of coffee. "It is done. The FBI and the Secret Service—"

"Secret Service?" Kaylin looked at him in surprise.

"They assist in kidnapping cases. So does the FDLE. Your cell phone is being monitored. No one official will contact you. And the information is being kept on a need-to-know basis."

"And if the kidnappers call? If they demand a ransom?"

"No one will interfere until after you, Lia, and Billy are safe," Shadee assured her. "Just make sure you keep your cell phone with you at all times. There's a GPS inside so the authorities can track you."

"Thanks." Kaylin reached out and squeezed his hand. "We really appreciate your help."

Shadee slipped back out to Becca and Kaylin watched the sun rise and hoped Lia was somewhere watching it come up, too. Although the idea of food made her stomach roil, she cooked breakfast. No one ate much, not even Shadee, who promised to stay with Mitzy and Becca while Kaylin and Sawyer drove to find Quinn, whom they'd found online. Kaylin MapQuested the directions and, relieved that Quinn Productions wasn't far from Riverview, decided to check him out.

They carried their cell phones and the data with them in case the kidnappers called. Sawyer drove and Kaylin navigated—not that he needed much directing until they reached back roads. They turned off Highway 301, drove past a few subdivisions, and then hit an industrial park.

"Third building on the right," she directed. The park was a mix of businesses, including a carpet cleaning service, auto mechanics, a boat trailer manufacturer, a roofing company, a martial arts studio, and a vending machine stocker.

Sawyer parked in front of a *Quinn Productions* banner that hung over a door. The lack of a permanent sign was the first clue that this wasn't a high-class operation.

They knocked on the door and a burly bouncer type in a gray muscle shirt and baggy shorts opened it and loomed over Kaylin, blocking her view of the interior. "You're late. Get inside and get your clothes off." He moved aside to let her pass.

"What?" Kaylin blinked, peering down a hallway where lights flashed against the tawdry green walls and threadbare carpeting.

"Aren't you Miss Cotton Candy?"

"Not in this lifetime."

Sawyer chuckled. As she stepped forward, she jammed her elbow into his rib. "Stop smirking."

"Sorry," he muttered, still grinning.

She ignored him as well as the sound of a high-pitched

woman's squeal and a man's deep chuckle. What was going on here? "I'm Kaylin Danner and I'd like to see Quinn."

The guy folded massive biceps and stepped forward to block them. "He's busy. Of course, if you wanted to take off your clothes he might—"

"That's not an option." Kaylin no longer had any doubts about Quinn's being a standup kind of guy. Clearly if he made porn films, he wasn't a pillar of the community.

Sawyer reached into his pocket and came up with three twenties. Mr. Bouncer eyed the cash and waited. Sawyer added another twenty and the guy pocketed the money and stepped outside. "If anyone asks how you got in, the door was unlocked and you never saw me."

"Whatever." Kaylin opened the door and the sound of a camera clicking hit her, then a man's voice directing, "Head up, turn, that's the angle I need. Beautiful. Hold it. Hold it. Give me that expression again."

Kaylin forged down the hallway that opened onto a huge set, filled with a black satin sheet-covered bed with women wearing lingerie, lights, camera people, assistants for hair and makeup and half a dozen other jobs she couldn't name.

Maybe she'd jumped to the wrong conclusion. They seemed to be filming lingerie. Not porn. No men were in sight—at least not on the set. None of the women were naked; they all wore a variety of lingerie.

The man she'd seen on the security DVDs was the same man who sat directing the shoot. Quinn. Her father's old partner, the man to whom he'd signed over half the rights to his future inventions. Quinn had thinning black hair with silver streaks, a straggly goatee, and wore clothes that looked as though they'd needed a washing two days ago.

He paid no attention to their entrance. He sat in a chair marked Producer, an unlit cigar hanging from his mouth. Every once in a while he directed the photographer. Mostly he stared at the models.

"People. People. You're supposed to be having a frickin' good time. You look like you're in pain, sugar puff."

"I need some more oil," Sugar Puff complained.

The model opened a jar and spread oil over the tops of her breasts. Right in front of everyone. Kaylin was no prude, but this setup looked raunchy. Yuck. There was no romance here. No magic. No spark. She doubted the photographer knew the models' names.

Kaylin ignored the set and marched over to Quinn. The man took one look at her and the cigar dropped from his mouth to the floor. "Kaylin? Kaylin Danner?"

"You know me?"

He closed his mouth. "Of course I know you. I bounced you on my knee. You used to call me Uncle Quinn. And," he stood and gestured for another man to take his place, "a lady like you doesn't belong here. That's why Henry wouldn't let me come over no more. He didn't want his girls mixed up with the likes of me."

He ushered her and Sawyer to an office and shut the door. He waved at the set. "I'm sorry about that. But I've got to make a living. And lingerie catalogues pay well. Can I offer you a drink?"

"No, thanks." Kaylin felt dirty from just being in the same room with him. She tried not to look at the posters on the walls of half-naked bodies in provocative positions. She wanted to wash her hands—no, make that her entire body. She wouldn't feel clean until she showered. Kaylin had watched dancers in tight leotards that showed just as much skin without batting an eye, but this creeped her out.

It might be a "lingerie" catalogue but she doubted anyone bought the lingerie. She suspected these pictures went into men's magazines or onto the Internet, and that it wouldn't be long before the lingerie came off.

The idea of accepting a drink from this guy made her stomach heave. She swallowed hard. "How did you recognize me?"

She watched his expression to see if he'd lie. Had he been watching their every move? Is that how he'd known who she was?

"You look just like your mother." Quinn's eyes softened, and his tone took on an almost reverent tone. Oh Lord, Quinn had been in love with her mother.

Suddenly his eyes narrowed and his tone hardened. "How did you get in here?"

Sawyer shrugged. "The door was open. We walked in." Sawyer's words might have been casual but no one in the room could have missed the possessive thread running through them. As he'd spoken, he placed a hand over her shoulder. Had Sawyer noted that the guy had had a thing for her mother?

Quinn frowned, opened a box on his desk and took out a cigar. He didn't light this one either. Just stuck it in his mouth. "So what can I do for you, Kaylin?"

The way he spoke, Sawyer might not have been in the room. But Kaylin was very glad of his presence. Quinn had this way of staring at her that made her want to slap him. And it didn't help that from the other room, the photographer's directions, "Yes, girls. That's it," continued in the background.

"You knew my parents since I was a kid."

"Since before you were born. I actually introduced Danielle to Henry. A big mistake. Once they met, she only had eyes for him."

"So can you tell me about the documents I found in my father's safe deposit box? Why would he give you half the rights to his projects?"

"I loaned him money and funded him for years. We made an agreement. A bad one on my part. Henry never came up with anything good after the paper mill invention. Your mother would have been better off with me."

Kaylin bit her lower lip. Antagonizing Quinn wouldn't help her find Lia and Billy. Sawyer leaned forward. "Can you tell us why you went to see Henry the week before he died?"

"I could." Quinn chewed on his cigar.

"Since my father's death, we've been robbed and my sister's been kidnapped."

Quinn's eyes widened. "Becca?"

"No, Lia. And we were warned not to go to the authorities, so—"

"Do I look like I'm the kind of guy who's in bed with the cops?" Quinn chewed the cigar some more. "You came here thinking I had something to do with—"

"We're exploring every option. Can you tell me what you and my dad spoke about before he died?"

"Yeah. I'll tell you. Your father was worried about security."

"Let me get this straight. You and Dad haven't seen each other for years—"

"What gave you that idea? We met once a month. In my line of business, he didn't want me around you girls. We met downtown in Ybor City at Pasha's Restaurant for lunch. Had a standing date."

It was hard for Kaylin to believe this man and her father were friends. He seemed so sleazy, but her father had found friends in places that didn't interest most people. However, if she could overlook what Quinn did for a living—and that was a huge *if*—she might obtain useful information from him. "Dad told you he was concerned about security. Why?"

Quinn tapped the cigar on his desk. "I sell my photographs in the Middle East to some fairly high rollers. Henry thought I might be able to get some Middle Eastern guys to back off."

"What do you mean back off? Did they threaten Dad?" she asked.

"They were pressuring him to sell. Not every Arab country has oil or refineries. Those that don't have it, want it. Biodiesel is right up their alley."

"Did he give you names?" Sawyer asked and Kaylin's heartbeat thudded.

"That's when we had a little disagreement."

"Is that why you didn't come to the funeral?" Kaylin asked.

"I was there. Sat in the back. Left early. Funerals aren't my thing." Quinn looked her straight in the eye. Had he really been there? She supposed she could look in the guest book, but not everyone signed in. And she'd been so upset she might have looked straight at Quinn and not even noticed him.

"What kind of disagreement did you have with Henry?" Sawyer asked.

Quinn sighed. "I suspected Henry had actually come up with something good. He had this shine in his eyes. He was all excited like back in the old days. I offered to lend him money, but he didn't want to give up more than half. We argued. I said good-bye and the next thing I heard, the lab exploded. I'm sorry. I don't know more than that."

Sawyer stood. "You have proof that you paid Henry in return for part of the proceeds?"

"We made the deal a long time ago. Henry's word was good. And to tell you the truth, I'm doing fine. Real fine. I don't need any rights to his ideas. I don't need the Sheriff's Office poking into my affairs either. So you go ahead and tear up those old papers and just forget about Quinn." He peered at her without blinking, his eyes cold.

Sawyer nodded and Kaylin stood, hoping she'd never have to see the man again. "Good-bye, Quinn."

Kaylin didn't speak until they were back in the car. "I don't know what to think. Why would he tell us to tear up the old papers?"

"Maybe he really thinks they're worthless and doesn't want the cops coming around. I'm not sure if what he does is legal."

"Or maybe he got Dad to sign new papers and gave him more money."

"It didn't sound like it. They argued. Still, have you checked your father's bank accounts?"

"I didn't go over them that carefully."

"Was there any unexplained influx of cash?"

She shook her head. "I would have noticed."

"Quinn's connection to the Middle East bothers me," Sawyer admitted. "He might fear that if word of his partnership with Henry comes out, that the men who went after Henry will come after him."

Before Sawyer could say anything else, the phone rang. She grabbed her purse, snatched out the cell, and checked Caller ID. "It's not the kidnapper. Someone's calling from home. Hello."

Becca spoke quietly. "Billy just came home. He took off all night. He didn't even know Lia was missing."

30

§

Becca didn't know if she wanted to leave the house, especially after Billy's sudden return. Billy had told them a story about staying overnight with a friend. When they'd expressed surprise, especially his mother, he'd insisted he'd told Lia and Mitzy ahead of time and that they'd forgotten. Suspicious of his story, Becca had wanted to stay at home to pry the truth out of him, but Shadee had suggested they leave Mitzy to deal with her son. The woman was so far gone into her booze that Becca wondered if maybe Billy *had* told the truth, that she had forgotten her son's whereabouts. However, Mitzy's drinking and Billy's whereabouts last night weren't Becca's primary problem.

Lia was. And Shadee had told Becca that if Middle Eastern men were behind the kidnapping, someone in the Arab-American community might have heard about strangers in town. So she agreed to accompany him. She'd dressed in her most conservative skirt and blouse and drove with Shadee to the Arab-American Community Center.

She'd never noticed the building before. Highway 301 was mostly commercial and retail establishments, but the occasional house from an earlier era still stood beside the highway. Shadee turned into a paved parking lot beside a large yellow stuccoed house that had been remodeled on a fenced corner lot.

Filled with anxiety that she wouldn't fit into the community and Shadee would drop her, Becca tried to remind herself that people were people. She heard kids playing out back. This place wasn't so different from the Boys & Girls Club. But when she spied several women with their heads covered walking through the front door, their long skirts swishing over the concrete sidewalk, she stopped.

"What's wrong?" Shadee asked.

"Will I be welcome here?" She tugged her skirt down an inch, but the hem still didn't cover her knees.

Shadee took her hand. "You'll be fine."

She appreciated his confidence, but he seemed more of a people person than she was. At the marina, he was one of the guys. At her home, he'd adapted, almost like a chameleon. It was a skill she admired. Becca had pretty much never been out of her middle-class Southern neighborhood. Unlike Kaylin, who dreamed of going to the big city, she would have been happy to live in the Danner house for the rest of her life.

She knew she had it good. She liked the Florida weather, enjoyed the slower paced Southern lifestyle. Why would she ever want to leave?

Shadee brought her inside and the scents of foreign food immediately made her mouth water. Women, many without headdresses, had laid out a buffet along one wall. Men stood in groups talking. Kids played tag and ping-pong and video games.

Several people greeted Shadee with nods, and none of them made her feel unwelcome with hostile stares, as she had feared. Despite her lighter skin and her more revealing skirt, the crowd pretty much ignored her, which was a good thing, giving her time to look around and adjust.

When a little girl ran over and hugged Shadee, he grinned and scooped her into his arms. "I thought Tariq was taking you to the beach."

"I am." Tariq came over and joined the conversation. "This afternoon."

Tariq shook Becca's hand. "Hello." His greeting and manner had a stiffness to them. A formality that he might be using to hide resentment of her. And his eyes burned with an intensity she didn't understand.

Every time she was with Shadee and Tariq, Becca sensed something odd, like she didn't belong. She didn't like feeling like an outsider and told herself she'd have to get to know his family better.

Uncomfortable, her gaze moved on to the child. She must be his cousin—a beautiful little girl with big brown eyes and curly black hair. The child handed Shadee a book. "Read me a story?"

Shadee hesitated.

"Brother, you neglect our family," Tariq spoke, his voice low.

Clearly Shadee felt bad about backing out of taking the child to the beach. But he had come to socialize with the men, see if anyone had heard about strangers in town, and he couldn't do that if he read to his cousin.

"I love to read," Becca said.

"Is this your new girlfriend?" the child asked with a bold curiosity.

Becca sensed Tariq's unusual interest in Shadee's answer, but Shadee paid no attention to his brother. "Lana, this is Becca. Would you like her to read to you?"

Lana smiled at Becca. "Yes, please."

Shadee handed her to Becca. In his arms the child hadn't looked heavy but she was a handful. "My, you're a big girl." Becca gave her a hug and then let her slide to the floor. The brothers walked away and Becca focused on the girl. "Where's a good place to read?"

Lana took her hand and led her to one side of the buffet. Tables and chairs awaited the diners. But apparently it wasn't yet time to eat, so they had the area to themselves. Becca opened the book and began to read. As she turned the pages, she kept an eye on Shadee and Tariq.

Together they moved from group to group, talking quietly, sometimes listening, at other times Shadee clapped a man on the shoulder or laughed at what appeared to be a joke. Today, of the two brothers, Shadee was the more outgoing. Tariq remained silent, brooding.

But the camaraderie here was obvious. And while she didn't feel comfortable, she didn't feel unwelcome, except when Tariq had been close. As she watched the men, Shadee occasionally met her gaze, but Tariq acted as if she didn't exist—which was fine with Becca. And no one seemed bothered by her presence or even seemed to notice her short skirt.

When Lana climbed onto her lap to turn the book's pages, several women preparing the food smiled at her. Becca nodded a greeting and kept reading. She'd almost finished the story when one of the women announced the food was ready. Sensing Lana's impatience, Becca quickly reached the end. Lana thanked her, took back her book, and joined the food line.

Becca looked up, pleased when Shadee rejoined her. His brother had disappeared. "Would you mind if we left?"

Praying he'd learned something useful, she shook her head but didn't ask questions until they'd reached the privacy of the car. "What's going on?"

"Maybe nothing. Maybe something."

"What's that mean?"

"One of the men I spoke to manages a popular Arab-American bank. He mentioned that funds have been wired to Pasha's, a Middle Eastern restaurant in downtown Tampa."

"Is that unusual?"

"It is when it's a great deal of money and it comes from Iran. The restaurant could be a front for a terrorist organization."

"Terrorism? But what would the owners of Pasha's want with Lia?"

"I don't know. But you described four men who invaded your house. My contact thinks he may have seen these men at Pasha's. If they are foreigners, they'd need a place to live and a place to eat. Unless they have family in the area, they'd stay at a hotel or a rental house. Either way, they need funds to operate, and who would notice Middle Eastern men in a Middle Eastern restaurant?"

"That's it?"

"The men are from an assortment of countries. One's actually Russian. One is from Morocco and the other two are Lebanese."

"You think these men are the ones who came to the lab, invaded the house, and took Lia?"

"It won't hurt to check them out."

"You have their names?"

He shook his head. "But I have a friend of a friend who works for the Federal Reserve. He should be able to track a bank wire from Iran."

"A friend of a friend?" He sounded vague. As if he didn't want to tell her exactly who his contacts were.

"In the military I did all kinds of networking."

Again, his comment seemed ambiguous. He didn't talk a lot about his past, about what he'd done in the service, or even where he'd served. In fact, he rarely spoke about his personal life at all.

"Why do I get the feeling you're keeping secrets from me?" she asked.

"We all have secrets. We wouldn't be human if we didn't."

He was playing games. Giving her hints. She recalled other things he'd told her. *I'm not what I seem. We all have secrets.* His words haunted her. What wasn't he telling her? And if he was keeping secrets, was she making a mistake trusting him?

31

§

Kaylin's phone rang and she jumped in her car seat, then checked Caller ID. "It's Shadee," she told Sawyer, then answered the call.

"I borrowed Shadee's phone," Becca said. "Call me back, because I don't want to run up his minutes, okay?"

Shadee had warned them not to say much over their cell phones, so a few minutes later Sawyer stopped the car and Kaylin called back from a pay phone. She held up the phone so that Sawyer could hear, making the call a four-way since Becca had them on speaker phone.

Becca sounded subdued, discouraged. "Shadee took me to the Arab-American Center. He's tied into the Middle Eastern community and he wanted to see if strangers were in town."

"Go on."

"We got a lead about large amounts of money transferred from Iran and into an account for Pasha's Restaurant that Shadee wants to follow—"

"Did you say Pasha's?"

"Yeah. Why?"

"Pasha's is the restaurant where Dad and Quinn had lunch once a month."

"They did?" Becca sounded as surprised as Kaylin had been to find out her father had maintained contact with his old friend.

"We should check it out," Kaylin said.

Shadee spoke up, his tone firm. "Kaylin, it's the kind of restaurant where you'll attract attention, possibly the wrong kind. I know some people. Let me do the checking."

"Thank-you so much, Shadee. I'd appreciate it." Kaylin hung up the phone and turned to Sawyer, but before she could say anything, her cell rang again. Caller ID wouldn't identify the number. "I think it's them. Lia's kidnappers."

Sawyer took her hand. "You can do this."

Fingers shaking, she answered the call on speaker. "Hello."

A voice with a thick accent instructed, "If you want your sister to live, bring the formula to Ybor. Sit in the square opposite Muvico Theater. At midnight. Come alone with your cell phone."

Before she agreed, the caller hung up. She knew exactly where he wanted her to go. A stone square with tables and chairs and surrounded by many stores, the site would be busy on the weekends and she could be approached from almost any direction.

"He said midnight." She frowned. "Why would he give us so much warning?"

Sawyer frowned. "Maybe they're already watching the site and want to make sure no authorities show up. Maybe they want you to worry. Maybe they told you to bring the phone because they'll give you more instructions after you arrive."

Sawyer started her thinking in other directions. "Or maybe they want time to learn if we've contacted help."

Sawyer squeezed her hand. "Pasha's is almost right across the street from the theater."

"That can't be a coincidence. I need to go there ahead of time."

"To Pasha's?" Sawyer shook his head. "Didn't you hear what Shadee said?"

"I don't want to go in blind tonight. Besides, Pasha's is our only lead to find Lia. She could be there. And we still don't have the formula."

Eyes concerned, face intent, Sawyer spoke softly, as if he held back his frustration. "Look, if these people have your sister, you can't just walk into their restaurant and start asking questions. If they have anything to do with Lia's kidnapping and they think you're on to them, they might get scared and kill Lia."

"I know. But Lia's their ticket to getting the formula. I have to believe my sister will be safe as long as these men want to trade her for the formula."

"But you don't *know* that."

She swallowed hard. She didn't even know if her sister was still alive. "I have to do something. Maybe I could get a job there."

"As a waitress? Do you speak Arabic?"

"No. But I can dance. And if I get a gig, I could wear

a veil. And stage makeup would prevent even you from recognizing me."

Sawyer gave her a hard look that told her he didn't think much of her idea. "The restaurant's probably just a front for the money people. But even if they're in the booth next to you, do you think these people will talk about their operation in public? Do you think they'll have Lia stashed in the back room? And even if they did, do you think you could get her out by yourself?"

"Fine." Kaylin threw her hands up as if she intended to give in, but she had no intention of giving up. If the restaurant was Lia's kidnappers' headquarters, they might slip up. Leave behind a clue. She might see some mail, a message, overhear a conversation at a table or at the bar or on the phone. And just maybe she might find Lia. She sighed to make Sawyer think he'd convinced her. "So I just wait for tonight, give them the fake data, and hope they give Lia back?"

He nodded. "I know waiting for midnight is hard."

Hard? He had no idea. Even if she handed over the data, she didn't know if they'd free Lia. Every time Kaylin moved or walked, she wondered if Lia was tied up. Every time she spoke, she pictured duct tape over her sister's mouth. Was Lia thirsty? Hungry? Hurt? She couldn't bear to think of anyone frightening her sister, injuring her, raping her. The longer they had her, the more time they had to mistreat her, and the less chance she had of coming back. A dozen times every hour, Kaylin wondered if she'd made the right decisions. Was Lia suffering because of Kaylin?

If her parents were still alive, would they have handled this better? Should she have gone to the authorities herself, immediately, instead of waiting for Shadee to do it?

And what about the instructions to meet at midnight? If the authorities slipped up, if the kidnappers fled, the exchange might not even happen. And if there was a chance that Lia was being kept nearby, it made sense that she could be in a back room at Pasha's.

Deciding what to do clawed at Kaylin. If she went to Pasha's and was caught, the kidnappers could retaliate and harm Lia. But if she disguised herself well, only her eyes would show above the veil. Of course, tribal dancers never wore veils but the restaurant's customers wouldn't know that. She'd have to be careful not to catch the veil on fire, but she could manage.

Sawyer drove back to the house, giving Kaylin time to think. She appreciated Shadee's willingness to help them and hoped the authorities were diligently working on Lia's behalf, but she refused to rely solely on others to find her sister. Dancing could be her way in. She'd have to make sure she wasn't followed. And if Sawyer didn't agree, he didn't have to come along.

She closed her eyes, planning what she would do when they reached the house. Although it was impossible to pick up a gig at the last minute in the restaurant of her choice, Kaylin knew the talent agent who booked the restaurant entertainment in Tampa. If Kaylin could find out who danced at Pasha's and pay the dancer to stay home, she could take her place.

Finally, they reached the house. Sawyer opened the front door for her and they went inside. "Want a sandwich?" he asked.

"No, thanks. You go eat."

He peered at her. "What's going on in that head of yours?"

"Nothing." She'd clearly been silent for too long, arousing his suspicions. "I'm just tired. And worried."

He placed a hand on her shoulder and gazed into her eyes. "Is there anything else I can do?"

"You've been wonderful. Maybe you could check on Becca and Shadee while I make a few calls."

"No problem." Sawyer took her into his arms and hugged her. "Hang in there."

While he went inside, Kaylin slipped out the front door and drove her car down the block to her dance studio. She hadn't been back since the night her father died. But she didn't have time to reminisce. Ignoring the blackened empty lot where the lab had been and the boarded-up Danner home, she parked and strode straight for her desk and her business directory. Last year at a recital, an acquaintance had given her a card and she'd saved it. After flipping through the file, she found the number and dialed.

"Hey, Karen. This is Kaylin from Danner Dance Studio."

"What's up?"

"I need a favor. There's this guy I want to meet who hangs out at Pasha's," she lied. "I'd love to dance there tonight. You think I could pay the regular to stay home?"

A few minutes later, the gig was set. Kaylin spent a

half hour carefully applying heavy stage makeup to her eyelids and another half hour packing her gear, picking out bras and belts, arm bracelets, head pieces, makeup, candles, footgear, music, and a face veil that would cover everything except her eyes. She would dance three sets and hoped she might pick up a lead during her breaks. While the odds were against her, she had to try.

Her major fear was that if another call from the kidnapper came while she danced on stage, she might not hear the ringer. Setting it to vibrate while she danced wasn't possible. Her costume had no pockets, no place to hide a phone. However, she planned to give her cell to one of the waitresses and if it rang, ask them to answer and signal Kaylin to take the call. She'd have to lie, tell the waitress that she had a sick parent in the hospital, but Kaylin was feeling no guilt. Lia's safety came first.

Eager to head out before Becca, Mitzy, or Sawyer tried to stop her, she picked up her dance bag. She turned out the light and was about to leave when the door banged open. At the intrusion, Kaylin jumped back, her pulse leaping at the sight of Sawyer. There was no mistaking his powerful shoulders, his lean waist, and his long legs that gobbled the distance between them until he loomed over her.

Uh-oh. With the makeup on her face and the costume bag in her hand, she couldn't deny her destination. One more minute, just one more minute and she would have been gone. Now she had to deal with him and her stomach knotted.

Talk about tense. Sawyer's eyed narrowed to a squint. His jaw clenched as if he were chewing rocks. Between his tight lips and the fire in his eyes, the man was angry enough to spontaneously combust. At any moment she expected steam to rise from the top of his head.

"You lied to me." He took her face between his palms, his powerful arms blocking any escape, and pinned her to the wall.

Her stomach twisted, refused to settle. "I omitted the truth."

"It's not safe to—"

She tried to slap his hands aside, to brush by. "My sister has been kidnapped. I don't care about safe."

His arms didn't budge. "Getting yourself killed won't help Lia."

She didn't bother saying she was simply going to dance. "They won't hurt me."

"Really?"

"They won't hurt me," she repeated. "Not as long as they think I have the formula."

"You don't know that."

"And you don't know what they'll do. They won't figure out who I am."

"What if they do?"

"I'll be in a public restaurant. The authorities are tracking my cell by GPS."

"Oh, I feel so much better now."

"Good." She pretended not to hear his sarcasm. "Let me pass."

He glared at her. "You're putting yourself in danger and I'm not letting you go."

"Excuse me?" Her own anger fueled her, whipped her into a storm of temper that pounded through her and fought for release. How dare he act as if he were in charge, as if she should obey him? Where did he get off thinking he could tell her what to do? Lia was her *sister*. Her family.

She couldn't have held back her anger if she'd wanted to. And Kaylin didn't want to. She blasted him in a voice of pure outrage. "What in hell gives *you* the right to tell *me* what to do?"

"This." He grabbed her shoulders, yanked her to him with hard hands that refused to accept her defiance, and branded her with his lips.

She'd expected a verbal response. So at first she was so shocked by his actions, she stood there like a dance student on her very first day, bewildered, uncertain, pliant.

Kaylin inhaled his scent and her mouth responded to his heat, his possessiveness. Damn it. His worry over her might be intoxicating, but her response was ridiculous, impossible, annoying. If he thought he would sway her with a kiss, he couldn't have been more wrong.

So what if her blood rushed to her head and her ears roared? So what if his tongue danced a tango that left her aching to follow his lead?

Her brain finally caught up. And she yanked away. "Are you insane?"

The pulse in his neck pounded. "I'd be insane if I let you go half naked into—"

She rolled her eyes at the ceiling. "It's a dance costume."

"—a hangout of suspected kidnappers."

"And I don't need your permission." She ducked under
his arm and marched out the door, anger vibrating through
her. Did the man think that when he kissed her she'd turn
into clay that he could shape any way he pleased? Better
he find out now that that wasn't the case. Kaylin might appear reasonable and easygoing, but she would not be told
what to do.

Although her mother had more than supported Kaylin's
efforts to become a Broadway dancer, she'd often told her
that her stubbornness would be her downfall, but her
father had disagreed. He'd claimed stubbornness had kept
Kaylin at the practice bar long after the other students had
gone home. Stubbornness had allowed Kaylin to push past
aching muscles, sore arms, and cramped toes to become a
damn good dancer.

As a child Kaylin had danced to please her mother.
As a teen, it was an activity they'd shared. Her mother
had sewn costumes, taken her to practice and recitals,
scrimped on groceries to make sure there was money for
Kaylin's music. After her mother's death Kaylin had carried on alone, but when she'd danced, she'd never been
lonely, not with her mother's presence so strong. Her
mother had approved of Kaylin's strength.

And it was time Sawyer learned she had a backbone,
too. Kaylin could stand on her own two feet.

Up until now Sawyer had been so reasonable. His

anger had seemed to roar out of nowhere, like one of those no-name storms that whipped the Florida coast and caused more flooding than a hurricane. She understood that worrying about her had set him off—enough to go all macho on her. But even as one part of her understood he wanted to protect her, she couldn't soften.

Lia was her responsibility.

32

The men hadn't shot Lia last night. Instead, they'd laughed at her fear and then dragged her somewhere. Somewhere awful. She'd heard a door clang, a lock click. They'd tossed her inside this cell with no more care than if she'd been garbage. She'd fallen and skinned her knees, then jammed her hip and pain shot through her body. Barefoot, her feet cut and bruised, and with her still wearing her urine-stained pajamas, Lia had never wanted a hot bath and her own clean bed so badly. The bastards hadn't even bothered to untie her or remove the duct tape from her mouth.

At first she feared they'd return. Then as silence engulfed her, she feared they would never return, but had left her in her grave. The idea that she might never be found, that Kaylin and Becca might never know what had happened to her, cleared her mind and stiffened her resolve. Suppressing her terror, she lifted her head, stilled her tears. Maybe, she could escape.

In the darkness, Lia had no way to judge the passing of time. But she squirmed, rubbing her head against the floor until she knocked off the headset. She listened hard, but couldn't make out anything beyond her own breathing. Next, she went to work with her tongue on the duct tape. During her struggle, the hood came off but it seemed like hours before she loosened the tape enough to scrape it away from her mouth. Not that either accomplishment did her much good. Wherever she was, it was pitch black and she felt terribly alone.

But she could breathe. And if she could have reached her wrists with her teeth, she might have ripped off the tape. Yet, with her hands behind her back, Lia couldn't reach her taped wrists. And she couldn't slip her hands down to her ankles, either. Too bad she wasn't as flexible as Kaylin. She'd have to find another way.

Inching forward in the dark, she bumped into a smooth, metal wall. The floor was metal, too. She must be in the back of a truck or inside a metal storage unit.

Sitting up, she propped her back against a wall. In her soiled pajamas, her hands and wrists numbed from the lack of circulation, she took a moment to rest. The air smelled musty, as if the place hadn't been open to fresh air in a long time.

Were there people around? Should she call for help or would that bring back her captors?

She placed her ear against the wall. Nothing.

She whispered. "Anyone here?"

But the metal walls just echoed her whisper. While she suspected all the shouting in the world wouldn't help, she had to try. For several long minutes, Lia shouted, then cursed at her raw throat.

No one came to investigate. Likely no one heard.

They'd apparently brought her to the middle of nowhere. She could be on the back acres of a huge strawberry farm, or out by the phosphate mines, or stuck in a cow pasture. Or a junk yard. She suspected that they'd brought her someplace so remote that no one would find her by accident.

She had only herself.

God. What would Kaylin do?

Lia ached to sleep. It would be so easy to give in to the weariness, to close her eyes and rest.

Her eyelids weighed a ton, and if she slept, she could forget for a little while. *No*. She had to stay awake. Find a way out. But she didn't know what to do, and she hated feeling helpless and vulnerable.

Lia shivered. Leaning her back against the metal wall chilled her, but what would happen when the sun hit this prison? Would she dehydrate? Die from lack of water?

Already she wanted a drink. Needed some water to ease her parched and raw throat.

Think. How could she free herself? She needed something sharp.

Lia spent the next few hours scooting around her

prison, trying to find a sharp edge. She succeeded only in wearing herself out, making her muscles scream in agony.

And when she returned to the spot where she'd started, scraping her elbow on the headset, she started to laugh. What an idiot. The headset had sharp metal. She smashed off the ear piece with her foot, then ignored the pain in her heel as she grabbed the metal and dug with the sharp edge at the duct tape.

Working efficiently with her hands behind her back was almost impossible. Especially with her numb fingers. But eventually, she ripped off enough tape to free her hands. Quickly, she removed the tape at her feet.

Exhausted, yet elated, she stretched out her fingers in an attempt to restore the circulation. Shoving to her feet, she explored the boundaries of her prison. She walked slowly with her arms outstretched in the darkness, but felt nothing. Heard nothing beyond the slide of her feet against metal and her harsh breathing.

Rectangular in shape, about eight feet wide and maybe thirty feet long, the metal container caged her. And for all the good it did her, she could have been still tied up. Because no way could she break down the steel door, which must be locked and barred from the other side.

All that wriggling and struggling had been for nothing. She wasn't breaking out. She wasn't going anywhere.

With the metal headset pieces, she began tapping against the floor. Maybe someone would come by and hear the noise.

As hours passed, she dozed, tapped and dozed some more. The heat sapped the rest of her energy.

And as more time passed, just as she'd feared, the rising temperature outside baked her in the metal prison. Moisture seeped from her skin until she could think of nothing but water. Pools of water. Rivers of water.

The very air seemed to suck the fluid out of her pores.

Lia prayed that Kaylin would find her soon. Because Lia's time was running out.

When it finally cooled again, she dizzily calculated that twenty-four hours had passed. Lia knew one thing for certain. Without water, she wouldn't live through another day.

33

Billy had so much anger in him that he wanted to hit someone. Instead he'd yelled at his mom. But damn, the woman was smothering him, acting like she hadn't seen him in years when he'd only been gone one night and part of a day.

And with Lia missing, Billy had no patience for his mother's clinging. When she'd asked where he'd been, her eyes full of accusation, he'd shouted at her to mind her own business, then run to the sun porch. He crashed on the couch and Randy jumped onto the mattress and curled beside him.

Absently, Billy petted the dog. "You miss Lia, too. Don't you, little guy?"

All of Billy's life people kept leaving him. First his dad. Then Henry. Now Lia. In his head, he knew Lia wanted to come back. She hadn't left on purpose. But he felt so empty. Lia was his best friend, the person who liked him even when he screwed up.

And he was scared for her. Scared for himself. Scared that nothing would ever be the same. Billy shook a few buds out of the last ounce of weed, placed it onto a screen, and rolled the pot to sift out the seeds. Careful not to spill, he took out his bong, placed the pot in the bowl, and lit up.

Smoke filled his lungs and he held it in tight. He needed this hit. My God. Lia had been kidnapped.

And none of the adults seemed to be doing anything to get her back. Or if they were, they weren't talking to him about it.

Becca and Shadee had disappeared. So had Kaylin and Sawyer. His mother had drunk herself into another stupor. She really should watch the booze. Sometimes Billy speculated that Mitzy had run his dad off with her drinking, that it was her fault they had to manage on their own. But all too often, he blamed himself. His father hadn't wanted him. And that hurt, so deeply it was like a wound that oozed daily doses of pain.

When Billy couldn't hold his breath any longer, he released the smoke, blowing it into Randy's face. The dog didn't appreciate his efforts. He whined, jumped off the bed, and hid under a chair.

"It's okay. The smoke will make the hurt go away, buddy."

Randy snorted but didn't come out.

Billy put away the bong, hiding it behind a drawer, and placed the last ounce in his front jeans pocket. He had one more sale to make and he'd once again be debt free. He'd worked his ass off, but he finally had the cash. Except he didn't feel good about it. How could he, with Lia in trouble? Lia *gone*.

Billy closed his eyes, embarrassed when a tear leaked out. The pot usually mellowed him out, but it had barely taken off the edge. He dragged out the bong, took a second hit, then a third. The room smoked up and he opened a window to air out the place.

He wished he could call Lia. Tell her she'd be okay. But guilt ate at him.

Billy had it good here. He had plenty to eat. They'd been with the Danners three years, but that wasn't long enough for him to feel safe. He still dreamed about being hungry and feared being homeless. Nightmares often awakened him. He remembered the string of motels and cheap apartments, not knowing how long it would be before Mom lost her job and they had to move again. It was a lifetime ago. It was like yesterday.

Sometimes he wished they hadn't landed in such a good place. Because every day he feared losing this home. This family. Lia. Stability was a huge concern. Billy liked going to bed with a full belly. He liked having food in the fridge. He liked knowing the lights wouldn't go out because his mother couldn't pay the electric bill.

He never forgot that if he screwed up big time, he'd end up back where he'd been—at the bottom of the food chain—or worse. But bad men had murdered Henry, robbed the Danner house, and kidnapped Lia. Maybe no place was safe.

Billy dropped his head into his hands. The dope hadn't done the job. His stomach hurt. His mother had told him that the men who'd taken Lia had wanted Henry's formula, the formula that might be on Henry's laptop.

No matter what he did next, Billy was in a shitload of trouble. Still, he had to come clean. Had to help Lia get home. And fear had him shaking.

Lia's kidnapping might be all his fault. And even if it wasn't, Billy had to make things right. Tonight he would pay off his debt. And then he'd go to Kaylin, tell her the truth.

If he'd waited too long, if those men hurt Lia, Billy would never forgive himself. No matter what time he came back, he'd wake Kaylin up. Tell her what he knew before something else happened.

34

§

Kaylin had left her car parked at Kmart. She'd used their restroom to change into her costume, donned a caftan to cover herself, and then jumped into a cab. Following the directions the other dancer had given her, Kaylin entered Pasha's Restaurant through the back. She headed straight down a hall and turned right into an empty office where the dancers changed their costumes between file cabinets, an old desk, and faded wall posters frayed and yellowed at the edges. Even here she could appreciate the scent of delicious food wafting from the kitchen, tickling her nostrils and teasing her appetite.

She removed her caftan and examined her costume and veil in a mirror behind the door. Unlike traditional belly dancers, tribal dancers often wore their hair up. She pinned flowers in her hair and attached long braids of multicolored yarn to hang from her flower-covered bun. The rest of her costume consisted of dull bronze coins sewn into a black bra and rimmed with white shells, and hip-hugging pants that began a few inches below her navel and flared wide at the knees. Over the pants, she wore a hip belt with chains that dangled from Turkish silver pieces.

She donned wide silver cuffs over her wrists, then slid more silver bracelets up both arms. Her fingers required rings to emphasize the dance. And she strapped flat sandals onto her feet—a necessity in a restaurant where the public brought in dirt on their shoes from outside. Last, she added the silver ornaments that would hold candles on the tops of her hands for the fire dance. But she wouldn't light the candles until just before her performance, so she tucked matches into her bra.

When Kaylin finished, she checked her eye makeup. Satisfied with her appearance, she began to warm up her muscles and stretch. She used yoga poses first, then graduated to a more specific warm-up for the hips, ribcage, and pelvis. Last, she stretched her calves and hamstrings. Finally loosened up, she was ready to work.

With ten minutes before her first set, she slipped down the hall. On the way in she'd seen two closed doors. One room was open and she glanced inside. Empty. The second door was closed. She didn't knock but walked right in as if she belonged, praying Lia might be inside.

A man sat at a desk, his back to her. Lia wasn't there. He looked up, questions in his eyes.

"Excuse me." Heart racing, she stepped back into the hall and closed the door. With no other rooms to explore from this hallway, she went out front to check the sound system. She hadn't taken two steps when the bartender, a man with friendly brown eyes hidden behind thick glasses, dark hair, a broad mustache, and swarthy skin shot her a warm grin.

He spoke with a thick French accent. "You are new to Pasha's. Yes?"

"Yes." She held up her music CD and took in the bar. Lined with glasses, slivers of lemons and limes, plus assorted liquor bottles on shelves, it looked no different from any other bar—except perhaps the smoke was thicker. Men spoke in English, Arabic, and French, maybe Turkish, or at least that was her best guess. While a few men drank hot tea, many drank alcohol, even those wearing Arab headdress. She'd always thought alcohol was against the Islamic religion. Apparently these Arab-Americans had taken up U.S. customs. For all she knew, maybe they were Christian. Frankly she didn't care about their religion or country of origin. She just wanted to find her sister.

She smiled at the bartender. "Can you show me the sound system?"

"Over here." He gestured to an area behind the cash register where waitresses rang up the bills. As she followed him, she glanced over the restaurant's interior layout. The place was already filling up with the five o'clock after-work crowd. A few couples sat at tables, but the majority of customers were men. They sat at the bar, and the only thing that struck her as unusual was there wasn't one blond among them.

"Where are you from?" she asked to make conversation.

"Algeria."

"Perhaps when I dance, you could hold my cell phone? I'm expecting an important call from the hospital," she lied.

"No problem. If it rings—"

"Signal me and I'll cut the set short."

She'd hoped the restaurant wouldn't be large enough to have a separate dance floor or stage. And she had lucked out. The aisles were wide and she had a space to work in within easy viewing of most patrons. Pleased that she'd have the freedom to move between tables and customers, where she could watch the comings and goings of the clientele and get a feel for the place, she searched for the management.

She saw a man, possibly a manager, conferring with one of the waitresses, but the dancer Kaylin had replaced had told her the owner, Ali Asad, was tall and thin in stature and wore traditional Arab robes. If Mr. Asad was here tonight, he had yet to appear. Waitresses in long skirts served the tables with quiet efficiency. The lighting was dim, the thick carpet beneath Kaylin's feet a deep red. The chairs and placemats, also a deep red, set off the shiny silver but reminded Kaylin of blood.

She shook off the image and noted that the restaurant had several dark booths of deep red leather with pristine cream-colored curtains that could close for privacy. Currently all the curtains were tied open, the booths empty. A hostess greeted customers at the front door and seated them. No one yet had food on the table, but from the aromas emanating from the kitchen it wouldn't be long before the waitresses served the meals.

Several customers arrived, and she recognized Quinn at once. Apparently the man not only dined here with her father, but frequented the restaurant for dinner, too. He entered with another man, whom she didn't recognize, and two women. She doubted Quinn would recognize her behind her veil and vowed to take a good look at his friends when she danced by his table.

The front door opened again, a bell lightly chiming, and another customer entered. Kaylin caught sight of the man out of her peripheral vision. She was busy changing the track of her CD to find her song and adjusting the volume. But the way the man moved caught her attention. He seemed familiar.

But when she turned back toward the restaurant to look at him more closely, he'd slipped into a dark booth. Although the curtains remained open, she couldn't see his face at all.

She planned to dance in that direction first. She took a deep breath, cued her music, lit the candles on her hand ornaments, then sauntered slowly to the beat. Conversations stopped. Male and female heads turned toward her, expectation and curiosity on their faces. The music began with an up-tempo beat. When she reached a location where all the customers could see her, Kaylin held perfectly still and fluttered one hand, drawing the eyes to her fingers and the flame. A good dancer knew how to begin, how to pace herself, how to grab an audience.

From the first unusual chord, she had their attention. Tension filled the room, an air of expectancy amid the sudden hush.

Ever so slowly, Kaylin let her hand movement connect

with and roll into her elbow, her shoulder, her ribcage. Until her upper half undulated, slowly, sensuously, like silk spinning from a cocoon. As she began to circle her ribcage in a horizontal pattern, she kept her hips and feet still, giving the audience time to take in her face, her costume, her flow.

On a crash of drums, she changed the pattern, holding her upper body still. She slid her feet forward and moved her hips, alternating up and down and back and forth. As she advanced her feet, she used a series of vertical hip circles, first right, then left. Her style was grounded, flowing, earthy. As the music streamed into her blood, Kaylin interpreted the beat with her body. Sometimes she allowed the cadence of the drums to set the rhythm, other times she floated with the melody.

She danced her way through the restaurant, taking her time, the candlelight on her hands leading the way. Quinn sat next to one of the women, but Kaylin paid more attention to his male dinner partner. The man looked Middle Eastern with his dark hair and eyes. He wore a business suit and otherwise possessed nondescript features. If she saw him again, she might not recognize him.

Next, she headed toward the rear booth. A customer tossed money onto the floor, a tip the waitresses would collect for Kaylin. This type of dance didn't permit touching. Customers showed their appreciation by clapping in time to the music and tipping her with coins and cash thrown into the air.

Swaying with timed precision, Kaylin advanced, her

steps smooth, sliding. Always emoting what she felt, she showed her fear through the dance, using it to give her the edge that kept her performance different from all others. Dance was nothing without emotion. When she reached the back booth, she might have stopped dead in her dance sandals if she hadn't been a professional. No wonder that customer had looked familiar.

Sawyer sat in the booth, his eyes narrowed and intent. With his lips tight, his jaw clenched, he obviously disapproved and still hadn't gotten past their former argument.

Damn, he was angry. Well, he wasn't the only one. Just seeing him caused her blood to slam her into a fury of hip drops and shimmies.

He'd followed her.

And now she had a complication she hadn't anticipated. Annoyance fought relief. On the one hand, she wanted to shout at him that she could handle this herself. On the other, she wasn't so angry that she wouldn't appreciate his backing her up if it became necessary. She didn't like Quinn being there. The man gave her the willies.

Besides, Kaylin wasn't too proud to accept help. Not when Lia's life hung in the balance.

But if she needed Sawyer's help, it might be to their advantage if no one knew he was there for any reason other than a meal. She just hoped Quinn didn't see Sawyer.

Unwilling to draw attention to Sawyer, she didn't acknowledge him. She didn't talk to him. Didn't reveal she knew him. She had a job to do and she was not about to break her cover by talking to him. Altering her plan would be foolish. During her next break, she needed to hang near the bar, the cash register, and the phone. Scope out the place as well as she could.

Maybe she'd have a chance to drop by Quinn's table and eavesdrop, or at least see the bill, and if his friend paid by credit card, learn his name. She might find nothing though, and she was prepared for disappointment. But she wouldn't know until she'd tried. She couldn't sit home and do nothing.

So in the split second she recognized Sawyer, she spun, gave him her back. Although many eyes followed her dance, Kaylin could have sworn she felt only Sawyer's stare burning holes through her.

Too bad. She tossed her head. She was here to put on a show. And that's exactly what she would do. Drawing on all of her emotions and professional expertise, she threw herself into the dance. Spun away her fears. Shimmied out her uncertainty. Let herself go with the flowing rhythm. Drawing in the music, she went to another place deep inside, where she stirred all her determination and let confidence emerge in her steps, hope shine through in the angle of her head, anticipation in the gestures of her hands. She let the dance rip, with no self-examination, no thought for the audience.

It was pure art.

And when she finished, held her last pose, and blew out the candles, the audience was absolutely silent.

Oh, God . . .

Sweat glistened on her skin in the lamplight. Obviously this audience had expected traditional belly dance—not the Americanized contemporary tribal version. If the owner tossed her out, didn't allow her to finish her set, then she wouldn't have time to scope out the place.

But someone in the bar began to clap. As if the noise broke a spell, others joined in. Dollars flew into the air. Some men actually stood to give her an ovation.

Hoping she hadn't revealed her uncertainty in her eyes, she waved and glided smoothly toward the back. Breathing returning to normal, she removed the hot metal and candles from her hands, uncapped a water bottle and rested near the bar, hoping no one would think her presence unusual or unwarranted. She drank the water slowly and searched the customers' faces.

During her dance, several new drinkers had joined the others at the bar. And while some men spoke English, they talked about their jobs, their wives, their children, and their girlfriends. Nothing unusual.

Still Kaylin didn't give up. And when the phone rang, Kaylin eased around so she could listen to whoever took the call. When Shadee came out of the back and picked up the phone, she choked on the water, mid-swallow.

She had no idea if he spoke English or Arabic. He kept his voice low, down to a murmur. Heart pounding, muffling her cough, Kaylin shifted her position until her back faced him. Had he recognized her? Had he followed her here? But why? Or was it just coincidence? He had said he would check out the place.

Before she could decide whether to confront him or try to remain anonymous, a hard object suddenly jabbed her in the ribs. A man's harsh voice whispered into her ear. "Don't call for help or Lia is dead. You will come with me."

Uh-oh. Fear streaked down her spine and a chill radiated through her. Someone had figured out her identity. Surely Shadee hadn't turned her in? What about Quinn? Could either man be working with the kidnappers? For all their sakes, she prayed not. But as the gunman forced her to walk past Shadee, Becca's lover didn't glance her way, giving no indication he'd recognized her or knew she was in trouble.

And from his angle at his booth, Sawyer wouldn't see the gun pressed into her side, either. The restaurant was too busy, too dark. Should she cry out? Yell for help? Or the cops?

At the realization she no longer had her phone in her possession, her fear quickly spiked back up and she began to tremble. If Lia hadn't been kidnapped, Kaylin would have taken her chances on shouting for help while still amid this crowd. Sawyer was less than thirty feet away. Shadee even closer. However, she couldn't risk escaping if it meant placing Lia in further danger.

Between her worry for Lia and the muzzle pressing into her bare flesh, crying out seemed stupid. She'd been careless. Overconfident. Being in public hadn't kept her safe. She should have listened to Sawyer.

And yet she might have been caught because she was on the right track. Or someone thought she was and felt threatened. Maybe she shouldn't have barged into that back room. Still, whoever this man was, he might know something about Lia.

Kaylin stilled her trembling and turned around in the costume room as if she didn't have a gun pressed into her kidney. When the man slammed the door behind her, she distracted herself from the fact that he had her trapped by taking in his features.

He wore dark sunglasses and a flowing white robe. A cord at his forehead kept the headdress in place, but she could make out a prominent nose over a thick gray and black mustache and beard. His brown eyes, cold and malevolent, assessed her as if she were a cockroach.

Kaylin addressed the man she assumed was the owner of Pasha's Restaurant. "Mr. Asad?"

"Yes." He seized her veil, tore it from her face, and let it flutter to the floor. He looked from a dance flyer with Kaylin's picture that he held in his hand to her face. "Kaylin Danner?"

Seeing no point in denying the obvious, she nodded.

In a swift powerful move, he raised his hand and slapped her.

Kaylin's quick reflexes helped deflect most of the blow. Still she fell away from the brutal force, staggering, her ear ringing. If she hadn't reacted, she might be out cold. As it was, her cheek burned hot enough that tears sprang into her eyes, but more than the pain, his cruelty slashed straight to the bone. If this man held Lia . . . God . . . even if she found her sister, she would . . .

She breathed hard, clenching and unclenching her fingers. "I want my sister."

"You ignored my directions," Asad countered. All she could see were tight lips, dark skin with no real identifying marks. But he'd just admitted he knew about Lia, that he'd made the phone call.

Unfortunately, she didn't believe he made foolish mistakes. Obviously, he thought he had total control of the situation and that she could do nothing with the knowledge. Either he didn't expect her to leave this room alive, or he knew she'd do whatever he asked to save her sister.

Maybe she could use that.

"I want my sister. I'll do anything to save her. You can have me instead."

"I already have you."

"What do you want?"

"You know what I want." He slapped her again. "Don't waste my time with foolish questions."

Her cheek felt like it was on fire. It took all her willpower not to cower, not to raise her hand to her face to soothe the burn. "You want the biodiesel formula?"

Asad smiled, pulling his lips back, reminding her of a cheetah about to pounce on its prey. Kaylin steeled her spine, prepared for another blow.

Instead he kept her off balance, demanding, "Who knows you are here?"

She ached to lick her dry bottom lip, but that would be a sign of weakness. Instead she shrugged. "No one."

He slapped her again, but the sting of her cheek was the least of her problems. The door opened and two men thrust Sawyer into the room. They held him between them, each man wrenching back one of his arms. His worried gaze found her and she mouthed, "I'm sorry."

She'd insisted on coming here and although he'd followed of his own accord, she felt responsible for his safety. Asad took the gun from her ribs, aimed the weapon at Sawyer's temple and her heart danced up her throat.

"Oh God. Don't shoot him."

Asad spoke to her, his voice harsh and impatient. "Give me the formula. Now."

Sawyer had the laptop in his vehicle, or at least he had when she'd left him last. If Kaylin revealed the information, Lia might never regain her freedom. But if she held back, Asad might shoot Sawyer.

The terrible choice weakened her knees. Her head spun.

Think. Think. And she came up with a desperate plan.

She forced words out her mouth. "The deal was, my sister for the formula. But if you kill Sawyer, you'll never get the formula, because only he has the computer password."

Asad frowned. "Is that true?"

Sawyer hesitated.

Asad slapped Kaylin again, splitting her lip. She gasped

at the pain, and Sawyer lunged toward her, but Asad's men held each of Sawyer's arms, preventing him from reaching her.

Slowly Kaylin straightened. Between the pain in her lips and her cheeks and the ringing in her ears, she swayed on her feet. As much as she feared Asad, she risked a glance at Sawyer. Earlier, she'd thought she'd seen him angry, but nothing compared to what she saw now. His eyes burned with a wild fury. Every muscle in his body drew taut with rage. His mouth pressed so tight, his lips formed a tense line.

Asad lifted his arm to strike her again.

"What she says is partially true," Sawyer ground out. "I have the laptop, but I no longer have the access code."

Asad pointed the gun at Sawyer again, and cocked it. "Then I no longer have need of you."

"Wrong." Sawyer grinned, his eyes defiant and Kaylin dared to breathe again. From the twinkle in his eye, she dared to hope Sawyer could outsmart Asad. "Knowing we might walk into a difficult situation, I asked a friend to change the laptop code. He's agreed to tell *me* the code—"

"Then call him."

"Only after Lia is free." Sawyer shrugged. "No matter what I tell him now, he won't give up the code until Lia returns home."

Kaylin realized she'd been holding her breath and slowly released the air in her straining lungs. If Sawyer had lied, he was damn good at it. If he'd told the truth, she would have kissed him if she could have, even if her lip had swollen to twice its normal size. Thanks to Sawyer's advance planning and/or quick thinking, they still had a chance to free her sister.

Asad's expression didn't change. He spoke to his men in a language she didn't recognize. They patted Sawyer down for weapons, removed his cell phone from his pocket, and shoved Sawyer into a chair. After cuffing his hands behind his back, through the chair slats, they left.

Now what?

Kaylin didn't dare ask. Asad didn't say anything. She prayed they had Lia safe in another room in this restaurant and that he would free her. But she couldn't predict what Asad would do. Every time he looked at her she went clammy and cold. Asad appeared to have no conscience, no compassion or kindness, as if the world had sucked all humanity from his soul.

She wished she knew where he'd sent his men. She wished she understood his orders. And she wished she knew for certain if Shadee was their friend, because if she'd been wrong to trust him, she and Sawyer were on their own and no one would be coming to check the whereabouts of her cell phone.

But most of all she wished that some good would come of her actions. That Asad would let her sister go free.

35

§

At first Lia paid no attention to the voices. After all, she'd been hearing odd sounds all day: a barking dog, a roaring lion, a baby crying, spiders whispering to one another. Every cell in her body craved water. Her lips were desert dry and her tongue swollen. In a rational moment she understood dehydration had led to hallucinations, and it took several long seconds to comprehend that someone really was outside.

Her throat, long past the point of shouting for help, hurt so much she couldn't utter a sound. Instead, she picked up the broken headset and pounded the floor. With little strength left, she created a few tiny dings.

She would have cried in frustration, but her body had no fluid left for tears. Moving her hand shot pain up her arm, but she made the effort. Her body was shutting down. Her kidneys hadn't worked all day.

But as the door opened, she summoned enough energy to turn her head. Bright lights blinded her.

She must have passed out because the next thing she knew, she was sitting up. A blindfold had been tied over her eyes, but someone held a cup to her lips. She drank greedily, blessed water running down her parched throat.

Lia had swallowed only a few sips and would have begged for more, except a gruff male voice with a Greek accent warned, "Not too much at once or you'll vomit."

Someone carried her to a car, thrust her into the back seat and gave her more water before blindfolding her again. Her brain started to work. They wouldn't have given her water if they intended to kill her, would they?

But Lia had been through too much to get her hopes up. For all she knew they were moving her to another location, another prison. She couldn't bear to go through that again.

Her mouth was still so dry. She could have downed a gallon or two more of water.

Since Lia had no clue where she'd been kept, she didn't attempt to memorize the twists and turns of the vehicle's route. However, if the car stopped and she listened hard, heard people outside, maybe she could summon enough strength to scream.

But if she did, would they put her back in her prison? She might be blindfolded and helpless, but the air conditioning felt like heaven. And she'd do anything for more water. She didn't want to make them angry.

They hadn't tied her hands or feet—they didn't need to. Too weak to stand or walk by herself, she didn't have the strength to escape. Instead she licked her bottom lip and the man gave her more water. Light-headed but feeling better than she had all day, Lia wished someone would tell her what was going on.

The not knowing what would happen, whether she

would live or die, was the hardest part. That and knowing her sisters would be worried sick over her and that she might never see them again.

As she'd agonized through the heat of the day, Lia had almost welcomed death. She'd wanted to be done with the suffering. So she'd given up. Despite all her vows to keep fighting, she'd quit.

She'd been weak when she begged God to either take her or save her. But what hadn't killed her had made her stronger. Already she knew that every day from now on would be a gift . . . and she would be up to dealing with whatever life threw her way.

Now she just wanted to go home.

36

For Kaylin the wait to see if Asad would free Lia took an eternity. Every second seemed an hour, every minute a day. Finally Asad's cell rang. He placed the phone on speaker. Kaylin heard Becca screaming, "My God. Lia's back! She's home. We've got her. She's safe." From the enthusiasm in Becca's voice, Kaylin believed Lia was really free.

A moment later Lia spoke into the phone, sounding hoarse. "I'm home, Kaylin. They let me go."

With all her heart Kaylin wished she could be there to hug and comfort Lia, but Becca would have to stand in for her. Maybe Becca would go to their grandmother and they'd be safe, but Asad snapped the phone shut, and Kaylin realized she was not going to be allowed to speak to Becca.

She braced for anything and tried to remember that no matter what happened next, at least Lia was alive. Free.

A huge weight lifted off Kaylin. She'd promised her mother to take care of her sisters. And she'd done that.

"Where's your laptop?" Asad asked Sawyer.

He didn't hesitate. "In my truck. It's parked on the corner. Keys are in my pocket."

A man took his keys and left. Quickly he returned with the laptop, opened it and set it in front of Sawyer. Kaylin's hopes soared. If Asad possessed the data, maybe she and Sawyer would also soon be free.

Asad nudged Sawyer with his gun. "The password?"

"You'll need to make another call." Sawyer looked Asad in the eye, then waited as if he hadn't a care in the world. If she hadn't known better, Kaylin wouldn't have guessed Sawyer was helpless, handcuffed to the chair. Composed and casual, he gave off a confident vibe.

"The number?"

Sawyer reeled off a number and Asad punched it in. A woman answered the phone: "Hillsborough County Sheriff's Office."

"Is this a joke?" Asad pistol whipped Sawyer, slamming his head to one side. Kaylin gasped. Blood seeped from a long cut. His eyes clouded as if almost losing consciousness.

Sawyer managed a shrug. "If you want the code, ask for Deputy Bryant."

Asad warned him, "I will not permit you to stay on the line over thirty seconds."

"I only need ten, twenty, tops." Sawyer asked for the deputy.

He came on the line almost immediately. "Deputy Bryant."

"It's Sawyer. What's my password?"

"WQYZEDLPSRX298WL."

Asad motioned one of his men to write. The other typed the code into the laptop, verified the data, and hung up. Her emotions on a roller coaster—up when Lia had been released, down when Asad pistol whipped Sawyer, now up again that they might go free—Kaylin tried to control the adrenaline surging through her. But at least Deputy Bryant knew they were in trouble. And if Shadee had recognized her, he could lead the authorities to Asad.

Sawyer stood, the chair coming up with him. "You have what you want, now let us go."

Asad kicked his legs out from under him. With his hands cuffed, Sawyer was unable to protect himself and went down hard. The slats broke and one of the chair's legs snapped beneath him. He groaned as he hit the floor but he must have been faking the injury because as Asad and his men laughed, Sawyer stuffed part of the broken chair leg up his sleeve. She tried not to watch, instead closing her eyes.

Kaylin had no idea what Sawyer could do with a broken piece of wood when his wrists remained cuffed, but she wouldn't give up any advantage, especially one he'd paid so dearly to gain. When she heard a vehicle pull up behind the restaurant, she prayed the Sheriff's Office had traced the call and was about to rescue them. She opened her eyes.

"Get them up," Asad ordered. "We're taking them with us."

What? Kaylin shook her head. "That wasn't the deal. We gave you the information. Now let us go."

Asad sneered. "We need him to interpret the data."

"You don't need her. Release her and I'll help you," Sawyer insisted as Asad's men picked him up from the floor, looping their arms through his bent elbows.

"You'll help us anyway. And she's our insurance." Asad smacked her once again across the cheek, then glared at Sawyer as one of the men freed him from the chair, then recuffed his hands behind his back. "With your woman in danger, you will work harder for us. Now no more talking. We go."

So Asad would threaten her safety to keep Sawyer in line. The rage apparent in Sawyer's eyes convinced her that Asad's tactic would work.

She prayed Asad would take Sawyer's cell phone with him so the Sheriff's Office could trace their location, but

Asad tossed the phone into the garbage. "Move out. We haven't much time."

Oh God. They wanted the data interpreted. But it was all fabricated. And if they found out, they would no longer have a use for either of them, since they didn't have the *real* data.

Face burning from Asad's slaps, she wobbled to her feet. His man grabbed her, thrust her into the corridor and out the back door onto a side street. Ybor City's main streets were well lit for club goers and tourists, but many restaurants backed up to dark alleys that reeked of old beer, garbage, and trash.

No one noticed as the men pushed them into the van. They rode east for several minutes. Then the van stopped in a warehouse parking lot. At this time of night, the area was deserted.

The men jerked them out of the van and within moments a helicopter landed and they forced her and Sawyer onto the floor of the chopper. Sawyer bent his head to hers, and she hoped the others couldn't hear them as the rotors cut the night air and the engines roared during takeoff.

"You all right?" he asked.

No. "Yeah," she lied. Her cheeks were on fire, her neck ached, and she'd never been more scared in her life.

She reached back to one of his cuffed wrists and slipped her hand into his, taking comfort in the contact. These men with their cold eyes and stares frightened her. They had no right to steal her father's work. No right to kidnap her sister. And now Kaylin and Sawyer.

"Any idea where they're taking us?"

"Let's hope it's not out of the country."

God. . . . If they transferred to a plane and these men took them all the way to the Middle East, they would stand little chance of ever coming home.

Kaylin tried to look on the positive side. Lia was free and Kaylin wasn't alone. She had Sawyer, and she couldn't imagine facing her captors alone. Couldn't imagine how she would have handled this whole situation without Sawyer's calm strength to support her. She'd never had anyone to rely on before, not since her mother had died, anyway. She'd been the one that her family looked to for support. But now Sawyer had stepped in . . . and she *liked* him beside her, liked that he'd helped her when her actions had placed them all at risk. His precautionary measures had alerted Deputy Bryant to their difficulties. Her cell phone's GPS system would confirm their last location.

But Kaylin couldn't ignore the clammy fear in her gut. They'd brought her along to coerce Sawyer into giving up information—information he didn't have. That meant he couldn't stop them from hurting her.

As a dancer, Kaylin was intimately acquainted with pain. She'd danced in toe shoes with bleeding feet, blisters, and open sores. She'd learned to stretch her muscles to the max, push her mind and body harder than she'd thought possible. But torture . . . the idea made her mouth go dry. For a moment she thought she might heave up lunch. But she swallowed hard.

Told herself she was no use to them dead. They would keep her alive—if only to force Sawyer to give up the secrets they thought he knew. But she didn't know which was worse, thinking they'd keep her alive when she wanted to die, or the possibility of them killing her when she wanted to live.

Her entire body trembled and a bitter taste filled her mouth. Kaylin had imagined her life going in many directions but not once, not ever, had she thought she'd be held hostage with a man she'd come to care about.

"Easy." Sawyer squeezed her hand. "Trust me a little. I'll keep us safe."

"How?"

"We'll escape and go home."

"They have guns. Or haven't you noticed?"

"We have brains."

She pictured their brains splattered against a wall and shuddered.

"We're going to make it. You have to believe that."

She didn't believe a word he said. And yet, the coaxing softness of his voice calmed her. Just a little.

She'd known dancers who practiced and trained for years, then got stage fright. They forgot their choreography, froze, burst into tears. Sometimes a positive mindset helped to make a reality. If a dancer thought she was good, she jumped higher, lifted her arms with confidence, cued into the music better. A positive attitude might be exactly what she needed to get through this.

"I'm going to make myself believe." She spoke in a

fierce whisper. One of the men eyed her bare shoulders and Kaylin wished she had a cover-up. Reminding herself that her costume showed no more bare flesh than a bikini top and yoga pants, she raised her chin.

"That's the spirit," Sawyer said with an approving nod.

"No talking." One of the men shoved Sawyer, who banged his head against the door. The wound on his forehead reopened and bled but he nodded to Kaylin, reassuring her he was okay.

He remained with his back propped against the door and they could no longer hold hands. But she took comfort in his presence and his glances bolstered her courage. She suspected she'd need plenty in the upcoming hours.

It was one thing to tell herself to be brave. It was quite another to act brave.

When the chopper set down, she had no idea where they were. She heard no city sounds. Saw no car lights. They seemed to be in the middle of a farm. Maybe a tomato or strawberry farm in Plant City or Ruskin or even Pasco County. She estimated their air time had been between ten and twenty minutes, so they hadn't gone far.

But when she spied the runway and small plane waiting for them, her fears almost spun out of control again. Telling herself the plane was too small to fly across the ocean didn't help. They might take them to Mexico or South America—if they stopped to refuel.

And even if they got away, she had no passport, no identification, no money. Her purse was back with her clothes at the restaurant.

She had to think positive. Maybe Sawyer had his driver's license and some cash in his wallet. And all they needed was to make it to a phone to call for help.

Besides, maybe the plane wasn't for them. Maybe Asad and his men intended to take off and leave them behind. From here, she and Sawyer would have a long walk back to civilization but she'd pick a hike through farmland over whatever Asad might have planned. She prayed that he and his men would climb into the plane and leave Sawyer and her behind.

No such luck.

Asad's men pushed Sawyer and her toward the runway. The plane, a twin engine that held six, plus two more seats for a pilot and copilot. Asad's goons stuffed her between two men on the rear bench. Sawyer sat in front of her, beside an armed guard.

Before liftoff, the men placed blindfolds over their eyes. Kaylin didn't dare try to rip it off. If they'd forgotten her hands were free, maybe she'd get an opportunity to grab a gun—not that she knew how to shoot it. But how hard could it be?

But the blindfolds told her Asad had been prepared to take her and Sawyer. She suspected that if he hadn't grabbed her at Pasha's, he would have come to her. She'd just made his job easier. But she'd gained Lia's freedom, so something good had come from her actions tonight.

Judging time with her eyes closed and no visible landmarks wasn't easy. But she figured they had flown for close to two hours before the plane bumped down on a runway.

The door opened and she smelled the ocean, heard seagulls call and waves crash on a not-so-distant shore.

Were they in the Florida Keys? The Bahamas? Or someplace off the Georgia or Alabama coast?

Without knowing which direction they'd flown, she had no idea of their location. And as they kept the blindfold over her eyes, she stumbled enough times to recognize sand and rough grass beneath her feet.

Whatever their location, she didn't hear the sounds of civilization, except one steady machine that purred louder than a car engine. A generator? After a hurricane, she'd heard many of them powering up her neighbors' homes. But this one sounded more powerful.

If this location required a generator, that meant they were somewhere isolated. Someplace Deputy Bryant wouldn't easily find them.

Kaylin stumbled and flung her hand out for balance. The men laughed at her. Hoping the movement appeared natural, she used her shoulder to nudge the blindfold up a bit.

In the dark, she couldn't see much but a sliver of sand and weeds along a stone path. Like that was helpful. Okay, what did she expect, a mat that said *Welcome to the Bahamas*?

The good news was they hadn't flown to the Middle East. And this climate seemed similar to Florida. Maybe a bit breezier, but that might be due to their proximity to the water. The salty tang and the sound of palm fronds rustling led her to believe they'd flown south or east, not north or west.

That probably narrowed their location down to the Caribbean and Bahamas, or islands off the Florida coast. If Kaylin and Sawyer kept working at it, perhaps they'd learn more. Every clue was important, but she didn't have time to see more before their guards shoved her into a room with Sawyer and slammed the door shut, leaving them alone.

Kaylin removed her blindfold. "Your hands are still cuffed?" She untied his blindfold.

"Yeah. I didn't think it wise to inform them of the oversight."

She didn't blame him. With a few exceptions, pretty much every comment they'd made to their captors had been answered with painful blows to her face and devastating punches to his head.

She looked around but couldn't see much in the dark. "I don't think we have windows." She felt with her hands. "Actually, there *are* windows but they've bolted shutters over them—from the outside."

She bumped into a table. On top she found a kerosene lantern and a pack of matches. Quickly, she struck a match, lit the wick and turned up the lantern. "Let there be light," she joked.

Their quarters could have been worse. Much worse. The room was about twelve feet by twelve feet. The floor was concrete, the walls the same. The furnishings consisted of a single bed with clean sheets, a working bathroom with a sink, toilet and shower, a table and two chairs. Above the table was a cabinet with canned food.

She saw no can opener. No knives, spoons, forks. No tools or weapons.

Sawyer, still bound, managed to shake the broken chair leg from his shirt sleeve and shove it under the mattress while she took inventory. There were no electric light switches and she doubted the room had ever been wired for electricity. In the darkness, she'd missed spotting some open windows near the ceiling, which she could now see in the lantern light. The windows set up a cross breeze and made the temperature comfortable. But even if they could lift themselves high enough to squeeze through, a closer look revealed metal bars over the openings.

She searched the cabinets, looking for anything that might be useful but came back empty handed. "I don't know what I was expecting, but this room isn't it."

She'd been bracing herself for torture. A long, slow death. And although those possibilities might still arise, she had a reprieve, a badly needed one. Too much fear had caused a knot in her gut that wouldn't go away, a gnawing hollow ache that she hated to acknowledge.

Sawyer pulled out the chair next to her with his foot and sat down. "You hungry?"

She shook her head. The idea of food made her nauseous. Her hands trembled and she twisted them together, trying to hide her reaction, but Sawyer noticed. "Hey. Come here."

She bit her lower lip. "What?"

"Come sit on my lap."

How did he know how alone she felt? How the fear ate at her? Kaylin didn't hesitate, she moved to Sawyer's lap, placed her cheek against his chest, listened to the steady rhythm of his heartbeat.

"This is so much better," she admitted, snuggling against him, taking comfort in his broad chest and his powerful shoulders. But best of all was knowing that if intelligence could get them out of there, Sawyer would find a way. And meanwhile, he was good company. Not once had he criticized her for dancing at Pasha's or said *I told you so*. Instead he'd been solid. There for her.

"Don't give up on me." He nuzzled her neck, whispered into her ear.

"I should be telling you not to give up on me," she replied, her voice shaky. "I'm scared."

"I know. If my hands were free, I'd knead the tightness out of your muscles."

As his heat seeped into her, she slowly relaxed. "I'm not scared of death. It's the dying part. Dying painfully."

"That's not going to happen." He spoke with conviction, in a tone she'd never heard him use before.

She tilted back her head to look up at him. "For such a man of science, you sure don't have any evidence to back up that claim."

"Actually, I do." His calm gaze twinkled as if he knew a secret. "I know what I'm capable of. Believe me." He ducked his head and his warm breath whispered into her ear. "We need to look around for bugs."

The room seemed clean enough to her. She frowned at him. "You're worried about bugs?"

"Not the cockroach kind. Listening devices," he whispered again.

She whispered back. "And what would those bugs look like?"

"A round shiny button. Or a bit of circuitry. Extra wires protruding from nowhere."

Kaylin didn't want to climb from his lap. But his strength and warmth had refueled her courage. Besides, Sawyer was brilliant. He'd already surprised her once by alerting Deputy Bryant and ensuring Lia's freedom by thinking ahead. Perhaps she should give him a real chance, rely on him like she'd never relied on anyone before.

He nodded. "Let's go check out the shower and see if we have hot water."

Kaylin noted the way his gaze followed her around the room. Sawyer had known she was scared, but he hadn't patronized her, hadn't told her her fears were groundless. Instead, he'd asked her to believe in him.

Sawyer might be a dreamer but he was reliable, steady, and if she had to be here, there was no one she'd rather be with than him. If anyone could find a way out, Sawyer would do it. If anyone could protect her, it would be Sawyer. And if this was her last night on Earth, she wanted to spend it with Sawyer.

Her hopes lifted, she searched under the table and bed,

on top of the cabinet, and inside the bathroom. She found nothing suspicious but kept her voice very low. "Could bugs be in the pipes?"

He followed her into the bathroom. After she turned on the sink's faucet he whispered. "Don't say anything you don't want them to hear."

She placed her palm on his cheek, trailed her fingers along his jaw line. "You have a beautiful face."

"I do?"

She traced his features. "Strong cheekbones, intense eyes, a kind smile. But you have a soft heart—"

"Hey, no need to insult me."

"And you always seem to know what I need."

"I wish I could do more."

"You've done plenty. You've given me comfort and hope. Then distracted me with your sexy body."

He grinned. "Ah, so my plan is working?"

"You really think they're listening?"

"Probably not. But we aren't taking any chances."

She turned her back to him, shut off the water, and winked at his reflection. "I don't have any secrets."

"Every woman has secrets," he teased and she really appreciated his efforts to keep the mood light. A heavy conversation wasn't what she needed right now—especially if they could be overheard.

"You want to know my secret desire?" she teased right back.

"Oh, yeah."

"I'd like a hot shower. You think it's safe?"

"Probably not. But we should take one anyway." He grinned, a sexy grin that indicated he wasn't the least bit concerned about tomorrow. He was in the moment. More than willing to share a shower with her.

"We?" She turned around and he was so close, if she'd leaned forward an inch, she could have kissed him. He might be a tad sweaty, but he smelled all male, hot and sultry. And very, very interested.

His eyes glinted with heat. "I can't wash myself with my hands cuffed. I'll need some help."

"That could be arranged." In fact, all kinds of possibilities leaped into her mind. Sensual possibilities. Sexy possibilities. Talk about a last-in-a-lifetime opportunity.

She didn't know what the hell was wrong with her. She should be thinking about escape. Planning how to defy their captors.

And yet . . . she couldn't deny herself, or him, in that moment. Besides, for all she knew they wouldn't make it through tomorrow. Why not live for tonight?

With a provocative swing of her bottom, she opened the shower door. "Follow me."

"That's the best offer I've had all day."

She looked back over her shoulder. "It had better be the *only* offer you've had all day."

He chuckled and nuzzled her neck. "If you say so."

Sawyer stood with his shoulders lodged in the threshold, casually leaning against one wall. His skin bronzed, a five o'clock shadow on his jaw, he couldn't have looked more sexy.

"Your skin's glowing in the lantern light," he murmured. "Do you have any idea how hot you look?"

She leaned forward and performed a subtle shoulder shimmy that made her breasts quiver. "So. You'd like to see more?"

"Damn straight." His gaze dropped to her flesh, exactly as she'd intended.

Sashaying over to him, she hooked her fingers into his jeans. "Tonight I'm in charge."

He cocked a haughty eyebrow but his lips turned up at the edges. "Is that so?"

She skimmed her hands over his stomach and lifted his shirt over his head. "We're not going to be able to take this all the way off."

"I can live with that."

"Your shirt will get wet in the shower."

"I'm hoping more than my shirt gets wet."

She angled her head and considered his chest. His broad shoulders and powerful pecs fired her blood to a heated simmer. Sawyer didn't have the lean muscles of a dancer or the thick ones of a weightlifter. He resembled an Olympic swimmer, his proportions pleasing to the eye, masculine and calling to her on a multitude of levels, both visual and tactile.

She couldn't wait to skim her hands over his bared flesh. Her mouth watered at the thought of having him when she wanted, how she wanted.

The tiny bathroom didn't leave her a lot of maneuvering room. But that made removing his jeans more interesting. The lack of space gave her the excuse to let her hair brush against his chest, and her fingers tease his hips as she unsnapped his pants.

But although he was clearly ready, she thought it would be fun to set the pace. Sawyer always seemed so cool and patient, in control. And she suddenly yearned to push him. Play with him. See how far he'd let her go.

Leaning into him, she kissed him lightly, teasingly, careful not to injure her already bruised lip. Meanwhile, she slid her hands down warm, hard abs into his jeans. She cupped him where he was soft, stroked him where he was hard. And all the while she kept her mouth fused to his, accepting the pain, using the pain to drive away her fear of this place and center her in this moment. Her free hand rested on his throat where his pulse thrummed to its own pace—fast and hard.

And Sawyer . . . let her do what she wished.

Damn, the man had control. The straining flesh beneath her hand and his elevated pulse told her how badly he wanted her to do more. And yet he hadn't made demands, letting her take the lead without one complaint.

A man had to be bold, secure in himself to give up so much and she found that his confidence fed her own. Sawyer was all male, raring to go, and yet, for her he held back, content to wait on her wishes.

Intoxicated by his sexiness, she grew bolder. For all she knew, this might be her last night. His last night. She ached to make it special.

"Tell me what you want," she whispered.

"You. I want you." His words came out throaty, needy, and a mischievous glint shone in his eyes.

"You can have me tonight. All night."

He cocked his head, leaning it against the door frame. "Suppose I want more than tonight?"

She chuckled, but didn't answer the question. "You're a greedy man."

"You have no idea."

37

Kaylin hooked her hands into Sawyer's jeans, shoved them from his hips and he kicked them off. Glad to finally be rid of his clothing, except for the shirt caught by his wrists in the handcuffs, he was more than ready for his shower. More than ready for Kaylin.

Letting her take total control while every cell in his body screamed at him to thrust into her heat might have been more difficult if Kaylin hadn't evaded his question. She had no idea how much he wanted her. In his mind Kaylin was already his woman. She just didn't know it yet.

Telling her would only make her pull back. His feelings too strong to reveal, he kept his plans for their future to himself. She wasn't ready to hear more yet. But he knew deep in his heart that one or two nights with Kaylin would never be enough. Not when he couldn't stop thinking about her. Not when he could barely think past her soft lips and her silky caresses.

They were in serious trouble. But he wouldn't waste one moment of this precious time. If this was all they had, he would make the most of it. But he fully intended for them to have many, many nights like this one.

He might not have free use of his hands, but Sawyer could be inventive. He skimmed his lips over her shoulder blade, down to her bra. Licking a path over her flesh, he refused to ask her to take off her top. He simply outwaited her.

He put from his mind the raging fire in his groin. Instead, he focused on her sweet scent, tasted her exotic flavor. And finally when he didn't think he could wait any longer, she unhooked her bra and belt, kicked off her pants, and tugged him into the shower.

He chuckled. "Don't you think you should turn on the water?"

"I'll get to that." She kneeled, her lips closing over him. "Eventually," she mumbled, her mouth full.

"Kaylin, sweetie, your lip is swollen," he protested, but she paid no attention.

He hadn't realized how badly he wanted to touch her with his hands until he began to shake. She felt too good. He strained to hold back. But her tongue and lips and hands all worked together, teasing him, taunting him, tempting him to let go.

His muscles strained with the effort to hold on. His breath came in harsh, hurried pants.

And just when he thought he couldn't hold back one more second, she turned on the shower spigot. Cool water sprayed all over him, and surprised, he yelped. But the distraction helped him to wait.

Thankfully, she didn't bother with the hot water. Instead, she grabbed a bar of soap and lathered her skin. "I'm going to wash you with my body," she murmured, a half laugh in her throat.

She slid up against him, around him, behind him. Between the water, the soap and her slippery skin, he'd never felt anything so wonderful and painful at the same time.

"You're making me insane."

"Good."

She had him so fired up, so slippery, so excited, he could no longer hold still. Even with her hands and mouth no longer in direct contact with his sex, he found his hips gyrating into the air.

She laughed with him, teased him, danced around him, flicking a hand against his buttocks, a palm along his ribs, all the while slithering her soapy body against him. "You feel like heaven," he murmured.

She didn't stop, spinning, whirling, humming. And then when he didn't think he could take another second of this wonderful madness, she placed her hands around his neck, lifted her legs to his waist and slowly lowered herself onto his erection.

He leaned his shoulders against the wall and spread his legs to brace them. "Oh . . . my . . . God. You feel great."

He knew she was strong but he wanted to help support her, an impossibility with the handcuffs. "Can you hang on?"

"I'm a dancer." She squeezed his waist with her legs, then lifted and lowered herself on him while water cascaded over them. Between her slippery flesh, her gyrating hips and water, water, everywhere, he closed his eyes and let himself go with her rhythm.

When he tilted his hips a certain way, she let out soft *ahs*. They moved faster. Harder. She took him deeper, and his head began to spin. She convulsed, contracting, and he shot over the edge with her in a massive explosion that stole his breath and rocked him back on his heels.

He had no idea how he stayed on his feet. Luckily the shower's tiny size kept him propped upright. Because making love to Kaylin was like nothing he'd ever experienced. First bliss, then bursts of pleasure, then the ebb of tension that led to satiation.

"You are amazing," he told her. "I haven't had fantasies this good." He dropped to his knees, backed her against the shower wall and nuzzled between her thighs. He didn't stop until her hands on his shoulders gripped him tight as she cried out.

By the time they left the shower, their skin puckered from staying so long in the water, he barely had the energy to stand. She dried him with a towel, then herself, and turned out the lantern light. Together they staggered to the single bed.

"I wish I could hold you," he muttered. With his hands still cuffed behind his back, sleeping next to her and being unable to gather her against his body bothered him.

She turned onto her side and scooted over, then wrapped her arms around him. "How's this?"

"Good. Very, very good."

When she drew the blanket over them and snuggled against him in the darkness, he smiled. He suspected many women in her position would be complaining and crying. Kaylin's courage amazed him. That she could be so giving and loving when they had no idea what tomorrow would bring made him all the more determined to protect her.

Today he hadn't done such a good job. Asad would pay for smacking her. Remembering the man's brutality kept Sawyer awake. Tomorrow he had to do better.

38

When the front doorbell rang, Becca obviously didn't want to leave Lia to get the door. Billy didn't volunteer. He didn't want to leave Lia, either. Shadee said he'd answer and Becca smoothed Lia's hair. She'd told Billy it had taken three shampoos to clean it and she'd spent another half hour putting antibacterial ointment on Lia's assorted cuts and bruises. She'd wanted to take her to the hospital but Lia had quietly said that she was fine, and Billy had breathed a sigh of relief when Becca had agreed she could stay home.

Billy shifted from foot to foot. Poor Lia. She'd had a rough time. He watched Becca tuck her in and Lia's even breathing suggested she'd fallen asleep.

Shadee called from downstairs. "Becca?"

Billy moved toward the bed. "Becca, I can stay with Lia if you want. Shadee needs you downstairs."

"Thanks, Billy. I'm sure if Lia wakes up she'll be happier if you're here."

Billy lifted Randy onto the bed and the dog cuddled up next to Lia. He sat in a chair by the bed. "Go. I'll call you if she wakes up."

"All right. Thanks." Becca nodded, then peered hard at him. "Is something up with you, Billy?"

"Don't think so." He shoved his hands into his pockets.

"You've changed in the last twenty-four hours—almost as if you've matured overnight. But Lia's going to be fine. Don't worry."

"All right."

The moment Becca walked out of earshot, he sat next to Lia on the bed. "She's gone. You can open your eyes now."

"How did you know?" Lia asked.

"When you sleep, you aren't that peaceful."

She rolled her eyes. "Next you'll be claiming that I

snore." Lia raised herself on her elbow and looked at him. "Becca was right. Something's up with you."

"You don't need to hear about my problems."

Lia shook her head. "Actually it would be a pleasant distraction from thinking about what happened."

"All right. But you can't tell anyone."

"So what else is new?"

Billy told her about his weekend. About almost getting caught by the cops. About finally paying off his debt.

"And now what?" Lia asked. "You going to keep dealing?"

Billy shook his head. "It feels good to be in the clear."

"Your job at the convenience store isn't going to pay for your habit."

Billy frowned. "That sounded like something Kaylin would say."

Lia grinned. "Kaylin's no pushover. She has a good heart but if she catches you smoking weed, she'll worry about your influence over me." Lia peeked at him. "I don't want to lose my best friend."

Billy took her hand. "I'm going to quit."

"You think you can?"

"Your father once told me that I would attempt more—if I knew I wouldn't fail. So I'm going to pretend I won't fail. I'm going to try—"

"That's all you can do sometimes. I tried and tried to get free. But I couldn't. Then I decided to be brave. I couldn't do that either, but I made up my mind that if I lived, nothing else was going to ever scare me again."

"Cool."

BECCA HEADED DOWNSTAIRS and stopped on the landing at the sight of the visitor waiting in the foyer. She looked like an older version of their mother, a much, much older version of Kaylin. But Becca had her regal nose.

"Becca," her grandmother said tentatively, as if awaiting a reaction, an invitation.

Becca recalled their grandmother had told Kaylin that she'd had a PI watching them. She knew their names, their faces, what they did for a living. That must mean she cared—didn't it? Regardless of the past, the trouble between mother and daughter, the lost time and poor choices, this woman wouldn't be here right now if she didn't care.

Her grandmother stared up at her. "Is Lia all right?"

Becca nodded slowly, and with the look of relief in the older woman's eyes, the worry she'd been holding back gushed like an unclogged waterspout after a hard rain. "But Kaylin's disappeared. Shadee saw men take her into the back room at a restaurant downtown. We haven't heard from her or Sawyer since then."

"Have you informed the police? The FBI?" her grandmother asked with a worried frown that creased her smooth forehead.

Becca shook her head. "Not directly. Kaylin feared contact with the authorities might make the situation worse. So Shadee has been the go-between."

"Kaylin isn't here." Her grandmother climbed the steps like a twenty-year-old. "However, we can still follow her wishes and ask Shadee to continue as the go-between. I'm also willing to hire a private security firm to search for Kaylin. The decision's yours."

"Mine?" Becca gulped. Shocked her grandmother had made the offer, she didn't know what to say. Ever since Lia had disappeared she'd been happy to let Kaylin make the decisions and bear the responsibility. Now, Kaylin was gone. And her grandmother had offered resources that might save her. But Becca knew those resources could also backfire and cause the people who'd taken Kaylin to kill her.

Becca wanted to go to bed, pull the covers over her head, and pretend this whole nightmare had never happened. But she couldn't. As if he realized how torn she felt by having to make such a huge decision, Shadee placed a hand on her shoulder. "You aren't alone, Becca. Tell us what you want."

His support meant the world to her, and her feelings for him had deepened. A few days ago she'd feared his family wouldn't accept her, but she no longer worried about it. Shadee would invite her to meet his family when the time was right. She trusted his judgment.

But not only was she certain he was the man for her, she realized she liked the woman she'd become when she was with him. Shadee gave her a sense of self-worth and contentment. Being with him brought out her best qualities. She was thinking about returning to school, maybe for computer programming. If she spent enough time with Shadee, perhaps Becca would someday be as successful and independent as Kaylin. Funny how loving a guy could make her feel more independent—but Shadee had made that happen.

Now if only she could use her newfound strength to do the right thing for Kaylin.

39

Kaylin opened her eyes to find Sawyer dressed in blue coveralls, his hands free. He gestured to a pile of clothes and a box of cereal and milk. "A guard dropped by and left us—"

"Is that coffee I smell?"

With a serious look in his eyes and a small grin, he kissed her, then placed the hot drink in her hands. She sipped, letting the flavor roll over her tongue, waiting for the caffeine kick. "What's going on?"

"No one told me anything." He paced from one side of the room to the other. "But the guards freed my hands and gave us food. I suspect they're treating us well to gain our trust. The moment we refuse to cooperate," Sawyer snapped his fingers in the direction of the food, "all this could be gone. Eat while you can."

His tone might have been light, but the news remained grim. She slipped back into her bra and donned coveralls that reminded her of a mechanic's uniform. Grateful she wouldn't have to prance around in her dance costume, she rinsed her mouth at the sink, then poured herself a bowl of cereal.

Dozens of questions spiraled through her mind, but instead of asking about things Sawyer couldn't answer, she finished her coffee and ate the cereal. Surprisingly, the food helped settle her stomach. Last night had been unreal. Sex had been a great stress reliever, but she'd gone through an entire gamut of emotions. Frenzied desire, losing herself in the moment, and afterwards, a tenderness that had enabled her to sleep. But today reality had returned.

She'd just finished the last bite of cereal when the sound of men's voices and footsteps approached. Kaylin strapped on her dance sandals, her heart tripping in her throat. She'd wanted to know what happened next . . . but now this room represented safety. Leaving meant reality—uncertain reality.

Not that she or Sawyer had a choice. Three armed men opened the door and led them outside. Kaylin looked around, encouraged when they weren't blindfolded again. Until she realized blindfolds weren't necessary. She and Sawyer couldn't escape.

Palm trees indicated they were still in a tropical area. A series of buildings suggested a military-type compound. She counted eight men walking, fixing two jeeps, and reroofing one of the outbuildings. Many were dark haired, dark eyed, and dark skinned. Middle Eastern. But others had light brown hair and green or blue eyes, and she suspected these people were mercenaries who represented many nationalities. Those who spoke kept their tones low, but she picked up several languages: French, Arabic, and maybe even Greek or Russian.

In the distance, white sand and the emerald sea clued her in that they might be in the Florida Keys or the Bahamas. As if it wouldn't be hard enough to get away, they were locked in by the sea. She wished she had the knowledge to spot a bird or flowers or plants that only grew in certain latitudes. But schoolwork had never been her forte. She didn't like sitting behind a desk, not even to invoice her students.

She must have dallied. A guard prodded her with a gun, reminding her that though the island might be tropical, this was no vacation package. The bright sunlight seemed to mock her as they marched across the sandy compound toward a gigantic warehouse. She estimated the size at about ten times that of her father's lab. About 80,000 square feet.

The building sat next to the water, about twelve feet above sea level. She couldn't be certain of the facilities on the other side because the building itself blocked the view. However, she heard engines and glimpsed a boat's wake.

Asad joined them with a nod to his men, then escorted them quickly into the warehouse. The reek of chemicals hit her about the same time Asad halted, turned around and spoke. "If you would like the same kind of treatment you've been given, you will follow orders."

The threat in his accented voice was in the subtext. His tone remained flat, unemotional. When he glanced over his shoulder and deeper into the warehouse, almost as if fearing what was ahead, a chill of fear shot down her spine. Asad was tough, and if he was afraid, then she had reason to shake.

For the first time, Kaylin had the feeling Asad might not be the leader. For all she knew, he held a minor position.

Sawyer nodded. She didn't say a word. She didn't like the way these men looked at her, as if she were no more than a bug to be squashed if she got in the way. But as they entered the warehouse, their escorts tensed, their eyes avoiding one another the way men did when uneasy.

At first, she saw nothing frightening. The warehouse consisted of huge tanks of many sizes. Lots of noisy pumps. Machinery whose purpose she could only guess at. She might not be an expert, but she recognized a biodiesel plant when she saw one. This facility had many similarities to her father's smaller one—right down to the metered lines through which yellow fuel pumped into tanks.

But there the resemblance ended. The tanks were gigantic and numerous. A loading dock with a pass-through to the water revealed men pumping fuel onto a barge.

She frowned. They were already making biodiesel

here. So why had they gone to such extremes to kill her father, kidnap Lia, and now Sawyer and her? What could her father have discovered that was valuable enough to warrant such violence?

A man watched them advance, clearly waiting for them, Sawyer's laptop in hand. White, bald, and with muscles that bulged from his black T-shirt, he stared at them with cold blue eyes behind silver-rimmed glasses, a Rottweiler with a spiked collar by his side. Tattoos on the man's arms suggested he'd spent time aboard ships. He looked familiar, but she couldn't recall ever seeing him. But the fear in her guards' eyes put her on edge.

He spoke without an accent, but his language was so formal she suspected he hadn't learned English in the United States. "I am Pavel. I trust your quarters were comfortable?"

Again Sawyer nodded. Kaylin didn't move. She recalled where she'd seen him. On her father's surveillance DVD. This man had visited her father's plant the week before his murder. A cold chill ran through her as she suspected she now faced her father's killer.

Pavel turned to Asad and petted the Rottweiler. "Kit had a sandspur between his toes. Who did you assign to groom him?"

Kaylin had expected the man to address them, but obviously his dog took priority. She didn't mind. It gave her a chance to look around. Not that she saw a means of escape. A chain link fence surrounded the perimeter and armed guards and cameras were everywhere.

Asad motioned one man forward. The guard trembled and sank to his knees. From his tone and posture, she gathered he was begging, but she couldn't be certain since he spoke a language she didn't understand. Despite his plea, Pavel's face remained icy.

When the man stopped speaking, Pavel casually withdrew a pistol from his side holster. He shot the man between the eyes.

At the loud ringing in her ears and the sight of the man keeling over, Kaylin gasped. Pavel had shot the man for failing to find a sandspur between a dog's toes. His actions, both outrageous and brutal, floored her, shocked her, swept her totally off balance.

And their fate was in Pavel's hands? Oh . . . God. She froze, unable to move, to think. Her entire body shook. No one paid any attention, except Sawyer, who slipped his hand into hers.

She hung on for dear life. What she'd just seen could have been a scene in a bad movie. She couldn't take in the reality that one moment a man had been alive, the next dead, his life ended as if he were no more important than a cockroach. But he was someone's son, maybe someone's brother, possibly a father.

Her cereal rolled in her stomach and she swallowed hard to keep down breakfast. Closing her eyes for a moment, she slowly breathed in and out, trying to find her equilibrium.

Asad barked an order and two men dragged away the body as if he were a sack of caustic soda. The killing happened so fast, it seemed unreal. However, the trickle of blood and the drag of his boots across the concrete were a solid reminder she had not dreamed the incident.

Although Pavel had made an example of the guard, no doubt for their sake, his ruthless action only made her more determined to escape—before he found out they'd faked the data, before he disposed of them, too.

Pavel ignored Asad and held the laptop out to Sawyer. "You will convert this plant to Dr. Danner's new specs."

Sawyer took the laptop. "His formula is just a theory. You realize it has never been tested?"

"You make it work or you die." Pavel turned to Asad. "See that he has what he needs."

Whether or not her father had ever created a successful formula didn't matter. Sawyer and Kaylin didn't have the formula. They only had the data Sawyer had falsified. Kaylin noted that Pavel issued the ultimatum without giving them a time frame for completion. She had no idea if he expected results in hours, days, or weeks.

Kaylin didn't ask questions. Instead she watched Sawyer go into action. Asad stayed with Pavel, but the remaining two guards trailed them to a section of the plant where the computers sat in a section walled off from the big tanks and chemicals.

Sawyer opened the laptop. "Where can I plug in?" When neither guard answered, he frowned and tried a second time, "Do you speak English?"

Again, neither guard answered.

Sawyer held up the cord. One guard pointed to a socket that Sawyer could have found by himself. Obviously he'd been testing the men to see if they spoke English. However, just because they hadn't answered didn't mean they weren't faking.

Kaylin decided to test them further and watch their responses closely. "After making love last night, my breasts hurt."

"What?" Sawyer jerked up his head, but she focused on their guards. Neither had reacted. Not a smile. Not a hint of understanding.

"I'm fairly certain these men don't speak English." She took a chair beside Sawyer. "What can I do to help?"

"Don't assume anything. Follow my lead and stay alert." He linked his laptop into their system. She saw him hack through a series of codes. Their guards paid no attention. Instead they watched as if fearing they would try to escape at any moment. Apparently, the loss of their former comrade had left a deep impression. These guys would not fall asleep on the job.

But as for her staying alert? She didn't need Sawyer to tell her that. At first, she jumped at every sound. But when nothing further happened, the heat began to mellow her out. Pavel and Asad disappeared, and watching Sawyer type code into his computer hour after hour was as interesting as watching the ants climb the wall.

So instead she watched the guards' routine. She counted how many minutes it took them to make their rounds. She noted when they hit the bathroom and when they took a cigarette break—always at one particular side of the building, far from the explosive materials.

Her father had never allowed smoking in the plant. Apparently one spark could set off the methane in its raw form. She kept an eye out for Pavel and Asad, but they didn't come by.

She counted the men coming and going, estimated the plant's fuel capacity, and wished she could talk to Sawyer. But he seemed busy, totally focused on his laptop.

Eight hours later, the same guards escorted them back to their quarters where a meal waited for them. Chicken and rice, a salad, and Jell-O. They ate without speaking. Finally Sawyer suggested they take a shower. Either he wanted sex or he wanted to talk. She was up for either.

40

§

Sawyer tugged her into the shower and kissed her. "I've been wanting to do that all day."

"Me, too." She leaned into him, enjoying his hands sliding up and down her back, and rested her palms on his hips, her fingers on his butt. "Did you bring me in here for sex or conversation?"

He grinned. "Both. Let's talk first."

"Pavel is the bald guy on Dad's security footage."

He nodded, obviously having made that connection himself. "I hacked into their books."

"How?"

"I had a keylogger program on my laptop. I installed the program on their computer and then traced every key stroke. That gave me their passwords and, like that, I was in the system."

Sawyer's exterior often distracted her from his intelligence. She'd known her father wouldn't have kept him on as a partner if he hadn't been brilliant, but she kept forgetting about his doctorates, probably because he exuded Southern charm. She eyed him. "Sometimes you scare me."

"Is that a good thing?" he asked.

"I haven't decided yet."

"Don't tell me you're one of those women who doesn't find nerds attractive?"

She caressed his chest. "Yeah. That's it. I have to force myself to touch you because you're smart."

At her sarcasm, he chuckled. "Nerdiness can be a good thing. Pavel and Asad acquired their tanks from Witman Container."

"So?" She narrowed her eyes, not seeing his point. "From the size of Dean's operation, I'd imagine they supply half the eastern seaboard with biodiesel tanks."

"Yeah, but Pavel and Asad didn't *pay* for the tanks."

"You mean they're short on funds?" That was kind of difficult to believe considering the size of their operation. From what she'd seen, they had to be selling tens of thousands of gallons of biodiesel every day.

Sawyer shook his head and water sprayed down her

back. "This plant has been here for over a year. Yet, they haven't paid so much as one penny for those tanks."

Pavel hadn't paid Dean Witman for the containers, yet he'd had plenty of time and had the cash to do so. She could only think of one reason why Dean Witman hadn't collected. "You think Dean might be an investor, one of the owners here?" Her eyes widened as she caught on. "If Dean's an owner in this place and he was trying to buy out Dad, then he's behind all our problems."

"Looks like it."

"You think Dean tried to buy out Dad, and when Dad refused he killed him, thinking I'd inherit and sell out to him?"

"I don't know. If that's the case, why didn't he ever e-mail us the offer?"

"Maybe he thought the price would go down if he waited—but he called the day after Dad's funeral. It doesn't make sense. Did you check to see if the message got caught in your spam folder?" she asked.

"I had a lot on my mind with Lia being kidnapped," he admitted. "But this new information about Dean won't do us any good if we can't escape this island."

"Are you sure we're on an island?"

"We're somewhere off the Florida Keys. I traced the satellite uplinks."

Of course he had.

"So what's our next move?" She leaned into him, expecting a physical response. His erection didn't disappoint her. But instead of returning her embrace, he shot her a serious frown.

"I can manipulate the computer program to cause an explosion in the plant."

An explosion? Like the one that had killed her father? From his tone she could tell he had problems with that idea, but probably not for the same reasons she did. She still recalled the horror of losing her father and had no wish to repeat the experience. Explosions weren't reliable. They killed indiscriminately. "Are you certain you can do it?"

"No problem. Methanol is very flammable. That's not the issue." He stared into her eyes. "It's the timing."

"We don't want to be inside the plant when it explodes."

"We also don't want to be locked up here, either."

"Oh. You want the explosion to be a diversion so we can get away. Makes sense. But we can't be certain if they'll bring us back here at the same time tomorrow night."

"Exactly." He nodded approval. "We have about a six-minute window if they keep the same schedule. And that's an *if* that might make the difference between us living or dying."

"We could wait a few days to see if they keep—"

"I'd rather not. Asad enjoys hurting you. And Pavel's no fool. He'll expect progress, and I can't deliver it."

"You want to set the explosion for tomorrow?" She shivered under the water and turned the temperature to hot.

He nodded. "But if we fail—"

"Don't say it. I don't want to think about it."

"Kaylin. I'm not going forward unless you agree. But the alternatives—"

"I know." She recalled Asad's slaps and Pavel's brutality toward his own men. These men had no mercy in them. "Can you make the explosion go off whenever you want?"

"Pretty much. Within a few seconds."

"And once you start the process, is there any way to shut it down?"

"Nope. That's why we're deciding now."

"Maybe we'll find a different way to escape."

"Maybe."

"You don't think so, do you?"

He shrugged and ran a hand through his hair. "I don't know. The longer we wait, the higher the chance that Pavel will discover we don't have the secret formula."

She took a deep breath and let out the air slowly. "Okay. Let's do it tomorrow. It would be nice to have a backup plan if they don't escort us out on time."

"I'll wait until the last moment to arm the trigger. Just try and stay sharp tomorrow. If I squeeze your hand, that will be my signal to be ready to act."

"You mean run?"

"Yes."

"What if we can't touch?"

"Then I'll wink."

She eyed him, afraid he might try something heroic, like staying behind to fight so she could get away. Like she would stand a chance of escaping by herself. Even if she found a boat with a radio, she wouldn't know how to use it. "We are running together, right?"

He pulled her tight and slid his hands down her buttocks. "You bet your sweet ass, we're running together. I'm not letting you out of my sight."

They ran out of hot water sometime during the next half hour. Kaylin didn't care. Sawyer projected enough heat to keep her warm. He knew how to get under her skin, excite her mind as well as her body. Tonight they'd replaced last night's playfulness with wild abandon. She didn't hold back. Not her body. Not her feelings. Not her essence.

And it felt good. Not just physically, but emotionally. For too long she'd held herself apart. She hadn't wanted to fall for anyone—not when she'd been so determined to leave Florida for New York and the stage. But none of that mattered now. Not when the future might not be there for them.

And if they lived? She'd deal with it then.

Later, after they'd made love, she tried to relax. But just thinking about tomorrow, about blowing up those huge tanks, set her on edge. For all she knew, everyone on the entire island might die in the explosion. She hoped Sawyer had calculated how far away from the blast they needed to be to survive.

She thought about asking, but changed her mind. Some things it was better not to know.

But one thing she knew for certain, without him, she

wouldn't have stood a chance. If he hadn't followed her to Pasha's, she might have been here alone. Having Sawyer to talk to, to make love to, to hold on to through the long hours of the night made her circumstances more bearable.

She'd wanted steady and solid. Sawyer was all of that. Funny how her definitions had changed. Steady and solid had once meant a regular paycheck and health insurance. Now steady and solid meant a man who would do his best to save their lives.

Being close to Sawyer no longer scared her. Maybe she was so frightened of dying that admitting she needed someone else no longer seemed like a big deal. Maybe she'd grown emotionally. Maybe she'd just lost her sanity. She suspected if her life ever returned to normal she would have a lot of soul-searching to do.

But for now, she was oddly . . . content.

41

Kaylin woke up the next morning with a sense of impending doom in the pit of her gut. For Sawyer's sake, she tried to pretend she had no doubts. She pretended she believed his plan would work, that they'd escape. But deep down, she said good-bye to her sisters, good-bye to her dreams of dancing on stage, good-bye to life.

Of the three, saying good-bye to her dreams of dancing on stage was by far the easiest. Kaylin had shared her love of dance with her mother. It was the thing they'd done together, where she'd felt special and close to her mom. Dance had been their mother/daughter thing. After her mom died, she'd hung on to the dream, but for the first time, she wondered if she would have pushed so hard to continue if her mother had lived. Was dancing her way of trying to keep her mother's spirit alive?

Kaylin didn't know. The thought made her uncomfortable. She'd been so busy looking out for her sisters and paying the bills, surviving, that she hadn't considered the choices she'd made or asked herself why she'd made them. But self-recriminations at this late date would serve no purpose. It wasn't as if she expected to live much longer.

Pavel simply had too many men on the island for them to escape. Even if the blast took out everyone in the building, he had armed guards on the perimeters, armed guards on the boats, armed men at the gates.

Escape seemed impossible. But she liked the idea of fighting back. Of doing something proactive. No doubt Pavel thought he had the complete upper hand, that he could force them to do what he wished, that nothing could stop him from stealing her father's formula. When Sawyer retrieved the broken chair leg from under the mattress and pushed it up his sleeve, she tried not to think about fighting off bad guys with a piece of wood.

She expected the hours until Sawyer set off the explosion to go by in a flash. But the day dragged.

Sawyer had work to keep him busy. He had to change the backflow of the chemicals running through the system and make sure the alterations didn't set off any warning alarms. She sat beside him with nothing to think about except dying.

She kept trying to relax, to save her energy, but unlike yesterday, Pavel didn't leave them alone. During the morning he strode past their work area twice.

The third time, during their lunch, Pavel, Asad at his side, peered at Sawyer's laptop, his eyes cold through his silver-rimmed glasses. "I expect to see results this afternoon."

Her sandwich lodged in her throat.

"I can give you the projections right now." Sawyer's voice remained upbeat as if he couldn't wait to show off his work. He hit a few keys. A series of equations scrolled down the monitor.

She had no idea what the numbers and symbols meant. Neither did Pavel. "That means nothing to me."

Sawyer nodded, his face grave. "Would you like to see a working diagram?"

"Of course."

"Bear in mind I have some minor fiddling to do and then we should retest—"

Pavel snapped his fingers. "Show me the projection."

"No problem." Sawyer ran a simulation. "Along the side of the screen, you can see the gallons per minute rate."

In the middle of the monitor's screen, Sawyer had configured a blueprint of the plant. Valves opened and oil pumped through pipes and into tanks, mixed with methoxide and then worked through the reactor.

The reactor slowly turned red. An alarm sounded on the laptop.

Pavel frowned at the red swirling gas in the tank. "What's that?"

Sawyer scratched the back of his neck. "I can fix it. The mix is too rich." Sawyer ignored his lunch and typed steadily. "Sorry. It's too late to change the mixture in this simulation. I'll have to start over."

On the view screen the tank exploded. The entire screen burned red.

Kaylin held her breath. Either Sawyer's plan would work brilliantly, or he was an idiot and Pavel would take out his gun and shoot him dead.

Sawyer didn't wait for Pavel's permission to proceed. He cleared the screen. "I'm lowering the ratio." He ran another simulation, this time it took longer for the tank to turn red, but again the plant exploded.

Pavel glared.

Sawyer shrugged. "I'm almost there. It's a fine balance. If the mix is too thin, the gallons per minute is too low. If the flow rate is too high . . . well, you saw—"

"What I saw is that you do not have your formula perfected." Pavel scowled at Sawyer.

"Henry died before that happened."

"You will succeed," he pointed at Kaylin, and it wasn't hard for her to look scared, "or she will pay for your failure. Am I clear?"

Sawyer nodded.

"And you will not test in this facility until that simulation runs perfectly and my engineers have triple checked your data."

"Understood."

Kaylin didn't dare glance at Sawyer. Talk about smooth. Pavel had not only stopped demanding they complete the formula by this afternoon, he'd delayed the testing until other engineers checked out the data.

Sawyer had taken a huge risk. The dangerous time was when the chemicals were mixed. Even she knew that flow rate had nothing to do with the possibility of an explosion. Obviously Pavel didn't have a clue about the manufacturing process of biodiesel. His ignorance and Sawyer's intelligence had bought them the time they required.

Three o'clock and then four o'clock passed, and she had to stop herself from glancing at the clock every minute. She didn't want to look anxious or suspicious, although if she did appear frightened their guards would likely attribute it to Pavel's threats.

If Sawyer noted her impatience, he didn't acknowledge it. All business, he typed furiously into his computer. As the guards approached to escort them to their quarters, he reread his code one last time, then shot her an are-you-certain-you-want-to-go-through-with-this look. They locked gazes. Her mouth went dry.

She nodded.

This was it.

Sawyer pressed the enter key. The countdown began.

If the guards didn't bring them out in time, they'd blow up along with the plant.

Sweat broke out under Kaylin's arms and between her breasts. Her pulse pounded as she walked through the exit next to Sawyer, trying to look bored while every muscle in her body shouted for her to run.

42

Sawyer wished he'd had more time to prepare. He wished he had a gun instead of a broken chair leg up his sleeve. He wished he knew the emergency procedures at the plant. He had no idea what would happen after the explosion. Would the guards form a tight perimeter? Would police and fire engines arrive? Since he wasn't certain of the size of the island or if it was inhabited by anyone other than Pavel and his men, he couldn't calculate the odds of escape.

In addition, he had no firm plan. Stealing a vehicle and getting Kaylin as far away as possible remained at the top of his priority list. But that could change. He intended to watch for opportunities.

He'd set the charge to go off at exactly six minutes

after five. Their guards shoved them out the door and Sawyer happily complied. He and Kaylin headed past the exit—just as they had yesterday.

So far, so good.

Two minutes until blast time.

Outside the sun beat down on their heads and he squinted. They still had plenty of daylight left, but he'd have preferred to make their escape in the dark. But at night, they were locked up. Men headed out of the plant for the shift change. The perimeter guards made a last security check as final loads of fuel were being pumped into ships at the loading dock.

One minute left.

Sawyer tensed. He was counting on the explosion distracting and disorienting the guards long enough for him to take them out. Too bad he'd only been in one prior fight, when the kidnappers had taken Lia. That hadn't turned out well. He much preferred chemistry and physics to boxing or the martial arts. However, even he knew a hard enough blow to the right place could knock a man unconscious.

He had to be swift, sure, decisive. At least he'd played enough computer games to know the proper sequence of action—disarm, disable, run. In theory it sounded easy. But his opponents outnumbered him and they had weapons. And time was on their side. He had to move fast. Pavel and Asad would send reinforcements at the first sign of trouble.

He glanced at his watch.

Thirty seconds.

He gave Kaylin's hand one final squeeze and decided they should make a run for the parked vehicles on the other side of the chain link fence.

Fifteen seconds.

Sawyer fingered the wooden chair leg up his sleeve. He reminded himself that if Pavel had ordered these men to shoot him, they wouldn't have hesitated. It was Kaylin and him . . . or them.

Behind them, the blast roared like an angry dragon. Sawyer didn't look back. He raised his arm and slammed it into the nearest guard's head, striking his temple. With a grunt, the man collapsed. As flames broke out in the plant and black smoke and hellish sparks shot into the sky, the second guard pulled his firearm.

Sawyer tripped over the downed man, slowing his forward progress. He wasn't going to get to the guard before he could shoot.

The man aimed.

Then Kaylin did some kind of spin kick, striking the guy's wrist and flinging the weapon into the dirt. Sawyer recovered his balance. He lunged, the piece of wood he'd hidden held above his head. The guard closed in and they struggled for control of the stick. Wrestling, they fell to the ground, and he abandoned the stick, which did little good in such tight quarters. Instead, he punched and jabbed, using elbows and knees.

It was taking too long.

Sawyer spat out dirt, tried for a choke hold.

Kaylin had recovered the gun. She swung it at the guard's head. Connected. The guard's eyes rolled to the back of his head.

"Is he out?" she asked.

"Yes." Sawyer began to shove the man off him.

To help, Kaylin tugged the guard's arm and finally Sawyer stood, grabbed her hand and they sprinted toward the fence. Other men ran too, shouting in a variety of languages. But no one appeared to pay attention to Kaylin and Sawyer. The fire burned brighter.

Heat had increased in intensity. Several more explosions, as one tank after another caught fire, rocked the dirt under their feet, making their balance precarious. His lungs burned as fire sucked the oxygen from the air.

They reached the fence and he cupped his hands. Kaylin placed her foot in his palms and he boosted her up the fence. Before she reached the top, he started climbing. Barbed wire at the top sliced him in a half-dozen places. He ignored the pain and jumped down ahead of her.

She'd been more careful going over the top and he could see only one cut on her hand. Thank God, she was an athlete, more suited for this kind of activity than he.

"Let's see if we can find an unlocked vehicle." They ran to the cars, but the perimeter guards had begun to recover from their initial panic. The ones at the gate spied them, pointing and shouting.

Sawyer checked the first car. Locked. The second was also locked.

Three cars down, Kaylin had the same problem. "They're all locked."

Sawyer spied a golf cart parked alongside the entrance gate. "Over here," he yelled.

They both raced toward the cart. The key sat in the ignition. He started the vehicle, pulled it through the gate and arbitrarily turned right onto a dirt road.

Kaylin glanced back over her shoulder. "Pavel's coming after us."

"You sure it's him?"

"It's hard to miss his bald head. Floor it."

"I already am. The top speed is around thirty miles per hour. They're going to catch us."

"So what's the plan?"

Wind whipped her hair. She had dirt smudges all over her face. Her coveralls were ripped. She'd never looked more beautiful. Her eyes glinted with a warrior's fire, and with that gun in her pocket, she looked sexy as hell.

"We put as much distance between us and them as possible."

"And then?"

"I'm working on it."

"Work faster. They just reached the cars."

The terrain ahead didn't suggest many choices. Thick vegetation along both sides of the road offered few places to hide. And it was so dusty, hiding their tracks would be impossible.

The road curved and she leaned into him. "I've lost sight of them."

He slowed and pointed. "Pick up those rocks as we pass by."

She scooted to the edge of her seat, grabbed a hand bar, leaned over and picked up rocks. When she had five or six good sized ones, he tapped her. "That's enough."

"Now what?" She looked back. "I can see their dust. They're gaining on us."

"Pile the rocks on the gas pedal."

She didn't ask questions and kneeled, piling the rocks on, wedging them tight. When she finished, he removed his foot from the pedal. The cart kept up its speed.

He ripped off one of his shirt sleeves and tied the cuff to the steering wheel and the other end on the cart's roll bar. "This should steer the cart down the road without us for a while."

Her eyes widened. "Without us?"

"We need to jump."

She shook her head. "We're going too fast."

"Jump, tuck, and roll."

Again she shook her head. "We're going too fast."

He should have slowed, let her jump, then done the rest himself. But it was too late now. "They'll see us soon. We have to jump now. And then hide."

"But—"

"You can do it." He prayed he was right. Even a minor sprain could be a death sentence, because Pavel would catch them. But he hadn't really expected to get this far.

He placed a hand on her shoulder. "Pretend you're doing one of those ballet jumps."

"You've got to be kidding." But she jumped. And he leapt off right behind her, watching to see that she made it. He hit hard and his sleeveless arm scraped across the dirt. Gritting his teeth, he tried to pretend he didn't hurt.

Kaylin rolled and bounced to her feet. "That wasn't so— you're hurt."

"I'm okay."

"Your arm—"

"Get down." He tugged her into the underbrush. From the way the dust was kicking up, Pavel, Asad, and his men were right around the last bend. He held his breath, hoping they'd take the bait. The golf cart continued down the road, then veered to the opposite side of the road from them. Perfect. They'd search inland and that would give them time to get away along the coast.

After the vehicles passed by, he and Kaylin walked deeper into the underbrush, past a burned out cabin half overgrown with weeds. A tree grew right through a rotted wall. Kaylin spied an aloe plant, tore off several of the thick fleshy leaves and as the resinous pulp leaked out, she spread it over his arm. Immediately the sting lessened.

"Thanks," he whispered.

Up the road they could hear Pavel issuing orders. Asad shouted, "It's a trick."

So they'd found his sleeve tied to the steering wheel. But they would have no idea where they'd jumped off or in which direction they'd walked. Kaylin reached into her pocket and pulled out the gun. "Here."

He took it as if he knew what to do. But in truth he'd never fired a gun. Sawyer checked the safety, removed the clip, counted the bullets, replaced the clip and slid it into his pocket. The weight of the weapon against his side reminded him that they were still far from safe. They needed water and a way to get off the island. They had no map. No knife. Not even a fishing hook.

"Which way?" she asked.

"We should head for the beach. If people live here, they probably live by the sea."

"Which way is the sea?" she asked.

He'd always had a good sense of direction. But he couldn't count on that. Just because the water had been on this side of the road back at the plant, they still might walk for miles and miles before they hit the ocean. The plant could have been in a cove or bay, the land could jut out in this area.

He might save hours of walking time if he got their direction right from the start. "I need to climb a tree."

She frowned at his arm. "You're in no condition to climb anything. I'll do it."

"You ever climbed a tree?" He kept his voice easy, but couldn't hold back a grin.

She scowled. "You think I can't?"

"After you kicked that gun out of the guard's hand and saved my life, I don't think there's anything you can't do."

"I might have got lucky on that one. But trees, I can climb." She spun around, looking for a suitable tree, eyed one bent at an angle and headed for it. She pulled herself up, high along the trunk, and although she made it look easy, he didn't take a normal breath until she'd descended, and set both feet back on the ground.

She pointed. "The sea is that way. About a half mile."

Her shirt looked funny and he frowned at the large lump between her breasts. "What happened?"

She followed the direction of his gaze and grinned. "I picked a snack on the way down." Opening the coveralls, she pulled out a coconut. "If we can open it, we can have a drink."

"Sounds good, but I don't want to pound it until we're certain Pavel and Asad have given up the search. Sounds can carry a long distance in the wild." He took her hand and together they walked through the vegetation. "Did you see anything else interesting while you were up there?"

"The plant's still burning. And I caught sight of Asad a long way down the road." She paused. "I also thought I heard a helicopter, but I didn't see it. You think they called out a chopper to search for us?"

"It's possible. We'll have to take care to stay off the beach as much as possible." However, if the choppers had sophisticated search devices, like night vision or infrared indicators, they could be spotted even at night. Sawyer didn't mention that though. No point in borrowing trouble. With the vegetation's increasing density, they had enough to deal with.

They'd resorted to walking single file. He kept their direction steady by keeping his left shoulder pointing west toward the setting sun. To prevent the saw grass from shredding their skin, Sawyer picked up a long stick and held it horizontally, bending the leaves downward to keep the sharp edges away.

In the heat, without water, he insisted they stop frequently and take breaks whenever they found shade. Finally, just as the sun began to set, streaking across the horizon in pale pink streaks and slashes of deep purple, they reached the sea. He'd hoped to find footprints in the sand, a boat, a town, some sign of civilization. But the beach looked as if no one had ever walked here. The last tide had deposited driftwood, seaweed and a variety of shells, but as for evidence of people—not so much as a candy wrapper.

At least there were no signs of pursuit and they could probably risk showing themselves on the beach. A breeze kept away mosquitoes and he longed for a swim. Kaylin ran toward the beach, without taking off her coveralls and he called out softly, "Wait. Don't get your clothes wet."

She slowed and looked over her shoulder at him. "They're filthy and it's still hot enough for us to dry them in under an hour."

"All right," he agreed. They dived into the water, frolicked a bit and rubbed sand on their clothing to clean them. Then he left her in the water, wrung out the clothing, and set the coveralls on branches to dry before returning to her.

"All this water and nothing to drink." She floated on her back. "Think we can crack that coconut?"

"I'll try. Those husks are tough. Without a knife . . ."

"We could always shoot a hole in it and drink the milk."

"If we shoot it, it might splatter everywhere. And the noise from a shot could lead Pavel here."

"Fine." She sighed. Her skin had turned red during their trek and he hoped they might find more aloe to soothe it. In addition, her split lip had opened again and bled into the water. He didn't mention sharks, but it was dusk, feeding time. They needed to get out of the water.

"Come on." He took her hand and tugged her toward shore. Although the cool water felt wonderful on his skin, and he hoped the salt had cleansed his wounded arm, which had started to bleed again, swimming was not a good idea. They probably shouldn't have gone in.

"Wait." She pulled back. "I think—" She tugged her hand from his, dived under and came up with a clam. "Look, dinner. This sandbar is full of clams." Before he could stop her, she handed him the heavy shell and dived down for more. Less than thirty seconds later, she surfaced with three more.

"That's enough." She must have heard the urgency in his tone because she didn't protest and accompanied him to shore.

But after they reached the beach, she searched the water, her gaze narrowing on the shadows. "Did you see anything wrong?"

"Sharks feed at sunset, and we're both bleeding," he pointed out now that they'd made it back to land.

"Yeah, I thought of that."

"You did?" And she'd gone in anyway?

She shrugged. "Shark attacks are rare and I needed that swim to revive me."

Totally unselfconscious about her nudity, she placed the clams on some driftwood. "Dad, Mom, Becca, and I used to go to the beach and do some clamming. Lia wasn't born yet. At night we'd make a campfire, sit around the blaze, and sing. After dinner, we'd make s'mores. Melted marshmallows over graham crackers and Hershey chocolate bars. Delish."

"You cooked the clams?"

"Sometimes we ate them raw." She must have read the squeamishness in his eyes. "They're good. Really. Dad said we couldn't eat them straight out of Tampa Bay because of the pollution, but the Gulf of Mexico was safe unless we had a red tide." She sniffed. "I'm sure this water is clean."

He supposed after all he'd survived, he could manage to ingest a raw clam. The shell was already partway open and he pried back the rest. Tilting back his head, he slid the clam into his mouth, but then as a light caught his eye, he forgot about food. "Do you see that?"

Kaylin turned her head. "What?"

"Over there." He pointed. "Those are lights reflecting into the sky."

Kaylin squinted. "You think?"

"Yes. Come on, get dressed. If we head down the beach, we should be able to hike there in a few hours."

The clams forgotten, both of them hopped into their damp clothing, then put on their shoes. They walked for hours. Sometimes the sea covered the beach, and they trudged inland where the saw grass whipped at them like a cat-o'-nine-tails, but their clothing protected them from the worst of it.

They scaled several boulders and climbed over fallen trees, but the light in the sky kept growing brighter, a beacon to keep up their hopes. When they heard a helicopter flying a search pattern overhead, they ducked under trees to avoid being spotted. Damn it. They hadn't given up. But after a few minutes, the chopper flew away again.

Finally, about an hour later, Sawyer and Kaylin came across a tiny wood cabin with a tin roof. Sawyer didn't stop. "This place doesn't have phone lines or electricity. Let's keep going."

He wanted to make certain they didn't accidentally walk into any of Pavel and Asad's people. In a city this close to the oil plant, Pavel might have excessive influence with the authorities. Sawyer hadn't journeyed all the way across the island to stupidly walk back into their clutches.

Kaylin remained silent. She hadn't complained during their walk, but he could feel weariness radiating from her. He didn't blame her. He estimated they'd walked over fifteen miles, and he ached just about everywhere.

Tired men made mistakes, and he slowed his footsteps as they neared several buildings. "Let's stop and use the cover of these trees for a few minutes."

"Okay." Kaylin slid her back against a trunk and sat in the sand.

They appeared to be near a marina. Several boats were moored in the bay. A nearby office building looked dark and empty. Lights had led them to the outskirts of a town, but along with civilization, they'd find attention that might prove dangerous.

"Stay here," Sawyer whispered. "I'll see if that office has a phone."

"You think we should split up?" Kaylin asked, her tone weary and uncertain.

"If I get caught, you'll be my best chance to find help," he told her, praying that wouldn't happen. They didn't both need to expose themselves. And if only one of them could get away, it should be Kaylin. Her sisters needed her. But even if her sisters hadn't needed her, he'd still want her to be safe.

Kaylin stood and flung herself into his arms, kissed him on the mouth. "Be careful."

"I promise."

He gave her a hug and then slipped into the shadows. The tiny office was unlocked. He stepped inside, banged into a chair and wished he had a flashlight. Sawyer felt around and eventually discovered a desk. And a phone.

Bingo.

He lifted the receiver and relief washed over him as he

heard a dial tone. He charged the call to his phone card and asked the operator to connect him with Deputy Bryant and the Hillsborough County Sheriff's Office. A few minutes later, Sawyer closed the door and made his way back to Kaylin.

She remained where he'd left her, and she jumped up when she saw him. "Are you okay? Did you find a phone?"

"You aren't going to believe this."

"What? Was the phone dead?"

"I got through to Deputy Bryant."

"Great!"

"That helicopter, the one we've been avoiding . . ."

"Yeah?"

"Your grandmother sent them. They've been looking for us. We hiked all night for nothing. They're coming back to pick us up."

43

§

When the helicopter landed on the marina's sand beach, Sawyer and Kaylin were only fifty yards away. Close enough to feel the wind of the rotors, close enough to hear the engine's whine. A man called out their names over a loudspeaker. "Sawyer Scott. Kaylin Danner. We are search and rescue specialists." The sound blasted through the tropical heat. "Kaylin's grandmother, Mrs. Carstairs, sent us."

"I was afraid to believe it until now." Kaylin's tone was happy. "But, Sawyer, you did it. You saved us."

He hugged her against his side and they hurried to the chopper. "I didn't do it alone."

A man opened the door and greeted them with a wide smile. "Kaylin Danner and Sawyer Scott?"

"That would be us." Kaylin held out her hand and jumped into the machine.

Sawyer followed, his adrenaline rush gone. Tired and happy, he couldn't contain his curiosity. Deputy Bryant had been brief on the phone. He had no idea how Mrs. Carstairs became involved in their rescue.

While the pilot radioed they'd been found, the other man handed them water bottles, sandwiches, and a tube of antibiotic ointment. "We'll have you back home in two hours."

"My grandmother sent you?" Kaylin asked, clearly as curious as Sawyer.

"She hired us to find you." The copilot shouted as the chopper soared into the sky.

"You searched for us after the plant exploded?" Sawyer guessed, putting the pieces together.

"Yeah. You guys sent up a great SOS signal. Every satellite in the region picked up that blaze. And since no permits had ever been pulled to build that plant, it caught law enforcement's immediate attention, and they suggested we search the island."

Sawyer didn't bother telling their rescuers their intent had been to get away, not send up a signal for help. He munched on his sandwich, downed the entire bottle of water, and happily accepted another.

Kaylin ignored her food and sipped her water. "Is my family—"

"They're fine, ma'am. And you needn't worry about those men down there coming after you. The appropriate government agencies have been notified of their illegal activities and will round them up. They won't bother you again."

"Great." Kaylin finally bit into her sandwich, her eyes mischievous. "Too bad you didn't wait a bit before rescuing us. Sawyer couldn't wait to eat the dinner we'd caught. He was really looking forward to his raw clams."

"We could go back," their rescuer suggested, catching on to the byplay.

"That's all right." Sawyer chewed his roast beef and grinned. "I can make do with this."

Although they'd swum in the ocean, his clothes still reeked of smoke and sweat. When they got back, he hoped to hit the shower, then crawl into bed, but he suspected they would be up for hours, talking to Kaylin's family. Taking advantage of a headset that drowned out all background noise, Sawyer closed his eyes and slept.

For the first time since they'd been captured, he slept soundly. He didn't even dream—or didn't remember dreaming. When he awakened, it took a few moments to regain his bearings.

That a herd of photographers surrounded the helicopter as it landed in his backyard didn't help. Apparently news trucks, both local and national, had interest in their story. He expected Kaylin to look as bewildered as he did by the fuss, but her gaze was trained on the back deck where her sisters and grandmother waited for them.

Jumping out of the chopper, she put her head down and marched through the crowd like a celebrity accustomed to dealing with the press. Meanwhile reporters shouted questions.

"Ms. Danner, were you held captive?"

"Did you blow up that plant in order to save—"

"Did the plant down there have anything to do with Dr. Danner's—"

"Why are you living with Sawyer Scott? What does he have to do with—"

Sawyer didn't answer any questions, either. That didn't stop the news people from shoving mikes in their faces or the photographers from snapping photos. But finally they reached the back deck. Kaylin's sisters flanked her, Mitzy guarded her back, and Billy stepped forward to open the door. Finally they all moved inside. Sawyer drew the blinds shut against the press, then stood back, folded his arms across his chest, and watched the tears flow.

Becca, Kaylin, Lia, Mitzy, and Mrs. Carstairs were all hugging, squealing, kissing, and crying. Shadee caught Sawyer's eyes from across the room full of emotional females and nodded. Billy hunkered down in a chair, right in the middle of the women. Randy sat on his lap and barked to add to the commotion. Sawyer breathed in the scent of the women and took pleasure in Kaylin's happy face, especially when she hugged Lia.

"You okay?"

Lia nodded. "A few nightmares, but otherwise I'm fine."

Mrs. Carstairs took over the kitchen, passing out fruit plates, gourmet cakes from a nearby bakery, and cookies. She fussed with the coffee and eventually everyone settled around the kitchen table.

"Grandma," Kaylin spoke softly. "How did you know we needed help? How did you find us?"

Her grandmother rubbed her forehead. "I had lots of help." She looked across the table at Shadee.

Shadee held Becca's hand and cleared his throat. "Deputy Bryant asked me to watch out for all of you. Because of my military background, law enforcement sometimes calls on me if they suspect trouble in the Arab-American community. And, of course, I wanted to look out for Becca's sisters. So I followed Kaylin and Sawyer to Pasha's that night. I saw men take them away by chopper. Deputy Bryant pulled some strings and we tracked the chopper to the airfield. But the plane they transferred you to flew under the radar and we lost you."

"So I hired a security team," her grandmother continued. "We found a migrant worker who'd seen the plane take off and head south, so we focused in that direction. But until you blew up that plant, we had no idea where to narrow the search."

"Hiring that helicopter to rescue us must have cost a fortune." Kaylin's eyes teared up again.

And then she saw Sawyer take a piece of cake. He *never* ate cake. He'd once told her that after his parents died, he'd thought he didn't deserve to be happy. But there he was drinking a cup of coffee with a big corner piece of cake on his plate, happily eating away. She longed to give him a big kiss, but first she had to hear everything her grandmother had done.

"I hired your rescue helicopter and several others. I had to help. Getting you back safe was all that mattered."

"Thank-you." Kaylin hugged her grandmother. "Thank-you so much."

"Tomorrow the deputies are going to need statements from everyone," Shadee warned them. "It'll take a while to get through the red tape, but—"

"We think Dean Witman's connected to the group of men on the island." Kaylin looked at Sawyer and he nodded. "He supplied the containers to the biodiesel plant and they never paid him—which makes sense if he's a partner."

"And we saw him inside the lab on the surveillance DVDs before Henry died," Sawyer reminded them. "He told us he intended to make an offer on the business and then never did. If he was in on the kidnapping, it would make sense not to make an offer. Why purchase what he could get for free?"

Shadee frowned. "So he's still on the loose. I'll notify Deputy Bryant." Shadee made a call on his cell. "He's likely too busy covering his tracks to bother us again. But I'm still checking all the door locks before we sleep."

Sawyer thought they'd covered everything when Lia poked Billy. "Tell them."

Billy squirmed in his seat, then stood. In his hand he held a black case. "This is Henry's laptop."

44
§

Kaylin stared. "You found it? You found Dad's laptop?" She hadn't thought she'd ever see it again, especially after they'd searched and couldn't find it. After returning home to find Lia safe, her family united, she couldn't have hoped for more. Seeing that laptop stunned her and filled her with hope.

"I didn't *find* it. Not exactly," Billy admitted.

"You stole it?" Mitzy accused.

Billy raised his chin. "I don't steal. Henry *gave* it to me."

"I don't understand." Why would her father have given Billy the laptop? And if he'd had it all along, why hadn't he said anything until now?

"Henry was worried about security. Apparently his visitors scared him. The morning the lab exploded, he told me to take the laptop to school with me, not to tell anyone, to keep it safe. I put it in my locker. He said the formula on it was his legacy."

Becca frowned. "But you knew we were looking for it. Why didn't you tell us?"

Billy hung his head in shame. "Because I used the laptop as collateral for drugs."

"Drugs?" Kaylin's eyes narrowed.

"I thought I could sell the drugs and get back the laptop before anyone really needed it. And I would have."

"Only those guys who vandalized the house stole the drugs," Lia said.

Billy raised his head. "I did what I had to do to get the laptop back. Then I heard Lia had been kidnapped and I would have given the laptop to Kaylin, but then Lia was back and Kaylin was gone."

Kaylin took in the frustration on his face, the fear in his tone. She believed that Billy had been terrified, that he hadn't meant any harm. "Billy, the drugs—"

"Don't send me away. Please." Billy's lower lip trembled and Kaylin's heart went out to him. Clearly, he felt remorse for letting the laptop out of his hands.

"Why didn't you say something to me after Kaylin and Sawyer disappeared?" Mitzy asked.

Billy's eyes flashed. "If I'd revealed I had the laptop, then Kaylin and Sawyer would have been no use to the bad guys. I was afraid they'd be killed. So I waited."

"Oh . . . my . . . Billy. You're amazing," Kaylin told him, realizing he'd been correct. "In the end you did the right thing." As Billy beamed with pride, she heaped on the praise. Kaylin hugged him and her sisters joined her, all of them talking at once. "Billy, I'm proud of you."

"You aren't going to send me away?" Billy asked.

"Only to rehab. But then you're coming back home. To us," Kaylin assured him.

"You did great," Becca told him.

Lia grinned so wide her cheeks hurt. "Who knew you were so smart? I can't believe you didn't tell me." She kissed him right on the mouth.

Billy's entire face and neck turned crimson. "I wanted to tell you, but I didn't want you to worry."

"Damn. My son is growing up." Mitzy hugged him, too, and tears of happiness trailed down her cheeks.

Eventually the celebration broke up. Her grandmother agreed to spend the night and retreated to the sleep sofa in the living room. Lia and Billy went off to the sun room, their heads close together, Randy on their heels. Shadee and Becca remained in the kitchen and Kaylin peeked out the window while Sawyer took a file from a kitchen drawer.

"Looks like the press have gone."

Sawyer set down the file and laptop, came up behind her and wrapped his arms around her waist. "Tired?"

"Exhausted. But I'm too wound up to sleep."

"Why don't we go out on the back deck?" he suggested, scooping up the laptop and file. Although Shadee and Becca paid no attention to them, she liked the idea of some alone time with Sawyer.

"All right," she agreed, but when she followed him,

tension gripped her. Dad's formula was probably on that laptop. And she honestly didn't know if she wanted it to work. If it did, then her father had died for something worthwhile. And yet if the formula really was there, if it did work, it would bring about all kinds of decisions— about the business, about her and Sawyer's future.

She didn't know if she was ready to define their relationship, but she didn't want to lose him, either. They'd been through a lot together. They'd saved one another's lives. Although the adrenaline rush had long since passed, she didn't want to say good-bye, either. She couldn't imagine life without him.

They strode outside and he set the laptop on the picnic table. But he didn't open it, as if sensing what they found on it might alter their future.

"What are you thinking?" she asked.

"I could erase the file."

"No." She gasped, shocked at his offer. His dreams were on that laptop. That he could even make such an offer told her his feelings for her. But the laptop wasn't just about Sawyer's future, it was all their futures. Her father had always asked, *What would you attempt if you knew you couldn't fail?* He'd lived by that, died by those words. No way could she erase his life's work. "I couldn't stand not ever knowing. Whatever is on there, we'll deal with it."

"Together?"

She nodded. "Go ahead. Let's see what Dad came up with this time." His last invention. His legacy. She prayed she wouldn't have to disappoint her sisters. She hoped their future rested in that case. A future that would send Lia to college and help Becca finish school and maybe put Billy through rehab. A future that would keep Sawyer in her life for years to come.

"You're certain?" he asked.

"Yes."

"All right." He sat at the picnic table, stretched his fingers and cracked a knuckle. It took a moment for the laptop to boot up and she reminded herself to breathe.

"No matter what's on there, I don't want to lose you," she said, the words rushing out unplanned, but never had she been so certain.

He ignored the laptop and turned sideways to face her. "What does that mean?"

"We're good together. I said I didn't want to get involved because I knew that meant giving up my plans for New York, but my dancing was an excuse."

He frowned. "You love to dance."

"Recently, I've spent most of my time on tribal belly dance. I can do that here."

"Look. Even if there's a formula in this computer that will turn dirt into diesel oil, I don't want you to give up your dream. We can build the plant anywhere."

"You'd move to New York? Didn't you tell me you hated the cold?"

"I'll buy a good coat," he joked.

"You'd move to another state . . . for me?" She couldn't believe she could be so lucky.

He opened the file and pulled out a piece of paper. "I've been waiting for the right moment to give this back."

It was her old plane ticket. The one she'd ripped in half and thrown into the bushes. He'd salvaged it and taped it together.

He waved it at her. "You can change the ticket. I checked."

He'd saved it for her. And all this time he hadn't said a word. A lump formed in her throat. "You don't have to move up north. Dancing in New York wasn't my dream. It was my mother's hope for me. It sounded exciting. An escape from everyday life. And after she died, I needed to hang on to that dream while I took care of my sisters. I think maybe it was my way of hanging on to my mother and what we shared. But now, I don't need those old dreams."

The laptop dinged, signaling it was fully booted. Sawyer kissed her. "We don't have to decide this minute, but I wanted you to know you don't have to choose between Broadway and me. You can have both."

She couldn't believe how lucky she was to have this man's love. Her throat tightened. It seemed she'd spent the last few hours crying happy tears.

"Kaylin?"

"Mm."

"Say something."

"There's this giant lump in my throat."

He grinned. "I like it when you get all emotional."

"You do?"

"Yeah. Actually I pretty much like you all the time."

"Oh, my God."

"What?"

"Here I've been thinking how great you are, but I've never told you."

"Sure you did."

"No, I didn't. I'd remember."

A teasing grin broke out and his eyes crinkled at the corners. "You risked your life to save mine. At least three times. Maybe four."

"I did?"

"You kicked a gun out of that guard's hand. You picked rocks up out of the dirt when that golf cart was racing down the road. You climbed a tree—"

"That's hardly saving your life—"

"So we could trek in the right direction. And you made up with your grandmother so she could save us."

"Now that's farfetched. I thought scientists were supposed to be objective?"

"There's no such thing. Not when I'm around you," he admitted.

"You still need to hear it. I love you."

"Actually, I've known for a while. You're the one who needs to hear it," he teased her, then entered the password on the computer.

"Why that's the most conceited, arrogant—"

"He did it."

"What?"

"Your father."

She snapped her head to the monitor. "The formula is there?"

"This is brilliant."

"What?"

"Henry came up with an algae-based biodiesel formula."

"I don't understand."

"Kaylin, right now the world is converting soybean, corn, and vegetable oil into biodiesel. But we can't grow enough crops to produce all the fuel we need. At least, we can't grow enough on land. But in the ocean, we can produce algae in enormous quantities. If this works, and I believe it will, you and your sisters are going to be beyond wealthy."

"I'll be able to pay our bills?"

He didn't answer. Sawyer tensed and lost his smile. He frowned at the computer screen. In a hushed voice, he muttered, "Your father left me a coded message."

"Coded?"

"Yeah. In case anyone else guessed the password."

"But what could be more important than his formula?" Kaylin peered over his shoulder.

"Let me extract the sequence and I'll—"

"What?" She couldn't read the message on the screen since it appeared as a series of numbers. But her pulse increased and she placed her hand on Sawyer's shoulder to steady herself.

Henry wrote, "*Quinn is a threat.* He wants to run the

show. And he's brought in a Russian partner, Pavel, who works with Asad. Beware."

"Quinn?" Kaylin looked at Sawyer in confusion. "But he told us to tear up the contract. Said he wasn't interested."

"He threw us off the scent with that comment. Maybe he had a duplicate contract. But he wouldn't need a contract if he stole the idea and murdered your father."

"Quinn doesn't have the money for a plant like the one we saw." Kaylin still didn't believe it.

"Quinn hooked up with Pavel, who must have had plenty of funding. The Florida Department of Law Enforcement may have rounded up Pavel and Asad by now, but no one's even looking for Quinn." Sawyer reached for his phone. "I'll call Deputy Bryant and he can alert the other government agencies."

"It's late."

"Bryant gave me his cell number and told me I can reach him 24/7."

Sawyer made the call and shut off his phone. "He's sending someone over to pick up Quinn."

"But Quinn isn't home." Two men with guns stepped out of the shadows. One man had a badly burned face. Kaylin gasped at the ugly scars. "Don't like what you did to me, bitch?"

This was the man she'd burned the night they'd taken Lia. Even in the dim porch light she could see the hatred in his eyes. The other man, Quinn, stepped forward, his gun aimed at Sawyer. "Move back. I'll take that lap-top."

Sawyer reached for it. Quinn cocked his gun. "Don't touch it."

"Take it easy." Sawyer raised his hands and the motion caused his elbow to knock the laptop to the deck. Kaylin suspected he'd done it deliberately but couldn't be certain.

Kaylin prayed her sisters stayed inside and asleep. The burned man grabbed her around the neck, choking her. Pain shot down her neck. Her lungs burned.

She clawed at his gun hand and slammed her foot down onto his toes, the motion like squashing a beer can. He roared in pain and loosened his arm from around her neck, leaving enough room for her to squirm out of his choke hold and drop to the decking.

Gasping for air, Kaylin scooted backward on her butt, crabwise, her palms supporting her weight. Her right hand landed on the laptop. As her scarred opponent pointed his gun at her, she swung the laptop, intending to strike the weapon away. She missed, but the laptop struck his burned face. He screamed in pain, dropping the gun as his hands flew up to cradle his face. He staggered and toppled over.

Quinn kept his weapon pointed at Sawyer. "Kaylin, give me the laptop or I'll shoot him."

The man beside her groaned. Holding the laptop in one hand, Kaylin rose, edging away from him and toward

Quinn. She kept her head bowed, her shoulders slumped as if defeated. "Don't hurt him. Don't shoot us, please. You can have the laptop. Here you go." Then she tossed the laptop right at him.

And she caught him by surprise. He tried to catch it with one hand, his other still holding the gun. Sawyer picked that instant to barrel into him, tackling him around the legs, slamming him to the ground. The two men rolled across the grass, wrestling for control of the weapon.

Kaylin picked up the laptop, whacked the burned man's head again, making sure he wouldn't get up anytime soon, then looked for the weapon that had gone skidding across the deck. She didn't see it anywhere, and suspected it had fallen in the rose bushes where she wouldn't find it until daylight.

Sawyer didn't have that much time.

She raced toward him, fear shimmying down her spine. In the darkness, she could barely tell one man from the other. The two men tangled and rolled in the grass, arms and legs kicking and punching. Grunts and groans punctuated the air.

Quinn was older, but he outweighed Sawyer. While Sawyer used knees and elbows slamming into Quinn's body, the man's fat seemed to protect vital spots.

She had to do something. But what? If Quinn's gun went off at such close range, Sawyer would surely be hit. She feared using the laptop as a weapon. With the two of them rolling she could hit the wrong man.

Suddenly Quinn rolled on top, aiming the gun at Sawyer. Sawyer's hands closed over Quinn's, but they rolled again and she couldn't tell in the darkness if Sawyer had managed to deflect Quinn's aim.

A shot reverberated across the river. Sawyer's chest bucked.

Kaylin screamed. "God . . . No!" She'd lost her mother. Quinn had murdered her father. Surely he hadn't killed Sawyer?

"Get back," Sawyer yelled and knocked the gun loose. When Sawyer shouted, she started to breathe again.

He jabbed Quinn's throat and the man doubled up in pain, choking and releasing his hold.

Sawyer scrambled out from under him and recovered the gun. Kaylin ran over. "Were you shot?"

"I'm fine."

"When he fired that gun, your body jerked. Are you certain?" She ran her hands over his chest, his shoulders, his stomach, searching for blood.

"Kaylin, I was trying to buck him off."

"I've never been that scared."

"Except for bumps and bruises, I'm fine."

Shadee and Becca stumbled out the back door with her grandmother just as the sheriffs arrived, their red and blue lights flashing, their sirens screaming.

Becca ran to Kaylin. "We heard a gunshot. Are you okay?"

"Quinn attacked us," Kaylin explained. "I think he

murdered Dad, too." Kaylin explained about the laptop and their father's warning.

Sawyer put down the gun and placed his hands over his head. But law enforcement seemed to know Quinn was their man. When Deputy Bryant stepped out of the car, Kaylin began to shake. The blood rushed from her head. "I don't feel—" she began, then fell to the ground.

Moments later she opened her eyes and found herself lying in the grass, her head in Sawyer's lap. "What happened?"

"You fainted."

She tried to shove herself to a sitting position. "I don't faint."

Sawyer whispered in her ear. "We didn't have protection on the island. Maybe you're pregnant."

She tensed, then counted backward. "It's highly unlikely."

"You don't seem too upset."

"I always planned to have a family," Kaylin told him. "Maybe not so soon, but what about you?"

"Me?"

"If I *am* pregnant—"

"I don't care if you want to have ten babies or none. I want you. I love you."

"That's awesome because I love you, too."

Deputy Bryant cleared his throat. "Excuse me, but we've got Quinn and his pal restrained in a vehicle. I need your statements."

"We're getting married soon," Sawyer told him, his tone husky, warm and sexy. "How's that for a statement?"

"Did you hear that?" Becca nudged Shadee. "My sister's engaged."

Shadee grinned. "Maybe we should have a double wedding."

"Huh?"

"Sawyer and Kaylin. You and me."

Becca whooped. "You mean it?" She flung herself into his arms and he spun her around.

Happy for her sister, Kaylin laughed. Becca had told her once she expected a traditional proposal, a ring, the guy down on one knee, but in her excitement, none of that mattered. Even under the sheriff's car's bright headlights, she glowed with happiness.

Kaylin pushed to her feet, pleased that although Sawyer hovered protectively and appeared ready to catch her if she fainted again, he let her get up by herself. Sawyer was good that way. She linked her arm through his. "What was that you said about ten children?"

"I'm not kidding. Whatever you want is fine with me."

Whatever she wanted? Kaylin finally knew what she wanted. Or whom she wanted. Sawyer. She wanted Sawyer for today, tonight, and all their tomorrows.

Epilogue

Two years later

"**R**eady?" Kaylin juggled her one-year-old son and looked over her shoulder at Sawyer. Husband, father, scientist, and her best friend, he was covered in dirt and grease. But he'd never looked better to her.

With a big smile, he shot her a thumbs-up and she threw a switch that started a pump and a continuous flow cycle. Beside Sawyer, her grandmother looked on with a loving gaze. She'd traded in her designer clothing for a set of coveralls. Not only had she funded the plant, she'd insisted on helping.

Becca tipped her hard hat. "Ready over here."

Lia nodded. "I'm set."

"All right, I'm letting her rip." Sawyer opened a pipe and their first biofuel poured through the system.

Mitzy came in with a plate of cookies and Billy handed out soft drinks and water. Mother and son had gone into rehab together, Mitzy for her drinking and Billy for his drug dependency. Both had been clean for over a year.

Lia's grades had shot straight up and she'd have no trouble finding a college. While Becca hadn't gone back to school, she was going to be a mom soon, too, and Shadee worked part time at the plant.

Kaylin offered up a prayer to her father. *Are you watching us, Daddy? We're doing it. We're making fuel. And no one is going to hurt us again.* Her grandmother's PI, Lyle Jackson, had taken several photographs which had provided additional evidence in court that Pavel and Asad had visited Henry shortly before his death. Quinn, Pavel, and Asad were in jail for life with no chance of parole. Dean Witman had been cleared of involvement, and they'd bought tanks from him to reopen Henry's plant.

Best of all, the algae formula made a superior grade of biodiesel fuel. The golden liquid was grade-A pure.

Sawyer came over and checked the meter by her pump. "Eventually, we need to automate the systems."

"Are you trying to make me obsolete?"

"Never. But I heard about a new dance troupe forming in town. They hire out to big companies to do commercials, amusement parks, and trade shows. Thought you might be interested." He kissed her.

She kissed him back. "I'm interested all right, in you."

Kaylin hadn't wanted a dreamer. She'd wanted practical and steady. But with Sawyer she'd gotten it all, practical, steady, *and* dreams—what could be better than that?

Their son pointed to the tank. "Oi. Oi. Oi."

"Oil," Sawyer corrected him and put his arm over Kaylin's shoulders. "That's oil, son. It's our future."